THE POPPY ORCHARD

There she was! A tall, nonchalant figure with her hiker's knapsack slung carelessly over one shoulder and a book grasped in her free hand.

Ellen was just as he remembered her: golden brown skin, clear grey eyes as bright as the open skies under which she had been reared, a smudge of freckles across her wide brow, and that big, all-embracing smile …

She spotted him almost in the same instant that he picked her out of the crowd.

'Stevie!' she cried, and flew towards him, her arms wide, the knapsack bumping about her shoulders. Despite their own preoccupations, those around stood back to stare as the two young people hugged each other.

'I wasn't sure I would recognise you,' he confessed, laughing. 'You haven't changed a bit!'

'You have, though.' She stood back, admiring his lithe, muscular body with its well-developed shoulders, noticing too the maturing lines about his eyes, a serious expression which gave him a dignified, confident appearance. Yes … she thought, every inch the doctor. Just as she would have expected him to look.

D0493938

Also by Mary Withall

BEACON ON THE SHORE
THE GORSE IN BLOOM
WHERE THE WILD THYME GROWS
FIELDS OF HEATHER

The Poppy Orchard

Mary Withall

coronet

CORONET BOOKS
Hodder & Stoughton

First published in Great Britain in 1999
by Hodder and Stoughton
First published in paperback in 2000
by Hodder and Stoughton
A division of Hodder Headline

A Coronet Paperback

10 9 8 7 6 5 4 3 2 1

A CIP catalogue record for this title is available
from the British Library

ISBN 0340 74870 2

Printed and bound in Great Britain by
Caledonian International Book Manufacturing Ltd, Glasgow

Hodder and Stoughton
A division of Hodder Headline
338 Euston Road
London NW1 3BH

Although Archie McIndoe figures largely in this book, it is in no way intended as a biographical account. I hope that I have offended none of his many followers by my interpretation of him as a man. It is to Mr McIndoe and his team at East Grinstead, and to the army of Guinea Pigs who regained their lives under his hand, that this book is dedicated.

ACKNOWLEDGEMENTS

My thanks are due to Mr Baker and the staff of the Argyll and Bute Public Library, Oban, Argyll, for their generous and unfailing support in my researches for this and other books in the Beaton series. Also to the Mitchell Library in Glasgow, the Imperial War Museum and the RAF Manston History Club.

Chapter One

Stephen felt the rush of air as his Westland Wallace gathered speed and shot along the runway. He pulled back on the joystick and the little biplane lifted her nose into the wind. With the slightest of judders, she left the ground and he watched the land drop away beneath his port wing as he made his first turn around the airstrip.

Two turns around the field then due west for fifteen minutes. Watch the compass . . . the needle swung crazily past west towards north . . . *correct, correct* . . . it swung back and settled on west.

Watch the altimeter . . . where's the horizon? Automatically he glanced back over his shoulder, expecting to see Middleton's head nodding but, of course, the trainer's seat was empty. The reality of the situation hit him at that moment. He was on his own, a thousand feet up and only himself to rely on if he hoped to return safely to terra firma.

Stephen fixed his eyes on the horizon. *Her nose is dropping . . . up . . . pull up. No . . . too much . . . gently . . . relax.* He eased his grip on the joystick, stretched his fingers and wriggled his shoulders. Then, settling back against the seat padding, he forced himself to breathe out. Immediately he could feel the release of tension and began to hum quietly to himself, the volume increasing as he realised that there was no one in the whole wide world to overhear him.

Alone, quite, quite alone in the universe . . . wonderful! Let's gain a little height and have a proper look-see.

He eased the joystick back into his abdomen, the nose lifted and he gained fifty . . . a hundred . . . five hundred feet.

Steady on west.

The tiny aircraft flew through the clear August sky towards a bank of white cumulus cloud drifting in from the Atlantic. Wisps of cotton-wool slid past him until suddenly he was enveloped in a dense white fog. Stephen panicked. He was flying blind . . . how was he to know where he was? *Instruments . . . watch your instruments . . .*

He manipulated the stick until she was flying straight and level, due west. He hoped that there was no other aircraft on the same flight path.

What's the time?

He seemed to have been airborne for hours, but according to his watch only ten minutes had passed since he had left the ground. Then, as suddenly as he had been blinded by the dense cloud, he was through it and out in the clear.

Allowing himself the luxury of a glance away from the instrument panel, Steve stared down at the scene below him. The silver ribbon of the Clyde, following his own path westwards, slid gracefully to the sea. From this height he could see a multitude of rivers and lochs emptying their waters into the mighty river. Cutting diagonally across the Clyde, the Erskine ferry plied between its banks, laden with vehicles and passengers. He could almost hear the familiar rasp as the chain was lifted, passed over the cogs and dropped again to the river bed.

He wondered if his father was aboard, on his way to the Southern General Hospital at Govan. It was Thursday, one of his consultancy days. He might be looking up even now and watching the biplane as she passed overhead. How surprised he'd be if he knew who was flying her!

Stephen had told his parents about joining the City of Glasgow University Air Squadron but they had no idea that he was learning to fly. His mother would have a fit when she heard he was going to be a pilot! If all went well, he'd tell them tonight . . . He thrust the thought aside. No point in tempting fate.

Below his port wing lay the Princess Louise Scottish Hospital for limbless soldiers and sailors. What about the RAF types? he wondered idly. When the hospital had been set up, pilots were attached to the army or the navy. The RAF hadn't been formed officially until after the Armistice.

The river began to widen beyond Dunglass Point and soon the endless shipyards gave way to rolling green fields sweeping up to the foothills of the mountains surrounding the familiar sea lochs: Loch Long, Gare Loch, and, in the distance, beyond the Isle of Bute, Loch Fyne.

For a few moments he allowed his mind to wander even further to the west, to where the Atlantic rollers swept along the Argyll coast, weaving a complex pattern of currents around the tiny islands of the

Sound of Lorn . . . those islands of Seileach and Eisdalsa where he had spent his childhood.

Stephen's fifteen minutes were up.

Banking steeply to starboard, he brought the tiny aircraft round to face in the opposite direction and as he levelled out saw, approaching fast from the east, three fighter aircraft, monoplanes whose petal-shaped wings and slim aerodynamic outlines made them instantly recognisable. Spitfires!

They flew towards him on a collision path for a few minutes more before peeling off, one to port, one to starboard, and the third climbing to avoid him at the last minute.

My God, he thought, this must be what it's like to be attacked by the enemy. A few months from now, this could be for real.

Stephen's emotions were a mixture of anticipation and apprehension. Looking back over his shoulder beyond the second cockpit where the figure of his instructor, Middleton, might once have obscured his view, he was in time to see the central aircraft waggle its wings at him in friendly mockery. They had all made their first solo flight at some time. Perhaps there was just a little sympathy in that derisory gesture.

On the approach to Dumbarton Stephen was able to relax sufficiently to take in the unusual activity in John Brown's shipyard. Once they had launched the *Queen Mary* the previous year, thousands of workers had been laid off and it had seemed then that there was little prospect of any work in the future. Since Munich, however, a new phase of activity had begun. Now two skeletal hulls were rising from the dry dock area. Towering cranes dipped and wove like prehistoric monsters as they manoeuvred enormous steel girders into position. Tiny black match-stick figures crawled all over the superstructure like an army of ants.

It was good to see the yards busy again, even if it was the threat of war which had initiated the change.

Stephen had witnessed so much poverty and deprivation during his first year of residency at the Western Infirmary. The first thing to suffer when there was a depression was the health of the ordinary people, and it was the old folks and the children who succumbed first.

Down below him, still on the north bank of the river, the tall chimneys of the Singer works were belching out clouds of white smoke. He caught a glimpse of the great clock which was a landmark to sailors and airmen alike, and as Brown's yard disappeared beneath his port wing, Barclay's and then Henderson's took its place and he began his sweep round to the south and west again, passing above the massive yards of

Fairfield's and Harland and Wolf on the southern bank. Around every dry dock there was the same feverish activity.

As he came in over the airfield at Abbotsinch, Stephen reduced speed and began his descent, rehearsing the familiar procedures for landing.

The wheels touched down at approximately the right moment but they hit a bump in the turf, causing the little craft to catapult six feet into the air before she made contact with the ground again and came shakily to a standstill.

With limbs trembling he talked himself through the shut-down as aircraftsmen appeared on all sides. He loosened the strap on his leather helmet and sat for a moment, dazed at the enormity of his accomplishment.

'What kind of a landing d'you call that, Beaton?' The voice had the familiar badgering ring. Middleton was hanging over the side of the cockpit, shouting into his ear. 'Go up and round again and this time see if you can come in like a pilot and not a bloody kangaroo!'

'What d'yer think, Doc, will she do?'

Ellen extricated her arm and wiped it on the soiled piece of sacking which the hired hand passed to her.

'Should be any time now,' she decided. 'Some time tonight, I reckon. Everything's in place . . . the old girl shouldn't have too much trouble.'

The roan mare turned her head, limpid brown eyes observing the veterinary surgeon suspiciously. Recognising the familiar figure of the boss's daughter, however, she blew softly down her nose and returned her attention to the manger where Tanunda was ladling out a supply of her favourite oats.

Ellen McDougal pushed her sun-bleached hair back out of her eyes and replaced her wide-brimmed hat as she strode into the yard and made for the water trough.

It was a scorcher, sure enough. A black and white collie, with just a hint of tan on his rump and behind one ear, followed at her heels. She reached for the dibber and took a deep draught of water. The dog lapped contentedly at her side.

'Yer pal's going to be all right, Al,' she told him. The dog touched her hand gently with his nose before trotting back into the stable to settle in the straw alongside the mare. The two animals were inseparable. Jack McDougal's horse and his dog . . . one of a long line of sheepdogs descended from his original bitch, Vicky, who had accompanied him from Argyll when he emigrated to Australia before the war.

Ellen hoped the mare would be OK. Her father was anticipating a good foal.

She shielded her eyes against the glare of the sun and scanned the horizon for some sign of Jack. He ought to be back by now. It was only thirty miles to Miles Hamilton's spread and he'd set off very early that morning.

'I hope to God that damned truck isn't playing up again,' she said. 'Dad can't walk miles through the desert if she does. He'll just have to sit there until someone comes by with a tow rope.'

She imagined her father hobbling stiffly on his tin leg across the red, dusty plain. Impulsively, she threw down the dibber from which she had been drinking and turned to the Aborigine at her side.

'I'm going to see if I can spot the old man, Tanunda. Tell Ma I'm a bit worried that the truck might have broken down.'

She hurried over to the shed and led out her own horse, an Arab stallion which stood over seventeen hands. Ellen, who had sat in the saddle before she could walk, could ride the most demanding of mounts and Grey Whisper was certainly that.

She swung her light frame up into the saddle, checked the water bottle she had filled only that morning, and took her medical bag from Tanunda, fitting it on to the saddle in front of her. Experience had taught her never to travel without it.

Although more than a quarter of a century had passed since this tract of land had been opened up for development, the road from Southern Cross down to Albany was still little more than a dirt track. The twenty-mile section which skirted Kerrera station was better metalled than some other parts, but no one had yet come up with any form of tarmacadam which wouldn't melt in temperatures of more than a hundred and twenty degrees. As a consequence, the surface of rough stone chippings was torn up by heavy vehicles which left huge potholes to trap the unwary traveller and buckle the wheels of lightweight trucks.

Normally, Ellen would have taken a short cut through the bush on horseback, but she did not want to miss her father who should be driving home along the main road.

The sun was low in the western sky and the dusty air made it glow red above the horizon, painting the red sandstone hills with mysterious figures, formed by the deep purple shadows. The gum trees rustled in the evening breeze blowing up from the coast. It was the first time that day that she had felt reasonably cool.

Throughout her childhood, Ellen had absorbed her father's colourful memories of the Hebridean Island where he was born. It would be autumn in Scotland now. Buzzards would have come down from the mountains to keep watch for carrion, perching on every convenient pole and gate post. Purple heather, sweeping across the hillsides, would highlight the rich brown of the dying bracken, and rowan trees in the hedges would be weighed down by their huge clusters of bright red berries.

Everything here at Kerrera station was designed to remind them all of 'back home'. The very name Kerrera was taken from the Scottish island where her grandmother had spent her childhood. The Pastor's tin church in town was called St Brendon's after the kirk in which her father had been christened.

As her grandfather had called his property after places in Scotland, so too had their neighbours. There was a Kilmarnock House and a village called Dalmally only a few miles down the road, while the very names of their neighbours identified them as coming from the Welsh hills or the Scottish Highlands. Joneses and Lewises rubbed shoulders with the McNabs and the McKinnons, but while the older generation maintained the accents of their home country, the youngsters, like Ellen herself, had assimilated that distinctive twang which separated her and her contemporaries from first-generation Australians.

She had never really thought much about the difference between her father's accent and her own until her cousin Stephen had come to stay, back in '32. When she had heard her father and her cousin talking together, she'd realised for the first time why it was that Jack McDougal sounded so different from the roustabouts who came to work on the station.

She had been forced to admit that Stephen's accent was perhaps more refined than her father's, which must be due in part to his Edinburgh schooling. He had been very proud of the fact that he had been a pupil at Watson's School, attended by both his father and his grandfather. She wondered what it was like to come from such solid foundations. Her own family seemed to have become scattered to such an extent that there were very few whom she could call close relatives. Her grandfather, John McDougal, had founded Kerrera and before he died had seen the opening of a school in the little township whose first teacher had been her aunt, Mary McGillivray, and a hospital where her cousin Flora was still Matron. Ellen supposed that if she were to have children, they too might grow up here to form some kind of a dynasty, but they would have to wait a long time before they approached anything like the Beatons.

She remembered how Stephen had once proudly run through the list of doctors in Scotland who bore the Beaton name. There was even a girl, Morag Beaton, who was, she believed, a surgeon. Stephen was going to be a surgeon too. He had been quite adamant about that. When Jack McDougal had suggested once that perhaps he might follow a different career, her cousin had been most determined. 'I must have iodoform in my blood,' he protested. 'I've never considered any other way of life.'

He had spent several months at Kerrera the year before he began his medical training. Ellen had already started on her university course, but since she was doing her farm practice on her own home ground at the time of his visit, they had managed to see quite a lot of each other.

Stephen must be nearing the end of his training by now, Ellen thought. She wondered where he would be working by the time she got to England . . . if she ever got there. Would he be pleased to see her? she wondered. They had got on well together when he was here, but of course at that time he had had no other distractions. She wondered how she might fare in competition with the sophisticated young women with whom he mixed in Glasgow. They must both have changed a lot since he was here.

The horse shied at a deeper shadow lying in his path. Ellen reined him in, stooping from the saddle to see what had attracted his attention.

A kangaroo lay at the side of the road. He seemed to have been injured . . . hit by some passing vehicle, she assumed.

She slipped from the saddle and approached the beast warily. The Big Red could be pretty dangerous when cornered.

In his alarm, the animal showed her the whites of his eyes and struggled to regain his feet. He forced himself up on to one leg but the other dangled uselessly and after a few seconds he toppled over again to lie panting rapidly, his neck stretched out, his tongue lolling.

White foam had gathered around his lips. The creature was clearly dying.

Ellen crouched down beside him and gently rubbed her fingers along his neck, all the while speaking quietly to him so as not to alarm him further. After a while he seemed satisfied that she meant him no harm and began to relax. Still stroking the soft red skin of the kangaroo's neck, she reached for her bag and searched with her fingers for what she required to ease his pain. She had to leave off for a moment in order to find the bottle she needed and to fill a syringe. When she did so, the animal raised his head to watch her, his limpid brown eyes no longer showing any alarm.

'OK, mate,' Ellen crooned, 'soon be over now. Just a little prick, that's all.'

With a pair of scissors she cut away a little of the fur from the back of one ridiculously tiny hand, and plunged the needle into bare skin. As she released the drug into his bloodstream, the creature closed his eyes. In a few seconds it was all over.

Ellen took out her stethoscope to make quite sure that he was dead. Then she repacked the bag and sat back on her heels, brushing away a tear as she did so. Used as she was to animals in all states of sickness and injury, she had never really come to terms with the harsh reality of death.

She consoled herself with the thought that there was nothing more she could have done for the poor beast. At least she had saved him from a lingering and painful death. She would have liked to move him off the road, but he was a granddaddy of a Big Red . . . must have stood six feet high at least and certainly weighed as much as any well-grown man.

She wished she could have buried him but as it was the carcass would provide food for a multitude of scavengers in a land where everything edible disappeared within hours of dying.

She crouched over the magnificent corpse for a few minutes more, her hand smoothing the soft fur of his cheek and brushing across the dog-like nose.

She smiled to herself. Even this poor, abandoned carcass reminded her of Stephen.

The Big Red's skin, its reddish hues enhanced by the rays of the dying sun, was the colour of her cousin's hair when he had been swimming in the creek. Close-cropped and tightly curled, she recalled how it had dried to stand out like a flaming halo around his head. His eyes were blue and strangely pale. They might have been quite menacing had not the creases, formed when he screwed them up as he stared into the sun, broadened and softened his generous smile.

The sound of an approaching motor vehicle caused her to straighten up and peer ahead to where a cloud of dust approached at speed. To avoid the truck, she walked the horse to the side of the road and waited for the vehicle to pass. Only when it was within a few yards was she able to recognise her father's vehicle.

She waved him down.

'What've you got there?' he enquired, climbing out of the cab and coming to join her. 'My goodness, that's a mighty big fellow. What happened to him?'

'Run down by a truck . . . his leg was broken. I had to give him a shot.'

Jack McDougal glanced at his daughter, searching her face for any sign of distress. He knew how she hated to lose a patient.

'Nothing else you could do for a wild creature like that,' he said. 'We'd better move him off the road. If something were to hit that, it could cause an accident.'

Together they were able to lift the animal to the side of the road. Somehow Ellen felt better for having prevented the possibility of the kangaroo's body being further mutilated.

'Anyway,' said her father, spitting on his soiled hands and rubbing them on his cords, 'what're you doing out here, girl?'

'Just wondered where you might have got to,' Ellen replied as nonchalantly as she could manage.

'Your mother sent you, I suppose?'

'As a matter of fact . . . no,' she replied. 'I was a bit worried about the truck. She's been playing up a bit lately.'

'You women'll be the death of me,' Jack protested. 'Anyone'd think I was a baby the way you both look out for me. Still, it won't be long before I have one less of you to bother me, that's for sure.'

Grinning, he pulled a yellow envelope from his breast pocket.

'This cablegram was at the Post Office, waiting for someone to collect it.'

'Oh, Dad, it's come . . . well, what does it say?'

'How should I know? You don't think I'd open your mail, do you?'

'Yes, I do!' she cried, exasperated. 'Oh, come on, let me see it.'

She found the flap undone and grinned up at him. Of course he knew the contents.

SECONDMENT TO BRITISH ROYAL COLLEGE OF VETERINARY SURGEONS APPROVED STOP REPORT ASAP FOR FINAL BRIEFING STOP SAILING FIFTEENTH INST STOP CONGRATULATIONS STOP GERRARD.

Chapter Two

Annie, concentrating hard upon her sewing and trying desperately to hold back the tears as she did so, was startled to hear the clock strike.

Could it be nine o'clock already? She would have to hurry or she would be late for her first appointment.

Snipping a thread, she laid the light blue tunic carefully across the back of a chair, smoothing flat the cloth badge on which she had been working. Much as she hated to see them there, the blue wings of the RAF pilot really did look very impressive.

Brushing the back of her hand across her eyes, she felt for her pocket handkerchief and blew her nose loudly. Then she struggled to her feet and placed the tunic over the back of a chair.

Annie was no lightweight. The spread of middle age had been added to a body structure which had always been of ample proportions. She stood five feet eight in her stockings and her childhood training had left her back ramrod-straight despite the privations of earlier days, when she had spent a period in Holloway gaol as a Suffragette. Starvation had taken its toll on a previously robust constitution but there was little sign now of the harrowing times through which she had once lived. Her hair, although pure white, was still thick and wavy, bearing the same gloss which had one made it glisten like a raven's wing.

She heard her son Stephen's eager step on the stairs.

He had been so excited when he had revealed his secret last night. It had reminded her of the time when Stuart had come home from university, just before the war, to tell his father he had enlisted in the Royal Navy. Just as his father David Beaton had had to accept that Stuart had relinquished the promise of an excellent posting in a London hospital to become a Naval Surgeon, so now Stuart himself was obliged to allow his son to forgo the opportunity of taking his Membership examinations in order to become a fighter pilot.

She hurriedly brushed away a tear as her son bounded into the room.

'You're going to be late,' said Annie, needlessly.

Stephen bustled around the table, spreading toast and pouring himself a cup of tea from the big brown pot.

'If you'd care to wait a few minutes more, I'll boil you an egg,' she suggested.

'No time, Mother, really,' he replied. Then, noticing his tunic, he picked it up and admired her handiwork.

'That's splendid!' he cried, delightedly. 'Thanks very much.'

He grabbed her to him in a bear hug which nearly took her breath away then set her down gently on her chair, carefully ignoring the tear-stained cheeks and reddened eyes. Although she had risen early to sew the wings on his tunic, he understood the pain that last night's announcement had caused her. Only by convincing herself that no military command would be so foolish as to risk the life of a fully trained surgeon by making him into a fighter pilot, had she been able to come to terms with the situation.

Stephen stepped back, regarding Annie proudly. None of his friends could boast such a handsome, intelligent creature for a mother . . . no one so understanding and so worldly wise. Despite her shock and disappointment last night, she had nevertheless been prepared to sew on his badges. That must mean she had accepted the inevitable.

Annie Beaton had always been a pillar of strength in her son's life. For the first few years of his existence they had lived together on Eisdalsa Island in the Hebrides, while Stuart Beaton completed his naval service. Even when, a civilian again, Stephen's father had taken up private medical practice for the first time, Stuart had remained a somewhat shadowy figure in his son's life. It was to his mother that the boy had always turned for comfort and advice at the most problematic moments.

He watched her now with affection and not a little concern as she busied herself, moving purposefully between the stove and the sink.

Annie was looking tired.

Stephen sometimes wondered what had produced the deep lines about his mother's eyes, and the furrows which appeared on her brow when she felt she was unobserved. What tragedy could have caused that tiny downturn at the corners of her mouth which at times made her seem so vulnerable?

'Dad not up yet?' he asked her, making a grab for his lab coat and books which he had left scattered across the dresser top the night before.

'He's in the surgery,' she told him. 'It's Govan day, today . . . he's just doing a few little jobs before he leaves.'

'Tell him I'll see him tonight.'

He kissed her lightly on the forehead then hurried out, pausing only to gather his hat from the hall stand before slamming the front door behind him.

Annie pursed her lips in disapproval and then her mouth softened. There was something comforting in having her big, noisy son about the house. He would not be at home for much longer . . . she should make the most of him while there was still time.

She picked up the tunic and folded it carefully. Perhaps she should get Mrs Brown to give it a press later on. There was no knowing how soon Stevie would want it again.

'Annie, have you seen my good pen? I was using it last night, I know. Must have put it down in here somewhere.'

Stuart Beaton poked his head around the door, hoping to see his son before he left.

'Stephen gone?'

'Just this minute . . . he was already late.'

'I only wanted to congratulate him again. I can't get over it . . . our son able to fly an aeroplane. If I was a few years younger, I reckon I would want to do the same.'

'Thank goodness you're not then, is all I can say. One idiot to worry about in the family is quite enough.'

He looked at her sharply, noticing the deep frown which always betrayed her when she was particularly concerned about anything.

'There's no point in wasting energy worrying about what might or might not happen in the future, Annie. Who knows what any of us will be doing in six months' time? Let's just make the most of what we have, eh? Stephen is no fool. He's not going to waste his life on some reckless folly. You wouldn't expect him to sit back and let others fight his battles for him, though, would you? Not when you have set him such a different example!'

Touché, she thought.

Annie Beaton had never been one to avoid a fight, so why should she imagine her son would be any different?

Stuart was pleased to see the deep furrows on her brow disappear.

'Well, I'd better be off.'

Annie followed her husband out into the hall and watched him place his Homburg hat at just the right angle. He looked every inch the prosperous consultant in his pin-stripe trousers and his short black jacket. She sometimes regretted that surgeons no longer wore silk hats and morning coats for her father-in-law had always cut such an imposing figure in his formal dress.

She took a brush and removed a little fluff from Stuart's shoulders. That was the trouble with black . . . it showed every mark. She noticed the dull tones of the loose hairs gathered up on the brush and realised that he was thinning almost to baldness. His once thick auburn hair had, over the years, turned a mousey grey. Only the bushy eyebrows and neatly trimmed moustache now gave an indication of the fiery colouring of his youth. Why should it matter that there were a few less hairs and a more pronounced stoop? He was still the most handsome man around in her eyes, and that was all that mattered to either of them.

She lifted her face to be kissed and as their lips touched she knew that no amount of years would dampen the fire, the excitement, conjured up by his presence. They lingered over their embrace until the moment was shattered by the sound of a key in the scullery door and the tap-tapping of Mrs Brown's heels on the quarry-tiled floor.

'Goodness, is it that time already?' Stuart exclaimed. 'I'd better be going.'

'Are you likely to be late in?'

'It was a pretty short list when I saw it last. I should be home in good time for evening surgery.'

'I just thought that we might have a special dinner tonight . . . a little feast to celebrate Stephen's success.' She smiled up at him, struggling to maintain her composure.

'Good girl, Annie,' he said, smiling down at her. She might have been five years old again, the way he applauded her acceptance of the matter. 'That sounds a splendid idea!'

She followed him down the steps to his black Wolseley, parked beneath the lime trees where a narrow service road separated their terrace of Georgian houses from the Great Western Road and the Botanic Gardens beyond.

She kissed him again before he climbed in behind the wheel and started the engine. With a quick wave he drew away from the curb. Annie waited until he had turned out into the flow of traffic making for the Clyde Tunnel before turning back to the house.

Mrs Brown was waiting at the open door, a bunch of letters in her hand.

'Good morning, Mrs Beaton.'

The daily help followed her employer into the kitchen, sorting through the post as she did so.

'They're mostly for the doctor as usual,' she said, 'bills and such like, I shouldn't wonder.'

She laid a pile of assorted envelopes on the chenille table cover, retaining two which she handed to Annie.

'Both from Australia,' she announced, with a suspicious sniff as though correspondence from overseas had no business landing in their letter box.

Annie, recognising her niece's writing, laid the letter from Flora McGillivray aside and examined the unfamiliar hand on the second envelope.

Mrs Brown, her hands thrust deep into the pockets of her flowery overall, looked on too. Her hair, which had been tightly wound in rag curlers all night, was completely hidden by a turban of Paisley-patterned cotton. Annie had never seen her otherwise, and would probably not have recognised her had they met under different circumstances.

The woman was excruciatingly thin, her true height disguised by a pronounced stoop, due to the arthritis in her spine. Her features, although perhaps a trifle bird-like, with a narrow beak of a nose jutting downwards to meet an upward-curving chin, were nevertheless finely chiselled. Her well-formed cheekbones, highlighted by the deep hollows beneath them, gave her a certain air of breeding.

Annie had often wondered how Maggie would look well dressed, carefully made-up and expensively coiffured.

It was clear now that she had no intention of going about her work until she had discovered who was writing to her employer from such a distance.

Annie tore open the envelope, scanned the first few lines and said, 'It's from my step-brother . . . the one who farms sheep near Southern Cross.'

'Isna that where your Stephen stayed a year or two back?'

'Yes, indeed. My parents and my step-brother went out there before the war.'

'I couldna do any such thing,' declared the other woman. 'I canna see why anyone in their right mind would want to go so far away.'

'They were hard times, Maggie. There was no work for the men where my family lived in Argyll. Emigration seemed the only answer. My people did very well out there, although life must have been tough in the early years.'

Annie thought of her mother as she had seen her on that last occasion, soon after Stuart was discharged from the Navy. They had taken the infant Stephen to visit the farm in the outback so that Anne McDougal might see her grandson. By then the farm had been well developed, the homestead and the other buildings were comfortable and her mother had seemed contented with her lot.

Annie and Stuart had found Perth to be a young, vibrant city with a great deal going on and many plans for the future. They were equally impressed by Kerrera, the sheep station of which John McDougal seemed justly proud.

Encouraged by a grateful government, veterans returning from the war had settled in the newly established township of Kerrera, bringing with them a multitude of skills and experiences. Lacking sufficient money to complete the building programme, however, by the time Annie and Stuart arrived, John had ceased to hope that he would ever see his dream project completed.

Her mother had suggested, a trifle wistfully, that Annie and Stuart might consider staying on. She had stressed the advantages to baby Stephen of growing up on a farm. Had explained that John McDougal planned to build a hospital . . . it was one of his top priorities. Would not Stuart consider being its first Superintendent?

At the time he had had other plans, however, and Annie could see little prospect of a good life for her infant son in that backwoods place with such an uncertain future.

They had sailed home from Fremantle only weeks before John McDougal died. His wife had followed him soon after, and Annie had considered that with her mother dead, there was little incentive for them to return to Australia.

Now her glance rested momentarily on Stephen's uniform jacket. She picked up her step-brother's letter, wondering as she did so if Stephen would not have been safer after all had they chosen to settle there when they had the opportunity.

Kerrera Station
Kerrera
Western Australia

31 October 1938

My Dear Annie,
You will be surprised to hear from me after all these years. I am afraid that I am not a great correspondent and usually leave it to the

womenfolk to keep in touch with things at home. Flora will tell you all our news as she always does, but I have a special favour to ask and must, on this occasion, put pen to paper myself.

My daughter Ellen, who took such a fancy to your Stevie when they met as infants, is now at university in Melbourne where she has just become qualified as a veterinary surgeon.

Annie recalled the curly-haired wean with her matchboxes full of beetles and caterpillars, her escort of dogs of many breeds and none, and a yard full of ducks and chickens which she mustered and commanded like a regiment of troops. It was hardly surprising that little Ellen had taken to agriculture as a career, but for a woman to become a veterinarian . . . that must have taken a great deal of perseverance against the tide of opinion.

Annie knew just how difficult it was for a woman to row against that tide. She herself had studied Law at university but had never been allowed to graduate, despite holding a number of important legal posts in the government during and after the war.

Ellen has obtained a post as a research assistant at the Royal Veterinary College in London and will be sailing from Fremantle in two weeks' time. Her appointment is for two years although what will happen should there be a war, I don't know.

I have suggested that she contact you on her arrival in England as I know that she is anxious to see Argyll, particularly Eisdalsa. Although we all talk of Scotland as *home*, we McDougals have no one left whom we can call family except yourselves. I would be very grateful if you and Stuart would try to keep an eye on her. I know that she is a grown woman but I cannot help being a little apprehensive about her travelling to the other side of the world without us.

Ellen still remembers your visit and often talks of you all. I know that she is looking forward to meeting Stephen again. He made a great impression upon everyone on the station when he was here in '32. Can it really be so long ago?

Ellen's ship is the *Southern Cross*, docking at Tilbury on 3 December. She has arranged to stay in London with a fellow student who will be travelling with her and who has relatives in Norbury, but she hopes to be able to travel north to sample a real Scottish New Year before taking up her post on 15 January.

I attach Ellen's address in London should you wish to write to her.
Jeannie sends her love to you both.
All good wishes,
Jack McDougal

'We shall have to invite her here for Hogmanay.' Annie spoke her
thoughts aloud, forgetting that she had an audience.

'A relative coming on a visit?' asked Mrs Brown. Visitors made extra
work, of course, but it would be nice to have a new face about the house
for a while.

'My step-brother's daughter . . . I suppose one might call her
my niece. It's all a trifle complicated.' Annie was not prepared to go
into details about the relationship between the McGillivrays and
the McDougals. Annie's mother had married her neighbour, John
McDougal, after they had both been widowed for years. Annie had
known her step-brother, Jack, as a school friend of her brother, Dougal,
for as long as she could remember. She had always found it difficult to
think of him as anything other than a good friend.

'Ellen is coming to London to study but she may visit us for New
Year, that's all,' Annie explained. 'I shall write straight away and invite
her.'

A letter to the address in Norbury should just about coincide with
the arrival of the *Southern Cross*. She turned over the other envelope,
intending to open it, then seeing the time, stuffed it in her handbag. If
she did not leave right away she would be late for her first interview. Her
niece's letter would have to wait.

The woman was every inch the solid Scottish matron; tall, broad-
shouldered, back stiff as a board, chest thrown out defiantly, her one
good, navy serge costume well brushed and smelling faintly of naphtha
balls. The iron-grey hair was dragged back and clamped firmly into a tight
bun. It sat just above her collar, and on it perched the brim of a shapeless black felt hat whose only decoration was a tiny bunch of linen violets
worn jauntily, just above the right ear.

The lad beside her was thin as a bean-pole and tall – five foot seven
or eight. His pallor was that of a child fed on porridge, bread and scrape
and little else, probably, since the day he was weaned. He wore grey
flannel trousers, carefully mended at the knees and reaching to a point

just above his ankle bones. By contrast, his tweed sports jacket was several sizes too big, the sleeves long enough to cover his hands completely. In his nervousness he frequently raised his right hand to pass his fingers through a shock of ginger hair which curled in unruly fashion across his forehead. When he did so, his over-wide sleeve fell back to expose a painfully thin and none too clean forearm.

'Well . . . ma'am,' the woman began, diffidently, 'if it was for m'self I would'na be askin' but it's for the laddie here, d'ye ken?'

'What exactly is the problem, Mrs McKechnie?' Annie Beaton sat behind the desk, her pencil poised. She understood how difficult it was for the proud poor to ask for assistance of any kind and in normal circumstances would have allowed the woman to come to the point in her own time, but there were ten more claimants waiting outside and Annie had hoped to be away before six.

'My Tam here has the chance of work in England, if he can pay the fare to London. If he isna taken on they'll gie him his fare hame . . . so it's just the fifteen shillings for the train down that we'll be needin'.' The final words came out in a rush as this well-rehearsed speech rattled off her tongue.

'I need just a little more detail,' Annie explained, gently. 'What sort of work is it that your boy has been offered? Is there a reasonable possibility that he'll be given employment?'

'Well, y'see, ma'am, my Tammy is a braw hand wi' the pencils and brushes and that, and his art teacher says he should go to Art College, but o' course I canna afford to send him . . . so the teacher sent away for forms to join the Civil Service as a map-maker in the Surveying Department. Tammy filled them in and did a wee test for them and they say they want to see him. There may be an apprenticeship for him.'

'That sounds like a fine opportunity, Tam.' Annie smiled at the boy encouragingly, hoping to get him to speak up for himself. She made a note on the sheet before her and then regarded him closely.

'Fifteen shillings for the fare, you say, Mrs McKechnie?' The woman nodded eagerly, almost unable to believe that their plea might be answered.

'For the Civil Service they will want you to wear a smart suit, Tam,' Annie said carefully, trying not to embarrass him. Clearly the youth was dressed up for the occasion in his father's best which meant that he had no other decent clothing of his own. 'I am able to make you a loan of, say, three pounds, which you may pay back when you are able . . . enough, I would think, to kit you out quite well.'

18

Nothing was said of the consequences were he to be refused the job. A loan seemed less patronising than a charitable gift.

'Thank you,' Mrs McKechnie blurted out. 'That will be most satisfactory.'

Annie wrote for a few moments and then passed the chitty across the table.

'This is a travel voucher. Just hand it to the clerk when you buy your ticket.'

With a muttered 'thank you', the boy pocketed the slip of paper before his mother could lay hands on it. She had insisted on coming with him thus far, but he was damned if he was going to have her collecting his ticket at the station!

'And if you will just sign here,' Annie showed him where, on the second sheet of paper, 'this is a receipt for the money for your clothes.' Incautiously perhaps she added, 'There should be sixpence left over for a haircut.'

The other woman pursed her lips and nodded.

The boy shuffled his feet uncomfortably but made no response. Soon he would be on his own . . . away from all these interfering women!

Annie took a key from her ring and opened a small drawer in the desk. She extracted two pounds ten shillings in notes and counted out a further ten shillings in coinage.

'. . . three . . . five . . .seven. . . ten . . . there you are, three pounds. Don't worry if it takes you a little time to repay the loan. The Society is very understanding.'

The boy pocketed the coins and carefully folded the notes, placing them beside the precious docket for travelling. Freedom at last!

As the two of them left, Annie caught snippets of their conversation once they were outside in the corridor.

'Would ye no' like me to put that money in ma bag, Tam?' demanded the mother.

'Naw, it's all right where it is!'

She smiled to herself. The boy was clinging fiercely to this first vestige of independence.

Annie got up and went to the waiting-room door. 'Next, please,' she called.

A man, stoop-shouldered and with the all-enveloping greyness which marked out the permanently unemployed, shuffled towards her.

She glanced down at the list in her hand.

'Mr Doran?'

'Aye.'

'Do sit down.'

Awkwardly he seated himself on the edge of the chair, clutching his flat cap nervously in thick sausage-like fingers.

'There's a chance of a start at Fairfield's,' he blurted out suddenly, 'for them as has a pair of steel-capped boots and a set of tools. Mine's in pawn,' he explained apologetically. Then, more defiantly, 'There isna ony use hanging on to a set o' tools when the weans is starving.' He drifted into silence. He had said all there was to say.

'What will it cost to redeem your tools?'

'Two pound is all,' he replied, slipping his finger inside the tight neckerchief which substituted for a collar.

'And the boots?'

'Fifteen shilling the pair.'

'You do appreciate that the Society makes loans only for clothing and travel as a rule?' Annie emphasised. 'It would not do for word to get around we were an easy touch.'

He shuffled his feet and stared at the ground.

'In the circumstances, however,' she continued hastily, 'I believe I can accommodate you. Please bring along the redemption receipt . . .' he looked puzzled '. . . you'll get one when you pay for the tools.'

'Oh, aye.' He nodded.

'And I'll expect repayment of the loan, interest free of course, as soon as you can manage it.'

'Ah, weel.' He'd just remembered what his wife had called after him down the stair.

'D'na forget there's the interest t'pay on the money for the tools!'

He glanced at Annie guiltily, aware that he had made a mistake in not saying straight out how much he wanted.

'Yes?' she enquired encouragingly.

'There's the interest on the two pounds . . .'

'How will it be if we make the loan two pounds ten shillings?' she suggested. 'Then you can clear the whole debt and start fresh.'

Relief flooded the man's face and for the first time Annie noticed a spark of internal fire, a flash of the spirited, intelligent person that Charlie Doran had once been, before the long years of depression and lack of employment had taken away his self-respect.

She counted the money and handed him the pen with which to sign.

'No interest?' He wanted to hear her say it once again, to reassure himself. He knew all about the loan sharks who charged so much money that their clients were never able to pay them back.

'No, no interest. But of course the sooner you are able to repay the loan, the sooner we can help someone else.'

He nodded, rose from the chair and touched his forelock.

'I won't let you down, missus,' he said determinedly. With a lighter step he strode from the room, his head high.

Usually these sessions left Annie drained and miserable but somehow this afternoon had been most rewarding. Perhaps things were looking up after all. She went to call the next client.

'Mr Robertson?'

'It catches me just there, Doctor.' The woman indicated a spot just below her breastbone. 'If you'll just give me ma usual pink bottle, I'll be a' right.'

Her words held no conviction and Stuart Beaton knew very well that there was more to his patient's condition than simple indigestion.

'Nevertheless, Mrs Fergusson, it's a long time since you came to see me. I think I should take a closer look, don't you? If you'll just strip off to the waist and pop up on the bed . . .' He indicated the white screen placed discreetly around a leather-covered couch. Stuart could never understand why people were so reluctant to be examined by their doctor. They came along expecting miracles, but were horrified when he asked to examine them thoroughly.

Mrs Fergusson rose hesitantly and hid herself behind the screen. The iron-clad matron could be heard heaving and grunting as layer upon layer of body armour was removed. Finally she called out, 'A'm ready the now, Doctor.'

Wordlessly, Stuart observed the pink Spirella stays with their steel support rods and multitudinous laces, thrown over the back of the hard wooden chair, and thought it was not surprising that these women were forever complaining of pains in the abdomen. The wonder was they managed to breathe at all. His mother, he recalled, had worn similar corsets and nothing would have persuaded her to forgo their rigidity for the relief and freedom of a less formidable undergarment.

He warmed his hands, rubbing them together briskly, before laying them on the mountain of flesh, deeply striated by the merciless corset from which it had escaped.

As he manipulated her abdomen with firm fingers, Mrs Fergusson winced but remained silent.

'Can you feel anything here?' Stuart demanded as he palpated the liver. 'Or here?'

With a loud screech, she shouted, 'Lord 'a' mercy! What are you trying to do?'

'It hurts when I touch you there?' he asked, careful not to do so, again.

'It's like a red-hot needle, Doctor.'

Nodding brusquely, absorbed now in what he was doing, Stuart fixed his stethoscope into his ears, and continued his examination, noting the condition of her heart and lungs. Finally he peeled back each of her eyelids in turn, looking for, and finding, a tell-tale yellow coloration.

'All right, Mrs Fergusson, you may get dressed now.' Stuart moved out from behind the screen and sat down at his desk to write.

At last, dishevelled and perspiring freely, the woman re-emerged and seated herself in front of him.

'I'm afraid that there is no doubt about your condition, Mrs Fergusson. You have an inflamed gall bladder and I suspect that surgery is called for. I am just writing a note to the specialist for you to take along to the Western Infirmary for an appointment . . .'

'Oh, no!' she interrupted sharply.

The doctor looked up, startled.

'I beg your pardon?' He thought he must have misheard her.

'I will not be seen dead in one of those places,' she declared stoutly, unaware of the pun. 'My sister and my mother both went into hospital and never came out. You won't get me in there!'

Stuart glanced at the patient's record card. 'I see you have just had your forty-ninth birthday,' he observed, rather coolly.

Reluctantly, she nodded in agreement.

'If you don't have surgery pretty soon, Mrs Fergusson, I don't give much for your chances of seeing your fiftieth.'

On hearing of this unpalatable truth, the woman hesitated for a moment only.

'No,' she declared, 'we couldna afford to go private and I'll no' take a charity bed . . . I've heard what they do with you in those. We did join the HSA once but with ma man out o' work for so long we couldna keep up the payments.'

'It's a pity about the Hospital Savings Association,' Stuart observed. 'That would have covered you for everything. However, I can assure you that even in a free bed you would get the best of attention, Mrs Fergusson.'

Frustrated as he was by her attitude, Stuart respected her reluctance to take charity. What he could not understand was a pride so fierce that it prevented her from accepting free medical aid, even at the expense of her own life. Pride, obviously, and a deep-seated fear which stemmed from the experiences of previous generations.

'No one ever laid a knife on me,' she declared determinedly, 'and no one ever will! No, Doctor, just you give me ma usual bottle and I'll be right as rain, you'll see.'

He reached for his prescription pad.

'I think we can do better than bismuth, Mrs Fergusson,' he said, writing steadily, 'but I do think that you should discuss this with your husband. Don't you think you owe it to him to tell him the truth?'

She snorted in disgust.

'Him!' she cried. 'He never made a decision in his life. What would he know about anything?'

'He might want you to take a chance of saving yourself for a ripe old age,' Stuart suggested, mildly.

'No one will ever lay a knife on me!' she repeated adamantly, and snatching up the prescription he had written for her, stormed out of the room.

The encounter with Mrs Fergusson had left Stuart dispirited after a day which had seemed relatively successful until his encounter with the wretched woman. Annie noticed it the moment he came into the kitchen.

'Tired?' she enquired as he rested his weight on the scrubbed wooden table and watched her peeling potatoes at the sink.

'Couldn't you get Mrs Brown to do the vegetables before she goes home?' he asked, ignoring her question.

'I can't ask her to stay on any later,' Annie explained, 'she has to fetch her little boy from school. Besides, I don't mind doing this one bit . . . it relaxes me.'

'Busy day?' He slipped off his jacket and poured water into the kettle, setting it on the gas stove to boil.

'A bit better than usual, as a matter of fact,' she answered. 'To begin with, I had two letters from Australia. One was from Jack McDougal . . . it seems that Ellen is coming over to London to work at the Royal School of Veterinary Surgery. Can you believe that? Anyway, he asks if we will make her welcome should she come north to visit Argyll. I wondered if we should ask her to join us for Hogmanay? We might even manage to go over to Eisdalsa and spend the holiday with Hugh.'

'Imagine that little scrap coming all this way alone,' Stuart mused, absent-mindedly.

'Hardly a little scrap!' Annie laughed. 'She is older than Stephen by about six months!'

'Well, I can't imagine her any other way.' He dismissed the topic abruptly then, realising that he was being rather boorish, continued half apologetically, 'You said two letters?'

'The second was from Flora. It seems that she is to be married at last, to a physician they appointed to Kerrera Hospital last year. I really thought Flora would remain a nursing sister all her life, but it seems she has found her ideal partner after all. I do hope she will be happy. We must find something suitable to send as a wedding gift.'

Stuart grunted a response. He seemed to have lapsed into his own gloomy thoughts once again so Annie continued brightly, 'There seems to be work about at last. I had three requests today for boots so that men could go and sign on at the shipyards.'

'It's a pity it has to take the threat of war to put people back to work,' he sighed. 'It was just the same in 1913. People poured out of the country, looking for something better in the colonies. A year later they were begging men to come back home to work in the yards or join in the fighting. The McDougals are a prime example.'

'I suppose if there is a war, they'll be expecting the women to take over from the men in the factories again,' Annie observed. 'The government was pleased enough to have their support during the crisis, but immediately the Armistice was signed all that was forgotten. Then the women were sent back to the kitchen sink with hardly so much as a thank you.'

She lifted a corner of the net curtain and glanced down on to the wide street below. Trams and horse-drawn vehicles mingled with motor cars and lorries, all moving in fits and starts along the Great Western Road as the city emptied itself for the night, dispersing its workforce into the mass of housing schemes which radiated from the city into the country-side for miles around.

From the far side of the road, the luscious greenery of the trees bordering the Botanic Gardens gave off a heavy scent of pine needles and elder flowers which, miraculously undiluted by the fumes of the traffic, wafted towards her on the evening breeze. Was it really possible that all of this might be wantonly destroyed by that maniac in Germany? A chill feeling in her spine caused Annie to shudder. Abruptly, she allowed the curtain to fall back into place.

'What was it that upset you this afternoon?' she asked as Stuart handed her the tea he had made.

'A woman so scared of hospitals that she refuses admission even though, without surgery, she is going to die. She has a husband and four children . . . one only ten years old . . . yet she is adamant that she won't have an operation.'

'They have long memories, some of them,' Annie murmured. 'You have to admit that hospitals used to be pretty gruesome. The common folk regarded them as places where you went to die.'

'Fifty years ago, maybe,' he agreed.

'Ignorance and fear are powerful allies,' Annie reminded him.

'A few months from now, one woman's gall bladder is going to prove pretty insignificant compared with the mutilations resulting from air raids and shelling,' Stuart murmured, and on this gloomy note, carried his cup into his study to work on the day's records before dinner.

Annie, taken suddenly with a fit of rage against those who were steering the world towards chaos, slammed a saucepan down on the stove with such force that she was obliged to pick it up again a moment later to make sure she had done no damage. She continued to vent her rage first upon the onions on her chopping board and then upon the carrots which she sliced with the determination of an axe man at the block!

By the time she heard the front door open and slam to, heralding the arrival of Stephen from the hospital, she was quite calm. Taking Jack McDougal's letter from the shelf where she had left it, she went out into the hall to meet him.

'Such a surprise, Stevie,' she greeted him. 'Your cousin Ellen is coming here for New Year.'

Chapter Three

A few moments before the station concourse had seemed almost empty. Now, slowly, it was beginning to fill as though, on some enormous stage setting, the cast was assembling. The London train was due at any moment.

A single porter hovered in desultory fashion near the Departures board. At the barrier to platform three the ticket collector was busily engaged in sorting his collection from a previous arrival. An old woman, dressed in layers of rags in the hope that what one garment failed to cover would be compensated for by another, visited the litter bins as a bee hovers over flowers, her quarry the carelessly wrapped remnants of a sandwich lunch, a half-consumed apple, a cigarette packet discarded still containing one last crumpled fag.

Stephen glanced up at the clock for the umpteenth time and cursed silently. The hand had hardly moved since the last occasion he had looked.

A small group of people had begun to gather around the barrier at last. More porters were lining up with their trolleys, ready to pour on to the platform the moment that the train entered the vast glazed dome that covered Glasgow's Central Station.

It was six years since Stephen had travelled alone to Australia to meet his cousins. Despite the fact that he and his mother had peered for ages last evening at the tiny snapshots he had taken with his box Brownie camera, he feared he would not be able to recognise Ellen McDougal.

The golden girl who had galloped beside him all day across the outback paddocks of Kerrera station would be nearly twenty-four by now, six months older than himself. She must be very different from that skinny tomboy with whom he had talked night after night on the high railway embankment, waiting to catch the evening breeze as the sun went down. He remembered how he had sat there under the stars, sharing with her his hopes and dreams for a future whose possibilities had seemed limitless.

He had loved every moment of his stay, almost regretting his commitment to five years of medical studies back home, before he could even think of returning to the wide horizons and the blazing skies of that extraordinary continent, the country which Ellen McDougal was able to call home.

The busy years between, so full of studies and rugby football and learning to fly, had put these thoughts right out of Stephen's head, but now, as he waited for her train to arrive, they all came flooding back . . .

There was a surge of activity around the barrier. Someone had spotted a signal falling and, yes . . . there . . . there she was . . . emerging from a cloud of dense white steam, her monstrous steamlined boiler growing larger by the second until she seemed to fill the entire concourse: the Coronation Scot.

Stephen waited impatiently for the steam to clear so that he could get a proper view of the people coming towards the barrier.

There was Ellen! A tall, nonchalant figure with her hiker's knapsack slung carelessly over one shoulder and a book grasped in her free hand.

She was just as he remembered her; golden-brown skin, clear grey eyes as bright as the open skies under which she had been reared, a smudge of freckles across her wide brow, and that big all-embracing smile . . .

She spotted him at almost the same instant that he picked her out of the crowd.

'Stevie!' she cried and flew towards him, her arms wide, knapsack bumping about her shoulders. Despite their own preoccupations, those around stood back to stare as the two young people hugged each other.

'I wasn't sure I would recognise you,' he confessed, laughing. 'But you haven't changed a bit!'

'You have, though.' She stood back, admiring his lithe, muscular body with its well-developed shoulders, noticing too the lines of maturity about his eyes, the serious expression which gave him a dignified, confident appearance. Yes, she thought, every inch the doctor. Just as she would have expected him to look.

'I can't believe it's really you!' he exclaimed. 'I would have expected you to be married to some farmer by now, mustering the jumbucks and raising a swarm of little diggers to feed the chooks and chase the goannas!'

Ellen was thrilled to hear him slip so easily into the kind of banter they had exchanged six years before. He must have thought quite a lot about the time they had spent together to come up with such expressions.

'Not too many Australian blokes show any interest in a female who spends her life with one arm stuck inside a pregnant cow,' she laughed. 'They prefer their Sheilas pink-cheeked and smelling of lavender.'

And how did Stephen Beaton prefer his women? she wondered. Maybe he too liked dizzy blondes. Or was it dark, mysterious *femmes fatales* for him?

'What about you?' she enquired lightly. 'Am I going to be introduced to the future Mrs Stephen Beaton this weekend?'

'Hardly,' he replied, laughing, 'I haven't had time to meet her yet.' She hoped her relief was not too obvious.

'With all those beautiful nurses you guys hob-nob with on the wards, one would think you might have found someone to suit your taste by now. You must be very particular.'

'I think you must have seen too many Hollywood versions of the medical profession,' he insisted. 'The Staff Nurses and above are as starchy as their cuffs and collars, and the new recruits are so frightened of Matron they daren't open their mouths.'

'Well, that's a relief,' said Ellen. 'It means the field is wide open for the rest of us.'

'Always supposing anyone would be interested in a penniless doctor who is nearly a surgeon but never likely to finish his training!'

'Why's that?' she demanded, suddenly serious.

'Oh, it's a long story,' he told her, and looked pointedly at her knapsack.

'You don't look like someone coming to stay in Scotland for a few months,' he said, grinning broadly. 'Have you got some more luggage somewhere?'

'Oh my God!' Her hand flew to her mouth. 'I forgot. There's a trunk in the guard's van. I was looking for a porter, then I spotted you and everything else went right out of my head . . .'

They collected a porter, a trolley and a trunk, in that order, and Stephen went off to find his father's car which he had parked in a road nearby. Soon they were threading a path through the noonday traffic, by way of Cowcaddens to St George's Cross, and out along the Great Western Road towards the Botanic Gardens.

'So you're a fully qualified veterinary surgeon, are you?' he asked as

Ellen settled back against the passenger seat and closed her eyes, relieved to have completed her journey at last.

'Yep.'

'I have to admit that when I left you back there at Kerrera, I never expected you to make it.'

'It wasn't easy,' she told him. 'Not everyone at Vet School thought it a suitable training for a young woman. I had the Devil's own job persuading the Dean that I could handle a sick cow just as well as any man my own size! They expected me to opt for a city practice with pampered poodles and Persian pussies, but I wanted to get back to the country where the real work is.

'In the end we compromised. They've sent me over here to do research work. I'm attached to the Royal College, but seconded up here to Aberdeen for a few months. They're doing some special work on cattle I want to have a look at.'

He turned into a service road and pulled up before an imposing terrace of four-storey houses, built in more affluent days to house the industrial magnates of the previous century. Ellen followed him up four stone steps to a front door and as she waited for him to find his key, took in their surroundings, crying out with delight at the prospect of the lush gardens across the road, and the tree-lined avenue that stretched out of sight towards the western boundaries of the city.

'My father always describes Glasgow as a hell-hole of a place, dirty, noisy and too full of people,' she explained, 'but this is absolutely beautiful!'

'I suspect that Jack McDougal saw little of Glasgow in his youth,' observed Stephen, 'other than Broomielaw Quay, where the Clyde steamers docked, and the railway station where he caught the train for London on his way to Australia.'

'Yes,' Ellen agreed. 'He always talks longingly of Argyll, though, the mountains and the islands of Lorn. I think he was envious when he waved me off on the ship from Fremantle.'

Stephen had the door open by now and was on his way back to the car for the rest of her luggage.

'Here, I'll give you a hand.' Ellen dumped her haversack in the hall and skipped down the steps, taking one of the handles as between them they lifted the heavy trunk into the house.

'Feels as if you've got one of your sick cows in there,' Stephen declared, wiping his brow which was damp from the effort.

'No . . . just books . . . and a few clothes, of course.'

Stephen eyed the trunk warily. He knew his mother had allocated a room on the second floor to their guest. The thought of carrying it up two flights of stairs was rather daunting.

'I think I'll wait until Dad gets home,' he said cautiously. 'He can give us a hand.'

'Aw, c'mon,' cried Ellen in disgust. 'Get it up on my shoulder and I'll take it meself.'

He had forgotten what a determined creature she was.

Together they hauled the heavy trunk up the stairs and into a bright room overlooking the street and the gardens across the way.

Stephen threw himself on the bed in mock exhaustion and Ellen ran to the window to gaze out on the scene below.

'This is just wonderful,' she cried, and came and sank down on the bed beside him.

He turned to her shyly, overwhelmed by her vibrant personality. He felt as brash and foolish as the boy who had arrived at Kerrera station all those years ago, his city clothes covered in red dust, his porkpie hat set square and his smart leather suitcase dangling from one kid-gloved hand.

Now he took both her hands in his.

'It's lovely to see you again, Ellen,' he said, warmly, and leaned forward to kiss her. She flung her arms around his neck and kissed him full on the mouth.

'Oh, Stevie . . . I've been so excited about this trip and seeing you again and meeting Auntie Annie and Dr Stuart! I can scarcely remember them.'

'Mother remembers *you* all right, though.' He laughed, the moment of tension gone. 'Last night she was recalling collections of creepy crawlies, pet lizards and other hazards with which you used to surround yourself. I couldn't remember any of that . . . but I was no more than four or five years old at that time. All I can recall of that first visit was a huge basket full of collie pups.'

Mention of her beloved dogs gave Ellen a sudden pang of home-sickness, but she was determined that nothing should mar this reunion. Thrusting aside any further thoughts of home, she jumped up and threw open the lid of the trunk. Rummaging among the contents, she came up at last with a strangely shaped parcel which she handed to Stephen almost reverently.

'Do you remember our stockman, Taffee? He took a real shine to you, you know. He made this 'specially when he heard that I was coming over to see you. It's a great honour for an Aborigine to give away his boomerang. It's like giving away a part of himself.'

Stephen well remembered the skinny black man with a limp, who had kept such a keen eye on all Ellen's movements. He had been her protector since the day that she was born, and during Stephen's stay Ellen's mother had not let them out of sight of the homestead unless Taffee was with them.

He unwrapped the parcel to expose a boomerang in polished eucalyptus wood. Flamboyantly decorated in glorious jewel-like colours, it was a work of art.

'That's beautiful,' he said, allowing his fingers to caress the carefully chamfered edges, smooth as satin.

She was glad. He had not disappointed her. Others might not appreciate the significance of the gift, but Stephen clearly understood its value.

'I will write and thank him,' he murmured.

There was some sort of commotion in the hall below and they heard his mother's voice protesting loudly in unladylike terms.

'Stephen . . . are you up there?' she called from the foot of the stairs.

'Up here, Mother. In Ellen's room.'

'Really, Stephen,' his mother complained when she arrived, breathless, leaning against the doorpost and rubbing her leg furiously, 'I do wish you wouldn't leave things just inside the door like that . . . I nearly fell over.'

'I'm sorry, Aunt Annie, that was my fault. I do hope you haven't hurt yourself?' The warm, soft voice of the girl startled her.

'Why, Ellen, my dear . . . how good to see you.'

Annie advanced into the room, catching Ellen in a big hug and turning her towards the light so that she might get a proper look at Jack McDougal's daughter. When she did so she gave a gasp of recognition, her arms falling quickly to her sides.

The long silky hair, struggling successfully for release from the tight knot into which Ellen had wound it, was the colour of ripe corn. The light grey eyes, high cheekbones and fresh complexion, she owed to her Highland ancestry. Only the golden tan, now fading slightly after a few weeks in London, suggested that she was from anywhere other than Argyll.

'For a moment you reminded me of someone else,' Annie stammered apologetically, cursing herself immediately for her impetuous outburst.

'Why are we all standing around here?' she demanded sharply. 'We would be so much more comfortable in the living room before the fire. I'm sure you could do with a cup of tea, Ellen?'

Glancing across at her son, she rebuked him for lingering in the girl's bedroom.

'Come along, Stephen. I expect Ellen needs to tidy up a little after her journey.'

Stephen, mildly amused that his mother should consider his presence there to be improper, muttered an apology and followed her out of the room.

'Stevie,' the girl called after him. 'Thanks for meeting me . . . it was lovely to see a friendly face in all that crowd.'

'Pleasure,' he replied, lightly and thundered down the stairs, returning a few moments later with the offending rucksack. He thrust it through the door with a conspiratorial grin.

'Better not let her fall over it twice in one day!'

Not understanding her aunt's reaction to her appearance, Ellen formed her own interpretation. Annie Beaton had left no doubt in her mind that so far as her niece was concerned, Stephen was forbidden fruit. She, like so many Australian matrons, must consider a female veterinarian to be a most unsuitable match for her son.

The morning of 31 December 1938 dawned bright and clear. As so often when least expected, the Highlands showed themselves off to perfection for Ellen McDougal's first sight of Loch Lomond.

Her excitement began to mount as soon as she glimpsed the waters of the loch through a gap in the trees, and while Stuart Beaton's black Wolseley continued along the perilously narrow, tortuous route, she cried out in delight at each fresh vista which opened up before them.

The hillside descended steeply into a drowned glacial valley. The depth below the surface, so Stuart informed her, was as great as the height of the surrounding hills. Snow, clinging to the highest peaks, was reflected in the still, black surface of the loch. Across the water, dark green stands of pines covered the lower slopes of Ben Lomond while, above the tree line, dead bracken and heather painted the harsh landscape with their chestnut and ginger hues. Close beside the road grey rocks, richly patterned by green moss and yellow lichen, littered the shoreline. Countless burns, swollen by autumnal rains, thundered down the mountainside to join the loch in silvery waterfalls.

They had loaded the car that morning with a hamper containing some of Mrs Brown's magnificent pies and cakes. This was strapped over the spare wheel while Annie and Ellen shared the rear seats with a pile of gaily wrapped presents for all the family. Although the day was bright, it was extremely cold and the two women snuggled under soft tartan rugs to keep warm. Stuart, happy to allow his son to undertake the driving, pulled his Trilby down to shade his eyes from the glaring, low-slung winter sun, and dozed contentedly.

Annie kept up a continuous monologue, describing the places they were to see and giving the lurid histories of warring clans. She punctuated her account with reminiscences of other journeys down the years, in ramshackle vehicles on rutted roads. There were anecdotes also about Stephen's youthful adventures. A wild creature of the countryside of Argyll until he was sent away to school at the age of eleven, he had roamed freely over the hills, chasing the deer, searching out where badgers had their setts, or crouching below the rocks along the shore in hopes of seeing otters at play.

'I never knew such a boy for coming home saturated to the skin where he had fallen in a lochan or else covered in mud from wandering into some bog. His cousins were so much more cautious than he . . . I don't know where his restless spirit comes from!'

Ellen believed she knew. Her parents had bombarded her since infancy with tales of Stuart Beaton's exploits during the war, and her grandmother had told her about Annie's fight for women's right to vote and her experiences when imprisoned for her beliefs. There was no doubt in Ellen's mind where Stephen had obtained his adventurous nature.

Nevertheless she listened, enthralled, to Annie's ceaseless chatter. The hesitancy she had displayed the previous day seemed to have been quite dispelled. As each bend in the road revealed some fresh marvel, Ellen's exclamations of delight made Stephen look again at the familiar scene, seeing it through her eyes.

As they topped the rise which is known to the locals as the Rest And Be Thankful, he drew off the road before a small timber building where scattered wooden tables and upturned chairs remained from the departed summer.

A single unshaded lightbulb, alight despite the bright morning, indicated that the café was open and they went in to coffee and hot scones, dripping with butter.

'I used always to stop here when I cycled out from Glasgow at the weekends,' declared Stephen.

'And I used the same resting place when cycling home to Eisdalsa in the school holidays,' Stuart capped the story with a wry smile.

'On your penny farthing?' Ellen demanded gleefully.

'I'll have you know that I had one of the first fixed wheel touring bicycles in the parish,' Stuart declared proudly. 'My brother and I were well known for our mighty feats of endurance. We cycled for hundreds of miles all over Argyll. Even took our bikes to the top of Ben Nevis on one occasion. Couldn't cycle all the way, of course.'

'Remembering the roads of those days,' Annie recalled, 'it was a feat merely to be able to stay in the saddle. Especially going downhill.'

They set off again and as they passed the junction with the road from Dunoon, Annie launched into the story of how Stephen had almost been born there, beside the road, when she and Stuart's father, David Beaton, had been travelling home from Dumfries during the war.

'How I managed to hold on, I shall never know,' she told them, laughing. 'No more than half an hour after we had reached Dr David's house at Connel, the baby was born!'

'Must be why Stephen still lacks caution and restraint,' observed Stuart, laconically.

It was an hour and a half later when the car rounded a bend at the top of Smiddy Brae and the panorama of Eisdalsa and the Islands of the Sea came into view for the first time. Stephen stopped the engine and got out of the car to lead Ellen to the look-out point.

As a child she had listened, enthralled, to her father's description of that scene. She had pored long over old sepia photographs, faded by the Australian sun, their edges curled in the heat. Nothing, however, could have prepared her for the panorama which lay before her.

In the clear December air the distant islands seemed to hover above a glassy sea, their sharp triangular outlines giving the appearance of a fleet of sailing ships. A cloudless sky was reflected in the calm waters, turning them blue as the Mediterranean Sea. Not a ripple disturbed that tranquil ocean. In the far distance she could distinguish the cliffs of Mull and recognised the cone shape of an ancient volcano.

'That must be Ben More,' she declared.

Stephen glanced at her in admiration. 'You really have studied the place, haven't you?'

'I have so looked forward to seeing it, but I never expected it to affect me so strangely. It's as though I have known it all my life.'

The crisp air had made her light-headed. She staggered slightly and Stephen took hold of her arm to steady her.

34

'Do you see down there, by the shore? That's the village, and across the strait Eisdalsa Island itself. Those whitewashed cottages are where the slate workers lived.'

'What happened to them . . . all the people?'

'Gone away, most of them. To other quarries or to the Lowlands, looking for different work. Some of them followed your father's example and emigrated. Only the old folks live down there now. There's no employment. The place is almost dead.'

'How sad,' she said. 'All the hard work, all the hopes and dreams which were formed in those little houses . . . all gone for nought. Will the place ever recover, do you think?'

'Who can say?'

'Oh, I do hope so.' Ellen turned to him earnestly. 'There must be a way of regenerating the village. There must be something people can do to make a living.'

'We really should be going, Stevie. Aunt Millicent will have the lunch on the table by now!' Annie was standing on the running board of the car, waving anxiously.

Reluctantly, the two young people turned their backs on the scene. They took the downward road at a pace which terrified Annie and thrilled Ellen. At the foot of the brae, Stephen turned right along the shore and in at the wide gateway which led to Tigh na Broch. As the Wolsey drew up in front of the house, Stuart's brother, Hugh Beaton, rounded the corner of the building and strode across the gravel towards them.

To Ellen's delight, he wore the kilt. His tweed jacket was patched with leather at the elbows; his high brown boots, polished in the early dawn, coated now in farmyard muck. Hugh Beaton looked every inch the farmer he had chosen to become after years of wrestling with a declining medical practice in the aftermath of the war.

Ellen was enchanted by the old stone house, white-painted under its many-gabled slate roof.

Stephen's great-great-grandfather, also Hugh Beaton, had come here to farm the land and to be the medical officer for the slate quarries in the 1860s. His original croft house still stood behind Tigh na Broch, and was occupied now by the present Hugh's stockman, Angus Dewar.

Hugh's wife Millicent awaited them in the brightly lit drawing room with its great stone fireplace where a fire blazed on this last day of the year. Not for one moment was Ellen allowed to feel like a stranger in this most welcoming of households.

She recalled her grandmother's vivid descriptions of the old house and recognised so many features of it that she felt she had known it always. Anne McGillivray had been a close friend of the Beatons for many years and her daughter Annie had been like family to Margaret Beaton, Stuart's sister. Ellen had read some of Margaret's work and was anxious to meet the famous authoress. Would she be there tonight? she wondered.

The light lunch which Millicent Beaton had to offer them was but a stop-gap before the main meal of the day. A large part of the afternoon was taken up with preparations for the festivities of the evening to come, and Ellen soon found herself in the kitchen with Annie and Millicent, helping with the Hogmanay dinner.

'Are you quite sure you don't mind?' Millicent asked anxiously for the third or fourth time. 'It seems a bit much to come all the way from Australia for Hogmanay and find yourself having to cook the meal before you can eat it!'

'Hardly that!' laughed Ellen, quite at ease with these amiable older women. 'I wouldn't call chopping a few vegetables and decorating a trifle, cooking.'

'Annie tells me you are a veterinary surgeon,' Millicent remarked, passing a hand across her forehead and leaving behind a smudge of flour. 'Is that a common occupation for a woman in Australia? I can't think what people would say to a woman vet over here. It's almost worse than a woman surgeon.'

Millicent had never quite come to terms with the fact that her own daughter was a surgeon. It was a pity that Morag could not be here for the party, she thought. The two girls would have got on so well together.

Hugh, coming into the kitchen at that moment, said, 'Woman or not, a vet is a vet and my cow has a cough. How about putting down that knife, Ellen, and coming outside to have a look at her?'

Eagerly she wiped her hands and made to follow him.

'Oh, Hugh,' Millicent scolded, 'you shouldn't ask her . . . what a cheek!'

'Nonsense,' said Ellen. 'I'll be pleased to have a look.'

Hugh fetched her outdoor clothing from the hall and wrapped her up warmly before allowing Ellen to go out into the cold evening air.

He steered her around the house to where a low barn crouched alongside the original crofter's cottage. When he pushed open the door, the strong sweet smell of hay mingled with the pungent scent of animal dung engulfed them, and Ellen felt instantly at ease. Hugh switched on the lights so that she could see the cattle in their stalls.

A row of gentle brown eyes, shielded by copious lashes of long coarse hair almost the colour of her own, turned to greet her. With gentle lowing noises, the cattle brought up their soft tan noses to be touched, and tossed their splendid horns in greeting. Ellen gave a gasp of delight.

'Highlanders,' she breathed, admiring their straight backs and silky flanks. 'Real Highlanders . . . at last. I've been looking forward to seeing some.'

'They are rather splendid, aren't they?' Hugh said proudly. 'Old Colomkil there won a first prize at the show this year.'

Ellen glanced up at a narrow glass-fronted wall cupboard in which were displayed trophies and rosettes, each a proud memorial to one or other of these gentle beasts.

The bull, on hearing his name, gave a bellow of recognition and placed his mucus-laden nose ring right into her hand. Ellen scratched his cheek and the space between his horns, wiping off the mess on the mop of hair. Hugh found it difficult to disguise his admiration for this slip of a girl. Millicent would have shrieked at such an advance by the animal, and run back to the house to wash her hands.

'Which is the sick one?' she asked, searching the row of eager faces for signs of one that was ailing.

'Eh? Oh, there isn't one,' he confessed. 'That was just a ploy to get you out of the kitchen. I wanted to ask after your father.'

He settled himself on a bale of straw, inviting her to join him.

'Jack and I grew up together, you know,' Hugh explained. 'After schooling we went our separate ways, but we remained friends.'

Suddenly very earnest, he demanded, 'How does he manage . . . without his leg?'

'Do you know,' Ellen told him, 'he manages so well that we seldom think to ask him about it. Of course, he spends much of every day in the saddle, and when he gets home at night he tends to sit for hours on the veranda, watching the sky. Sometimes, if his stump is sore, Mother insists he has a day in bed. Otherwise . . . no one would know there was anything amiss at all.'

'Did you know it was me who had to cut if off? In a field hospital beside the River Scarpe it was.' Hugh watched Ellen closely, anticipating some reaction from her.

She returned his gaze calmly. Clearly there was something troubling this rather sad but kindly man.

'My father has nothing but praise for all those who cared for him,' she assured. 'He always declares that but for the treatment he received, he would have been denied the happiest years of his life.'

'Even without his leg?'

'Even so.'

Hugh let out a long sigh. Absently he rubbed his fingers over the knobs where a young calf would soon begin to sprout the curved horns of his breed. 'I used to wonder,' he murmured as though she were not there, 'if I should have let him die.'

Ellen looked up sharply. So that was it. He felt guilty because he had been unable to do more for her father. Maybe it was these feelings of inadaquacy which had subsequently caused him to abandon his medical practice. Could that be the reason why he now concentrated so single-mindedly on his cattle?

'Well, I for one am very grateful to you,' she said, deliberately cheery. 'And I am sure that my mother would agree, even though she screams in agony whenever they dance together. Dad doesn't realise when he's stepping on her toes, you see!'

Hugh was forced to laugh at that and Stephen, looking out for Ellen, was surprised to find his usually rather dour uncle in such good humour as the three of them left the byre and returned to the house.

'Did you see that glorious sunset?' he demanded of them as he helped Ellen to struggle out of her coat.

'No,' she replied, 'we were in the byre, visiting the Highlanders. Aren't they beautiful?'

'Oh, I don't know so much,' Stephen replied. 'I prefer my females a little less shaggy.' He tugged playfully at a tress of her hair which had slipped out of its careful pinning. 'But then again,' he continued glee-fully, 'you're looking a trifle shaggy yourself this afternoon!'

Laughing and joking they went into the drawing room to join the remainder of the guests who were beginning to gather for the festive dinner.

Angus Dewar piped in the haunch of venison which was the main dish of the evening, and Hugh, still exhibiting the good humour which had resulted from his conversation with Ellen, performed surgery upon the joint to a tirade of banter from the medical men in the company.

It was a merry party that had assembled around the creaking table.

Hugh's two sons, Iain and David, had both managed to be free for Hogmanay and had travelled together that morning from Ian's Edinburgh digs. Margaret Brown and her husband Michael, Stephen's aunt and uncle, had arrived from Oban while Ellen and Hugh were in the byre. A rather elderly couple, Katherine and Archie McLean, had driven over just before dinner, bringing with them Ellen's Aunt Martha and her cousin Iain.

Here at last were real relatives.

Approaching her father's elder sister a trifle shyly, Ellen found herself instantly engulfed in a pair of well-padded arms, crushing her to an ample bosom.

'My, but you're a braw wee lassie!' Martha exclaimed, and turned excitedly to Annie. 'Does she no' have the look of oor Ellen about her, Annie?'

Annie blushed. So she had not been mistaken. Ellen did resemble her aunt, Jack's sister. But the subject was embarrassing, and she wished that Martha had not brought it up.

'You're talking about Ellen McDougal, aren't you?' the girl demanded. 'I know my father had a sister, but there has always been some secret about her. Is she the skeleton in the family closet?'

'Not that, no,' Annie said. 'It's a sad little story, though. If Martha agrees, I'll tell you about it some other time.'

'What harm can it do to tell the child? Ellen's long dead. Talking about it cannot harm her now.'

So excited was Martha to meet her niece at long last, that her broad speech became unintelligible to the unaccustomed ear of the Australian girl who struggled with her answers. Somewhat overcome by her aunt's enthusiastic welcome, Ellen was almost relieved when she found herself seated at dinner next to her cousin, Iain McDougal.

She found him shy, and quite difficult to talk to, but at least he spoke slowly and she could understand him. At one point during the meal, however, the conversation turned to the subject of trees. This topic sparked a remarkable change in the man who suddenly became extremely animated, demanding to know in minutest detail the properties of the different gum trees on her father's holding, asking if she thought that Eucalyptus might grow in Argyll.

'They are a species which survive drought and the occasional bush fire,' she told him, 'but they're not used to frosts and harsh winds, of course . . . I think you would have to import a few to find out which variety would grow best here.'

'There isna that much frost here, d'ye see?' he told her, excitedly. 'Do they no' have a hard cuticle on the leaves to keep in the moisture? That would protect them from the salty air too.'

Ellen hesitated for a moment. She had had to study biology, of course, but had taken little interest in botany and had to think hard before answering.

'I believe they have,' she agreed at last.

'Then the salty air'll no affect them,' he decided, nodding with satisfaction.

'Look, if you like, I'll write to Dad and get him to send you some young trees. They should survive the journey if they're properly packed. As I say, they can overcome drought in a remarkable fashion.'

'Oh, would ye? Would ye really do that?' His effusive thanks were almost more embarrassing than her aunt's greeting.

'I'll write home about it just as soon as I settle in at Aberdeen,' Ellen replied. She was beginning to wish that trees had never been mentioned when the elderly gentleman at the far end of the table began to roar with laughter.

'You've hit upon the only subject that Iain ever talks about,' cried Archie McLean. 'It's a pity you have so little time here, Ellen. I would have liked to take you around our gardens up at Johnstone's. Iain has spent nearly thirty years planting out our woodland. Some of the original trees are giants now.'

Annie was amused at the understated manner in which Archie spoke of his great passion in life, the garden that he and his head gardener had created. Originally a quarryman himself, Archie had purchased Johnstone's croft at the end of the last century with a fortune made mining diamonds in Africa. His gardens were now renowned throughout Scotland and were a great attraction for tourists.

'Ellen will be around for a few months,' Annie assured him. 'We'll bring her down to see the gardens in the spring . . . when the Rhododendrons are at their best.'

Hugh, questioning her now about the work she would be doing in Aberdeen, steered the conversation in a direction with which Ellen felt more at ease.

'We're trying to develop a strain of cattle able to withstand the changing conditions of the Northern Territories,' she told him. 'Although the days are hot and dry, the nights are very cold sometimes and when it rains . . . it's wet! We're looking for a breed which will thrive whatever the conditions.'

He held her in earnest conversation for a time until at last the meal was finished and the floor could be cleared for games and dancing.

Having at last succumbed to pressure from his sons, Hugh had installed a new electric gramophone for the occasion. Until the midnight hour, the young people waltzed and foxtrotted to the current favourites played by bands with names like Joe Loss, Geraldo and Tommy Dorsey.

As midnight approached, glasses were charged and on the stroke of twelve a toast was drunk to 1939. Dewar piped in the New Year in traditional fashion and Archie McLean produced his fiddle as the company exchanged kisses and expressed their hopes and wishes for the future. No gloomy thoughts were allowed to intrude upon this moment of euphoria. For a short while at least, the darkening clouds which hung over Europe were ignored.

The dancing now was of the traditional Scottish kind. Ellen soon found herself being whirled around the room to the music of Archie McLean's fiddle and Angus Dewar's penny whistle. She was surprised to find how well she could manage the unfamiliar steps when guided by the firm hands of these Beaton men and their friends, both young and not so young. As she was passed down the line each smiling face beamed upon her and she was struck by the similarity between them. Tall, auburn-haired and almost uniformly attired in the Campbell tartan, they made a strikingly handsome bunch. Her father had been right when he had said that she would be made welcome here. For a moment she found herself overwhelmed by a fierce longing to be a part of this company forever.

Stephen steered her away from the confusion which followed the ending of the dance.

'Let's go and sit under the stars,' he suggested. 'You look as though you could do with a drink.'

'Something long and cold,' Ellen agreed.

'There's lemonade . . . or I might find a little bubbly left over.'

'A beer would be lovely, if you don't think your aunt will be shocked.' She grinned as he raised an eyebrow in some surprise. In this company the ladies were expected to drink fruit juices. Champagne or cocktails were suitable in moderation, even a wee glass of whisky perhaps, but not ale.

'OK.' Stephen leaped to his feet. 'Beer it is. I think David put a crate outside to keep cool.'

In moments he had returned with her coat over his arm and carrying two foaming glasses. They let themselves out by the front door and cuddled together on the garden seat for warmth, while they drank their beer.

Overhead the stars, shimmering against the black velvet of the night, seemed close enough for them to reach out and pluck.

For a moment they were silent, their senses acutely tuned to the music of the night; the low murmur of waves breaking gently along the shore, the soft lowing of cattle and the scrape of a hoof as a beast shifted for comfort in the byre. And from the dark hillside above, the occasional bleating of a sheep separated from her fellows.

'What will you do if there is a war?' Ellen asked suddenly.

'Oh, that's all settled,' Stephen told her. 'I got my pilot's licence a short while ago. I'll be in the RAF.'

'You'll give up medicine then?'

'Just till the war is over. After all, it'll only be a matter of months, you'll see.'

'I don't know what I shall do,' said Ellen, thinking aloud. 'Go home and raise sheep for the war effort, I suppose. War is always good for wool producers. The entire settlement at Kerrera was built on the proceeds of the last one.'

'When do you have to leave for Aberdeen?' he asked. 'If you can make it a Friday, I'll be able to drive you up there myself.'

'That would be marvellous,' she cried enthusiastically. 'You can help me to find somewhere to live. I could stay in one of the Halls of Residence, but I'd prefer a little place of my own.'

'Yes, I'm sure you'd be better on your own. Students can be a bit irritating at times.'

Both nodded sagely at this, having only recently been a part of the wild undergraduate fraternity themselves.

'I can come up and see you whenever I'm free,' Stephen decided. 'Only if you want me to, of course?'

'That would be wonderful. I shall probably be a bit lonely at first.'

'Not for long, I'm sure,' he protested, strangely envious of the young men with whom his cousin would be associating.

'I shall probably spend a good deal of time travelling around. Part of my schedule is to visit remote hill farms to study their cattle. I'm really looking forward to it. It's a wonderful opportunity to see something of Scotland for myself.'

'Maybe I'll have a chance to discover a few places with you.'

Ellen, remembering other nights under a different sky, wondered if, after all, some of those dreams they had woven together so long ago, beneath the Southern Cross, might yet be fulfilled.

Chapter Four

Annie shivered and drew her fur coat closer about her. The wooden bench on which she had been asked to wait was getting harder by the minute.

What exactly was she doing here? she asked herself. She had managed to exchange a brief word with Stuart after she had read the Provost's rather cryptic note that morning, but her husband was already late for an appointment and couldn't give her dilemma his full attention.

'There's no harm in finding out what he wants,' he had told her. 'You can always say no.'

She took the sheet of expensively embossed notepaper from her handbag and read it again.

> Your name has been brought to my attention as someone with the organising skills and local knowledge to be of service to me in my task of devising a contingency plan to deal with problems that might arise as a result of enemy action . . .

Whatever could he mean? Annie knew nothing about air-raid precautions, and anyway they had seriously considered moving out of Glasgow altogether if war was declared. Stuart was close to retiring age and ready for something less onerous than a consultancy in a city hospital. Millicent had invited them to stay at Eisdalsa for as long as they liked, once the bombing started. They had watched the newsreels and had seen what aerial attacks had achieved in Spain and in China. It would be foolish to stay put and simply wait for the Blitzkrieg.

'Mrs Beaton?' the receptionist called from across the sweep of cold marble floor. 'The Provost will see you now.'

Annie got to her feet, glancing about her uncertainly.

'Up the main staircase and along the corridor to your right.'

'Oh, thank you.' She tucked the letter back into her bag and crossed to the wide staircase which led up to a first-floor gallery.

Halting before a heavy door, panelled in oak and marked in gold letters, Annie tapped lightly. Hearing a muffled response from within, she turned the brass knob and pushed.

The door opened smoothly, revealing a bright, airy room the window wall of which was filled almost entirely by the largest desk she had ever seen. She felt her feet sink into the deep pile of the carpet as she advanced towards a grey-haired gentleman in his shirt sleeves who appeared lost in the vastness of his surroundings.

Spread on the desk before him were piles of papers. One telephone handset was held to his ear, whilst another rang incessantly, demanding his attention. With a wild gesture he waved her to a seat, barked some incomprehensible commands into the telephone which he held in his hand and, as he slammed it down on to its cradle, reached for the other.

'Just one minute,' he commanded the disembodied voice which Annie could hear distinctly from the far side of the desk. 'Hang on, can't you!' Still holding the phone in his left hand, he half stood, extending his right towards her. 'Mrs Beaton? I'm Graham Waterstone. It was good of you to respond so quickly to my invitation. If you will just wait while I deal with this call, I'll be ready to give you my undivided attention.'

For a few seconds he listened. He gave a series of staccato instructions then dismissed the caller brusquely. Afterwards he flicked a switch on the intercom. 'No more calls until I tell you, Mabel. Absolutely none, d'you hear?'

There was a rapid and plaintive-sounding reply.

'No, not even *him*! Oh . . . say I've gone to lunch.'

He sat back in a massive leather-upholstered chair. Quite suddenly his harassed demeanour fell away and, clasping his hands together, the Provost beamed at Annie.

They had told him that he should expect to meet a formidable lady, but he had not been prepared for such a good-looking one.

Nearing sixty years of age, Annie still held herself erect, although her fine figure owed much to the Spirella corsets she wore. Her black hair had long since turned to a becoming silver grey but her dark eyes had lost none of their sparkle and the broad white brow suggested a more than average intelligence.

'I have been hearing remarkable things about you, Mrs Beaton,' he began. 'They tell me you were one of the very first women to graduate in law from Glasgow University.'

'It was all rather a long time ago,' she replied, embarrassed by his unwavering stare.

'Oh, come now, why so modest?' he insisted. 'How many of your contemporaries actually practised once they had qualified?'

'At the time, I suppose most of us were simply making a gesture . . . to prove that women could sustain study at that level was the important thing. Unfortunately I was the one who had to work for her living. The others were able to go back to their comfortable middle-class lives, having made their point.'

The Provost nodded wisely. Some of his colleagues had been critical of his proposal to invite Annie Beaton to join them. There had been talk of her having served a prison sentence in 1913 whilst working for the Women's Suffrage movement. If anything, this revelation had increased Graham Waterstone's determination to gain Annie's co-operation.

'I won't beat about the bush, Mrs Beaton,' he said, paying her the courtesy of pulling on his jacket at last. 'We are both very busy people.'

Annie smiled, accepting his compliment with a slight nod of the head.

'You should know that, despite the Munich agreement, the government has instructed civil authorities to prepare for war. With this in mind, I have begun to recruit a number of key personnel who will plan our local response to the anticipated enemy action. Naturally the emergency services will be involved in this; the Police, Fire and Ambulance Services have been placed on alert and are already in the process of recruiting and training volunteers, while the Women's Voluntary Service has undertaken to provide sustenance for the crews and immediate comforts for those civilians rendered homeless by the bombing. We are also trying to recruit for the Air Raid Precautions outfit, although strangely people seem reluctant to come forward for that.'

Annie knew all about the emergency medical services proposed. Stuart had been very much involved in drawing up and carrying out a programme of First Aid instruction and she and her friends had been roped in to act as casualties on several training exercises.

'In the coming conflict, Clydebank is going to be vital to the war effort,' the Provost continued. 'If we come under attack from the air, no matter how serious the damage, the factories and shipyards must be kept operating at the highest possible levels. It will be the task of this office to see that everything is done to get people back to work.'

He paused long enough for Annie to interrupt. 'I understand what you are saying, Mr Waterstone, but I fail to see what all of this has to do with me?'

'Let us suppose that there has been a serious bombing raid,' he went on, ignoring her question. 'Several streets around the dockyards have been devastated. Some people have been injured, others are shocked, dirty, left with only the clothes they stand up in. They are wandering around the streets, searching for their friends and family, everything they possess gone . . . how would you handle that situation?'

Annie looked at him hard for a moment, trying to understand where all this could be leading. Then she applied herself to his question.

'People who are so shocked and distressed are going to be worried most of all about their closest relatives,' she said. 'The sooner they are able to satisfy themselves that their nearest and dearest are safe, the sooner they will be willing to get back to work. I believe that one very important task will be to set up a good communications system, perhaps a control point for every few streets, manned by locals who know the area well, where folk can go for information about casualties, damage to property and so on. To maintain the confidence of people it's very important that this information should be issued as accurately as possible.

'I think that anger will play a large part in the way in which people react to air raids,' she continued. 'So I don't believe that there will be much difficulty about getting them back to work if only to spite the bombers, but they won't be able to do that without food and sleep, and they can't expect either if their houses have been destroyed. It will be necessary to provide temporary accommodation, and some kind of communal feeding system . . .'

She came to a halt, her mind still working on a dozen other possibilities. Waterstone seemed entirely satisfied with what he had heard so far.

'Mrs Beaton,' he declared, 'you asked me earlier what all this had to do with you. The suggestions which you have just outlined require a major exercise in logistics. Sites must be found for your local information centres. Temporary accommodation must be prepared for those rendered homeless, with beds and bedding, spare clothing and food, and there must be a system for requisitioning transport to and from work should the public transport services be rendered inoperable.'

He stopped suddenly. Annie remained silent, still unsure why they were having this conversation.

'Well,' he demanded, 'will you take the job on?'

She was thunderstruck. 'What do you mean?' she demanded.

'Look,' he said, leaning forward and gripping the edge of the desk in his enthusiasm, 'there are half a dozen men I could call upon to set this up, but none of them has had your legal training and experience in finding accommodation for the homeless. The chairman of your own organisation has told me about your work with the unemployed, your tenacity in acquiring homes and furniture for those in dire need, and about your work with underprivileged children in the Borough. I need both a cool head and an understanding heart for this job . . . and I believe you can supply both.'

'You make it very difficult for me to refuse,' she replied.

'There is of course the other aspect of the work,' he added hastily. 'Requisitioning of privately owned buildings could leave the Authority with a great many legal wrangles to clear up at the end of the day. I would like to see everything tied up properly, so that we can avoid any unnecessary expenditure.' He observed the frown which passed across Annie's brow. 'After all, I am the guardian of the public purse.'

She accepted what he had said with a brief nod before making her position plain.

'You appreciate that I cannot start immediately? I have certain obligations to fulfil to the Friendly Society, although it does seem that the threat of war has reduced my responsibilities in that direction very considerably. I have had the great pleasure of seeing many long-term clients returning to work during the past few weeks.'

'I have already taken the liberty of addressing your chairman on the matter,' Waterstone confessed. 'He it was who first drew my attention to you as a suitable candidate for this post. I can see no difficulty should you need to take time winding down your charitable activities, while beginning to set up the new organisation. It doesn't seem as though the bombing is likely to begin tomorrow!'

Annie hesitated. No matter what her chairman had said, it would not be all that easy to set aside her commitments to the society . . . and there was Stuart to consider. He had never stood in her way before, in fact he had positively encouraged her to take on the social work which she had been doing all these years, but he was entitled to be consulted over such an important offer.

'If there are to be no objections from the society, and if my husband agrees to it,' she told Waterstone, 'then I will be happy to consider your proposition.'

He stood up, offering her his hand as a signal that the interview was at an end.

'I have every confidence that you will make the right decision.' He beamed at her. 'Please don't take too long over your deliberations, though. I shall be looking forward to hearing from you very soon.'

Having shaken her hand, he led her to the door.

He closed it behind her and returned to his desk with a satisfied smile on his face. One thing at least had gone right this morning. He had no doubt that Annie Beaton was the woman for the job!

The basement rooms of the library in Dumbarton Road were filled with row upon row of floor-to-ceiling shelves, stacked with huge dusty ledgers, rolls of plans, sheaves of documents in untidy piles, and thousands of books of every description.

'The archives I can understand,' Annie observed after the caretaker had opened every door on one particular corridor, 'but the old books . . . is nothing ever discarded?'

'I've worked here since the last war,' said her guide, 'and I never knew anyone to throw away a single sheet of paper.'

Annie would have given anything to have had the time to sort through this mass of old documents, but the job that she had to do was far more important.

'Well,' she declared, 'it will all have to be shifted.'

The caretaker closed and locked the door behind him, leading the way along a narrow passage to the far end.

'This is a door which hasn't been used in many years,' he explained as he sought through a huge bunch of keys and withdrew one, somewhat older and larger than the rest. He fitted it into the lock and, much to Annie's surprise, the key was turned without difficulty. The door swung back to reveal a flight of stone steps leading up to street level.

'Mr Scott said you'd be wanting to see all the exits to the building, ma'am,' the caretaker explained, 'so I've been oiling the locks to make sure everything works.'

'Well done,' she replied, smiling. 'We may be very grateful for an alternative escape route one of these days.'

The old man acknowledged her compliment with a broad grin.

Annie had recognised in Bobby McGreggor a useful ally. If she was to take over the library premises, his co-operation would be essential.

'You must have an architect's blueprint of the original building somewhere in all that welter of documentation, Mr McGreggor,' Annie said, as she shook hands with him.

'I have a detailed plan of every floor, in my office,' he told her.

'Perhaps you will be kind enough to send round a copy of both the ground-floor and basement levels to the City Hall as soon as possible? Once the space has been cleared of all that paper, I can get the architects working on alterations to the layout. We shall have to provide suitable facilities for the large number of people who will work down here.'

The old man shook her hand.

'I'll send along your plans, Mrs Beaton, and I'll try to indicate where I think your facilities can best be installed with the minimum of work.'

Commandeering property already owned by the Council was one thing; negotiating the requisition of the disused garage belonging to the Clydebank Motor Buses Company, further down the same road, was a different matter entirely.

The owner, Angus McQuarrie, had agreed to meet her at the yard, but when Annie arrived there was no one to be seen. She was obliged to force an entry by tearing away a piece of corrugated iron which was loosely attached to the dilapidated gate.

The space which lay before her was about fifty yards square. Along one side, facing the main gate, was an open-sided shed large enough to house a number of double-decker buses. Its corrugated iron roof covering looked rather precarious in places, but the timbers supporting it seemed sound enough. It wouldn't take much to clear the rubbish and the owner could hardly claim for loss of earnings . . . the site already appeared derelict.

'I see ye found a way t' break in, lassie?'

Annie turned, startled, to find herself confronted by a wizened little man who swayed gently as he spoke. The reason for this instability became apparent the moment she approached to within a few feet and put out her hand.

'Mr McQuarrie?' she greeted him. 'Thank you so much for agreeing to see me.'

Taken aback by this pleasantly open approach, the man could do little else but mumble some kind of a greeting in reply. The simple act of opening his mouth was enough to confirm Annie's worst fears. He was clearly inebriated. She just hoped he was capable of conducting the interview she had planned.

'As you must know, Mr McQuarrie,' Annie began, extracting her letter of authority from her handbag, 'the Council is empowered under the emergency arrangements now in force to commandeer premises which it requires for the maintenance of essential services in time of war . . .'

'Eh? What's this . . . commandeer?' McQuarrie seemed taken aback. His mates in the Black Swan had sworn he would get a good price for his yard and he could certainly do with the money.

'. . . but we would prefer to come to some more amicable arrangement with the owners of property, if we can.' Annie paused to let this last sentence sink in.

'We would, of course, prefer to rent your property for the duration of hostilities,' she concluded.

'Y'mean, ye dinna want te buy it?' McQuarrie could not contain his disappointment.

'No. What we propose is an open-ended lease . . . for the duration of hostilities only. We would pay you a small annual rent, refurbish the building to our own requirements, cover the cost of insurance on your behalf, and return the property to you in good order when the war is over. How does that sound?'

The man's piggy eyes seemed to diminish to such an extent that they nearly disappeared altogether beneath his furrowed brow.

'Naw jus' a minute,' he slurred. 'Aa'm thinking of a straight sale . . . eight hundred poun's is wa' I'm askin'. No' a penny less.'

'I can requisition the building outright, Mr McQuarrie,' she told him firmly. 'In which case you lose all claim to the premises after hostilities are over, and the rate of compensation you receive will be at our discretion . . . nothing like eight hundred pounds, I can assure you.'

He was getting angry now. He began rambling on about how it was all the fault of the trolley buses. They had taken an honest man's trade and left him bankrupt.

In Annie's opinion it was the *uisge-beatha* which had been his downfall and nothing else, but she allowed him to vent his rage for a few moments. When he finally paused for breath, she again enquired, 'Well, Mr McQuarrie, what's it to be? A repairing lease with a reasonable rent paid to you annually, or straight out requisition at our assessment of the value?'

Her proposal seemed to have sobered her protagonist remarkably. He actually appeared to apply some thought to his next question.

'Wa' kind o' rent d'ye have in mind, hen?' he enquired now, his voice oily with greed.

'One hundred pounds a year seems a fair rent,' Annie replied smartly. 'Think of it, Mr McQuarrie. If the war lasts for eight years, which Heaven forbid, you will get your eight hundred pounds and still own the yard!'

Her logic finally convinced him. They shook hands on the deal and

Annie went away to have the lease drawn up. Within a fortnight, the yard was cleared and builders began to work on restoring the roof of the garage. The old petrol-holding tanks were cleaned out and filled with motor spirit. Two large water tanks were erected to ensure a small local supply should the mains fail, and vehicles commandeered from all around the city were brought in to be overhauled and distributed to outlying smaller parks from which they could be summoned in an emergency. Half the buildings, including the former office block, would be suitable for the headquarters of the local ARP section. Apart from her new job with the City Council, Annie had, much to the amusement of both Stephen and Stuart, enrolled in the ARP to become a voluntary Air Raid Warden. It would be to the bus garage that she would most likely have to repair on most evenings, after a day's work at her office in the Dumbarton Library Communications Centre.

Stuart followed her activities with genuine admiration and not a little relief. The suggestion that they might retire to the country had alarmed him for, knowing that it was going to be left to old fogeys like himself to carry on after the younger doctors had all been called up, he had anticipated his enhanced role in the community with growing excitement. He had no wish to be left out of the action!

Stuart Beaton strode along, hands clasped behind him in the best Naval tradition – a habit he had never managed to lose in civilian life. His head was bent to catch the words of the shorter, balding gentleman who had so courteously agreed to show him around.

'You will appreciate,' Stuart felt bound to point out, 'that it will be necessary for us to store a considerable amount of equipment here on the premises. I'm afraid that we shall need a large part of your space on a permanent basis. In an emergency, of course, I would require the main hall as a casualty ward.'

The Reverend Neil nodded understandingly.

'Of course, Doctor,' he replied, throwing open a door to a suite of rooms hitherto undisclosed.

'I thought this might be suitable.'

A narrow corridor led to a series of small rooms at the rear of the church hall. Some were completely empty. Two had the appearance of theatre dressing rooms, with long, wall-mounted dressing tables and mirrors and, at the far end, there were two sets of cloakrooms with wash basins and toilet cubicles, sufficient for a fair number of people.

'There will not be much call for amateur dramatics once all the young people have left us,' the Minister explained. 'Such meetings as are normally held in these rooms can be accommodated elsewhere.'

'This will do splendidly, Mr Neil,' Stuart assured him. 'Please express my appreciation of their generosity to your congregation.'

'The parishioners will be only too happy to see the building being put to good use. I dare say quite a few of them will be offering their services for First Aid duties anyway. I understand that you are still looking for volunteers?'

'All the time,' Stuart agreed. 'In fact, I was going to ask if I might use the main hall for a recruitment drive within the next week or two? And we also need a suitable venue for the blood transfusion service. The team will be visiting Clydebank the week after next . . .'

It was Annie who had told him that Minister Neil would be happy to let him set up a First Aid post at the hall in Radnor Park. With the Boquhanrhan School hall as a collecting point and Radnor Park church hall as a treatment centre, Stuart would be well set up to deal with whatever casualties the enemy decided to inflict on Clydebank.

The telegram was waiting for Stephen when he came off the ward after his final round of the night. He was exhausted and ready to fall into bed, too tired even to see what they'd left him for supper, keeping warm in the residents' pantry.

He tore at the little yellow envelope and extracted the sheet, his hands trembling with fatigue and anticipation.

FLT LT S J BEATON UAS REPORT FOR ACTIVE DUTY ABBOTSINCH FIELD STOP MAY FIRST NINETEEN HUNDRED HOURS LATEST STOP

But 1 May was tomorrow! He groaned as he sank into an overstuffed leather-covered armchair which had seen better days. Remembering too late, Stephen felt his backside hit bottom where the springs had been broken and bent aside, leaving nothing between his coccyx and the wooden base of the chair. Well, that was one good thing . . . they couldn't have worse chairs than this in the Air Force!

He glanced again at the telegram, still not convinced that what he had read was true. He had about twelve hours to settle his affairs here at the hospital, contact his parents, collect his flying gear and get down to

Abbotsinch. He didn't want to leave it until the last minute.

So the balloon must be going up at last . . . well, it was none too soon for him. He'd had about as much as he could take of this place.

His father had considered that a surgery residency at the Western Infirmary was about the best experience anyone could have. 'Well, Pop, I've got news for you,' muttered Stephen as he folded the telegram form and stuck it in the top pocket of his white coat. Instead of falling into his bed, he took a quick shower and changed into his street clothes then made his way to the main reception area and spoke to the night porter.

'Any chance of locating the Prof at this hour, George?' he demanded.

The uniformed porter looked down at his list of contacts.

'He'll be awa' hame for the night, Dr Beaton, a shouldna wonder.'

'I need to contact him urgently,' Stephen explained. 'It's government business.'

'You don't mean t' tell me they're taking you wee laddies right awa'?' The old man seemed genuinely distressed. Generally George McBain had little time for the young doctors who knew nothing and tried to convince everyone they knew everything. He spent much of his time taking them down a peg or two but young Dr Beaton was different. . . he was a good lad who knew his stuff all right. In any case, George had been a young porter at the hospital when Stephen's father, Mr Stuart, was doing his residency. Now *there* was a doctor and no mistake!

'I've got a number here for the Professor, sir,' he said with an unaccustomed measure of respect in his tone. 'I'll try to get him . . . if you'll just go to cubicle number two over there.'

Stephen did as directed and in a few moments the telephone rang in his kiosk.

'Yes . . . what is it?' The voice was petulant, irascible even. It had been a long day for all of them in the theatre.

'It's Beaton here, Professor,' Stephen told him. 'I'm sorry to have to bother you but I've had my call-up notification and I have to report before seven o'clock tomorrow evening. It looks as if I shan't be seeing you again for some time.'

'You appear to be in an inordinate hurry to go and get yourself killed,' observed his mentor, though his tone had softened. He would be sorry to see the Beaton lad go.

'Do your people know yet?' he asked.

'No, I need to get home right away . . . some of my gear is stored there.'

Stephen knew he would be lucky to catch his parents at home. They always seemed to have things to do these days, even after a long day at work.

'You cut along home then, Steve. And give my best to your father . . . and, Stephen, take care, lad.'

The line went dead and he was left staring at the telephone in his hand. The Old Man had sounded genuinely upset. He'd never shown a chink in his armour before. Suddenly it occurred to Stephen that what was about to happen was real and not some adventure out of the *Boy's Own* paper.

He hurried on foot along Byres Road, going over in his mind all the things he must do before leaving tomorrow.

Suddenly he stopped dead in his tracks and threw his hand to his forehead. So abrupt was his movement that others following behind, were forced to divert, casting angry looks in his direction.

Ellen . . . he was supposed to be driving up to join her at the weekend! She had a farm to visit on the Black Isle and he had promised to drive her. They had planned an overnight stay in Inverness . . .

Stephen turned abruptly into the Post Office, open late on this Friday evening, and selected a telegram form from the rack. He scribbled in his illegible doctor's writing and walked over to the counter, his hand in his pocket searching for coins.

Behind the counter the postmistress glanced at his writing, frowning. Stephen was startled when the woman proceeded to read the contents of his message aloud:

TO ELLEN MCDOUGAL 76 COLLEGE BOUNDS OLD ABERDEEN STOP REPORTING ABBOTSINCH FRIDAY STOP WEEKEND OFF STOP SORRY STOP STEVE.

'Nine words for sixpence plus a penny for every additional word. That will be one shilling, thank you.' The counter clerk looked up expectantly.

He glanced about him, suspecting that other customers might be listening in. Should he be broadcasting the fact that he was about to join up? he wondered. He need not have worried, for they all seemed to be concentrating upon their own affairs. He pulled out the required coin and paid.

Ellen would understand. They had already discussed the possibility of his being called up at a moment's notice.

Stephen felt a sense of mounting excitement as he thrust open the door of the shop and set off with a determined stride for home to begin his packing.

Chapter Five

Stephen was surprised to find himself on the end of a long queue which wound around the Company Office block behind the Officers' Mess Hut and stretched far across the parade ground. He had had no idea that there were so many young men in the area who had already signed up for some kind of preliminary training with the RAF.

Apart from those like himself, who during their time at university had reported to the field regularly, first for basic training and later for flying training, there seemed to be countless younger chaps he had not expected to see. Public schools ran their own Air Training Corps, so presumably some of these boys would be no more than seventeen or eighteen years of age.

He watched their eager young faces and listened to their excited chatter, and felt quite old.

For an hour last night he had talked quietly with his father in the study overlooking the Botanic Gardens. Stuart Beaton had coloured his son's young life with stories of his own adventures on the high seas when he had been a naval surgeon in the Great War, but last night for the first time he had spoken of the darker moments, the reality of a kind of warfare in which there are no winners or losers, only bloody casualties. Last night, Stephen had listened with much closer attention than had been normal during his teenage years, a period in which he had learned to apply the correct degree of youthful cynicism to his father's reminiscences. Yesterday he had heard for the first time of the comrades lost at sea, the maimed and disfigured seamen whose young lives had been blighted in a moment of madness. As he looked about him now, he wondered how many of these young men would still be around, joking and boasting, in a year's time . . .

'Flying Officer Stephen James Beaton!'

The WO called the name off from a list which he held stiffly in his right hand. His lips scarcely moved. The upper part of his face was hidden beneath the darkly gleaming peak of his cap which descended almost vertically over his eyes and nose, stopping short of his jutting chin a few millimetres above a heavily waxed moustache, ginger in colour and a good seven inches from tip to tip. Were it not for the occasional barked command, one might have suspected this rigid figure of being a tailor's dummy.

The Warrant Officer was not a regular member of the station's training staff; presumably he had been called in especially for the task of mustering recruits.

At the sound of his own name, Stephen stepped forward one pace and executed what he considered to be a reasonable salute.

'Papers!' the WO ordered, and Stephen bent forward to place his UAS documents and his Pilot's A certificate on the desk before the CO. He straightened up, grinning broadly. The CO had signed the certificate himself only a few months before.

'Attention!' yelled the WO.

Startled, Stephen pulled himself into the regulation stance and stared across the top of the CO's head, fixing his eyes on a poster which depicted a Spitfire soaring into a blue heaven dotted with sparkling white puffs of cloud and, in the foreground, a handsome young fighter pilot, his helmet casually unclasped. **JOIN HIM!** read the caption.

'Ah, Beaton . . . finished your Medic's course yet, have you?'

Nonplussed, Stephen nodded. What had his studies in Medicine to do with his being a fighter pilot? He caught the beady little eye of the WO upon him and hastily explained, 'I have my first degrees in Medicine and Surgery, sir, and I'm halfway through my second year as a Resident in Surgery at the Western Infirmary. I have another year or more to go before I can take my MRCS.'

'Shouldn't you be staying on to complete your training?' demanded the CO.

'I'm already qualified for general medical practice, sir. Registration can wait until the show's over,' he added, suddenly apprehensive. He was going to look a right 'wally' if they sent him back to the Western now!

Stephen allowed his gaze to rest once again on the Spitfire in the poster and his imagination soared. He was so enthused by the thought of being behind the controls of that superb aircraft, that he only half heard the CO's next remarks.

'. . . need some extra help at the recruitment centre at Blackpool. You'd better cut along there and report to the Chief MO. See to it, Warrant Officer, will you?'

'Sir!' The WO made a quick squiggle on his paid and stood, pencil poised waiting for the next command.

'OK, Beaton, carry on . . . and the best of luck!'

In a daze, Stephen gathered up the orders which were handed to him together with his other documents, saluted smartly and retired to read what he could not believe he had just heard:

FLYING OFFICER BEATON S J 3702594 BREVET RANK
FLIGHT LIEUTENANT TO REPORT TO MO RAF BLACKPOOL
FOR MEDICAL DUTIES.

He stood on the steps outside the recruiting office and wondered if he should turn back, demand a further hearing. The CO had mentioned something about junior pilots being two-a-penny, and that what the Service needed at the moment were more 'sawbones' to deal with the tremendous influx of new recruits.

That Warrant Officer was the true face of the Service. Stephen understood that now. 'Orders is orders,' he told himself, and thrusting the documents into his tunic pocket, went along to the Mess to drown his sorrows in sweet tea and sticky doughnuts. His travel warrant was for a train leaving Glasgow that evening . . . there might just be someone about who would give him a lift into the city.

The RAF Medical Assessment Centre at Blackpool Camp consisted of a series of Nissen huts linked together by draughty walkways, roofed but without side protection of any kind. As February's continuous rain gave way to the gales which are so prevalent along Lancashire's Fylde coast during March, the medical staff found themselves obliged to huddle into their Winter Warms merely to move from one examination room to the next.

Fortunately it was more often the recruits who were obliged to move. Stripped to their shorts, they were sent scurrying from one set of doctors to the next. With careful organisation of the procedures it had been possible to create a circuit by which the men ended up where they had begun and could struggle thankfully into their clothing while waiting for the outcome of the day's investigations.

Occasionally, however, some strange phenomenon would strike one of the specialists as being not of his field and he would send for a colleague for a second opinion. Then it was that the hapless expert was expected to don additional protection and scurry around the unprotected complex to give his judgement.

The medical assessment was intended to sort out the recruits into those in top-class physical condition who were suitable for air crew, as opposed to those who, while lacking 20/20 vision and A1 physical status, would nevertheless be suitable for ground duties. The system was simple but seemingly effective.

Sophisticated equipment indicated a man's ability to withstand changes in the force of gravity when whirling through space, flying upside-down and diving steeply. Ear, nose and throat specialists looked out for evidence of breathing defects and autic imbalance, and opticians looked for night and colour blindess; blood men searched for dicky hearts and defective kidneys, while the internists were relegated to the bowels and VD department.

Stephen met the recruits only when they had been passed through the system. His surgical skills were hardly taxed at all. Having been trained to the scalpel, it was thought he would be the one to do the least damage with a hypodermic syringe. Consequently he spent his days vaccinating and inoculating the long and the short and the tall, and catching the burliest of individuals as they keeled over at their first sight of a needle.

'Next!'

Stephen hardly glanced up as yet another upper arm was thrust under his nose. He grasped hold of the spindly limb with its thin layer of skin and muscle over bone and looked into the face of the eighteen-year-old youth before him. The lad was ashen, and although Stephen had become accustomed to the scared reactions of some of the toughest-looking recruits, this one had a pallor which suggested not just apprehension but extreme privation.

'OK, son,' Stephen murmured, 'it'll be all over in a second, just hold on.' He signalled to his orderly who stood on the recruit's other side, supporting him lest he fall . . . . it was easier to keep them standing than to scrape them off the floor once they had keeled over.

'Sit this one down over there.' Stephen glanced towards a row of hard chairs against the wall of the waiting area. 'I want another look at him before we pass him along.'

The orderly led the young fellow away and Stephen continued with the endless round of injections. After half an hour the queue came to an end and he threw the last of the syringes into an enamel kidney dish which was immediately whisked away by the orderly.

Stephen washed his hands deliberately at the sink and then turned to the young man who had caused him so much concern.

He took a chair alongside the hapless recruit and consulted the sheaf of reports which the boy had been given to carry round with him. The title page read: Aircraftsman Gage, Barnabus Aloysius George, 673894.

'What do they call you . . . Barney?'

'I answers to all sorts, sir,' said the recruit, 'but Baggy is what the boys call me . . . me initials being B.A.G.G., y' see, sir.'

'How are you feeling now, Baggy?' Stephen enquired.

'OK, sir. Thank you, sir,' came the reply. Apprehensive at being singled out in this way, the young man was anxious to be on his way.

'Seen the other MOs, have you?' Stephen asked, rather pointlessly, since he held all his colleagues' reports in his hand.

'Yes, sir!' Baggy replied without hesitation.

'Anybody show any surprise . . . express any doubts about your health?'

'No, sir!'

Stephen glanced through the notes again. There was nothing there that was inconsistent with the A1 category the boy had been given.

'Give you a chest X-ray, did they?' he enquired casually.

'Sir?'

'Good God, man, you know what an X-ray machine looks like, don't you?' In his exasperation with the system within which he was operating, Stephen had begun to lose patience. The kid wouldn't know an X-ray machine if he saw one, he told himself . . . he'd probably never been inside a hospital in his life.

'They didn't get you to stand behind a screen and take a photo of your chest?'

The boy gazed at him, uncomprehending.

'No, sir.'

'Wait here,' Stephen ordered. 'Don't move until I get back.'

Grasping the boy's documents in one hand, he threw his heavy over-coat over his white overall and strode out into the storm raging outside.

'It doesn't take a stethoscope, let alone a set of X-rays, to see that this recruit is suffering from advanced TB.' Angrily, Stephen threw the documents down in front of the Senior Medical Officer.

The SMO looked up, startled by the vehemence of Stephen's tone. It had been some years since a junior officer had addressed him thus.

Wordlessly he glanced at the document before him, read the summary sheet and handed back the papers.

'Your colleagues seem to agree . . . the lad's A1. If I might say so, they're all senior to, and with considerably more experience than, yourself. I see no reason why I cannot confidently accept their assessment.'

'But that's just it, sir. Each of the specialists in the group is looking for specific indications related to suitability for air crew. No one is seeing the whole man. Day after day we're passing hundreds of these lads through the system . . . how many more like this one have got through the net? Imagine what a case of TB could do in an ill-ventilated, overheated barrack room.'

'This man must have seen an MO on enlistment. Are you suggesting that the initial screening system is not working?' demanded the SMO.

'Oh, come, sir.' Stephen's tone was scathing. 'If a recruit can find his way into the examination room, he can see. If he removes his cap when the WO tells him to, he can hear. And if he can slap his feet together and come to attention, he can walk. And that makes him A1?'

Stephen noted the anger suffusing the SMO's face and knew that he had overstepped the mark. Well, there was no going back now. 'I'm not blaming any of my colleagues, I'm blaming the system. We're not given sufficient time to do our jobs properly. There's more to a medical examination than counting fingers and toes, as you well know!'

The SMO knew that this matter would not be allowed to rest until he had heard the whole story.

'All right, Beaton, sit down and tell me all about it.'

'I'd rather not, sir, if you don't mind.' Stephen looked appropriately apologetic while insisting, 'I would prefer that you accompany me to my office to see this particular recruit for yourself.'

Reluctantly, the SMO drew on his overcoat and together they staggered outside to be buffeted by the wind and soaked by the rain which was sweeping horizontally across the covered way.

Eventually they half fell into the hut which contained Stephen's consulting room.

The young recruit had not moved from his chair, but confronted by two officers he rose to his feet, apprehensively.

The SMO shrugged off his coat and Stephen took it from him.

'Here, boy,' the senior man said, not unkindly, and the recruit stood

before him, trembling, partly through fear and partly from the chill . . .
he was still in his shorts and nothing else.

'Stethoscope!' The SMO put out a hand and Stephen, anticipating,
thrust the instrument into it.

The SMO listened to both lungs and heart, tapped around the back
then below the shoulder blades, and muttered an oath which was barely
audible.

'Sit down,' he barked, placing a chair conveniently for the recruit.
'Sphygmo,' he ordered and Stephen obliged.

'Humph . . .' He grunted at the abnormal blood pressure reading,
and the boy's pulse.

'Night sweats?' he barked.

The boy looked abashed.

'Do you wake up in the night, pouring with sweat?' Stephen
intervened.

'Sometimes.'

'Cough?'

This time the recruit sought Stephen's assistance with an anxious
glance. The younger doctor nodded encouragingly.

'Yes, sir, on and off.'

'Spit into that!' The SMO proffered a kidney dish and the youth
obliged by coughing up a sizeable dollop of phlegm.

Stephen took the proffered dish and smeared a little of the sputum
on a slide. He ran a few drops of stain under the cover slip and placed
the slide under a microscope, studying it intently for a few minutes. Not
knowing whether to be relieved for himself or concerned for his
patient, he quickly surrendered his seat to the SMO, who glanced down
the binocular microscope, adjusted it to his own sight and uttered
another oath.

He looked hard at Stephen, then turning to the recruit, said, 'Cut
along to the dressing room and get your uniform on. Then report to my
office.'

The boy turned to the door, ready to face the storm ill-clad as he was.

'Just a minute,' said Stephen, and placed his greatcoat over Baggy's
shoulders.

'Bring it back to the SMO's office when you're ready.'

Totally bemused by the whole affair, the boy shot out into the rain.
It was probably the only time in his life he would wear an officer's coat.

Left to themselves the two doctors eyed one another cautiously.

'You're right, of course,' the SMO agreed without Stephen's having to make any further observation. 'It's a case of rampant TB, and it should have been spotted straight away. What I don't understand is how the lad was ever allowed to enlist in the first place. Surely his own doctor should have warned him off? A medical certificate from a civilian doctor would have been sufficient for him to avoid call-up.'

'Youngsters like that don't have family GPs,' Stephen reminded him. The SMO had joined the Service within months of completing his medical training soon after the Great War. For years he had lived the cushioned life of the Officers' Mess in a well-equipped and fully staffed RAF hospital. He knew nothing of the ways of the working men of cities like Liverpool, Sheffield or Glasgow.

'By the look of him, that boy has scarcely ever had enough to eat,' Stephen observed. 'He probably lives in a two-roomed apartment with a family of half a dozen kids . . . dad on the dole, mother scrubbing clothes for a living. Such families can't afford doctors' fees and are too proud to seek free treatment at the clinics. The boy probably left school the day he was twelve and has been scraping a living for himself ever since. Recruitment into one of the Services can mean only one thing to a chap like that: three squares a day and a clean bed to sleep in. The worst thing we can do for him now is to turn him out!'

'But we're going to have to,' said the SMO.

'Yes . . .' Stephen agreed thoughtfully. Then added, 'Of course, he *has* been passed A1, and he *is* an enlisted man. As such he's entitled to the services of an RAF hospital. We could recommend him for the necessary treatment. If he recovers, he might still be suitable for ground staff.'

Blackmail as such had never entered Stephen's head, but the SMO knew that this smart young doctor could make a few waves were he to report that a recruit suffering from advanced tuberculosis had been passed A1 by his medical team. There might be an enquiry, and the SMO's comfortable existence could be threatened.

'Look, Beaton,' he said now, thinking rapidly, 'you seem to have a pretty clear idea of how things could be smartened up around here. Write me a report on the present assessment system and how you see it being improved.'

'What about Aircraftsman Gage, sir?' he persisted.

'Leave it to me,' the senior officer snapped, retrieving his coat and hat and buttoning himself up against the wind.

'So far as improvements are concerned,' Stephen observed, daring to smile, 'we could ask for a properly covered walkway between the buildings . . .'

'Put it in the report,' said the SMO, and then at the door turned to exert his authority belatedly with a clipped, 'on my desk, Monday morning . . . latest!'

'Aircraftsman Gage wishes to see the Flight Lieutenant on a personal matter, sir,' the orderly announced smartly.

Stephen looked up from his desk, searching his memory for the name. Of course . . . Gage . . . Baggy Gage.

The aircraftsman, now fully dressed, looked if possible more sickly than when clad only in his shorts. His uniform, despite being neatly pressed, hung limply from his wasted frame. Stephen could see why the name Baggy was so appropriate.

'I just came to tell you, sir, I'm being transferred to Wroughton RAF hospital for treatment.'

'Good show. They'll soon get you sorted out there,' Stephen said.

'I came to say thank you, sir.' Baggy looked a little embarrassed. 'The SMO told me what you did for me . . . keeping me in the Service and that.'

'Nothing to do with me, young feller,' he insisted. 'Thank the SMO.'

'Well, goodbye then, sir.' Baggy grinned at him. 'Hope to see you again sometime. Once they've cured me of this rotten cough.'

'Yes, well . . . good luck, Baggy. Just stick to the regime at Wroughton, keep your spirits up, and I'm sure they'll be able to put you right.' He stood up and shook the lad's hand, wishing he felt as confident as his words suggested. Baggy's was a bad case. It would depend on the efficiency of the staff at Wroughton how quickly he would recover, if at all. But at least the boy would get proper care where he was going.

Baggy saluted stiffly and turned on his heel, winking broadly at the orderly as he went out. In his mind Dr Beaton was entirely responsible for keeping him in the Service and if determination could cure him, Baggy Gage would soon be truly A1 and ready for action!

As the summer advanced, the British working man, able to jingle a few extra coins in his pocket due to increased productivity in preparation for war, took his family to the seaside. Under a blazing August sky he protected his head using a knotted handkerchief, and dozed in his collarless shirt and braces in a striped canvas deck chair, while the children made dams to trap the sea and Mother scraped sand out of the sandwiches.

At the RAF Reception Centre a few miles away, Stephen watched the passing of more and more recruits for the coming conflict, gazing enviously after each contingent of the brightest young men who had been selected for air crew training. As they marched away, proudly wearing their officers' flat caps with the white band denoting a trainee pilot, he wished he could simply tag himself on at the end. After six months in the service he had scarcely seen an aircraft, let alone been allowed near one.

It was with a sense of enormous relief, therefore, that he at last received his orders to move on.

'Your transfer has come through, Beaton.' The SMO greeted him in friendly enough manner. 'You are to report to Manston Air Station in Kent on September the first. That gives you the chance of seven days' leave. How does that suit you?'

'That's splendid news, sir. Thank you.' Stephen replied. Then, realising that he should not appear too eager, added, 'Of course, I shall be sorry to leave here.'

'Of course,' echoed the SMO with just a hint of sarcasm. He knew that the majority of his staff were only too anxious to get away to more exciting duties.

The SMO's response to Stephen's list of recommendations had been cool to say the least, and although he had followed most of them to the letter, there had been no acknowledgement of the fact that the changes introduced to improve the screening of recruits were at anyone's suggestion but his own.

It mattered little to Stephen. The awkward situation which had arisen between himself and his CO had proved to be a blessing in disguise. No doubt his transfer had been speeded up as a result of his chief's anxiety to get shot of him, and this eagerly awaited switch to an active service unit was the welcome outcome.

The CO shook his hand cordially enough now that his particular thorn in the flesh was about to disappear.

'Best of luck, Beaton,' he said gruffly. 'Looks as though you might be seeing a bit of action where you're going.'

'Yes, sir. Thank you, sir.'

Stephen made for the door, anxious to be on his way. As he took the three wooden steps from the hut in one stride, he spotted his orderly hurrying towards the canteen.

'Craddick!' he yelled.

The aircraftsman came to an abrupt halt and turned somewhat reluctantly at the command.

'Sir?'

'I'm posted . . . get my gear packed and ready to go, pronto, will you?'

'Sir.'

Craddick watched the young doctor swinging off in the direction of his own consulting room. It would take him half an hour to collect up the stuff he had in there . . . books, instruments and such. Still time for a cuppa before he got started. Craddick continued on his way to the canteen.

In the privacy of his own office, Stephen lifted the phone and dialled home. After a few moments he heard his mother's voice.

'Doctor's Surgery.'

'Hi, Mum. It's me.'

'Stevie? Where are you?'

'I'm still at the camp, but I've got a few days' leave. I'll be catching the first available train . . . should see you this evening sometime.'

'That's wonderful.' There was a pause. Mentally, Annie was frantically rearranging her commitments for the next few days. 'Ellen said she might be coming down for the weekend, isn't that lucky?'

'Great! Perhaps we can get tickets for a show or something?'

'I'll see what I can do,' Annie replied. Now she was intimately connected with the City Council, complimentary tickets for various events fell on her desk from time to time. She would have to see if there was anything she thought they might enjoy.

'See you later then,' he said, and put down the phone.

Stephen couldn't wait to get home, and put behind him if only for a few days this mindless drudgery. His father had never mentioned this aspect of Service life.

It would be so good to see Ellen again, too. What with the Air Squadron training and his hospital commitments, despite his promises he had been unable to visit any of the hill farms with her. Since his call-up they had scarcely exchanged a letter, and he had seen nothing of her since February.

Ellen was such good fun . . . they got on so well together. Even if his mother couldn't get them seats for a show, they would go dancing. Ellen loved to dance. He recalled her at the Hogmanay party, collapsing in giggles when she found herself lost in the measures of some unfamiliar

Scottish reel. Hot and dishevelled, she'd seemed to radiate happiness on that occasion. She had fitted into the tight-knit Beaton family with such ease . . . everyone had taken to her.

The only women he had met since being posted to Lancashire had been bimbos, interested in nothing but clothes and sex. It would be great to exchange experiences with Ellen, who always came armed with a plethora of amusing stories about her work.

That night, Stephen managed to have his first really comfortable sleep for months. In camp, junior officers did not warrant interior sprung mattresses. In place of the bugle and the harsh commands of the Drill Sergeant on the parade ground outside his window, he woke the next morning to the familiar sounds which had surrounded his boyhood.

Climbing out of bed, he went to the window and for a few moments simply enjoyed the view across to the Botanic Gardens. There had been a shower during the night and a heavy scent of roses wafted to him on the morning breeze. The avenue of lime trees planted to either side of the Great Western Road added their cloying scent after the summer rain.

The gritty, sand-laden, salty winds of the Fylde coast were behind him now. Other than an occasional trip to the capital, he had seen nothing of the South East of England and imagined its soft green landscape, white cliffs and blue seas. He was really looking forward to his first sight of the Kent coast. Stephen breathed in deeply, then grabbing sponge bag and towel, set off for the bathroom on the floor below.

He could smell the porridge from halfway down the stairs and rubbed his hands in anticipation. Not the lumpy glutinous mess produced by RAF cooks, this. Mrs Brown knew exactly how to make his favourite breakfast dish and today was no exception.

'We could do with you in the Officers' Mess,' Stephen declared, scraping the bowl after his second helping. 'Any bacon?'

Annie watched him devour the plateful of eggs, bacon and potato scones in a few seconds. Anyone would think he hadn't eaten for a week.

'What are you going to do today?' she asked. 'Ellen won't be here before tomorrow morning at the earliest.'

'I thought about driving up to collect her?'

'Sorry. Your Father has so many calls upon his time at present, I don't think he can spare the car. I only managed to get out to see friends by Loch Lomond last week because he had a consultation at Alexandria.'

'Will Ellen come by bus or train?'

'Train, I expect. There's no telling how long it will take her. Troop movements have priority. We'll just have to expect her when we see her.'

'If there's no chance of her arriving today, I'll take a stroll down to the Infirmary and see if I can have a word with the old Prof. I'll be back at lunch time.'

He wandered off, taking a circuitous route to the hospital by way of the Kelvin Bridge and the University. Many things had changed in the few months he had been away. Walls of sandbags covered the entrances to official buildings. Signs indicating Air Raid Shelter, Fire Hydrant, First Aid Post, were much in evidence and it was clear that people had been busy putting in train the preparations insisted upon by a government no longer willing to be hoodwinked by the smooth-talking diplomats at the German Embassy in London. Everyone knew that war was coming. It was merely a question of time.

At the hospital he found his old mentor emerging from the theatre after a morning's work. Stephen knew that the Professor preferred to operate in the early hours, giving himself ample time for lectures at the University and ward rounds at a reasonable time during the afternoon.

'Stephen!' he greeted his ex-pupil warmly. 'How are things?'

'Pretty dull at present,' he replied, 'although there is a possibility I shall see some action shortly. I've been posted to an airfield in Kent.'

'Well, it so happens that I've some good news for you,' the Professor told him, placing a hand on his shoulder and steering him towards the office.

Once inside, with the door closed, he waved Stephen to a chair.

'The Royal College has agreed that, in view of the necessity to provide sufficient surgeons to cope with the casualties of war, in certain cases we may recommend advancement to qualification within two years instead of three. It means that if you can find sufficient time for study in the next few months, you may take your examinations early next year.'

Stephen had achieved his first degree jointly in Medicine and Surgery, MB, ChB, two years before. To become a surgeon he should have worked under the direction of a consultant surgeon, as a houseman, for a further period of three years before taking his Registration examinations. When he had been called up in February, he had had a further twelve months to serve.

'The trouble is,' he explained now. 'I have had little or no experience of surgery since I went down to Blackpool. They stuck a hypodermic syringe in my hand the day I arrived, and for the past six months I've done little else but give injections!'

'What about your new posting?' demanded the Professor.

'Well, I imagine I shall have a bit more to do on an airfield in Kent . . . but whether or not I shall be allowed to operate myself, I don't know.'

'My experience of the last war was that if you knew one end of a stethoscope from another, you could perform brain surgery.' The Professor laughed rather cynically. 'In any case, I would put forward my recommendation based on the work you have already done with me. Provided you can cope with the theory papers, and I have no doubt that you can, I see no reason why you should not become registered without further supervised practice.'

'I suppose it will all depend on how things go when I get down to Kent,' said Stephen. 'Provided things don't blow up in our faces in the meantime, I'd like very much to take the examinations. Thank you, sir, for thinking me capable.'

'As you know, Stephen,' the Professor replied, 'I seldom express any great confidence in the abilities of my students, but I would happily allow you to operate on a member of my own family.'

'I pray that may never be necessary, sir.' Stephen smiled. As the Old Man had observed, he was never lavish with his praise. Stephen could not help being pleased at what had been said. If they were not going to allow him to fly, he might as well complete his qualification as a surgeon and get his advancement in the RAF that way.

'Good.' The Professor indicated that the interview was at an end by standing up and coming around his desk to shake Stephen's hand. 'If you will give your new address to my secretary, I'll see that you get all the relevant documentation in due course. It's been good to see you, my boy. Come back again when you get some more leave.'

When Stephen arrived home, rather later than he had expected, it was to find Ellen and his mother already seated at luncheon.

'I managed to get an extra day off when Aunt Annie phoned to let me know you were coming,' the girl explained. 'Actually, I have a call to make at the University this afternoon, but after that I'm all yours.'

There was an awkward silence. Ellen hadn't meant it to sound as though she was pushing herself at him. She blushed and concentrated on her rice pudding.

Stephen, completely unaware of his cousin's embarrassment, said cheerfully, 'I'll walk down with you. There's a couple of books I need to collect from the library. After that we can decide what we are going to do with our weekend.'

'You hadn't planned anything . . . with some of your friends?' The last thing Ellen wanted was for him to feel obliged to entertain her. 'I don't want to intrude on your leave. You get little enough of it.'

'Good heavens!' he replied. 'I can't think of anyone I'd rather spend the time with. Anyway, if we manage to meet up with some of my old crowd it will be all the more fun, don't you agree?'

She smiled, relieved to feel that he really wanted her around.

'What do you want library books for?' Annie asked. 'Will they let you take them away to Kent?'

'The Prof's arranged for me to take my exams next spring after all,' he told her. 'It's to do with the lack of qualified surgeons in the armed services. He seems to think I've had sufficient practical experience already so he's recommending that I be allowed to sit.'

'Oh, Stevie, I am pleased!' cried Annie. 'Your father will be delighted. He hasn't said much, but I know he was disappointed that you didn't finish your training before joining up.'

They finished their meal and the two young people set out for the University building. Ellen went off to report to the department of Agricultural Science, while Stephen made for the library.

He moved confidently through the shady cloisters, as one familiar with the complex of buildings, now almost deserted during the summer vacation. In the library, he wandered around the packed shelves for a while before he found the books he needed, and by the time he had settled a little tussle with the librarian, in which she insisted upon telephoning the Professor to establish his bona fides, he was late for his appointment with Ellen.

The lady in question was waiting on a bench overlooking the River Kelvin. In the park down below the hill, trees drooped languidly in the heat of the afternoon and the shrill voices of children at play came to her above the noise of the traffic along Argyle Street. The surrounding hills, as yet still green and uncluttered by the advance of the city, shimmered in the clear air.

How different was the scene from the railway embankment at home . . . not another building in sight and nothing but widely separated gum trees and a few lumps of Spinnifex grass to break the monotony of the endless acres of red, dusty plain.

Ellen shaded her eyes, hoping to see Stephen approaching along the wide gravel pathway in front of the University building. She shed her woollen cardigan, exposing her bare arms to the afternoon sun. Back home the temperatures would be about the same as this, she thought, no more than seventy or eighty degrees towards the end of the Antipodean winter.

Ah, there was Stephen, at last. She waved to attract his attention.

How smart he looked in his RAF uniform. His usually unruly mop of red hair had been tamed with Brylcreem so that his forage cap could be worn at just the right jaunty angle. The sunlight caught the bright buttons on his tunic, and the two blue rings of a full Flight Lieutenant on his sleeve. He took more pride in the wings sewn over his breast pocket than in the two lapel badges which indicated his role as a Medic. He had been disappointed not to become a pilot, Ellen knew, but like Annie was secretly relieved that he was not allowed to fly. Stephen sat down beside her on the bench, placing the books beside him.

'Very impressive.' She grinned. 'They're almost as heavy as the veterinary bibles I had to carry around!'

'They'll probably do to prop up the corner of my operating table.' He laughed and glanced at his wrist watch. 'Crikey, is that the time? I'm sorry to have kept you hanging about,' he apologised.

'I've just been sitting here enjoying the scene,' she told him. 'I'm glad to have had a moment to see Glasgow as it is today. Who knows what it will look like a year from now?'

Stephen looked westward along the Clyde to where great derricks in the shipyards towered above the buildings of Govan and Clydebank.

'That's where the bombers will make for,' he said with conviction, 'the shipyards and oil refineries. My mother has been working for the Council, you know. They're expecting to be hit, sooner or later.'

He was proud of his parents' role in the preparations for war, but concerned for their safety. 'I can't believe they've called on my mother for such a job. She's getting on a bit, you know.'

'No one would guess,' said Ellen. 'She's so full of energy she puts the rest of us to shame.'

'How are your folks doing?' he asked. 'They must be worried about you being over here. If the balloon goes up, you're going to be stuck here for the duration.'

'I had a letter from Australia the other day,' said Ellen. 'Dad wants me to take the next boat home but I don't feel that I can do that . . . it would be like a rat leaving a sinking ship. There must be something useful I can do here when the war starts.'

'We're going to need all the help we can get. I remember my dad telling me how important it was, last time, to grow as much of our own food as possible. I don't doubt the Ministry of Agriculture will be able to find you a job!'

'I do hope so,' Ellen replied. 'I've written to them, offering to help in any way I can.'

'What about your research project? Will that still go on?'

'Probably. They're saying up at Aberdeen that it's all the more important now to keep the experiment going. Several more hill farms have been included in the pilot scheme, and farmers are being encouraged to stock cattle, even those who only kept sheep before.'

'At least your work will keep you out in the country,' he said. 'We'll not have to worry about *you* getting bombed.'

'What are we doing tonight?' asked Ellen, changing the subject. 'Your mother has some tickets for us for the King's Theatre, if you would like to use them? It's a musical show, I believe.'

'Sounds fine to me,' he agreed.

'We'd better get a move on then. I'd like to take a bath and change into something a little more glamorous.'

'You look perfect just as you are,' Stephen insisted, admiring her pastel blue cotton dress with its full skirt and square-cut neckline. Ellen really was a very attractive girl.

Long hours in the open had restored her tan and her skin glowed in the afternoon light. Her wheat-coloured hair had become bleached as much by exposure to strong winds and mountain air as to the unpredictable sunshine of a Highland summer. Ellen was a picture of good health.

'I know what you girls are,' Stephen declared. 'You'll want to take an hour or two getting ready. We can catch a tram from Kelvin Bridge, and I might even run to a taxi to get us to the theatre . . . after all, the tickets'll cost us nothing!'

The Isle of Thanet constitutes the south-easterly extremity of the British Isles. In 1939 its coastal towns of Ramsgate, Broadstairs, Margate and Westcliffe on Sea were linked together by a network of inadequate, poorly maintained roads, making the London and South Eastern Railway their main lifeline to the county town of Canterbury and to London itself.

At the centre of the promontory which is an island in name only, Manston RAF base was ten minutes' flying time from the coast of France, and England's first line of defence against enemy air attack.

On this first day of September, hops were still being gathered from the fields, and the trees in the orchards were bent almost to the ground under the burden of their fruit.

Mile upon mile of rolling downland, covered by vast open fields, was beginning to take on a uniform brownness from the autumn ploughing.

Stephen's train, which half an hour before had thundered through deep cuttings in the chalk, now slowed as it passed through the green valley of the Weald. Open fields gave way to cool woodland where oak and ash, chestnut and sycamore, hung heavy with nature's bounty, their tired leaves just beginning to suggest the glories of the coming autumn.

At last the countryside gave way to a sprawling conurbation and as the train drew to a halt, Stephen recognised the towering pinnacles of Canterbury Cathedral, a picture of which he had been staring at on the carriage wall ever since the train had left Charing Cross. The artist had used plenty of licence in his portrayal of the fine Medieval building shown towering above a town surrounded by willow trees and water meadows. Nowhere in the picture had he depicted the mean little Victorian villas at its feet, bordering the marshalling yards to either side of the track.

The steam train quickly disgorged its passengers. The bulk of servicemen alighting from the carriages wore RAF uniform. These made their way outside to where a series of trucks bearing the familiar roundels of the Royal Air Force, and painted the appropriate shade of blue, awaited their arrival.

There were very few civilians amongst them and Stephen, commenting upon this fact to the pleasant clerical gentleman who had shared his carriage for most of the journey, was informed that apart from essential workers, most of the civilian population of Thanet had already been evacuated in case of an invasion.

'There aren't a lot of folk left living on the coast now,' the priest had explained. 'Only those of us with a specific job to do really, people running the essential services and a few publicans for the boys in uniform . . . that's about it.'

He had been amused at Stephen's expression of relief.

'For a moment there, sir, I thought you were going to tell me that all the pubs were shut!'

They alighted from their carriage and shuffled towards the ticket barrier where a smartly uniformed RAF rating stepped forward and saluted Stephen.

'Flight Lieutenant Beaton, sir?' he enquired.

'Yes, Leading Aircraftsman.'

'The CO sent his car for you, sir . . . if you'll just follow me.'

Stephen turned to his new aquaintance. 'It's been a pleasure travelling with you,' he said, holding out his hand. 'I do hope we shall meet again.'

The aircraftsman, recognising Stephen's companion, interrupted with, 'Well, bless my soul if it ain't the Vicar. Was you looking for a lift, Mr Dobbie, sir?'

The reverend gentleman, a trifle embarrassed by the greeting, glanced from one to the other. 'Well . . . if the lieutenant has no objections, Fred?'

'You two know each other?' asked Stephen.

'Mr Dobbie is the Vicar of Manston Parish Church, sir,' the aircraftsman explained. 'We usually gives 'im a lift from the station, the CO and me.'

'In that case,' laughed Stephen, 'who am I to interfere with accepted practice? Carry on, Leading Aircraftsman!'

Fred picked up the larger of Stephen's two valises and led the way to a Humber saloon in Air Force livery. Deftly, he threw Stephen's gear into the boot and opened the door for his passengers.

Fred drove the sedate motor out of the station yard, now clear of military vehicles, and turned into a crowded narrow street. To Stephen, who was used to the rugged red granite and stark outlines of Scottish architecture, the sight of the ancient cathedral and the cobbled lanes, lined with timber-framed buildings of the thirteenth and fourteenth centuries, was like something out of a picture book.

'What a beautiful old place,' he sighed. 'I'd like to come and have a proper look round some time.'

'If you do,' said Dobbie 'you must pop in and take a look at the Cathedral . . . It's worth a visit.'

Out on the open road and heading towards Thanet, Fred glanced into the rear-view mirror, assessing his passenger.

'You'll be the new MO, I believe, sir?' he risked, at last.

'Yes, that's right.'

The Vicar viewed him with renewed interest.

'My goodness,' he exclaimed. 'Doctors, like policemen, seem to be getting younger . . . or else I'm getting older, one of the two.'

'I am qualified, I can assure you,' laughed Stephen. 'And in view of recent experience, a seasoned RAF Medic.'

'Where were you?'

'Blackpool Assessment Centre,' Stephen explained. 'I must have seen every RAF recruit since the dawn of time, up there!'

'You'll find things a little tame here, I'm afraid,' commented Dobbie. 'They're all exceptionally healthy young men. Except for a broken nose or two from the rugger pitch and the odd sprained wrist during the cricket season, there won't be a lot for you to do.'

'I hope you're right,' Stephen replied.

They both fell silent. News from across the Channel was bad. Troop movements had been reported along the Polish frontier with Germany. Britain had signed a pact with Poland to come to her aid should she be attacked. There was no question now that were Germany to invade, war would be declared.

They turned off the main A 253 and headed towards a village lying in a hollow, only the roofs of the cottages visible between the trees. To one side of the road an untidy hedge marked the limits of Manston Field. In the distance Stephen could make out a huge complex of Nissen huts and wooden single-storey buildings.

'That's the headquarters block and crew quarters,' explained Fred, 'and over on the far side, the hangars of the maintenance and repair depot.'

Stephen, sitting forward on his seat, was anxious to miss nothing of his first view of Manston. An active service unit at last! He could still hardly believe his luck.

The road swung away from the field and entered the village, past a row of farm workers' cottages. At the centre of the green stood a war memorial and to one side was a rambling barn-like public house. A sign, faded and indistinct, announced the Malt Shovel.

Opposite the war memorial stood the church. Its square, ivy-covered tower suggested Norman origins, but the greater part of the building was much more modern, bearing all the signs of Victorian Gothic Revival at its worst.

Beside the church stood an old flintstone house, ivy-clad, with beautifully proportioned Georgian windows below a low-pitched grey slate roof. It was here that the driver drew to a halt and stepped out quickly to open the door for his passenger.

'That was very kind of you, Lieutenant,' said the Vicar as he alighted. 'I hope that once you have settled in, you will bring a few chums along for tea one afternoon? My wife loves to entertain the boys from the camp. Wednesday is usually a good day . . .'

'Thank you, sir, that's really very kind of you.' Stephen stepped out in order to shake the Vicar by the hand. 'You make a stranger feel very welcome.'

'All part of the service.' The elderly priest smiled as he took Stephen's hand. 'And, thank you, Fred,' he said as he waited for the driver to open the gate for him. 'I'll see you again soon, no doubt. Please give my best to the CO.'

The aircraftsman allowed the gate to swing shut and latched it before climbing back into the driving seat. Stephen made to join him in the front passenger seat but he shook his head.

'Best not, sir. Not when we've to go past the guard at the gate. Likes things done proper, does the Orderly Sergeant . . . if you don't mind, sir.'

'Oh, very well, Fred . . . Leading Aircraftsman,' said Stephen, thankful to have someone willing to show him the ropes.

'Oh, Fred'll do between ourselves, Doc. . . Mr Beaton, sir.'

'Doc will do between ourselves, Fred.' Stephen grinned as he settled into the back seat.

He quite enjoyed his reception at the main gate to the camp, where the guard on duty and the Flight Sergeant each threw a smart salute. Had Flight Sergeant Wilson realised beforehand that the new MO was a mere Flight Lieutenant, he might have been just a little less energetic about it!

The Humber came to a halt outside a wooden building, distinguished from a row of similar structures by the addition of a narrow veranda. Before this was a neatly dug flower bed, edged with large flintstones, painted white. A board to one side of the main door proclaimed:

NO 11 GROUP
FIGHTER COMMAND
HEADQUARTERS

Fred opened the door smartly and saluted as Stephen stepped out of the car.

'The CO requested that you report to him on arrival, sir,' he said. 'The 'orspital is just over there to the right.' He pointed vaguely into the distance. All the buildings looked alike to Stephen. 'You'll know it when you see it,' Fred explained, seeing his concern. 'I'll dump your gear in the MO's office.'

He climbed back into the vehicle and pulled away, leaving Stephen alone to negotiate the short flight of steps on to the veranda. He pushed open a glazed door and reported to the NCO seated behind the desk.

'Medical Officer reporting for duty,' he declared, handing the man his transfer documents.

Warrant Officer Pritchard had joined the airforce in 1917 when it was the Royal Flying Corps. Deeply suspicious of every man under the age of thirty who wore the uniform of his beloved Service, he made a rapid appraisal of this new medic. Very young, he decided, but didn't seem quite so cocky as most. Reasonably well satisfied, he picked up the telephone on the desk before him.

'Flight Lieutenant Beaton, reporting for duty, sir.' He listened to the reply and replaced the handset.

'The CO will see you right away, sir. Down the corridor . . . last on the right.'

Chapter Six

As Stephen moved towards the inner door a very large sable-coloured German Shepherd dog emerged from behind the desk and wandered over to inspect the new arrival, brown eyes expressive and alert.

Trying hard to ignore the dog's penetrating gaze, Stephen bent down to retrieve his Gladstone bag.

'Don't worry about the dog, sir,' said Pritchard, 'he's trained to attack Germans only!'

The dog escorted him along the corridor to a door marked Station Commander. Stephen knocked smartly and stepped inside, coming to attention before the Station Adjutant's desk.

'Ah, welcome to Manston, Beaton. I see that you and Shep have met already.'

'Station mascot?' Stephen asked.

'You might call him that,' replied the Adjutant. 'He's the CO's dog actually. Anyway, he seems to have taken a shine to you which has to be a good sign.'

As though to confirm the Adjutant's assessment, Shep tucked his muzzle into Stephen's free hand. He was instantly rewarded when the doctor's fingers found just the right place behind his left ear and rubbed at the spot, firmly. Introductions completed, the dog moved to the inner door which bore the name of the Station Commander: Wng. Cmdr. Harold E. Calcutt, DFC. Squatting before it, Shep thumped his tail on the ground and looked appealingly from one to the other of the two men.

The Squadron Leader rose from his desk to introduce himself, extending his right hand. Stephen was startled to find himself grasping a gloved prosthesis.

'. . . accounts for my flying a desk,' explained the Adjutant. 'Lost my hand pranging a kite a year or two back. Hence the name – Stumpy Miles. It's Derek, actually.'

'Glad to meet you, sir.' Stephen released the false hand respectfully.

'No need to be too lavish with the "sirs" around here, Beaton. Not between ourselves at any rate. Stumpy will do.'

'Thank you, sir.' Stephen stumbled over his words. 'My friends call me Steve.'

'It'll do for now,' observed the other, 'but don't be surprised if they find another moniker for you very soon. As a matter of fact, a sawbones is lucky if he can get away with merely being called Doc.'

At that moment the door of the inner office flew open to reveal the Station Commander himself.

'Here you are,' he said gruffly, automatically stepping aside to allow his dog to sidle past him into the inner sanctum. 'Half an hour ago they said the new Doc was on his way in, so I hypes up m' blood pressure and gets m' palpitations goin' nicely and then, blow me, if I don't find Stumpy, waylaying him with his own bloody aches and pains as usual.'

Stumpy Miles grinned. They played this game of hypochondriacs regularly, in a pretence of trying to find a way out of the Service. Although the CO, at least, was old enough to retire, he prayed nightly that the authorities would continue to find his experience valuable.

Group Captain Harold E. Calcutt, although already past forty, appeared to be in robust health. Standing no more than five feet two inches in his socks, his chunky body was more like that of a prize fighter than the slender, Brylcreemed RAF types depicted on the posters. His dark hair, which curled close to his head, had turned grey at the temples, giving him a distinguished and somewhat severe appearance. This was, however, belied by the twinkle which was ever present in his startlingly blue eyes, sheltering beneath craggy brows. Shrapnel had pockmarked his skin with bluish-purple dots, while beneath the left eye an ancient bullet wound had left a white scar which traversed his cheek from nose to ear.

The CO stretched out his hand and greeted Stephen warmly. 'Good to have you aboard, Beaton . . . knew your father, were you aware of that? Soon as I saw your name the old memory cogs started churning . . . made a few enquiries . . . knew I was right!'

'I learned to fly with a pal of his,' he continued, 'fellow called Rosencrantz or Rosenstein or something. Poor devil went down with the old Hampshire in 1915. The three of us poured a few pints down our throats together in Portsmouth Docks in those early days.' He paused, savouring the memories of his youth.

'You were in the Navy in the last lot, sir?' Stephen enquired politely.

'The air-defence arm of the Navy, yes. We flew out of Westgate on Sea . . . coastal patrols, spotting submarines, worrying enemy shipping. You know the kind of thing. People like Rosenstein were the real heroes. They were catapulted from the decks of ships in light aircraft, to observe enemy fleet movements. Very few of those chaps survived.'

Nodding to the Adjutant, the CO led his newest member of staff into his inner sanctum and closed the door. Shep was already curled up in the only comfortable armchair in the room, nose over tail in apparent repose. One eye was fixed upon the newcomer, however, and both of the velvety black ears were cocked, alert to any change of tone, any alteration in his master's demeanour.

Stephen was ushered to a hard Windsor chair set before the desk.

'Not long qualified, are you?' observed the CO, casting a glance over the documents which Stephen had handed to him. 'This will be your first posting to a combat group?' He knew the answer, but it was an opening.

Stephen nodded. 'I can't tell you what a relief it is to be shot of all those inoculations and so on. The last three months have been pretty boring to say the least.'

'Don't expect any Dr Kildare stuff now you are here,' observed the CO. 'The worst complaint our men have been suffering from is inaction. Until now, cricket and athletics have been taking their minds off the hanging around, but once the weather changes there'll not be much chance of sporting activities. Then you can expect to find your daily sick parade busy with men complaining of all kinds of imaginary illnesses. A few sniffles and a touch of 'flu is all you're likely to encounter at the moment but the men'll try every angle imaginable to wangle a few days' leave. The fact is that I can't risk having the station under strength, so I don't expect to see a long list of non-combatants emerging from the sick-bay!' He paused to allow this order to sink in. Stephen accepted it for what it was.

'What's the usual method of dealing with the shirkers?' he enquired, hoping for some lead.

'Your predecessor, a Scotsman like yourself, was all for a quiet life. He suffered from cramp in his fingers from signing the men off work. A great believer in whisky as a cure for all ills, was MacIntyre.

Unfortunately he took too much of his own medicine . . . it was necessary to stand him down.'

So, he was not even to meet his predecessor. If there were to be no hand-over period Stephen would be obliged to find out the wrinkles for himself. On reflection, perhaps that was just as well. It meant that he would begin with a clean sheet. Irritating conventions could be ignored if he didn't know what they were.

The CO dug deep into his pocket and withdrew a pipe which he began to fill from a battered leather pouch.

'Our allies' experience of the Germans' method of attack so far has been surprise raids from the air, so sudden and so devastating that the victims have no opportunity to respond.' He leaned forward earnestly. 'I'm short of planes and my pilots are without combat experience . . . I'm just praying we can manage to get in sufficient daylight patrols over the Channel so that they all get a feel of the aircraft at least once before the real fighting begins. I want my men fit and ready to fight, Doc, both mentally and physically. If you can find ways of occupying them to that end, I shall be eternally grateful.'

'There seem to be plenty of aircraft about today,' Stephen observed as, one after another, a line of fighters started up engines, taxied down the runway, turned through 180 degrees and returned to the hangars.

As the sound of the Merlins died, the CO replied, 'I need to keep everyone on their toes, so we have maintenance drills for the ground crews and tactical lectures for the pilots. When the U-boat activity gets going in the Channel, the major threat will be to our oil supplies. I've been instructed to conserve aviation spirit, so the only flying practice the lads get is a coastal patrol twice a day and the odd ferrying job when some VIP has to be flown over to France. For the most part it's a question of waiting until the balloon goes up and hoping we'll be ready.'

Stephen glanced out of the window and observed a two-seater biplane about to take off. Recognising it as one of the Westlands on which he had trained, he asked, 'There won't be any chance of my having a spin in one of those then, I suppose? I have my Pilot's A licence.'

'So I see,' observed Calcutt. 'But even if you were expendable, which you're not, there's not enough fuel to spare to clean the oil off my trousers, let alone joy-riding in a Westland. Sorry!'

Calcutt's amiable mood changed suddenly as he addressed Stephen urgently.

'When things start to hot up a bit, it will be a very different story. You will have to be prepared for severe casualties once the field becomes actively engaged. I have no illusions about our ability to withstand continuous air attacks here, and you can be sure we are going to be a convenient target for Gerry. We have to be prepared for almost anything, and I'll be grateful for your suggestions about any preparations you feel you can make towards that end.'

'I'll do my best, sir.' Stephen, anxious now to see his own domain, rose to his feet. 'Will it be all right if I go and take a look at the hospital, now?'

'I'm afraid *hospital* is rather a grand title for what amounts to a First Aid hut,' the CO explained, apologetically. 'We have an arrangement with Margate Cottage Hospital to make use of their facilities if there are any serious cases. Here on the field the team consists of yourself and a couple of medical orderlies.'

Stephen's heart sank. He had been so looking forward to being in charge of his own unit and had conjured up grandiose ideas of the kind of establishment he would be heading. Now it seemed that he must go cap in hand to the local civilian doctors in order to get the use of any decent facilities at all.

As though reading his thoughts, the CO continued, 'You'll be meeting the Vicar and the local sawbones in the Mess for dinner tomorrow . . . they often join us on a Saturday night. It'll be a good opportunity for you to make Dr Lewis's acquaintance, and to sort out a few practicalities about the use of the hospital. There is one great advantage,' he offered as an afterthought. 'The Officers' living quarters are situated conveniently just across the road from the Cottage Hospital.'

'We don't live on the camp then, sir?' Stephen asked, surprised.

'Lord, no,' came the reply. 'When the balloon goes up the last thing we want is all our pilots in one basket so to speak . . . something we learned from the last war. By the same token, we have set up a stand-by command post at Westgate in case the airfield gets shot up. The duty squadron sleeps on the base, of course, but all the fellows have permanent digs in town where they can get a good night's rest when they need it. You'll be living at Doone House,' he continued. 'Once you have seen the infirmary here and settled yourself into your office, I'll get my driver to give you a lift into Westgate. You'll need to find yourself some kind of transport, by the way . . . for getting between here and the hospital. I can't offer you an official car, but if you can buy a vehicle of your own, we'll maintain it and provide the petrol.'

Stephen could envisage the dashing little sports car he would acquire for careering about the countryside . . . something flashy to impress the ladies.

'Actually the last MO had quite a nice little vehicle,' Calcutt observed casually. 'I think he left it behind to be sold off. Why don't you ask Fred about it?'

Surprised that his CO should take such a personal interest in his method of transport, Stephen replied, 'Thanks, sir, I will.'

He picked up his bag and coat, tucked his cap under his arm and turned to the door.

'Beaton.' The CO halted him in his tracks.

'Sir?'

'This period of idleness can't last forever . . . I hope we shall all be ready to face up to it when the trouble starts.'

Stephen nodded. 'I don't think you'll find the Medical Section wanting, sir!'

'No, I don't think I shall.' The CO waved a hand dismissively and Stephen closed the door behind him.

In seconds it was opened again. Stumpy Miles stood there, an anxious look on his face.

'He's a bit young, but I think he'll do,' observed Calcutt.

Ignoring the observation, Stumpy Miles laid a communication form on the CO's desk.

'Bad news, I'm afraid . . . the Germans have invaded Poland. It's only a matter of time now before we declare war.'

'Right!' It was almost a relief to know that things were about to start happening. 'Put the station on full alert,' Calcutt ordered. 'Cancel all leave until further notice.'

'We've had a request from the Westgate ARP,' said Stumpy. 'It seems that a load of Anderson air raid shelters have been delivered to Manston village. They wondered if we could spare a few men to help erect them?'

'Why not? I see no reason why the off-duty men shouldn't be usefully occupied. Get together a few volunteers right away. Better make sure they take their own picks and shovels . . . we don't want any of them standing around with nothing to lean on.'

Stumpy Miles snorted at the quip, returned to his own office and picked up the phone.

Between the two wars, while Westgate on Sea was still the main centre in the South of England for the newly created Royal Air Force, Doone House had been purpose-built to accommodate the officers stationed at both Westgate and Manston Air Bases. Built in red brick, with large Georgian-style windows, the building bore Queen Anne dormers in its upper storey, and concrete columns supported gabled porches over the two main doors. The architecture was typical of that introduced country-wide during the 1930s, in the building of secondary schools and hospitals. Whether or not Doone House had been designed deliberately to be indistinguishable from more innocuous buildings it was difficult to say, but Stephen, observing the Officers' quarters for the first time, was moved to comment, 'It doesn't look much like a hotel, does it?'

Fred, who had driven him over from the field on the CO's orders, suggested that he would be more comfortable here than in some of the quarters that he had experienced around the countryside.

'You don't want to be put into none of these stately homes, Doc,' he observed. 'All stonework and ivy on the outside and great draughty places inside without decent heating, and the officers' rooms carved up from huge ballrooms and that. At least in this place you gets a decent room to y'self.'

'You sound like an expert, Fred,' Stephen laughed. 'Been around a bit, have you?'

'I was the CO's batman right through the last lot,' he confessed. 'After we was stood down in 1919, I went into the garage business with me brother-in-law, but as soon as he's recalled to the colours 'imself, the Old Man gets on to me. "How'd you like to come back in as my driver, Fred?" he asks. Well, what was I to say? Couldn't have the Old Man fending for 'imself, could I? Came back like a shot, I did. Never regretted it for one minute.'

'That reminds me,' said Stephen. 'The CO mentioned that you had charge of a car I might be interested in . . .'

'Oh, yes.'

Did he look just a trifle shifty when the car was mentioned? Stephen wondered.

'When can I get a look at it?'

'I'll bring it round this evening if you like,' came the prompt reply.

There was no time for further discussion of the matter for at that moment a group of officers emerged from the building and, seeing Stephen alight from the CO's car, crowded around to introduce them-selves.

There was a certain amount of cheerful badinage between Fred and two of the young Lieutenants who between them relieved the driver of Stephen's gear. A third man, tall and willowy, whose Squadron Leader's insignia showed him to be the senior officer, stepped forward with hand outstretched. 'You must be the new Doc,' he drawled, indolently.

'Flight Lieutenant Beaton, sir,' Stephen saluted smartly.

'Good Lord,' observed the other, 'we don't have any nonsense of that sort around here. Save it for the Old Man! Piper's the name.'

'Answers more readily to "Squeaky",' observed one of the others, brandishing Stephen's Gladstone bag as he did so. 'I'm Bolton . . . and that weaselly little runt over there is Digger Sheen from Down Under!'

A giant of a man with blond hair and huge, widely set eyes grinned happily at this introduction. 'G'day, mate,' he greeted Stephen with a shake from a hand the size of a wicket keeper's glove.

Stephen winced with pain, but nevertheless managed a smile. 'Beaton,' he replied, 'Steve Beaton.'

'C'mon, Doc.'

Digger took hold of his heavy valise. Lifting it on to his shoulder as if it were a feather pillow, he said, 'I'll show you to your quarters.'

He led the way, Stephen following on with his precious Gladstone bag and a small attaché case, while the others trailed behind.

'Don't be too long sortin' yourself out, laddie,' Squeaky Piper called after him. 'Time for a snort in half an hour!'

Digger led him to a door at the end of the first-floor corridor.

'Dunno why the Doc gets such palatial quarters,' observed the Australian as he pushed open the door which already bore a neat label with Stephen's name and rank, as well as the designation MEDICAL OFFICER, painted on the wooden panelling in large gold letters.

To Stephen's amazement he had been allocated a suite consisting of day room, bedroom and bathroom. He had never known such luxury.

'Know how to treat their Medics in peacetime,' observed his companion. 'Lucky you, sport. I should make the most of it if I were you. You may find you don't get much time for lounging about here in a week or two.'

'What part of Australia d'you come from, Digger?' Stephen asked.

'Somewhere no one's ever heard of . . . a little outback town called Salmon Gums, south of Norseman in Western Australia.'

'I've stayed out near Southern Cross a couple of times,' Stephen told him. 'My mother's family emigrated before the Great War and settled a small township called Kerrera. I went out there as a kid for a few months and then again in '32, just before I went up to university.'

'What d'you think of Oz, mate . . . ain't it a great place?'

'It's big, certainly,' Stephen grinned, deliberately misinterpreting the question. 'It's also dry, dusty, hot and alive with sand flies.'

'But that's what we love about 'er!' declared the Australian, laughing loudly. 'You and I are going to find we have a lot in common, sport.'

'I hope so,' said Stephen, sincerely. He had taken an instant liking to this open, pleasant man. 'Look, you'll have to excuse me. I've been travelling all day and I need a shower.'

'OK, I'll push off and leave you to it,' said Digger. 'Dinner's at 1900 hours. Bar opens at 1830 . . . last one in buys a round of drinks!'

Despite the CO's having persuaded Stephen to see the previous doctor's car before looking elsewhere for transport, it was nearly a week before Fred reappeared.

'I thought it best to let the mechanics take a look at her before handing her over,' he explained, patting the shiny bonnet with some pride. He had personally attended to the chromium-plated bumpers and to the only slightly damaged paintwork.

Stephen regarded the sedate Morris Ten saloon with some disappointment. He had hoped his predecessor might have had a slightly more imaginative taste in cars.

'I don't know, Fred,' he said, doubtfully. 'It isn't quite what I had in mind . . .'

'She's a good little runner, Mr Beaton, sir,' the aircraftsman urged. 'Easy on the petrol. You can't afford to have a guzzler these days.'

'How much?'

'The CO was thinking along the lines of twenty-five,' Fred suggested, hopefully.

'I'd say she was worth no more than fifteen at the outside.' Stephen, although reluctant to make any offer at all, sensed that a certain compulsion lay at the back of this transaction.

'I might be able to get the Old Man to accept twenty.' Fred hesitated. 'Truth is, the old Doc left owing a hefty Mess bill. The car was left behind in settlement of his debts.'

'And twenty-five pounds would just about cover that, I suppose?'

Fred nodded, sheepishly.

Stephen realised that if he was going to keep on the right side of the CO he was really obliged to buy the car. 'It's not worth it,' he insisted, 'but I'll give you twenty.'

'Done!' Fred was so quick to accept the offer that Stephen wondered if he should have stuck to fifteen. Twenty pounds represented most of the money he had managed to squirrel away in his Post Office savings account. Still, the car was a good idea, and he would certainly be needing it when things hotted up a little.

He climbed in, switched on the engine and was gratified to discover that she fired first time. He sniffed at the leather seats, noticing a distinct odour of wet dog.

'Did the MO have a dog too?' he enquired, vowing to give the vehicle a thorough airing before taking any passengers.

'No, but Shep used to like a ride now and again . . . he gets bored hanging around the Station Office all day.'

Stephen wondered, not for the first time, who really ran the base – the CO or his dog!

One of Stephen's first moves on taking over, was to make a thorough inspection of both the camp and off-site accommodation. What he found confirmed his suspicions that his predecessor had completely neglected the hygiene of the living quarters and the duties of the domestic staff. All minor misdemeanours now warranted a punishment involving bucket and brush. Inspections of huts, ablutions and messes became a major event in the daily round, and those men responsible for the cleanliness of the base suddenly found that their cushy number did not look quite so rosy in the cold clear light of Doc Beaton's day. In his demand for cleanliness, Stephen had accidentally hit upon a way to occupy those men suffering from under-employment. His lead was taken up by other officers and NCOs responsible for discipline, and soon there was a general air of smartness and purposefulness about the place which Stephen had certainly not observed when he first arrived.

His overhaul of the so-called camp hospital was also a suitable occupation for punishment details. Soon the floors, their twenty-year-old linoleum replaced, were shiny enough to reflect the sharp outlines of newly painted doors and windows.

The one small ward, with its four pristine beds and neat lockers, was bright and welcoming, while the consulting room and Stephen's small dispensary were transformed by soap and water, white paint and a few decent pieces of new furniture. Even the red cross on the outer door and the sign saying Camp Dispensary were legible from fifty yards.

Stephen's first encounter with Dr Lewis, the Superintendent of the Cottage Hospital, proved to be unexpectedly agreeable. Lewis, a physician of considerable experience, welcomed the young surgeon with open arms.

'With half the civilian population of the area gone, there's little enough call upon our services,' he had explained to Stephen when the CO had diplomatically left the two doctors to discuss matters over the port on that first Saturday evening. 'I've lost my two young assistants to the RAMC, and I'm down to a couple of staff nurses, a few volunteers, Matron and myself . . . two old codgers for whom nobody can find a better use. The good thing,' he had continued, dismissing Stephen's polite protest, 'is that because we are now providing services for the RAF, we can get all the supplies and equipment we need. You can't imagine what a relief it is not to have to spend half my time sitting on bloody fund-raising committees with a lot of well-meaning, flowery hatted members of the Mothers' Union!'

Stephen had quickly taken up Lewis's invitation to visit the hospital and had been relieved to find that, although small, it contained every facility he could hope for.

The Cottage Hospital had been built and equipped by the people of the Thanet towns over an extended period, prior to the First World War. Whist drives and garden parties had paid for an excellent operating theatre and X-ray facilities, whilst the staff quarters were more comfortable than any he had encountered in Scotland's major hospitals.

With the CO's agreement, Stephen arranged to carry out minor surgery for both civilian as well as service personnel on one day each week. Dr Lewis was patently relieved to have a competent surgeon to call upon in any emergency, while Stephen was grateful for this initial experience which gave him an opportunity to familiarise himself with the hospital's facilities in preparation for more serious work.

Stephen had been at Manston two days when Neville Chamberlain's government at last ceased prevaricating and declared war on Germany. Within hours, Australia, Canada and other members of the Commonwealth followed suit. When the news came through in the Mess that Australia's Prime Minister had followed Mr Chamberlain's lead, everyone cheered, thumping Digger on the back and shaking his hand despite the danger of crushed fingers.

For a few days Calcutt had his men on constant alert. His aircraft were ready for take off at any time of the day or night. At the slightest sign of aerial activity in the Channel, planes took off to investigate, returning hours later with their crews dispirited after yet another false alarm.

In the town of Westgate on Sea, ARP Wardens had chivvied the population into preparing a complete blackout weeks beforehand. Now they patrolled the streets on bicycles, shouting out at any chink of light inadvertently allowed to escape from behind hastily constructed paper screens and heavily dyed curtains. Civilians carried their gas masks at all times, giving rise very soon to a new fashion in elegant cases.

Housewives, stocking up with tinned and dried food to ensure that there would be sufficient to feed their families, were accused of hoarding and the government, learning from the experiences of the Great War of 1914, distributed books of stamps ready for food rationing.

The streets of Westgate had been strangely quiet in the days leading up to the declaration of war. Although at the time there was no compulsion to do so, many people had evacuated themselves to friends and relatives inland.

The government, anxious to avoid the pitiful trek of refugees which they had seen taking place across the face of Europe, in which families on the move blocked the roads, inhibiting troop movements and exposing themselves to aerial attack, organised an official evacuation of the larger conurbations. Oddly, such places as Westgate were at first considered suitable as reception areas, so that as the town's natural population diminished, empty accommodation was taken by families from the East End of London.

Stephen, after spending that first weekend in September frantically preparing his medical facility at the base for the onslaught, found himself within days in demand at the Cottage Hospital, dealing with minor injuries to over-enthusiastic street urchins from Hackney who had never before climbed cliffs or bathed in the sea, and were learning the hard way to come to terms with the dangers of their new environment.

At the end of his second week at Manston, Stephen was summoned to the CO's office.

'Ah, Beaton.' The CO looked up from his desk and beamed. 'I popped into the dispensary yesterday . . . splendid job you've done there, very impressive.'

'Thank you, sir,' Stephen answered warily, sure that he had not been summoned merely for a pat on the back.

'Want to try out your new bus?' Calcutt asked, pointedly.

Stephen had only just taken possession of the Morris. He was not surprised, however, to find that the CO already knew of its new owner. He raised one eyebrow, enquiringly.

'The Vicar's niece, Grace Dobbie, has been recalled to duty. She's a nurse in one of the London hospitals. Anyway, she needs a lift into Canterbury this evening to catch the train. I try to supply the old boy with transport when I can . . . good public relations, y'know, but I daren't allow any of the aircrew to leave the station at present. The Padre usually obliges, but he's busy assisting with a special service in Margate this evening. I hoped you might be able to help out.'

Torn as he was between the need to complete his own arrangements in the camp and a strong desire to try out his newly acquired car, Stephen's objection was mild to say the least.

'There's still a lot to be done here on the base . . . but I must say that the proposition is a tempting one.'

'Good lad!' said Calcutt enthusiastically. 'You won't be disappointed, I can assure you. Our Gracie is a bit of a looker.'

As Stephen drew to a halt opposite the war memorial, he noticed a Panama-hatted head pop up on the other side of the hedge. With a cheerful wave of his secateurs, Mr Dobbie came to the gate and opened it.

'This is very good of you, Doctor. I don't know what Grace would have done without your help. There are no taxis to be had, and she must report for duty this evening at the latest. She'll be ready in just a few moments . . . come along in and meet my wife while you're waiting.'

He held the gate wide, allowing Stephen to pass through into the enchanting garden which was hidden behind a dense yew hedge.

The Vicar led the way round the side of the house to where his wife was seated under a rose arbour which provided much needed shade on that hot September afternoon.

Mary Dobbie was a woman in her early-sixties, round-bodied and round-faced, with the polished look and rosy hue of a ripe apple. Her bobbed curly hair was pure silver and shone in the bright sunlight like a halo about her head. She was nanny, mother, Women's Institute chairman and parson's wife, all rolled into one benevolent being. Stephen was instantly reminded of his grandmother, Annabel Beaton.

'Mary, my dear, may I introduce Dr Beaton?' said Dobbie, coming to stand beside her chair. 'Stephen . . . may I call you Stephen?' The doctor nodded pleasantly. 'This is my wife, Mary.'

Without thinking he took hold of one soft pink hand and drew it to his lips. 'This is a very great pleasure, Mrs Dobbie. It was most kind of you to invite me.'

If the lady was surprised, she did not show it. In the past few weeks she had been introduced to pilots from Poland, Czechoslovakia, and Holland. She was becoming quite accustomed to this courteous form of address.

On a wrought ironwork table before her stood a large teapot together with several cups and saucers. She motioned him to a chair and offered him tea.

From the kitchen garden, separated from the lawn by an ancient brick wall, there came the sounds of merriment. Mr Dobbie left them, and soon the drone of deep masculine voices was interrupted by a quick burst of laughter. For a time Stephen heard nothing but the chink of spade upon flintstones accompanied by someone whistling *You Are My Sunshine*. The musician seemed to have got stuck in a groove, for he repeated the same phrase over and over.

Mary Dobbie grinned at Stephen's pained expression.

'That's Bertie,' she explained. 'He only knows the one tune! Grace will be a few minutes yet with her packing,' she went on. 'The dear girl has been helping me with the blackouts all day, and I'm afraid she left it rather late to get ready.'

She waved a hand in the direction of a large wooden clothes horse over which were draped hugh swathes of material in various shades of dingy black. The surrounding grass appeared to have received more of the treatment than the cloth.

'The instructions made it seem easy enough,' Mary Dobbie explained. 'One pound of concentrated size, three pounds of lamp black and half a gill of gold size . . . it's supposed to cover eighty square yards of material but it obviously wasn't going to be enough to do all the Vicarage curtains, so we watered it down a bit. The result, as you can see, is rather patchy. Will you have a cup of tea?'

She had been pouring as she spoke, adding milk at Stephen's request.

'No sugar, thank you,' he said, accepting the delicate bone china cup, carefully.

At that moment Dobbie himself reappeared with four airmen, stripped to the waist and perspiring freely. It would seem that the CO's volunteer force was at work here, sinking a steel Anderson shelter unobtrusively in the Vicar's vegetable plot.

The men looked a little uncomfortable when confronted by an

officer, but when Dobbie introduced him as their new medic they seemed to relax a little. The Doc was normally accepted as the one member of the Establishment who need not be avoided.

They squatted on the grass while Mary fussed over teacups and cream buns. Stephen was hard put to it to contain his mirth at the sight of four tough RAF squaddies, trying to manipulate fine china cups in one hand while attempting, rather unsuccessfully, to bite into the soft, chocolate-covered choux buns without squirting cream all over their faces.

'Mrs Dobbie,' said Stephen, 'I have been admiring your beautiful garden. It must take a tremendous amount of work.'

'Well, yes it does,' she agreed. 'Until last month we had an excellent young lad from the village to help us. Unfortunately he has gone off to sea. I suppose it will be left to me now.'

'We'll probably have to dig up the grass and plant extra vegetables,' declared the Vicar. 'Better make the most of it while we still have a lawn.'

'Oh, not the croquet lawn, surely?' pleaded Mary. 'The boys do so enjoy playing . . .'

'We'll see, my dear.' Dobbie patted his wife's hand affectionately. He always humoured her if he could. Perhaps they could preserve the lawn and grow vegetables in the front . . . yes, that would be the answer.

'What's this about the croquet lawn?'

The clear bell-like tones seemed to hover on the still air. Every man's eyes turned towards the newcomer. The men put down their cups and struggled to their feet.

Stephen recalled the CO's words. The term 'a looker' hardly did justice to the delicate skin, the finely chiselled features and softly rounded, deliciously petite figure of Grace Dobbie. Despite her dainty high-heeled shoes, the top of her head scarcely reached the shoulder of any one of the squaddies who had instinctively gathered around her. Her fair hair was almost hidden beneath the blue cap she wore as part of her nurse's uniform. Her dark dress and the cloak of RAF blue, thrown carelessly over her arm to reveal its scarlet lining, confirmed her calling.

'Oh, there you are at last, dear.' Mary Dobbie lifted the teapot once again.

'No tea for me, thank you, Auntie,' she said. Then, sinking into the empty deck chair beside the Vicar, 'What's all this about digging up the croquet lawn?'

'Your aunt has managed to dissuade me,' was her uncle's reply. 'It will, however, mean growing cabbages amongst the roses in the front garden.'

'Oh, that could look rather nice, don't you think, Dr Beaton?' Mary Dobbie nodded contentedly, seeing in her mind's eye red and green cabbages grouped together for best effect. 'In fact, I don't know why we don't do it already.'

Stephen had got to his feet at the approach of the young lady. He hovered uncertainly now, waiting for an introduction.

'Grace, this is Dr Beaton who has kindly offered to take you to the train.' As Stephen took the delicate little hand in his own, Dobbie took off his Panama hat and mopped his brow. 'This really is extraordinary weather.'

'Yes, indeed,' agreed his wife, 'especially with the war and all.'

Stephen was struck by the fact that this was the first reference anyone had made to the morning's broadcast by the Prime Minister.

'Oh, really, Auntie,' the girl laughed. 'Were you expecting thunder and lightning like *Götterdämmerung*?'

'Something like that, I suppose,' came the reply. 'I know I'm a silly old woman . . .' Her voice faded rather pathetically.

It was a cue for the airmen to return to their digging. Mary began to collect the cups and saucers and her husband lifted the tray to follow her into the house.

'Well,' Stephen addressed Grace, 'if you are to catch the London train, we had better be on our way. I should tell you that I arrived from Glasgow only two days ago and have never been to Kent before. I hope you know the way!'

'So do I,' replied Grace. 'They have taken away all the signposts!'

The signposts had indeed been removed or obliterated, just as Grace had predicted. Within half an hour they had become hopelessly lost.

Approaching a crossroads, Stephen pulled over to consult his map. For a minute or two they both pored over the cumbersome sheet, unable to identify any landmark. At last, confused and frustrated, he turned off the engine.

'The only thing we can do,' he decided, 'is to walk to the top of that knoll and see if we can spot anything to show us where we are.'

In eerie silence they crossed a field yellow with late-ripening wheat. Even the birds were still on this sultry evening. Not a breath of wind stirred the leaves. There were not even the country sounds of farmers busy with their harvest. It was as though the entire universe was holding its breath, waiting for battle to begin.

At last they reached the hedge on the far side of the field where a stile led them on towards the grassy bank which was their goal. To their dismay they found that it was surrounded at its base by a dense thicket of hawthorn and hazel saplings. Underfoot the ground here was still boggy and Grace was forced to hop from one muddy patch to another to avoid spoiling shoes more fitted to paved streets in town than a country ramble.

'Here, give me your hand.'

Stephen, having leaped across a small brook, turned back to help her. She sprang towards him and he caught her deftly in his arms. For a moment they stood clasped together as he steadied her . . . he caught a whiff of lavender and perspiration mingled with carbolic soap. The analysis seemed mundane and yet the scent lingered in his nostrils, a memory which would lie dormant in his brain to be recalled in the future at moments when he least expected it.

Grace gave him a sharp, almost reproving look and took a pace backward. It was clear that she felt he had gone too far. He allowed his hands to fall to his sides and from then on preceded her along the overgrown path, holding back the branches which threatened to spring back into her face but otherwise ignoring the difficulties of her progress. They emerged on the open hillside at last and Stephen almost ran the last hundred yards to the top. He drew out the map once more and was already feverishly scanning the horizon when Grace reached him.

The spire of Canterbury Cathedral stood out against the skyline to the north-east and far away to the north and north-west lay the softly rounded contours of the Surrey Hills. In the foreground the fertile clay valley of the Weald was dissected from east to west by a series of sandstone ridges like the one on which they now stood.

Below the hill, they could just make out the roof of Stephen's car parked beside the crossroads. The road they must take ran like a serpent, skirting parish boundaries, following the hedges which separated the apple orchards from the hop fields, but travelling always in a generally north-easterly direction.

'That's our road,' said Grace, decisively, and started down the slope towards the trees.

'Hang on a minute,' Stephen called after her. 'Now we can see how far we have to go, it's clear we shall be in plenty of time. I could do with a few minutes' breather.'

Reluctantly she retraced her steps, resting against a large boulder and keeping him at a distance.

Stephen was nonplussed. He had never found it difficult to form relationships with the opposite sex. Nurses in particular were wont to throw themselves at his feet. Grace's attitude was something quite new to him.

In her distant perch, she seemed to relax a little as she remarked, 'It's quite a view, isn't it? I can remember picnics in spots like this . . . years ago, when I was a kid. Uncle used to bring us out, usually on a Saturday of course. Sunday was a working day in our household.'

'Have you always lived with the Dobbies?' he asked.

'Most of my life . . . all of it that I can really remember anyway,' she answered. 'My father, Uncle Andrew's brother, was killed in France in November 1918, a few days before the Armistice.' She paused, then added thoughtfully, 'That seemed to make it all the more heartbreaking.'

'I was born when my father was away at sea,' Stephen volunteered. 'He was missing for a long time, presumed drowned, then one day, right out of the blue, he came home. I was only an infant, but I distinctly remember being lifted up by this enormous stranger. I knew I was expected to be pleased to see him, but his deep voice and grizzly beard scared me to death!'

Grace continued her monologue as though he had not spoken, 'I can vaguely remember flags out in the streets and people singing and dancing. There were bonfires lit all along those hills . . . we were watching them from the church tower when the telegraph boy arrived on his bicycle and everyone went quiet. Then my mother began to scream . . . I have never heard a sound like it. It used to haunt my dreams for years afterwards.'

Grace was surprised to find herself opening her heart in this way. She did not usually discuss her life history with anyone, let alone a perfect stranger.

'So you and your mother came to live permanently with the Dobbies?' Stephen coaxed her.

'I had lived with them on and off for some time because my mother was a VAD, helping nurse the convalescent wounded in a nursing home at Hastings. Then she fell ill. They said she had a broken heart. You'd find that hard to believe, I suppose, but I think it was partially true. We both moved into the Vicarage permanently, and I went to the village school with all the other five year olds.'

He remained silent as she summoned the courage to tell him the rest of her sad story.

'There were people in the village recuperating from the 'flu epidemic which was sweeping through the cities. Mother had been feeling a lot better and Uncle Andy persuaded her to give a hand with the nursing. He thought it would bring her out of herself. She certainly perked up in a day or two and it was quite like old times . . . then she went down with 'flu herself. It was 1919, just before my sixth birthday. We were going to have a splendid party in the church hall. Auntie had made me a new white organdie dress to wear. It had little blue bows all around the hem. I remember her and my mother sitting together in the bay window, sewing them in place. That was when Mummy said she had a headache and would go and lie down. She died at ten o' clock in the morning . . . on my birthday.'

Stephen felt strangely in tune with the poor little orphan whom Grace had conjured up. He could have gone on sitting there but time was wearing on.

'We really ought to be going,' he admitted, reluctantly. 'You don't want to miss your train.'

Grace surprised him by taking his arm.

It was as though their conversation had raised him to a different level in her estimation for she no longer appeared to regard him as a threat. At the touch of her fingers on his arm, Stephen too relaxed and it was in a much lighter mood that they returned to the car, running the last few yards through the cornfield.

They had travelled the tortuous road in comfortable silence for some time before Grace suddenly asked. 'Were you always destined to be a doctor?'

'Well, put it this way,' laughed Stephen, 'it would have been very difficult for me to have been anything else!'

'It's a family thing?'

'I'm one of the fourth generation of Beaton doctors to be born and bred in Argyll. My three cousins and myself . . . we all wield the scalpel in one way or another.'

'It must be wonderful to be part of such a dynasty.' She said it with a kind of longing in her voice. 'I'm the only one of my generation – Auntie and Uncle lost their only child, a boy, when he was a few months old. I suppose that was why they took me in so readily. They've always been like proper parents to me.'

'Family expectations can be a bit of a bind at times,' Stephen suggested. 'If it hadn't been for my medical training, I'd have been a fighter pilot now. I had set my heart on it, you know, when I joined the RAF. Had I known I was only going to be an MO, I might have stayed on at the infirmary and taken my Fellowship exams.'

'Anyone can be a pilot,' said Grace, a trifle harshly, he thought. 'It takes brains to become a doctor.'

'If you regard us so highly, why do you dislike us so much?' Stephen's question had come from nowhere. He hardly knew why he had actually asked it. It was true however. Clearly she disliked doctors . . . that must be why she had held him at arm's length.

They had reached the outer suburbs of the city now and were crossing the water meadows which all but circled the ancient walls. Stephen was obliged to pay more attention to the directions which she gave him and a few moments later they pulled into the station yard. Their circuitous journey and the interlude on the hillside had taken longer than he had estimated. They barely had time for Grace to purchase a ticket and for them to hurry to the barrier before the London train departed. He would not, after all, be hearing what it was she had against doctors . . . or not today at any rate.

While her ticket was examined at the gate, she turned and held out her hand.

'Thank you so much for the lift, Doctor,' she said. 'I hope we shall meet again, although it may be some time before I get back to Manston. I could be sent anywhere.'

'Do get in touch . . . let me know when you're coming home.' He hesitated for a moment. 'And Grace, please call me Stephen. Or Steve if you prefer.'

She laughed, that delicious little sound which sent tingling sensations down his spine. 'What does your mother call you?' she asked.

He hesitated. Wrestling with the disclosure then grinning sheepishly, he replied, 'Stevie.'

'OK then, Stevie,' she said, 'I'll ask Uncle Andrew to let you know when I'm due for a leave. Goodbye!'

She was gone, lost in the turmoil of last-minute passengers boarding, the hiss of steam spewing from beneath the wheels of the locomotive blotting out the shouted orders of guard to porters.

With a light heart, Stephen retraced his steps to the car and drove off, negotiating the cobbled streets with care. At last he crossed the causeway and was plunged into darkness as blackouts excluded any light from buildings along his route. Unable to see anything ahead at first, he drove blindly for a time, imagining all the while that he could still see a reflection of Grace's delicate features in the dark windscreen. Soon the full moon gave enough light for him to speed up a little and by the light of the stars he headed for home.

*

'It's definitely mastitis, Mr Green. No doubt at all, I'm afraid. The poor old girl must be in agony.'

Ellen withdrew her hand from the cow's udder and wiped it on the damp towel the farmer offered her.

'All we can do is try hot fomentations . . . that sometimes shifts it. You'll have to take the calf away, of course.' Her hand went automatically to the wet nose thrust at her by a hungry infant, trying to reach its mother.

The farmer took hold of the little beast and lifted her bodily in his arms.

'She's a good little heifer,' he observed. 'Wouldn't want to lose 'er.'

'Nor will you,' Ellen assured him. 'I'll give your wife a formula that should see her right . . . a recipe given to me by an old stockman. The thing is, a new mum produces excess colostrum that the calf needs to survive. What we must do is provide a suitable substitute.'

Mr Green disposed of his burden, placing the calf in a stall at the end of the barn, and returned to Ellen's side.

'You'll be needing boiling water then?' he enquired.

'Yes . . . and an extra pair of hands to steady her. Where's young Victor?'

'Joined up. Left me in a right pickle 'e 'as too. Silly young duffer!'

'He would have got exemption if he'd tried, wouldn't he?' Ellen knew that farm workers could avoid being called-up because their work was of national importance.

'You know 'ow it is . . . lad thought 'e might be missin' something. I'd 'ave gone meself at his age. Can't blame 'im really. Farming's a dull old life.'

'You could apply for a Land Girl,' Ellen suggested.

'What . . . 'ave a bunch of lasses mucking out the milk shed and castrating the pigs? I should say so!'

'Some of those I've seen have been very competent,' Ellen corrected him. 'It would be better than no help at all.'

'What use would a girl be, handling my old Trooper there?' the man objected. 'Takes two of us to get 'im into 'is stall when 'e's in a frisky mood.'

As though understanding that he was the subject of their conversation the bull shattered the comparative quiet with his bellow.

Ellen, as though to prove a point, went to his stall and opened it. She moved inside, holding out a handful of sweet-smelling hay with one hand while, at the same time, twisting the bull's tail around her other wrist.

His head came round, fury and suspicion clouding his gaze. For a moment they glared at one another, girl and beast, then Trooper tore the hay from Ellen's hand and, still staring at her just a trifle suspiciously, munched contentedly, shifting his enormous head languorously under her hand as she rubbed firmly at the base of his truncated horns.

'Well,' breathed the farmer, openly relieved, 'I've never seen anyone do that with old Trooper.'

He glanced at the slip of a girl with renewed interest. When they'd told him the Ministry Vet was a woman, he'd been disdainful. In the weeks in which they had come to know one another, however, his scepticism had slowly diminished. He had been wrong in his initial judgement, he knew, but had satisfied himself that Ellen's background was what made the difference. She had told him of the Australian sheep station where she had grown up. Anyone from such a background would be bound to have extraordinary skills in handling animals.

'Most women would run a mile rather than go into Trooper's stall,' he observed defensively.

'And so would a lot of men we both know,' she added, laughing. 'The point is, Mr Green, we all have our strengths and our weaknesses. A couple of Land Girls could at least take some of the work off Mrs Green's hands. And you never know . . . you might even find one who can handle old Trooper as well!'

The boiling water was fetched from the kitchen in a pail and Ellen stooped again to the task of relieving the suffering cow. When she had done all she could, she got to her feet. Pushing a lock of hair out of her eyes, she wiped an arm across her forehead and grinned at him.

'Anything else I can get you, Veterinary?' he asked.

'I could murder a cup of tea,' she told him.

'Missus 'as got it all ready in the house.'

He led the way across the muddy yard and in through the kitchen door. Both of them stopped automatically in the entrance to discard their wellingtons before entering the house.

'Come in, Miss McDougal, do,' the cheery woman greeted her, pulling out a chair from beneath a table whose white damask cloth was laden with good things.

'What a spread,' exclaimed Ellen, her teeth sinking into hunks of freshly baked bread spread with delicious home-made jam. She found herself marvelling that a prudent housewife could make so much of the meagre rations at her disposal.

'We do have an advantage over the townies,' laughed her hostess. So saying she produced a box containing six large brown eggs and placed it on the table beside Ellen's plate.

'I'm sure you'll find a use for them in those miserable digs of yours.'

Ellen had been unfortunate enough to be billeted with the Vicar's wife in Bennington, a sparsely populated village in the heart of Warwickshire. The woman resented having to take any strangers into her rambling Rectory, and a female vet was just as distasteful in her eyes as an actress or an artist. She ignored her lodgers as much as possible and made little effort to provide more than the basic allowance of food.

Ellen was more than grateful for Mrs Green's thoughtfulness. If she presented the eggs on her return, maybe they would all have a decent supper for once.

The other guests at the Vicarage, a couple of Land Army girls and a schoolteacher from London, evacuated with her class of thirty ten year olds, were gathered in the parlour when she arrived.

'You're late,' observed the teacher. 'The old girl was having a moan.'

'I can't help the work I do,' said Ellen. 'Pigs and sheep don't get sick to a timetable.'

She went out to the kitchen, prepared to apologise.

'You're late,' Mrs Watchet greeted her disdainfully.

'Yes, I'm sorry,' Ellen said, and placed the box of eggs on the table. 'I thought perhaps we might all have one for our breakfast,' she suggested.

On seeing the eggs, the woman modified her tone. At least these girls working on the land made some contribution . . . not like that silly little schoolmarm who did nothing but complain about the hard mattresses and the lack of hot water.

She acknowledged the gift with a curt nod.

'I hope they're fresh,' she muttered. 'You never know with these farmers. Sometimes a clutch'll lay in the hedge for weeks before anyone collects them.'

Ellen wondered how it could be that the wife of the village priest was so uncharitable in her attitude towards her fellow men.

'There's two letters for you.' Mrs Watchet indicated two envelopes stuck behind the clock. 'One from Australia by the look of it.'

Ellen's tiredness dropped away instantly. She grabbed the letters, eagerly examining the handwriting on each envelope. One was from her mother. The other, bearing an Ashford postmark, was from Stephen.

She ran up the steep flight of stairs to the room she shared with the schoolteacher and, throwing herself on the bed, tore open Stephen's letter first.

Kent is every bit as beautiful as the travel guides tell us. They say it can be jolly cold here in winter but for the moment the days are long and sunny and the harvest is in full swing. Bumper crops all round, so it would seem . . . probably all for the best considering what the new year may bring.

They are a good crowd on the base. Disgustingly robust, so there is little need for a doctor at all. I sometimes wonder if I shall ever be able to make use of the splendid facilities in the little hospital in town. Cuts and scrapes and the odd minor fracture are the order of the day!

How is Shakespeare country? Do you ever have time to get into Stratford? I believe they are still putting on a season of plays despite the war . . .

She scanned the letter to the end. Full of chatty news, it gave no indication that he missed her. Still, he had kept his promise and written. She supposed that there was a limit to what he could tell her about his work.

Do write and let me know how you are getting on. Should you get a posting nearer to London, we will have to meet up sometime for a night out.

He had signed it 'kindest regards'. In his last letter it had been 'much love'. What had happened, she wondered, to have changed his mind?

As autumn advanced, winds from the east cut across the unprotected expanse of the airfield, penetrating every crack in the wooden structures in which the men worked. When the wind dropped, lashing rain gave place to heavy sea mists which rolled in from the Channel, muffling all sound and reducing activity to nought. Heavy weather did not prevent the movement of shipping around the coast, however. Nor did it deter the German U-boats whose attacks upon coastal shipping were already taking their toll of Britain's merchant fleet. In the North Sea, vessels were coming under regular attack from German aircraft stationed in north-west Germany.

Manston was well situated to protect shipping passing around the North Foreland, and fighter aircraft, patrolling in threes, now swept the area for enemy ships and planes during daylight hours.

The spring of 1940 came late to the Kentish hop fields. At Manston pilots fretted as, day after day, plans for practice flights and patrols across the Channel were thwarted by bad weather reports. At long last the rains ceased and the winter mud dried in the forest of the Ardennes. The German tanks moved forward, skirting around the northern end of the much vaunted and supposedly impenetrable Maginot line. They tore through Holland and Belgium, barely giving the governments of those two countries time to pack up their offices and depart. While monarchs and politicians fled to Britain, the British Expeditionary Force, supported by a dwindling French Army which all too rapidly laid down its arms, moved back towards the French coast, fighting every inch of the way.

From Manston a few fighters managed to fly across to tackle the German aircraft which were strafing the beaches of northern France. Here, assembled in orderly lines along the wide beaches, the British Army awaited an opportunity to escape by sea.

Within days, orders were received to retain all available aircraft to defend the mainland of Britain. The army must get away as best it could, for the next part of the war was going to take place in the air and Britain was ill-equipped to defend herself against the whole might of the German Luftwaffe.

Chapter Seven

This was more like it. Flying Officer Colin 'Digger' Sheen relaxed as he settled back against his parachute-pack and stretched his legs in the limited space below the control panel. They had certainly not designed these beautiful machines with six foot, two inches of Australian jackaroo in mind.

Ahead of him the neat little nose cone of the Spitfire was blurred by the whirling blades of the propeller. He made a routine search of the skies . . . above . . . over the left shoulder . . . down the port side . . . then to starboard. Denny Bolton had closed up beside him. He glanced again to port. 'Squeaky' Piper was indicating the coast below them. He waved in acknowledgement. Now he could see for himself the waves breaking along the flat sandy beach.

He began to whistle softly, stopped suddenly to check that his RT was switched off, then resumed his tune. He'd been in trouble once for leaving his helmet microphone switched on. Never again. The CO's wrath had been terrible.

'Do you realise, Sheen, that your stupidity could have prevented some other poor devil in trouble, and wanting to land, from getting any assistance from base? Do we have to wait until you've been in that position yourself before we get you to obey the rules? Keep your bloody RT switched off unless you really need to use it!'

He had sworn meekly never to do it again, and he never had.

They were flying east into the rising sun. The coastline had given way to a low-lying area of dunes and marshes. To the north lay the town of Zeebrugge, to the south Ostende. Linking the two was a stretch of railway line along which was snaking an electric train, looking for all the world like some monstrous caterpillar.

The dozen or more trucks seemed to be heavily laden and two small detachments of soldiers, armed with rifles and machine guns, were perched precariously upon open flat-beds, one behind the engine and the other at the rear of the train. They indicated the movement of some kind of military equipment.

Digger took note of the train but concentrated for the moment on the barges lined up, three abreast, along both sides of the canal. These too carried armed guards. Some barges were empty but others were well loaded. These were the day's main targets.

Each selecting his own area of operation, B flight swooped down upon the enemy barges.

Ignoring the tracer bullets soaring towards him from an oerlikon mounted on the prow of the first vessel, Colin strafed the deck and had the satisfaction of seeing the gunner throw up his hands and fall backwards across the deck. The second barge must have contained explosives because a small fire caused by the aeroplane's gunfire seemed suddenly to fan out into a sheet of flame and the subsequent eruption caused the Spitfire's wings to shake. Had she not been going so fast and swerving up and away at the moment of the explosion, she must surely have been damaged by the blast.

Over his shoulder he could see that the line of barges was burning freely. It was time to turn his attention to the train.

He flew up into the sun and, coming round in a tight curve, attacked the armed truck with the sunlight shining full in the face of the enemy gunners. Digger's cannon shells exploded, silencing two of the machine guns just as they began to stutter into action. He raked the entire length of the train with his fire, breaking off and swerving away in time to avoid flack from the anti-aircraft gun on the last truck.

The train, burning from end to end, had come to a standstill, its driver wounded or dead. Digger caught sight of Squeaky following in his path, making short work of a number of men who had clambered out on to the roof of one of the carriages and were firing their rifles in a hopeless attempt to ward off the devastating onslaught.

Satisfied that he had used all the ammunition it was safe for him to expend – there might still be a need to fight off enemy aircraft on the way home – Digger pulled out of the battle, and set a course for the Kent coast.

He had been going for some minutes before he noticed an oily smear appearing on the left-hand side of the canopy. Taking his eyes off his instruments for a second, he tried to make out where the leaking fuel was coming from. He saw a neat line of bullet holes which had penetrated the tank on that wing of the aircraft.

The rate of fuel loss did not appear to be excessive but he had little enough to spare. The English coast could not be far away now . . . even if he could not make it all the way back to Manston, he should be able to land somewhere nearer.

Instinctively he felt down his right boot and was comforted by the presence of the stiletto knife which he kept there in a specially constructed scabbard. He recalled the words of the veteran flyer who had had them all enthralled with his advice on how to survive in the face of the enemy. He had told them of a pilot who had been forced to abandon his machine over the North Sea. He had landed safely enough but had become hopelessly entangled in the shrouds of his parachute. The water-logged silk of the canopy had dragged him under the surface while the cords had prevented him from inflating his Mae West. When the rescue craft caught up with him, he was found head down in the water, his life-less body kept afloat by the parachute silk.

Digger always carried the knife these days, so that he might release himself should such a thing happen to him.

He glanced anxiously at his watch. He ought to be seeing something of the coast by now, surely? He took a reading from the compass. Yes, no doubt about it, he was on the right course. Making a further rapid calculation he realised that if his course was correct, he should have sighted the Thames Estuary three minutes before.

Something must be wrong with the compass.

Where the hell was he?

Even if he was off course by just a few points, he could be heading away into the English Channel and missing the Kent coast altogether.

The engine petered out, its final few stutters ending in an eerie silence. Almost immediately the plane lurched and plunged seawards, the increasing air-speed producing an ominous screeching which increased in pitch as the fighter lost height, diving rapidly towards the waves.

Terrified now as every additional sound of the disintegrating super-structure jarred upon his nerves, Digger clung to the controls, fighting to level out as the waves leaped up to meet him.

With all the strength he could muster, he pulled back on the joystick. It seemed to be stuck fast. The aircraft was not going to respond . . .

Then, very gradually, he felt the nose come up, and the Spitfire, whose design had been inspired by a seagull's flight, began to glide like a bird on the currents of air coming off the surface of the sea. She was still travelling fast, but was under control when she touched the water. For a few moments Digger found himself riding the waves as though he was in a speedboat, but at last the tiny craft plunged into a particularly large breaker. The engine folded into the cockpit like a concertina as the fuselage rose up from behind so that the aeroplane was standing on its head. At the moment of impact, Digger had experienced a fierce jarring sensation on his left side, but now as the aircraft sank back on to the waves and water began to pour through the holes torn in the superstructure, the pain from his leg receded and the instinct for survival took control. He was conscious that the aircraft was floating . . . if only she would continue to do so until he could free himself from the wreckage.

He reached up and released the canopy above his head. The rush of fresh salty air revived him. Taking hold of the cockpit's sides, he tried to heave himself up. His damaged foot was caught in a tangle of metal and wires underneath the control panel. Despite the pain, he tugged at it but to no avail. After a few seconds of struggling, he remembered the knife in his other boot. Sweating from his exertions, he reached down and pulled it from its concealed scabbard. Thank God he had had the foresight to carry it!

He began to slash at the stitching of the soft leather, haphazardly at first but then, realising that a more systematic effort was needed, he began to tackle the stitches a few at a time until he felt his ankle coming free. His boot was now sopping with blood and as he pulled the injured foot free, there was a sickening squelching sound which was accompanied by an ear-splitting scream. It was a moment before Digger recognised this agonised response as his own.

For a few moments he lost consciousness.

He came to convinced that there was something important that he had forgotten to do. For a moment he gazed blankly at the knife still held in his right hand. Then, slipping it back into its scabbard, he reached for the RT microphone in his helmet.

'Mayday . . . Mayday . . . B2 MANSTON . . . B2 MANSTON . . . Digger calling . . . do you read me? I'm in the drink.'

He managed to read off his last set of co-ordinates and switched to receive . . . nothing.

'Mayday . . . Mayday . . .' He repeated the distress call and his own call sign with little hope of a response.

Again he switched to receive. Still nothing.

He tried once more, and then, looking over the side, found to his horror that the wings were already half under water and that he must get out or drown.

Ignoring the awful pain in his leg, he grasped the edges of the cockpit and hauled himself free. He rolled out over the wing just as the fuselage began to sink beneath him.

With his life jacket inflated, Digger paddled himself clear of the wreckage and floated on his back. The water supported his legs and the cold had already numbed the pain. He thanked Providence that it was summer. In winter, he knew, he would have had little hope of survival.

Had his message got through? he wondered. He would know soon enough . . . With the waves lapping gently around him and sea birds gathering to wheel and dive for a closer inspection of the small pieces of floating wreckage which were all that remained of the Spitfire, he felt himself drifting into sleep.

No . . . this wouldn't do. To lose consciousness now would mean certain death.

He must stay alert.

He began to recite poetry to himself, poems learned for School Certificate . . . *'A wet sheet and a flowing sea, A wind that follows fast'* . . . no, that was too near the mark. How about, *'Once more into the breach, dear friends, once more, Or close the wall up with our English dead!'* He went through all the pieces of Shakespeare, Milton and Robert Browning that he could remember, and it was not until he was reduced to nursery rhymes that he began to despair. He lay back in the water, his hands folded across his chest. His lower body was now numb with cold. It felt as if there was nothing of him below the waist.

Giving in at last to an overwhelming desire for sleep, Digger allowed his eyes to close.

'Rocked in the cradle of the deep . . .' he intoned. The sound of his own voice droning in his head, drowning out any noise from the approaching motor vessel.

The sound of an aircraft coming in to land caused Stephen to put down his pen. He went to the door of the dispensary and looked up. This should be B flight back from their early-morning foray. He watched as the leader taxied to a halt and slid back his canopy. Immediately a small army of mechanics crowded round. No time was lost these days in rearming and refuelling aircraft, ready for immediate action.

The attacks upon the German invasion fleet, massing along the

French coast, were a desperate attempt to delay the enemy. With insufficient aircraft and men to wage a full-scale onslaught on the enemy barges, the RAF could only hope to disable communications and pick off the most vulnerable objectives. 'It's like a horde of midges trying to kill an elephant,' the CO had commented only last night in the Mess. 'All we can hope to do is irritate Gerry and hope he'll hold back just a little longer to give us time to get ourselves properly organised.'

There was a second plane approaching. As Stephen scanned the horizon for a sight of the third, the telephone rang sharply.

He returned inside and lifted the receiver.

'Medical Officer speaking.'

'The CO says you're to get over to Dover harbour as soon as you can, Doc.' It was Stumpy's voice. He sounded particularly anxious.

'What's up?' demanded Stephen.

'There's a Spitfire down in the drink. A Mayday message was picked up by a trawler off the North Foreland. The ASR launch has gone out from Dover to look for him but the reporting officer seemed to think the pilot may be injured . . . apparently the message was weak and disjointed.'

'Are you sure it's one of ours?' Stephen asked, carrying the handset to the window.

'We're the only station in the sector with aircraft unaccounted for,' came Stumpy's reply, his concern obvious.

Stephen leaned out of the open window so that he could see the pilot of the second aircraft push back his canopy and remove his helmet. . . . Denny Bolton. Then the missing pilot could be Digger. He felt a chill in his spine despite the warmth of the spring day.

'I'm on my way!' He slammed the telephone into its cradle, grabbed his Gladstone bag and ran out to the little Morris which was drawn up on the tarmac outside the Dispensary ready for just such an emergency.

As he opened the door, Shep appeared as if by magic. The doctor was rarely allowed to use his car without the dog insisting upon travelling with him.

'Not this time, old chap,' he said, and Shep, sensing that this was not a moment for further discussion of the matter, slunk away to his former position in the shade of the CO's veranda.

There was no real point in hurrying. The rescue boat would take some time to reach the downed flier, and if the position had not been given accurately it could be hours before they found him. Nevertheless, urged on by anxiety for his friend, Stephen put his foot down on the accelerator once he had left the camp gates behind him and he was doing nearly fifty miles an hour by the time he was forced to brake and change gear in order to swerve around the Manston village war memorial and tear past the Malt Shovel. Startled by the noise of rapidly changing gears, Mary Dobbie glanced over her hedge and watched the doctor's car disappear around the corner beyond the farm cottages.

'Wherever can Stephen be going in such a hurry?' she wondered, returning to her planting. The introduction of cabbages to the flower beds had been such a success the previous year that she was now sowing beetroot between the clumps of saxifrage and transplanting lettuces in between the peonies. These nasturtiums would not only brighten up the onion patch, she thought, admiring the bright picture on the packet, they would make a useful salad vegetable as well . . .

Outside the village, Stephen was brought to a sudden halt. Blocking the road was an enormous tree trunk and standing before it an elderly farmer whom Stephen recognised as a regular in the Malt Shovel. He held an old Lee Enfield rifle at the port, bayonet fixed. The man wore ordinary civilian clothes and black-painted tin helmet. His black armband with the letters LDV in white indicated his role as a member of the Local Defence Volunteers.

'Good morning, Mr Proudy,' Stephen called out, winding down his window.

'Papers!' came the sharp reply.

Nonplussed, Stephen reached into his pocket and fished out the various documents he kept there.

'What do you want to see . . . paybook . . . camp pass . . . Mess bill?' he asked. In normal circumstances the situation would call for some amusing quip, but today he was too anxious to be on his way.

Tom Proudy glared at him severely.

'It's no joke, Doctor,' he replied. 'You might be a Fifth Columnist.'

'I might be,' said Stephen, 'but you know I'm not!'

'They dresses themselves up like ordinary folks, y'know. Sometimes like nuns or policemen . . . anything.'

'Yes . . . yes,' said Stephen, becoming irritated. 'Come along, man. I have an emergency to attend to in Dover.'

'Oh, my word, anyone we know?' Proudy enquired as he handed back Stephen's documents and went to remove the barrier.

'We believe it's Mr Sheen,' Stephen replied, restarting the engine.

'Oh, the Australian gentleman . . . I hope he's not too badly hurt.'

One end of the great log was supported on a contraption which included an old bicycle wheel. At Proudy's push, it swung aside easily, pivoting on an equally ingenious construction at the far end.

'Let's hope not!' called Stephen as he revved his engine and took off down the lane.

Scarcely a mile further on he was confronted by a pair of hastily constructed pill boxes, set to either side of the road. Between them was an eccentric barrier of concrete blocks. The two overlapping spurs which together made up the line, had a gap left between them which was scarcely wide enough to allow the passage of his vehicle. With deft manipulations of the steering wheel, Stephen negotiated this in low gear. To his relief the post was unmanned, although he knew that at the first sign of the enemy, the gun emplacements would be bristling with weapons. Shotguns probably. He wondered what effect tree trunks and old sporting rifles would have against Tiger tanks and Krups sub-machine guns.

Everywhere there were signs of hurried preparations for invasion by the enemy. On the base, Calcutt's men were armed and ready at all times to repel enemy landings on the airfield. In the past week anti-aircraft guns had appeared along the front at Margate and Westcliff, while at Manston, Vickers machine guns had been mounted on armoured cars and now made regular patrols of the perimeter of the field to defend the base against low-flying aircraft. Or, indeed, to ward off any attack by ground forces.

So far Manston had not undergone any bombing of the runway, an ominous sign that the Germans had other uses for the largest landing strip in the south of England. Calcutt's orders were to destroy the installations and blow up the runway should they be forced to retreat.

Three more times before he reached the outskirts of Dover, Stephen was stopped, his papers examined and his vehicle searched by members of the LDV. At the harbour entrance a Naval Policeman flagged him down, asked for his credentials and directed him to the berth which had been allocated to the Air Sea Rescue vessels.

The interruptions to his journey had seriously delayed Stephen and by the time he had parked his car and found his way to the waterside, a small crowd had gathered to watch the RAF launch unloading its survivor on to the quay.

Stephen knelt beside the stretcher, his fingers anxiously seeking for some sign of a pulse. Colin Sheen was scarcely breathing. His skin was grey, the veins standing out like rivers drawn on a map.

The doctor looked about him helplessly. An RAF ambulance had drawn up close by and its driver approached at a run.

'Let's get him under cover, quickly,' Stephen ordered crisply. 'I'll take a proper look at him once he's on board.'

The ambulance was a very basic vehicle, lacking all but the barest necessities. It was designed to carry four stretcher cases with two tiered bunks to each side. The space between was too narrow for Stephen to work on his patient.

'Can't we have these other stretchers dismantled?' he demanded.

Startled by the request, the ambulance driver hesitated.

'Oh, for heaven's sake, man! I'll write a chitty for your CO if that's what you're worrying about. But I have to do something for this poor fellow here and now, and I can't work in this space!'

'OK, Doc.' One of the crewmen had been standing by to lend a hand if required. Signalling to a couple of his pals, he pushed the ambulance driver aside and began to dismantle the other stretchers.

Soon Stephen had a clear space in which to work. There was no oxygen available, of course, but he had injections of adrenaline in his bag. That should stimulate breathing for the time being. If he began to fail they would have to take Digger to the nearest hospital, but Stephen would prefer to get him back to Margate if he could.

The seamen had stripped off the flier's outer clothing and wrapped him in blankets. His wet clothes, together with a single boot, were piled on top of him on the stretcher.

Stephen pulled back the blanket to expose Colin's injured leg. A rough bandage had been applied to a deep gash on his upper thigh. The wound was clean, and the soaking in seawater should ensure a minimum of bacterial infection. The shock of the cold water had stopped the bleeding quite successfully so that a tight bandage had been sufficient to prevent too much blood loss. Stephen swabbed the torn tissues liberally with antiseptic and tied off the damaged blood vessels. With strips of sticking plaster he pulled the cut edges together. He could do more work on this under better conditions. He turned his attention to the lower leg.

The impact had caused both lower bones to fracture, with the free ends of tibia sticking out through the open wound. He would have to try and immobilise the leg to prevent further movement. As he tried to manipulate the broken bones so that they were sufficiently straight for him to apply a splint, Digger groaned.

'All right, old chap,' Stephen murmured. 'I'll give you a shot of morphine in a minute.'

Digger, suddenly aware that it was none other than Stephen who was ministering to him, let out a yell.

'By Christ, Doc! What the hell do you think you're doing?'

'You should be glad it's me,' replied Stephen grimly. 'Imagine how much more painful this would be if some other Pommy bastard, who didn't like you, was doing it!'

'With allies like you . . . who needs Germans?' muttered the Australian, eyes drooping as the morphine began to take effect.

The ambulance driver had come alone. Stephen looked about him. 'I need someone to travel in the ambulance to see he doesn't fall off the stretcher,' he said. 'Whose got a girl in Margate, then?'

A young seaman who looked scarcely sixteen stepped forward. 'I don't mind goin', sir,' he volunteered.

At the thought that this scraggy kid might have the love of his life secreted in the seaside town, the other men chortled.

'Me mum lives at Westgate, sir. I'd like the chance to look in on 'er. If it's orl right with the skipper?' He cast around, his eyes coming to rest enquiringly upon a bronzed figure in waders and thick Aran sweater. Only the tarnished gold filigree on his battered cap distinguished him from his men.

The skipper nodded, amiably. 'Be back by o-seven hundred hours, Bellamy. Not a minute later.'

'Aye, aye, sir,' the boy replied, and hopped up lightly into the ambulance.

'Thanks,' said Stephen. 'I'd have travelled with him myself but I had to bring my own transport.' He indicated the Morris. 'I'll see your boy gets back in time tomorrow.' He shook hands with the officer. 'Thanks for taking care of him . . . silly bastard's always getting himself into trouble.'

The skipper touched his cap in salute and Stephen wandered round to the front of the lorry and spoke to the driver.

'I'll lead the way, but when we come to any road blocks, sound your siren to give a sense of urgency. It might wake these LDV types up a bit. It took me ages to get here.'

'OK, sir,' replied the driver. 'Leave it to me!'

So effective was the ambulance driver in persuading the guards to let him through quickly that at every road block he was waved on while Stephen, much to his annoyance, was stopped and his papers examined minutely each time. He soon fell far behind the ambulance and gave up any attempt to catch up.

As he turned into the forecourt of the Cottage Hospital he found that Dr Lewis was already on the scene and with the help of young Bellamy and the driver was lifting Digger on to the hospital trolley.

'Here, let me do that,' Stephen exclaimed, taking the boy's place. The huge Australian was no lightweight, and the lad looked relieved to be able to relinquish his position.

At the sound of Stephen's voice, Digger opened his eyes.

'Hiya, Doc,' he croaked, 'didn't expect to see me like this, did you?'

'We've met already today,' said Stephen, pleased to find his friend awake and not in too much discomfort. 'I didn't know they expected you fellows to swim home.' He took the pilot's pulse as he was speaking. It was thready and the hand felt very cold.

'Come on,' he said, urging them all to get a move on. He addressed his friend once again. 'The sooner we get you into a nice warm bed, the better.'

'Just so long as she's the one to tuck me in,' Colin managed, indicating the young woman who had just appeared in the doorway and was holding it wide for the trolley to pass through.

'We'll see what we can manage,' Stephen replied, surprised to find Grace Dobbie here, in her nurse's uniform. He looked enquiringly at Dr Lewis, but the Superintendent was too concerned with the patient to provide any explanations at this stage.

The two doctors followed the trolley along the highly polished corridor to a small ward at the end.

'Seems to have lost a lot of blood,' observed Lewis.

'Not as much as he might have,' said Stephen laconically. 'He was too hypothermic to bleed much when they fished him out. We'll have to get his temperature up before we attempt to tackle the injuries to his leg.'

'What kind of injuries are they?' Lewis enquired.

'The lower leg is badly mangled but in the circumstances in which I examined him, it was impossible to say if the injury was due to bullet wounds or the impact of the crash. He had been afloat for a couple of hours when he was picked up.'

Lewis stepped back to allow Stephen to precede him into the room where Grace, who had been joined by Matron, was systematically removing the remainder of the flier's clothing.

'Cut that trouser leg,' ordered Matron as the nurse began to work on Digger's injured side. She herself unzipped the remaining boot and withdrew it from Digger's uninjured leg. As she did so she gave a little yelp and withdrew her hand, indicating a tiny cut on her finger.

'Whatever have we got here?' she demanded, withdrawing the thin-bladed knife which had saved the pilot's life.

'I'm told a lot of the men carry those,' observed Stephen.

'Well, I just wish they would give us some warning,' replied Matron, sucking her finger and examining it minutely for damage.

'Right,' said Stephen, taking command. 'Plenty of blankets and hot water bottles, please, Matron. We must get the patient warmed up before we start to interfere with that leg.'

Immediately the nurses responded and within minutes the Australian was muffled up and tucked in tight. Soon his drawn face began to colour up satisfactorily and Stephen took his temperature for a second time.

'It's looking a little better,' he observed, showing the thermometer to his colleague. 'A couple of points below normal . . . I'll give him another shot of morphine and we'll take a look at the leg.'

As Stephen had indicated, the effect of the sea water and intense cold had been to stem the flow of blood. His repair to the torn thigh muscles had held up well, but as the flier's temperature approached normal, bleeding from the mangled lower limb had begun again in earnest.

When Grace approached with a tray of dressings, Stephen ordered a light bandage only, sufficient to stem the flow for the time being.

'I'd like to take an X-ray and get the bones set as soon as possible,' he told his colleague. 'I'll tidy up the rest once that part of the job is done.'

Lewis, unfamiliar with this kind of wound, observed the torn skin and underlying muscle which had been gouged out by the impact of the machinery.

'What kind of a job will you be able to make of that?' he demanded. 'It looks as though that calf muscle has had it.'

'It may be possible to save a substantial portion by grafting,' said Stephen, measuring with his eye the extent of the open wound and trying to decide on the most satisfactory area from which to take skin grafts. 'Let's get him into theatre and see what we can do.'

David Lewis had once fancied himself an aspiring young surgeon. He had spent several years in hospitals as a registrar, assisting some of the best in the land. He had come to realise that surgery was three parts skill and knowledge of the human anatomy, one part intuition and flair. While he soon came to appreciate his own shortcomings in the latter, he was quick to recognise it in others. He had watched Stephen operating before and had recognised in the Scotsman that special extra ability that marked him down as a born surgeon.

Despite the difference in their ages and despite the years of experience which he had amassed, David Lewis gladly assumed the role of anaesthetist and assistant to Stephen Beaton.

The X-ray showed that the tibia had snapped under the impact of the crash, about three inches below the knee joint, and that the two broken ends were badly displaced. The fibula, being thinner and more flexible, had bowed, receiving a stress fracture, but the bone had not broken. It was difficult to say why so much muscle and skin had been torn away . . . there were no burn marks commensurate with a bullet wound.

'I suppose that either on impact, or in climbing out of the cockpit, some sharp object has taken a slice off him,' observed Lewis. 'The left boot's not here so presumably it was damaged and fell off.'

'We'll have to apply some force to set the tib straight,' said Stephen, 'I'm not sure that the girls will be up to it.' He glanced at the gowned figures of the theatre sister and her assistant and saw the flash of indignation in Grace's eyes, visible over the top of her mask.

Lewis grinned at the challenge, and the girl's unspoken response. He interceded with, 'I think you will find Miss Dobbie measures up to your requirements. It's not the first time she has assisted us in the fracture department.'

Sister too put in her six penn'orth. 'There's more to this job than brute force, Mr Beaton . . . some of us have the knack!'

Outnumbered three to one, he was forced to concede that the women would have to cope. He allocated them positions around the table, giving precise instructions on where and when to take a grip on the patient's leg. At his word each applied the necessary force to draw the crenellated ends of the bone apart sufficiently for him to relocate them correctly.

Once the tibia had been set in position, the twisted fibula resumed its normal shape.

'I'll use a plate to secure the tibia,' he decided, selecting a suitable piece of titanium alloy and preparing to screw it into place.

The basic engineering operation completed, Stephen turned his attention to the severe damage to Digger's soft tissues. Because the wounds were clean, he was not unduly concerned about the ability of the healthy young Australian to heal quickly.

He glanced up at Lewis who had resumed his role of anaesthetist as soon as the bone setting was completed.

'I'd like to take my time on this,' Stephen explained. 'A good job at this stage could provide at least ninety per cent recovery. How do you think he is holding out?'

Lewis, who had already performed the necessary checks meticulously, nevertheless examined the patient once again before replying.

'I think I can give you an hour,' he said, studying the electrocardiogram readings carefully. 'I'll have to bring him out of it after that . . . we don't know what damage all that sea water might have done to his lungs.'

'I'll try and finish before that,' said Stephen, taking up his scalpel and working with delicate strokes to tease out the torn muscle before stitching what he could back inside its sheath. Tendons, partially dislodged from their attachments, were delicately stitched and reattached. At last the repair work on the muscle was completed and only the skin remained.

'I shall have to take a couple of grafts from inside the other thigh,' Stephen determined. 'Clean up a good-sized area for me, will you, nurse.'

He appeared to have forgotten his earlier reservations about the girl's ability, standing back while Grace Dobbie swabbed the area with ether before shaving it carefully with an old-fashioned cutthroat razor, to remove all the hairs.

While Grace worked he took a closer look at those wide-set deep brown eyes, the only part of her face remaining exposed above the white mask, and was not disappointed when she flashed a smile at him, indicating she was ready for the next step.

With infinite care Stephen sliced away a thin sliver of skin about two inches square, laying it immediately across the worst of the gouges on the injured limb. Two more such grafts were removed from the inner thigh and placed in position. A neat row of tiny stitches secured the grafts to good skin along one side of the wound, leaving the remaining edges free to grow across the damaged tissue.

With gauze and tight bandaging to secure the grafts in place, the repairs were completed.

Stephen stripped off his mask and Lewis moved aside for him to examine his patient. Digger was breathing easily and his colour was good.

'I think he'll do, for now at any rate,' declared Stephen. 'Let's get him back to the ward before he wakes up. He's going to be in considerable pain and it's essential that the limb is completely immobilised for at least ten days.'

Remembering the predictable antics of the pilot's comrades, he called after Grace, 'No visitors for the time being, nurse. Absolutely none, d'you hear?'

'I'll let Matron know,' she replied.

Did he detect a touch of frost in her answer? Oh, well, he probably deserved it. Grace Dobbie had exceeded his expectations professionally. He hoped he would soon find an opportunity to apologise for having doubted her.

Since the day that Digger Sheen had been admitted to the Cottage Hospital, Stephen had visited him each morning after Sick Parade, to check on his patient but also in hopes of meeting once again the delicious Grace Dobbie.

For one reason or another, the nurse had not reappeared during any of his visits. He still did not know what she had been doing there on the day of Digger's operation. Her efficiency in the theatre suggested she had had training in that sphere. He had hoped to find out more about her on the occasion he had given her a lift into Canterbury to catch the train, but other events had forestalled any questioning on his part. There was still so much he did not know about her . . .

'Aw, c'm on, Doc.' Digger, obviously feeling much better after three days of careful nursing, and bored with his enforced inertia, was becoming querulous. 'Can't I get back to the House? There's no one to talk to here . . . the girls do their best, but they all have too much to do, bustling about like a bunch of blue-arsed flies!'

'You need rest, and you must keep that leg still,' Stephen explained, trying to maintain an air of detachment despite the pathetic pleadings of his friend. 'You know as well as I do that if I let you go back to the House you'll have idiots performing God knows what antics all around you, and in no time you'll be joining in. I have no wish to see my beautiful embroidery ruined by a bunch of nitwits.'

'How long then, Doc?'

Patiently Stephen explained, yet again, that it would be another ten days before they could remove the bandages and assess the success or otherwise of his grafts.

'I'll have a word with Matron about suitable visitors . . . one at a time,' the doctor relented. 'But at the least sign of activity on your part, it stops, OK?'

'OK, Doc,' came the eager response.

When Matron was approached she explained that she had in fact

already persuaded one or two regular hospital visitors to call upon the
pilot who, far from home, had no family members available to visit him.

'Mr Dobbie is always good for an hour on a Thursday,' she explained,
'and there are one or two ladies on the list who have chosen not to leave
their homes. I'm sure I can find someone to cheer him up.'

Stephen was pretty sure that a few middle-aged matrons, with
nothing better to do with their time than visit a lonely stranger in hospital
once a week, was not exactly what his patient had had in mind. He
decided, however, to leave it to the nursing staff to sort the matter out.
Digger was quite capable of making his feelings known if the arrangements did not suit him.

Grinning at the thought of the Australian's first encounter with
official hospital visitors, Stephen swung down the corridor and carelessly
thrust open the outer door, nearly colliding with Grace.

It was the first time he had ever seen her not wearing her nurse's
uniform.

Her pastel pink linen dress was a perfect foil for the sun-tanned skin
of her bare arms, and that tantalising portion of slender neck which was
exposed by her softly revered collar. Her flaxen tresses, which previously
had been neatly tucked up beneath her nurse's cap, fell in smooth, natural
waves to spring lightly on her shoulders as she moved. In her arms she
carried a bunch of cottage garden flowers: scabious and delphiniums,
cornflowers, asters and gypsophila. The white and blue blossoms had
been carefully chosen to blend together into a perfect bouquet.

'Good morning, Doctor,' she said brightly, acknowledging him
politely while at the same time making it very clear that her presence was
urgently required elsewhere.

Lost for any appropriate remark which might stay her passage for a
moment, Stephen murmured, lamely, 'Miss Dobbie . . .' And she was
gone.

He watched her striding down the corridor and was not a little
disconcerted to note that it was the Australian's room which she entered.

Chapter Eight

In hopes of seeing Grace again, Stephen decided the following Wednesday afternoon to take up her uncle's offer of afternoon tea at the Vicarage.

An air of breathlessness hung over the hop fields and apple orchards of Kent as Stephen parked his Morris Ten beside the village war memorial and stepped out on to the hot tarmac.

He breathed in deeply, savouring the sweet fragrance of summer meadows. The distant chalk hills shimmered in a thin haze which hung above the hedgerows where pink and white dog roses mingled with heavily scented elder flowers. Across the fields, like the buzzing of angry bees, aircraft engines revved and died as mechanics prepared their charges for an evening sortie.

The wrought-iron gate creaked as Stephen pushed it tentatively and took a few paces along the path. He could hear the sound of voices and the chink of china coming from the rear garden, and decided to go around the side of the house. As he did so he distinctly heard the clear tones of Grace's voice followed by the sound of her soft laughter.

His courage left him at that moment and he would have turned on his heel and retreated the way he had come, but she must have spotted his blue uniform through the tumble of clematis which covered this side of the house for she called out immediately.

'Come on, we're having tea out here this afternoon!'

There was a flurry of white tulle then she was standing, breathless, before him.

'Why, it's Dr Beaton! This is a surprise.' Grace sounded a little disappointed, as though she might have been expecting someone else.

'Good afternoon, Miss Dobbie,' he stammered. 'The Vicar suggested I might call . . . I do hope it's not inconvenient?'

'Not at all,' she insisted. 'My aunt had just about given up waiting for visitors from the camp. It seems that everyone is too busy today.'

'There is a bit of a flap on,' Stephen explained. 'I shall have to report back myself if there is any sign of activity.'

In the past few weeks, the immediate threat of invasion appeared to have receded, but the Luftwaffe, which had been concentrating its attacks on merchant shipping in order to prevent vital supplies from reaching the British Isles, had recently begun the systematic destruction of RAF bases situated around the coast, from Portsmouth to the Wash. It was only a matter of time before Manston came under attack.

'Well, come along,' Grace said, a trifle impatiently, 'Auntie's out at the back.' She waited for him to precede her along the red brick path.

'How's my poor Colin?' she asked. 'I had hoped to get in to see him today, but Auntie needed me here.'

He started, wondering for a moment. Of course, she was referring to Digger Sheen. It was odd to hear his proper Christian name used. 'Complaining as usual,' Stephen answered. 'A sure sign of a rapid recovery.'

They had rounded the corner by this time and there was no opportunity for any further exchange.

As they approached the elderly Dobbies, who were as usual seated in the rose arbour, the Vicar rose somewhat awkwardly, brushing away crumbs from his clerical stock.

'Ah, Doctor, how good of you to come,' he cried with genuine pleasure. 'Mary, my dear, it's Stephen Beaton.'

If Mary Dobbie was surprised, she gave no sign of it. Standing on tiptoe, she planted a motherly kiss on the surgeon's cheek, and made him blush.

'You're embarrassing the lad, Mary,' warned her husband.

'Nonsense,' she replied. 'Stephen is a long way from home and no doubt missing his mother.'

She waved him to a chair and lifted the tea pot.

'Tea? Milk and sugar?' she demanded.

'A little milk, no sugar,' he replied easily.

Soon he was helping himself to Mary's delicious fruit cake and answering her stream of questions about his home, his parents and his job, so that the Vicar and his niece could not get a word in.

'Oh, come on, Grace,' the old man said at last. 'Let's leave them to it . . . how about a game of clock golf?'

As they moved in leisurely fashion around the course, Stephen watched, paying only scant attention to his hostess's ceaseless chatter.

'I suppose clock golf is a little tame for a true Scot,' Mary Dobbie observed. 'No doubt you are proficient at the real game . . . don't all Scotsmen play?'

'I certainly try,' agreed Stephen. 'In Scotland it's easier to choose some undulating ground for a golf course than it is to find an area large enough, and flat enough, to lay out a cricket pitch. However, I must admit, given a choice, I would prefer to play cricket or tennis any time.'

'Do you hear that, Grace?' her aunt called out. 'Stephen plays tennis. You must invite him to the club some time.'

'Does Miss Dobbie not have to return to her hospital . . . Hammersmith, wasn't it?' he asked. He was still wondering what she had been doing working at the Cottage Hospital on the day Digger was admitted.

'Oh, they've evacuated the West London to Park Prewit near Basingstoke,' Mary told him, 'but Grace is awaiting a transfer to the Royal Masonic. They gave her a few days' leave before moving her on to her new posting.'

'I just wondered what she was doing working at the Cottage Hospital last week,' he explained. 'I was very surprised to find her on duty when I got back from Dover.'

'Ah, well, you see, she began her nurse's training at the Margate Hospital when she left school. It was the Matron there who persuaded Grace to go to London to study for State Registration. She always likes to help out when she can.'

Carrying her putter, the girl returned to where they were sitting.

'You won't get much of a game at the club now,' she said. 'Most of the members have been called up or else evacuated.'

'What? Oh, tennis.' Stephen had quite forgotten Mary Dobbie's ramblings for a moment. 'I'd love a game sometime.'

'Well, I shall be on my way very soon,' Grace told him. 'The day after tomorrow unless the raids get any heavier . . . in which case I have to report immediately.'

Mary Dobbie glanced from one to the other of the young people, her outwardly benign expression disguising the shrewdness of her examination. The doctor was undoubtedly smitten, so why was her niece behaving in such an offhand manner?

The questions which arose from this observation were to go unanswered, however, for at that moment the air raid sirens began their familiar wailing warning.

Mary started, spilling her tea in the saucer. Her voice trembled only slightly as she said, 'Oh, dear, how inconsiderate . . . on a Sunday afternoon too.'

'I must get back to the airfield,' said Stephen, drawing on his gloves and picking up his cap. He glanced questioningly at Grace. 'Will you be needing a lift into Margage?'

'I'll wait here until the raid's over,' she said, and gave a nod in the direction of the old people, indicating that she was loath to leave them on their own for the time being. 'I might call in at the hospital when it's all over . . . in case I can be of help.'

'Don't you worry about Grace,' said Dobbie. 'I'll get someone to give us both a lift into town if necessary.'

'I'll be off then.' Stephen held out his hand. 'Thank you so much, Mrs Dobbie. I have enjoyed this afternoon.'

'Come again . . . soon.' Mary kissed him lightly on the cheek and watched him disappear round the side of the house. They heard his car start up and the roar of the engine as he reversed into the lane and sped away towards the airfield.

Stephen reached the main gate as the first of the bombs began to fall. Braking suddenly, he jumped from the car and lay spread-eagled on the perimeter road as debris flew all about him. He could hear the roar of aeroplanes taking off in an attempt to avoid destruction while still on the ground.

He lifted his head and turned in time to see the last of the enemy bombers pass across the field, disgorge its load and disappear into the clouds at the far end of the runway.

The raid was over almost as suddenly as it had begun. Had they intended to destroy the field? If so it had been only a moderately successful attack. Or was it perhaps some stratagem to test the strength of their defences? Well, at least most of the fighters had managed to get clear in time . . . hopefully they would have had some redress as they chased the enemy back across the Channel, but the lack of anti-aircraft fire must have been all too apparent. Stephen doubted if the next attack would be as short-lived.

There had been no warning of an enemy approaching until the group of three dive-bombers had been sighted crossing the coast at low altitude. The Observer Corps seemed to have been taken completely by surprise.

Stephen could see that a number of planes had failed to escape the onslaught. One of the Defiants, recently brought in to replace Spitfires lost or destroyed over the Channel, stood forlornly in the centre of the runway, its wing sagging like an injured bird's. It had never even got its engine going. A second had made it a few yards down the runway before catching the blast from a nearby explosion and slewing around to plough headlong into the front of the WOs' mess. At the far end of the field, just beyond the control tower, a heap of newly turned earth indicated that one at least of the bombs had fallen harmlessly in the patch of marshy ground which was known to all as the Crimpton Mire.

Had there been any others? he wondered. The village of Manston lay directly in that path . . .

One or two of the station's fighters were now returning and circling the field in hope of finding sufficient runway left on which to land. As the All Clear sounded across the field, Stephen climbed back into the Morris and steered carefully through the debris towards the dispensary.

His orderlies were already attending to a number of minor injuries, patching cut faces and binding up torn limbs as best they could.

Stephen set about restoring order and soon had a chain of activity going which ensured that he saw all the casualties and allocated tasks according to the skills and experience of his team. They had practised such exercises often enough during the past months, but there was nothing like the real thing for testing arrangements.

He did not know how long they had been working when the first of the ambulances drew up beside the infirmary, summoned to remove the two most serious casualties: one a WAAF with a broken shoulder, the other a possibly serious head injury.

Stephen looked up as the stretcher bearers entered the hut. They were accompanied by a nurse in the cape and cap of the Princess Mary's Royal Air Force Nursing Service. Preoccupied as he was, it was only when she spoke that Stephen recognised the newcomer as Grace Dobbie.

Taken off guard in this way, all he could manage to say by way of greeting was, 'Hello . . . where did you spring from?'

'There was some trouble in the village,' she told him. 'The Malt Shovel received a direct hit. There were no casualties,' she added hastily, forestalling his question, 'so I left Uncle trying to sort out the mess and thumbed a lift into town to see what I could do to help.'

A transfer, Mrs Dobbie had said . . . not a word about Grace's having joined the Service. Treating her now as though he had known this all along, Stephen explained the situation.

'These are your patients, Sister.' He addressed her formally for the benefit of the two stretcher bearers. 'Two WAAFs.'

He opened the door of the smaller side ward.

'The shoulder injury will do very well until I get down there myself, but you might ask Mr Lewis to keep an eye on that head injury . . . there could be a skull fracture.'

She nodded her understanding and gave a few terse instructions to the stretcher bearers.

'We can expect you shortly, then?' she asked.

'Just as soon as I've finished patching up these fellows.'

Stephen watched her supervise the loading of the stretchers and then climb into the back of the ambulance herself. One RAF orderly followed her inside, while the driver made for the cab.

As Stephen watched the ambulance draw away, one of the aircraftsmen appeared, staggering under the weight of the CO's massive German Shepherd. The dog's limp body was almost as much as the man could carry and the way that his head lolled over his bearer's shoulder suggested that Shep might already be dead.

'He's still breathing, sir,' the airman insisted.

Stephen doubted it. Rather more bluntly than he intended, he said sharply, 'Good God, man, I'm not a vet. What do you expect me to do about it?'

'Nearest vet's in Deal, sir. I don't think the old boy can last that long.' The fellow's silent appeal was more than Stephen could bear.

'Does the CO know?' he demanded, fingers already pressing the dog's neck, searching for a carotid pulse.

'No, sir. The CO was over in the control tower when the raid started . . . he hasn't come back yet.'

As the dog was lowered to the ground at Stephen's feet, he knelt down and put his ear to the animal's chest. Yes, there was the very slightest indication of a heart flutter.

'Bring him inside,' said Stephen quickly.

Those men remaining in the dispensary, their wounds now neatly bandaged, were quickly dismissed and Stephen turned to his canine friend in some concern.

He stretched the warm body out on the table and made a thorough examination of all Shep's injuries. The fur along one flank was matted with blood and plaster.

'Where did you find him?' Stephen demanded. 'Had he been crushed . . . or buried?'

'He seems to have been hit by the Spitfire which collided with the WOs' mess,' explained the airman. 'It was only by chance I spotted his tail poking out from a heap of rubble.'

Stephen's hands told him that the dog's ribs had been crushed, and as though to confirm it, pink bubbles of bloody mucus began to form around Shep's lips.

'The slash in his side I can cope with. A punctured lung is quite another matter,' Stephen pronounced.

Turning abruptly to the airman he said, 'Get through to the exchange and see if they can contact a vet . . . I need to discuss this with someone who knows something about dogs. I wouldn't know what kind of anaesthetic to use . . . or how much!'

While the airman went to do his bidding, Stephen cleaned the dog's wounds with antiseptic and sutured the worst of the gashes in his back leg and side. Unused to dealing with such a hairy patient, his biggest problem was to get the surrounding skin sufficiently clear of fur to ensure the wounds would heal properly. When finished, he dusted his handiwork with Sulphanilamide powder to prevent infection and reached for the telephone as the airman said, 'The Royal Veterinary College for you, sir.'

Stephen look at him, surprised.

'Well, sir,' returned the young man defiantly, 'nothing but the best for our Shep.'

Stephen nodded abruptly, and took the handset.

'This is Stephen Beaton, Medical Officer at Manston RAF Station. We've had a few bombs here this afternoon . . .' It all sounded so matter-of-fact. 'I can cope with the human injuries, but I have a rather important dog here with crushed ribs. I'd like to save him if I can, but I need some advice . . .'

He listened patiently to the answers to his questions about procedure, use of anaesthetics and so on, then as he was about to put down the phone the speaker at the other end said, 'You did say your name was Beaton . . . Stephen Beaton?'

'Yes,' he confirmed.

'There's someone here who says she knows you. Ellen McDougal.'

Ellen? What was she doing in London . . . she was supposed to be safe in the Midlands.

There was a pause and a whispered discussion before the familiar Western Australian twang assured him this was indeed she.

'Hello, Stephen. Bet you're surprised, eh?'

'You could say that . . . yes,' he agreed, breathlessly. 'What are you doing at the Royal College. You shouldn't be in London now.'

'I'm not. We've been evacuated.'

'Where are you then?' he demanded, still unbelieving.

'I thought it was you who made the call,' she said, laughing.

'No, I got someone else to contact a veterinarian for me. I wasn't expecting him to call the Royal College.'

'We're in Arborfield, near Reading,' Ellen explained.

'Look,' said Stephen, catching sight of the anxious frown on the airman's face, 'I'll get in touch with you very soon . . . I have a four-legged patient awaiting my totally inadequate attentions.'

'So I hear,' she replied. 'Take care with the dog.'

'I'll do my best.' And Stephen put down the phone.

'Walters!' he shouted. The senior orderly put his head around the door.

'Sir?'

'Come here, will you . . . you're about to become a veterinary nurse!'

Following the vet's instructions Stephen relieved the pressure which had built up as a result of Shep's injuries, by inserting a long needle into the pleural cavity and withdrawing the excess fluid. Immediately the dog began to breathe more easily. As he manipulated the crushed rib cage with his hands and gently bound the bones into position, Stephen hoped that there would be no further bleeding into the cavity. The light anaesthetic which he had been advised to use to keep the animal calm while he performed this operation, began to wear off very quickly. Shep opened his eyes, stared at Stephen for a few long moments and then closed them again as he dropped into a calm and natural sleep.

'Well, there's nothing more to be done now,' said Stephen, rather gratified to hear the congratulations of the two men beside him. 'We'll bring his basket into my office for the time being . . . so that I can keep an eye on him. Let the CO know, will you, Williams?'

'Sir!' The aircraftsman saluted smartly and left.

'I'll have to leave you to keep an eye on things here while I go down to the hospital,' Stephen told his orderly. 'The dog should sleep for a while. Try to prevent him from moving about too much when he does wake up.'

In the NAAFI that evening the orderly and the CO's clerk exchanged views on the quality of their MO, now that they had seen him in action under fire, as it were.

'Well, all I can say is,' said the aircraftsman, 'if the Doc can put old Shep to rights, he can have my appendix any day!'

'I distinctly remember reading on your medical record that you had your appendix out when you was sixteen,' observed the orderly, dryly.

'Aw . . . shut up,' said his companion. 'You know what I mean!'

After that first raid on the airfield, such attacks became a regular occurrence.

It seemed as though the enemy waited only as long as it took to have one set of craters filled in along the runway, before sending over another wave of bombers to open them up again. Warnings of impending raids were becoming more and more efficient, although it was some time before it became generally known that this was due to a new device known as Radio Detection Finding.

When the RDF station on the promontory at Foreness gave warning of the enemy's approach, Manston's fighters would take off, leaving as few targets as possible on the ground. Casualties amongst ground staff were heavy, though, and those fighter planes which chased the attackers back across the Channel frequently crashed into the sea. Like Colin Sheen, many of the pilots who survived suffered from exposure as well as bullet wounds and burns. Stephen became very experienced in handling such cases whilst struggling to cope with a long list of more commonplace injuries.

In this he was assisted on the field by his two medical orderlies, while at the hospital in Margate, Dr Lewis, Matron and her staff were always there to help him.

He had fully intended to return Ellen's surprise call, but a suitable moment never seemed to present itself. Nor had he heard anything more of Grace Dobbie since she had collected those first casualties from the airfield.

It was not until he had had a chance encounter with the Vicar, more than a week later, that Stephen discovered she had been obliged to report for duty on the day of that first raid, to the RAF unit at Hammersmith's Royal Masonic Hospital.

Stephen's most seriously wounded cases were quickly transferred to other hospitals further inland, so that Manston's limited facility was kept available for the immediate treatment of casualties from the field and the surrounding area.

It soon became clear that early treatment of burns, particularly to the hands, was vitally important if the damaged appendage was to retain an acceptable degree of flexibility. Stephen sought information on the treatment of burns from every possible source, and in his researches discovered the work of an eminent plastic surgeon from New Zealand, Sir Harold Gillies.

Intrigued by what he had read of this gentleman's work, Stephen was pleased to discover that Gillies was actually working in England, and wrote to him, listing a number of queries. In the midst of his twenty-hour days Stephen received a reply to his letter, not from Gillies himself but from another surgeon claiming to be the eminent man's pupil.

> The Queen Victoria Hospital
> East Grinstead
> Sussex
> 4 August 1940

Dear Dr Beaton,
Your letter to Sir Harold Gillies concerning recent experiences with airmen shot down over the Channel and suffering severe burns has been handed to me since Sir Harold is not at present available for consultation.

As you yourself have observed, it is the first few hours which are the most important for a good recovery. Once tendons and nervous tissue have been allowed to atrophy there is little hope of any return to normality. I enclose for your attention some recent observations of my own which may be of some assistance to you.

Here at East Grinstead we are setting up a special burns unit to deal with injuries not only to Service personnel but also to those civilians severely burned as a result of the bombing.

While I appreciate that the wheels of bureaucracy may turn rather more slowly than we would wish, I hope that in future you will be able to refer your most problematic cases directly to me.

Bearing in mind the importance of good co-ordination between those who are party to the management of severe burns cases, I would suggest that you visit this establishment at your earliest opportunity to discuss ways in which we may be of assistance to one another.

A copy of this letter, together with your own to Sir Harold, has been sent to the Air Commodore, Medical Services. Hopefully this correspondence will help us towards the degree of co-ordination which is necessary if our work in rehabilitating the severely burned is to have any success.

Yours sincerely,
Archibald McIndoe

Stephen felt strangely elated, as well as relieved, to find that he was not alone in appreciating the importance of swift action in the case of burned aircrew. Although it was up to the central clearing office to decide where his patients would go on transfer from Margate, as surgeon in charge of the cases he was permitted to make recommendations about their further treatment. In the case of severe burns, this resulted in his sending to East Grinstead a steady flow of patients during the months which followed. Unfortunately it was to be a long time before Stephen was able to make the suggested visit, and then the circumstances were other than he would have wished.

Only the delicate nature of Colin Sheen's grafts and the need for his leg to be immobilised kept him from being transferred with the rest of Stephen's patients once the air raids began in earnest.

When the daily visits of Grace Dobbie ceased, the Australian became very restless. He was always pleased to see Mr Dobbie and for a time even the attentions of well-meaning female hospital visitors, bearing gifts of magazines and fruit, broke up the days for him satisfactorily. After a while, however, such visitations began to pall, then to irritate.

It was Dr Lewis who finally pleaded with Stephen on his behalf to allow some of Digger's fellow officers into the hospital for a visit.

Much against his better judgement Stephen finally agreed, insisting they should be allowed in only one at a time.

The intention was there right enough. They arrived one by one, but the first visitors, reluctant to leave and miss the next part of Digger's enthralling tales of hospital life, lingered, so that by the time it was the turn of Squadron Leader 'Squeaky' Piper, there was a goodly crowd gathered about the bed.

'I'll just sit here,' said Squeaky, perching on the edge of the mattress in the absence of a suitable chair. The expression on the Australian's face was one of intense surprise and considerable agony. The Squadron Leader jumped up as though he had been scalded.

'Oh, I say, I'm awfully sorry, old chap . . . did that hurt?' he enquired.

A clean-cut young Flight Lieutenant, who looked hardly old enough to be out of short trousers, glanced warily at the cradle which protected Digger's legs from the bedcovers and asked in hushed, respectful tones, 'Is it true you had to cut off your own foot before you could get out of the plane?'

'No . . . only the boot,' another of the pilots chipped in. 'Look here's the survivor.'

He pulled the boot from behind Colin's locker and swung it over his head.

'What am I offered for this fine, barely worn right boot? Only one reasonably careful owner . . .' There was a loud clatter as the stiletto knife fell to the floor.

The roar from the group around the bed was quickly stifled when they realised they had been joined by the CO.

Wing Commander Harry Calcutt advanced into the room carrying a brown paper bag. The smile with which he had intended to greet the invalid had been wiped away by the sight of the stiletto knife. He stooped to pick it up, then studied it for a moment in silence before demanding, 'Tell me, Sheen, were you carrying this knife in your boot when you went down?'

'Jolly good job he was, sir,' offered Denny Bolton, cheerfully. 'It saved him from drowning.'

'And sent him off course in the first place,' said Calcutt, harshly. 'A valuable aircraft and an expensively trained pilot, wasted unnecessarily. I'll have more to say about this when you're out of here, Sheen. In the meantime you'd better make a pig of yourself with these. It'll be bread and water when you get back to the field!'

He tossed the paper bag on to the bed, turned on his heel and was gone before Colin had managed to get out a belated, 'Thank you for coming, sir.'

As his mates began an onslaught upon the CO's gift of chocolate biscuits, Digger appealed to his Group Leader.

'What the hell was that all about, Squeaky?'

'A simple lesson in Physics actually, old chap,' replied Piper, feeling rather foolish himself for having sanctioned the carrying of the knife in the first place.

'If a steel blade becomes magnetised, which it invariably must, it affects other magnets around it . . . as in a *compass*!'

'Oh, heck!' exclaimed Colin. 'You mean, I'd have reached home if I hadn't been carrying the knife?'

'Precisely.'

A chill had fallen upon the company. The younger men departed, sympathising with the chastened Digger, while the Squadron Leader, realising he had failed in his duty by allowing his men to carry knives, worried about his next encounter with the CO.

Towards the middle of August, both of Stephen's long-term patients appeared to be recovering from their wounds. Colin's grafts had been slow to take, and in one case the added skin had sloughed before the area beneath could heal. Stephen was obliged to remove a second sliver of skin from the uninjured thigh and begin the tedious process all over again. It had been this problem in particular which had prompted him to make his initial contact with the plastic surgeons.

He was still not entirely satisfied with the results of his work. The tear in Digger's thigh had healed beautifully without any puckering. The absence of suture scars meant that only a white line remained to show there had ever been a wound there and Stephen was to use the device of tiny 'butterfly' plasters, to draw the skin together, for many similar wounds in the future. It was the Australian's lower leg which gave cause for concern. The calf muscle was seriously disfigured where lumps of tissue had been gouged out, leaving deep holes beneath the new skin. Stephen felt there should be some way of replacing this kind of tissue, just as he had been able to replace the skin which covered it.

When Digger was at last discharged from the hospital, he was assigned to light duties on the ground. Much to his chagrin, during a period of intense activity at Manston, the Australian found himself posted to the operations room below the control tower. Here he assisted Stumpy Miles and his team of WAAFs in co-ordinating the activities of the Manston squadron and following those of other air bases on the PLOT. It was the next best thing to being aloft himself, and Colin was forced to concede that he was fortunate to be this close to events as they happened.

Shep, too, recovered well from his injuries. Within days his breathing had improved and he had been returned to the CO's office from where he managed to crawl out of his basket and waddle uncomfortably, with his plastered leg and stitched side, out on to the veranda to take up his customary position.

In a couple of weeks he was almost back to normal: making his rounds daily with the CO, supervising the comings and goings in the Company Office and, with his uncanny instinct, presenting himself beside the Morris Ten at precisely the moment when Stephen embarked for his daily visit to the hospital in the town.

Here the dog was received royally in the hospital kitchen where the scraps appeared to be of a higher quality than those accumulated by the RAF chefs.

The Morris never did lose its wet-dog smell. In time Stephen became inured to it.

Shep showed little psychological disturbance as a result of his experience of bombing, except in one particular. When the siren went, the dog made for the nearest dugout, and since some of these reinforced holes in the ground were scarcely large enough to hold more than half a dozen people, the presence of a huge hound in addition, particularly if it had been raining, made such moments pretty uncomfortable for all concerned. Not one of the station's personnel resented Shep's presence, however, for he had indeed become their mascot. Like the ravens in the Tower of London, it was the conviction of every man on the base that while Shep survived, the station could not fall!

The German air offensive which had begun with a concerted attack upon Britain's fighter bases around the coasts, now switched to bombing raids upon London. Calcutt's squadron of Defiants was soon engaged in daily skirmishes with wave upon wave of German bombers and their long-range fighter escort. It soon became very clear that these outdated aircraft were no match for the Germans.

'Signal from Headquarters, sir,'

Pritchard laid the sheet on Calcutt's desk and stood back, awaiting further instructions.

As the CO read the words, a look of disbelief clouded his countenance. The communication from Commander Air Forces was dated 15 August . . .

In disbelief, Calcutt read it through a second time before barking at his WO, 'Pritchard, take a letter.'

WO2 Albert Pritchard could tell that the old man was angry. Squatting on the bentwood chair beside the desk, he held his note pad in readiness.

'Take a letter to HQ. Air Marshall . . .' Pritchard's pencil flew across the page. Line after vitriolic line filled one sheet and he barely had time to flip over the page before the next tirade began.

There was a knock on the outer door. In the absence of Stumpy Miles who was occupied in the control room, the visitor entered and approached the CO's inner sanctum. He knocked and, without waiting for a reply, pushed open the door.

'Do you have a minute, boss?'

Calcutt stopped speaking, abruptly.

'Oh, it's you, Piper . . . come in, sit down.'

He turned to the WO2.

'All right, Pritchard, you can tear that lot up . . . I'll give you something more diplomatic later on.'

Wordlessly, the Warrant Officer gathered his belongings and left. It was a pity that these cries from the heart would never be despatched. Later in the day Calcutt would find some more acceptable formula with which to attempt to stir those in authority into action, but as with all the others, it would do no good. He sometimes wondered what would happen if he did send them one of the old man's ranting communiqués. He glanced through his notes, tempted, then tore up the pages and committed them to the waste paper basket.

'How was it?' demanded the Wing Commander.

'How do you think?' Piper's reply was defiant. 'I'd like to see what one of those "brass hats" at High Command would make of a Messerschmitt coming straight at him, all guns blazing.'

'Who bought it this time?' Calcutt asked, quietly.

'Denny Bolton.' Piper paused, noting the skipper's sharp intake of breath. Another of his best lads wasted.

'What happened?'

'Turret jammed : . . he didn't have a chance . . . never got off a single shot. Gerry got him in his sights and – wham!'

The two-seater Defiant fighter had been designed with a turret-mounted weapon which required the gunner to train his guns manually upon the target whilst the pilot carried out the complex manoeuvres required of any aircraft in close combat. It was almost impossible to attain any degree of accuracy in such circumstances.

The German fighters, the Messerschmitt and the Heinkel, carried their guns fixed in the wings. A pilot need only attack his enemy head-on and press one button to fire all eight machine guns. Such aircraft achieved a deadly accuracy.

Aerodynamically the Defiant was a well-designed plane which could outmanoeuvre both types of enemy fighter, but without the equivalent fire power it was at a considerable disadvantage in combat.

'When are we going to get the new aircraft they promised us?' demanded Squeaky Piper.

'We're not.' Calcutt almost spat out the words. 'See this.' He tossed Piper the offending letter from High Command.

'"It must be appreciated",' Piper read, '"that considerable numbers of fighter aircraft must be held in reserve for use against a possible invasion force. The rate of production is insufficient at this time to replace existing serviceable aircraft with more modern machines . . ."'

Angrily he punched the wall with the hand which still held the offending signal. 'What use will a row of nice new Hurricanes be to us when we're down to our last trained pilots and our airfields have been bombed into ploughed fields?' demanded Piper. 'Are you going to reply to this crap?'

'I already have,' replied the CO. 'You heard me tell Pritchard to tear it up. There's no use trying to blaspheme our way into an understanding with the big brass. I'm going to demand an interview with the Air Marshall . . .'

The telephone rang, and at the same time the Medical Officer poked his head around the door.

Lifting the receiver, the CO signalled to Stephen to enter while Squeaky Piper, having unloaded his complaint on to the shoulders of his CO, growled a low 'Morning, Doc!' to Stephen and, scowling at the world in general, made his departure.

'Commanding Officer,' Calcutt barked into the mouthpiece.

'Things are beginning to hot up.' It was Stumpy Miles, speaking from the control room. 'Looks as though they may be headed for coastal towns . . . or the docks at Southampton again.'

'OK, I'm on my way.' Calcutt lifted his cap.

'Sorry, Doc . . . walk over to the control tower with me.'

'I only need a moment of your time, sir,' said Stephen, half running along the corridor in order to keep pace with his CO. 'Dr Lewis needs my assistance with a civilian injured in last night's raid. May I have your permission to leave the base?' Then, seeing Calcutt's doubtful expression, he continued, 'In a sudden emergency the Medical Orderlies are very competent to carry out first aid. If I should be caught at the hospital, I shall at least be ready to receive the worst casualties.'

'You know best, Doc.'

Calcutt stopped as he reached the outer door.

'Pritchard, alert the standby ops room crew. In case it's us that's target for tonight, they'd better be ready to take over at Muffins . . . we haven't needed to switch command posts yet, but this could be the day.' The alternative operations room had been located in the basement of a baker's shop in Westgate.

Stephen stepped into his car.

'Can I give you a lift to the control tower?' he asked.

'No, thanks, I'll commandeer this waggon.'

As he spoke the CO waved down one of the airfield run-abouts and climbed in beside the driver. Without invitation, Shep leaped into the back seat, looking back at Stephen and sniffing the air as if in apology. A dog cannot serve two masters . . . not both at the same time!

Half an hour before sundown the air raid sirens sounded again all along the coast.

Personnel in the control room had barely left their posts all day. Empty coffee cups and the remnants of a sandwich meal, hastily snatched, was the only evidence of their having taken any kind of a break.

'Hostile aircraft approaching Thames Estuary . . . Angels . . . one . . . eight,' sang out the WAAF communications officer. Stumpy and Digger exchanged anxious glances. If they were going to climb above twenty thousand feet before attacking, the pilots would need to wear oxygen masks – a further disadvantage in a small aircraft with a limited field of vision.

Her colleague pushed a black model of an aeroplane across the huge map. Alongside it a coloured counter indicated the number of hostiles expected. As she listened intently to the information coming through her headphones, the WAAF placed the Fighter Command squadron in their attacking positions. There seemed so very few of them pitted against the might of the enemy forces.

The CO leaned across the controller's desk.

'General alert,' he called through the Tannoy microphone. His message would be heard across the field. 'Every serviceable aircraft to take off . . . immediate.'

He turned to Stumpy Miles.

'I'm taking up the Hurricane. Keep them in the air as long as possible and give instructions for landing on other fields inland . . . I have a feeling there won't be a lot of runway left after this little lot.'

Even as he spoke, the WAAF operator moved the hostile aircraft into a position which made it certain their destination was this station.

Like all the experienced pilots, Colin Sheen had had a trip in the new Hurricane which had been placed on the base for training purposes. It had been a tussle to get Stephen to agree to his flying again, but since there was no threat of enemy action at the time, the MO had consented.

That had been a few days ago, when everyone had believed that it would only be a short while before the entire squadron was equipped with the new machines. Eagerly they had all taken a turn, appreciating the improvements, decrying the drawbacks, passing on warnings of particular foibles to one another. Now Calcutt would have to tell them there was no chance of their getting the Hurricanes in the foreseeable future . . .

As the CO reached for his flying helmet, Colin interrupted him.

'With all due respect, sir,' he began, and grinned because it was well known on the base that the CO considered all observations which began thus as likely to be insubordinate, 'I think I ought to take her, don't you?'

The Old Man was well aware that his young pilots considered him to be in his dotage.

'The Doc's grounded you, Digger,' he observed.

'Only until the beginning of the week . . . what difference can three more days make?' Colin failed to mention that Stephen had merely suggested they wait until Monday before he made his final decision about the pilot's fitness.

Calcutt hesitated for a moment only. He was well aware that his own eyesight was far below requirements for an operational pilot. He should have been officially grounded long before this, but since experienced Station Commanders were in short supply and he was unlikely ever to be required to fly, the matter had been ignored.

'OK, Digger,' he gave in and handed the helmet to the Australian. 'The fitter has had instructions to get her warmed up when there's a red alert . . . she should be fully armed.'

Grabbing the helmet and goggles, the Australian hurried out of the bunker into the bright sunlight and was forced to pause for a moment for his eyes to adjust. Across the tarmac the little machine was indeed ready for take-off. Limping only slightly, he hurried across, grateful for the help of the rigger who positioned his foot in the stirrup step for him and shoved with his shoulder to get the ungainly body up. With his good right foot firmly planted on the wing, Colin was able to swing himself into the cockpit. The rigger pulled his harness tight as Digger stretched his injured leg into the limited space beneath the control panel. He felt a twinge of pain and understood Stephen's reservations. But no time now to be concerned about trifles. Signalling that he was ready, he waited for the chocks to be drawn away and taxied down the runway. Ten miles behind him, the German attacking force was lining up for its most concerted raid yet on Manston airfield.

★

As Digger departed, the CO lifted the microphone to his lips.

'This is Manston – Manston calling. Message to all our chickens. Hostiles approaching the airfield. Do not, repeat *not*, attempt to land until All Clear is given. Use alternative fields if necessary.'

The familiar voice of his Commanding Officer gave a measure of security to a lonely pilot with nothing between himself and eternity but a thin shell of aluminium alloy and perspex, and a few spars of wood.

The control room fell quiet, the tension in the atmosphere increasing as an occasional report indicated the hostiles were nearly overhead. To every individual, fiercely concentrated upon his or her specific task, the sound of falling bombs came almost as a surprise.

Experience had taught them to expect sticks of six high-explosive bombs to be dropped at a time. The first five they heard, distinctly. First there was a terrifying shriek as the bomb fell. This was followed by a dull thud which was accompanied a moment later by the rumble of rushing air as the vacuum created by the explosion was instantly and forcefully filled, the blast carrying buildings, vehicles, people, any and every movable object, in its wake.

They did not hear the approach of the sixth.

It fell directly on the roof of the control tower, sucking massive panes of plate glass from the third-floor observation room and demolishing all three of the floors which stood above ground.

On the roof the Vickers machine gun, which had continued to fire at the approaching enemy planes until the last moment, was blown to smithereens and the men manning it consigned to eternity.

Below ground, buried beneath tons of concrete and steel reinforcement, the control room was eerily silent. With the main aerial mast gone, there was no longer any contact with the outside world. Only the generator, gasoline-operated and independent of the main electrical supply, continued to hum.

The lights flickered dimly for a short while as cables, broken by the effects of the blast, touched and parted. Suddenly there was a blinding flash which for one instant lit up the whole scene of devastation.

It illuminated the twisted metal of furniture, upturned and shattered. It picked out countless sheets of paper which floated on the currents of disturbed air, landing at last like fallen leaves upon the mangled bodies scattered in grotesque attitudes both above and beneath the piles of dust-whitened debris.

Chapter Nine

Shep, having accompanied the CO to the control tower, had had to be persuaded that his presence was not required inside.

'Go on, Shep,' Calcutt had told him as the dog waited patiently for his master to open the steel door that gave access to the basement room.

Despite his appealing stare, Calcutt would not relent and the Alsatian had been obliged to watch as his master descended into the gloomy space beyond. When the door was closed in his face, Shep ran back up the steps and trotted off to the cook-house for his elevenses.

More than satisfied with this visit, he set off for the camp office, visiting a number of favourite ports of call on the way. Having reported to WO2 Pritchard, he settled down on the veranda for his customary siesta.

He watched the aircraft taking off and returning throughout the afternoon, hardly lifting his muzzle from the warm boards to greet his pilot friends as they passed by on their way to the debriefing hut.

When towards evening the base siren sounded its warning, it would be difficult to say who responded the fastest: Shep or WO2 Pritchard.

Both dived into the nearest dug-out and had barely settled themselves in the chill darkness when the first bombs began to fall.

Pritchard squatted on the duck-boarded floor with his arm around the dog's thick ruff. As one explosion was followed instantly by another, he whispered in his companion's ear, 'All right old fellow . . . we'll be safe enough in here.'

Shep's ears were laid back in fear as the first screeching missile flew to earth, but in the silence which followed the last of the explosions, he turned his attention to the airman, licking his cheek clean of the grey dust which had settled there.

Suddenly the dog's ears pricked.

Pritchard wondered what it was he could detect that the human ear could not pick up? He was not left for long in doubt. Seconds later fire and ambulance waggons tore past on their way to the far end of the airfield.

At almost the same moment, across the fields from the Manston village siren came the steady note of the All Clear. There was no corresponding signal from the station's lookouts. The observation post and siren no longer existed to give it.

Man and dog emerged from the dug-out to survey the scene of devastation all around them.

Workshops and hangars, ranged along one side of the runway, lay in smoking ruins. Behind these the living quarters were empty shells. Curtains and clothing festooned the sagging telephone wires and electricity cables; odd chairs and tables stood alone in a sea of indistinguishable debris.

The camp office appeared to be relatively undamaged. Pritchard pushed open the door warily, half expecting the roof to cave in above him. He found the interior strangely light and realised that the boarding which had covered windows from which the glass had long gone, were now empty holes. He had a clear view to the far side of the runway.

In the distance he could see a number of buildings which were burning freely. Beside them a large fuel store was in imminent danger of going up in flames.

The station's two fire appliances were engaged in quenching another blaze, further over. It was clear that they needed help from some other source.

In the absence of any officer – all those not airborne were, he believed, gathered in the control tower – Pritchard sought authorisation to call in the civilian fire services.

Climbing over scattered furniture, he reached his desk and tried the telephone line to the control tower. It was dead.

He got up and went outside to where he should be able to see the tower, at the far end of the runway. He could make out only a charred and smouldering skeleton of a building.

There was nothing else for it. He must take it upon himself to summon aid.

Returning to the switchboard, he plugged into the outside line and was rewarded with a satisfying humming.

He tried dialling Margate Fire Station. The line was engaged, but at least he now knew that he had access to the outside world.

Pritchard used a second number. This time there was a response.

'Emergency Services.' The voice was cool, precise, impersonal. 'Which service do you require?'

'All of them, of course!' He realised that in his desperation he was shouting.

'Where are you speaking from?' The female operator remained calm despite his outburst.

'RAF Manston,' he replied, more controlled now.

There was a momentary pause. He wondered if the line was still functioning. Then, in a strangled voice, she spoke again. 'We saw the bombs falling over your way . . . is it very bad?'

'About as bad as it can be,' Pritchard replied.

The girl glanced up at a photograph of a thin-faced, smiling young man, his hair slicked down with cream, a jaunty angle to his forage cap, wings worn proudly on the breast of his Service tunic. There was a catch in her voice as she said, 'Just leave it with me. Stand by.'

Gratefully, he replaced the handset.

Every instinct suggested that he get out there to see what he could do to help, but he knew that his job was to remain here and relay whatever messages came through.

While he waited for the telephone operator to call back, he obtained a line through to Fighter Command Headquarters. With the station's control room out of action, those aircraft at present in action, were without instructions. He must inform HQ. Someone must make radio contact with them.

Shep sniffed the air, hoping for a familiar scent and finding none.

He cocked one ear in the direction of the main gate, and his heavy tail began to sway from side to side, slowly at first but gaining momentum when he recognised the unmistakable note of the doctor's Morris Ten, approaching at speed. By the time Stephen had pulled up and opened the driver's door, the dog was ready to jump in. His friend would know where to find Calcutt. Even when the doctor disappeared inside the hut, Shep waited, nose pressed against the windscreen, impatient little whining noises indicating his anxiety to get going.

'Glad to see you, sir.' Stephen found Pritchard's obvious relief more disturbing than the scene of devastation outside. The Warrant Officer was a stalwart among the station's personnel.

'Where is everybody?' he demanded. 'I was just on the outskirts of town when the bombers flew over. I could see that it was the airfield which was copping the worst of it . . .'

Pritchard swallowed in order to control his wavering voice.

'Most of the officers cleared the field of aircraft,' he explained. 'Those left on the base were in the control tower . . .' His sentence tailed off as Stephen followed his glance towards the distant scene of destruction.

He gasped. 'How bad is it?'

'I don't know,' came the reply. 'We have no communication with the tower. I called the Civil Authorities for help.'

Stephen had never been particularly well versed in the etiquette of camp life but was quick to understand the significance of Pritchard's confession. In the absence of any officer, the Warrant Officer had taken the initiative. Seeking to reassure the man, Stephen took upon himself the mantle of authority while feeling totally incompetent to do so.

'You've done well, Pritchard,' he said. 'Stay here to operate the outside lines. I'll send you a runner to relay messages . . . when I can find somebody. Meanwhile, I'll get over to the tower myself and see what's happening. Try to contact Dr Lewis at the hospital. If you can't speak to him directly, leave a message. I'd be grateful for his help, and for any other medical assistance he can muster.'

He paused. There must be something more he should do. Of course . . . it was just as well he had remembered to carry out Calcutt's suggestion and alert the standby control team.

He had done as the CO had requested, and had himself seen the Executive Officer's second in command, tousled from sleep after his night watch, mustering his team and leading them into the basement of the barber's shop at the end of the High Street.

'Ring this number.' Stephen searched the list of emergency numbers which was pinned to the notice board, and pointed out the right one.

'Explain that the MO is the only officer in a position to give orders here on the field. Tell them they will have to operate the control plot and get someone of appropriate rank to take over from me as soon as possible.'

While he spoke, he watched an ambulance unloading stretchers which were being arranged in front of the dispensary. His two orderlies were systematically examining the casualties. Some they were carrying inside, others remained on the ground. The row of motionless bundles lengthened with the arrival of a tractor and trailer carrying more stretchers.

He must get out there and help.

Stephen jumped back into the car and, with Shep urging him on, sped around the perimeter track, avoiding newly made craters and piles of debris. A dazed-looking aircraftsman was attempting to clear part of the end wall of a hut from the roadway. Stephen drew to a halt.

'What's your name, Aircraftsman?'

The man looked up, recognising the doctor. He straightened himself before replying.

'A/C2 Denis Woolley, sir,' he replied, speaking in the measured tones of an automaton.

'Are you all right, Woolley?' Stephen enquired.

This sympathetic enquiry was sufficient to cause the young man's eyes to well with tears and his hands began to shake so that the length of timber he was holding fell to the ground.

'OK. Pull yourself together, laddie,' said Stephen, not unkindly. The airman would recover faster if he was given something specific to do.

'I want you to report to the camp office, to WO2 Pritchard. Tell him I sent you and act under his orders. Get along now . . . at the double!' he added, goading the zombie-like figure into action.

Woolley lifted the offending timber to one side of the road and stood back, raising his hand to salute. Realising suddenly that his cap had blown off in the blast, he lowered his hand, confused, then seeing Stephen's encouraging nod, doubled away in the direction of the main gate.

Further along the track, Stephen pulled up before the dispensary. Shep, understanding that this was as far as the Morris was going, leaped from the passenger seat and charged in a direct line across the tarmac towards the ruined control tower.

Stephen stooped to remove the rough covering over the first of the corpses. It was a man he had come to know well, a keen athlete and a good cricketer. The beardless face looked child-like in death. The other coverings were lifted back to reveal more sad remnants of the once-living, breathing community which he had come to regard as his family.

There were girls too.

Gently he lifted a lock of yellow hair which had escaped its regulation bun, and tucked the strands behind a delicately shaped ear. Her face was dirty from the blast, but she seemed uninjured and merely asleep. He took out his stethoscope, hoping against hope that he would find some spark of life, but there was none. Sadly he replaced the waterproof cape which covered her and moved on.

Having confirmed that each member of that silent queue was indeed dead, the doctor pushed open the door and went inside.

He was gratified to find that, although crowded, the waiting area was a scene of orderly activity. The senior Medical Orderly, Patrick Devlin, was engaged in stitching a particularly nasty gash in an airman's forearm, while his assistant was bandaging a wounded scalp. Two of the WAAF officers had taken it upon themselves to carry out First Aid on some minor injuries, while a third girl was carrying round cups of hot sweet tea. She approached him as he entered.

Absent-mindedly Stephen took one of the proffered mugs and sipped at the scalding liquid.

Of the room in general he asked, 'How many were rescued from the control tower?'

The two Medical Orderlies exchanged glances, while the girl with the tea tray put it down abruptly and ran weeping into the kitchen.

Flight Lieutenant Sally Peters, whom Stephen had met briefly at one of the station dances, took him aside and, speaking very quietly, explained.

'All three floors of the building were demolished. Everyone in the observation and radio rooms were killed. They haven't found the fellows who were manning the gun . . .'

'What about the ops room?' Stephen demanded, thinking of his friends Stumpy Miles and Digger Sheen.

The WAAF officer shook her head and her glance shifted towards the kitchen where the other girl was hastily drying her eyes before returning to her tea round. 'Several of her roommates are buried under the rubble. There's no knowing if they're alive or dead. The rescue squads are out there now, trying to find out.'

Stephen made a quick examination of the injured still awaiting attention.

'Nothing here that you can't deal with, Devlin,' he decided. 'I'm expecting Dr Lewis from the hospital to look in shortly. I want you to hand over to him when he gets here.'

Devlin acknowledged the order and Stephen continued quietly so that his deputy alone could hear.

'It looks as though I'm the only operational officer on the base at the moment, so I think I should go and find out what's happening. Will you be OK here?'

'We'll be fine, sir,' Devlin replied in his thick Irish brogue, and waved the doctor away. 'Sure an' the lads'll be just as happy not to have you sticking the needles in . . . won't you, men?' he demanded, throwing a hypodermic needle, javelin fashion, at his victim's buttock. 'Can't have you getting a dose of tetanus, lad, now can we?' he enquired, not expecting, and not receiving, a reply. The injured man winced and then rubbed vigorously at the spot where the needle had gone in. They said it didn't hurt so much that way, but he hadn't noticed it.

When Stephen observed the remains of what had been the control tower, his heart sank. He had seen those bodies which had been recovered from the ruins. None of the control room staff had been among them. That could only mean that those below ground at the time the bomb fell must still be there.

The underground room was reinforced, he knew. Stumpy had told him once about the amount of steel and concrete which had gone into its construction. There was a chance that those below ground had survived the explosion, but unless this rubble could be moved in time, they might well die from suffocation. Stephen knew the room had been made practically air-tight as a defence against gas attack.

Hearing a familiar yelp of excitement, he looked across the piles of rubble to where Shep was padding backwards and forwards across the dusty mounds, picking his way daintily between shattered concrete beams and shapeless pieces of rusted steelwork.

The dog took quick little running steps, pausing every few seconds to stand with his head to one side and his ear close to the ground.

He began to work persistently at one particular spot. He tested the loose material with his forepaw, turning his head to listen. Then, nose to the ground, he began again alternately scrabbling with his feet and sniffing.

Stephen called to him, 'What is it, Shep? What have you got there?'

The dog lifted his head at the sound of the doctor's voice, then with renewed frenzy he tackled the rubble again.

Stephen hurried towards him, stumbling as he ran.

'Over here,' he yelled to the men working on the far side of the ruined building. 'The dog has found something!'

The RAF rescue squad had been working furiously ever since the dust had settled on the demolished building. Their earth-moving vehicles swarmed around the site, endeavouring to clear the mess. Traumatised by the sight of their dead comrades as they had hauled the broken bodies from the wreckage, the RAF men were not taking kindly to receiving orders from a civilian demolition team which had turned up only a short while before, summoned by Pritchard's appeal for help. The Civil

Defence boys had brought with them specialised lifting gear and since they were the only people proficient in its use, WO2 Ross had been obliged to concede command of the operation to their foreman. While both men understood the urgency of the situation, neither was happy with this chain of command. The civilian issued his orders, but the RAF men responded only when these were relayed by their own NCO.

The machines worked to remove fallen concrete beams from one side of the pile, while RAF men and civilians, working with their hands to clear smaller chunks of rubble, suddenly found the ground caving in beneath their feet.

'Stop!' yelled the civilian foreman. He turned to Stephen recognising him as an officer. At last! Here was someone capable of getting this mess under control . . .

'This is no good, sir,' he declared. 'If there's anyone alive down there, we're in danger of capsizing the whole structure and burying them for good. This is a job which will have to be carried out by hand, and if I might say so, sir, my men have had more experience.' His glance wandered over the remainder of the field. His unspoken thoughts were quickly seized upon by Stephen who turned instantly to Sergeant Ross.

'You must have pressing duties elsewhere, Sergeant?' he suggested.

'There is the runway, sir.' Reluctant to leave the fate of his colleagues in the hands of this civilian, Ross nevertheless knew that it was important to get the field operational as soon as possible. 'My men should be concentrating on filling in the worst of the holes,' he affirmed. 'I imagine the CO will be wanting to land his planes.'

'Very well, Sergeant,' the doctor replied. 'Take your men and get cracking on repairing the runway. Our friends here will manage without you, I'm sure.'

The Civil Defence foreman, relieved to be left to do the job for which he had been trained, without having to refer in all things to the Sergeant, nodded his agreement and turned to his own men.

'All right, lads, it'll be a hands-on job from now on. Slow but sure . . . that's the ticket.'

As the Sergeant's mechanical diggers moved over to the runway, the rescue team began the task of shifting concrete beams and tangled metal, a piece at a time, from the seemingly endless mound.

Stephen watched for a few moments then, alerted by Shep's frantic little yelps, turned to see that the dog, tail wagging furiously, was concentrating on one particular spot. For a few moments he pawed ineffectually at the rubble then, with his ears laid back, squatted on his haunches and let out a howl loud enough to make every man on the field stop what he was doing.

Stephen hurried towards him. He stooped and attempted to lift a heavy piece of masonry which seemed to be in Shep's way. Immediately the dog was in underneath it. He began once again scrabbling at the loose material beneath.

Stephen called across to the foreman.

'I say . . . sorry, Mr . . . ?'

'Tuffnell, sir.' The demolition foreman moved over to where Stephen was attempting to pull away another huge beam. 'If I might say so, you'd best leave this job to my men . . . they're all construction workers in peacetime. They do know what they're doing.'

'I'm sure they do, Mr Tuffnell,' Stephen replied, trying to remain cool in the face of mounting frustration. 'The fact is, the dog here is a particular favourite of the senior officers . . . in fact of the whole camp so far as that goes. He seems to have something to tell us about his friends. Perhaps we should investigate his find?'

The older man, his ruffled feathers considerably smoothed by the departure of Sergeant Ross, took a pipe from his pocket and thrust it between his teeth. The stem was so short after several snappings and repairings that the bowl nearly touched the tip of his nose. He rubbed a flake of tobacco between his palms and stuffed the mixture into the bowl, all the while observing the dog's antics.

Suddenly he removed the unlit pipe, and tucked it into his waistcoat pocket.

'Bill, Jo . . . over here. Looks like the dog's digging a tunnel. We'll need a bit of shoring.'

Relieved to see some purposeful activity at last, Stephen allowed his thoughts to range to other duties he might perform in the absence of his superiors.

Some of the ratings had begun the process of clearing essential access pathways through the piles of rubble. Others were wandering aimlessly. He yelled to a corporal he recognised.

'Maitland . . . over here . . . at the double!'

The man looked up, surprised at the doctor's tone. The power of the uniform was sufficient, however, to bring him up smartly before the officer.

'Sir?'

'Collect all the men not already occupied with vital work, arm yourselves with picks, shovels, whatever you can find, and report to Sergeant Ross for runway repair duties.'

'Sir.' Dishevelled and without a cap, nevertheless the Corporal saluted smartly. All he had needed was someone to tell him what to do.

'Oh, and, Corporal, see that skinny fellow over there?' He pointed out one of the youngest of the airmen on the base. 'Send him to me. He looks as though he ought to be a good runner.'

The Corporal went about his duties and in a few moments the young recruit reported.

'Name, lad?' Stephen demanded.

'1704592, Aircraftsman Barker, sir,' the boy replied.

'No, not that . . . your Christian name.' Stephen had not meant to sound so harsh.

'Daniel, sir.'

'Well, Dan, you can see the problem. We have an airfield in ruins, no senior officers to set it to rights, and no communications system except between the Company Office and outside. You are going to be my eyes and ears. I shall want you to run messages and gather information . . . is that OK with you?'

'Sir.' The boy waited patiently for his first assignment.

'Now, cut along to the Company Office and tell WO2 Pritchard that we need more fire appliances, construction teams to clear the runway and whatever additional help the Civil Defence people can spare. We have personnel trapped in the control room . . . hopefully still alive. Have you got all that?'

'Sir!'

'Right then . . . off you go!'

The airman went off at a fast sprint. Stephen had been right to pick him out as a good runner.

He turned back to assess the progress of the demolition workers and found that two of them had already disappeared under the heap of rubble. It seemed that the dog had indeed discovered a way in, and the men were busy shoring up a narrow passage in his wake. Stephen could see that progress was going to be slow. He was doing no good hanging about here. To the foreman he said, 'I'd be grateful if someone would come and let me know when you break through. I'm going across to see how they're coping with the fire and then I shall be at the casualty station.' He indicated the dispensary. 'I'll be back to assist with the injured.'

On seeing the man's puzzled expression, Stephen explained, 'I'm the camp's Medical Officer.' He climbed back into the Morris and set off across the tarmac to where the fire appliances seemed at last to be getting the conflagration under control.

The civilian stared after him.

'Blimey,' breathed the man, 'I thought he must be the Commanding Officer at the very least!'

It must have been twenty minutes before Stephen was summoned by one of the civilian workers.

'Mr Tuffnell has reached the door to the control room, sir,' he said. 'They're about to force it open.'

'OK,' said Stephen, 'I'll be across right away.'

He called Ross to his side.

'How long before we can say the runway is cleared for landing?'

'I'm just having markers put out to show the extent of the new flight path. Best warn the pilots that they'll have to take care to avoid the craters at the sides of the runway . . . there's no room for any sloppy steering!'

'Dan!' The runner appeared at Stephen's elbow. 'Get over to WO Pritchard and tell him that the runway is now ready for landing. Pilots to follow the markers. He'll know who to inform.'

'Sir!'

The boy sprinted away and Stephen turned to the fire fighters.

'Do you think you can save the fuel store?'

A blazing hangar was sending out sparks which, diverted by the wind, were falling dangerously close to a huge petrol tank nearby.

'We're keeping a hose trained on it all the time, sir,' replied the fire officer. 'We should be able to keep the tank from going up.'

'Good man.'

They both looked up to see a small staff car come belting across the field, careering dangerously around any obstacle in its way.

Stephen did not recognise the officer but he displayed the insignia of a Wing Commander and his presence filled Stephen with relief. He saluted as the car came to a halt.

'Flight Lieutenant Beaton?' snapped the senior man.

'Sir!'

'What exactly is going on here? I arrived at the camp office to find one WO2 on duty and no sign of an officer anywhere.'

'Yes, sir,' Stephen replied. 'That would have been the case. As you can see, we've had a bit of a flap on. All personnel capable of taking up an aircraft did so when the raid was imminent. The remaining officers appear to have been either in the control tower or the operations room when the raid began. As you can see, we are trying to reach those trapped in the ops room now.'

'I see . . . that's why your man said something about the MO having taken command?'

'There was no one else,' he replied flatly. 'I'd be grateful if I might hand over to you, sir? I shall be needed when they begin to bring people out of the basement.'

'Yes, of course,' agreed the Wing Commander, gazing about him, trying to sum up the extent of the problem.

'Sergeant Ross will put you in the picture, sir,' said Stephen and began to walk away.

The Wing Commander called after him, 'Need a lift?'

'It's OK, sir, my bus is over there.' Stephen pointed to where the Morris, covered in dust and looking somewhat the worse for wear, stood on the edge of the runway. 'Thanks all the same.'

The Wing Commander acknowledged this and added: 'I'll see you back in the CO's office when you're ready . . . and, Beaton . . .' Stephen turned back once more, impatient to be on his way. 'You did very well, son, very well indeed.'

'Thank you, sir.' Stephen climbed into the driving seat and sped across the runway just as the first of the returning aircraft appeared over the horizon.

Digger wriggled his shoulders, adjusted his harness for comfort and tightened the straps on his oxygen mask. These small aircraft gained height so rapidly that even when rising to levels below twenty thousand feet, pilots were advised to use oxygen when taking off, to compensate for the sudden difference in atmospheric pressure.

He must be quick . . . even as he began the take-off routine he saw the last of the Defiants leave the field. 'Steady, feller,' he told himself as his hands began to shake on the controls. He must carry out the procedures correctly if he were not to bungle this . . .

Prime the engine . . . The Hurricane's Kestrel engine required nine strokes of the pump.

Switch on . . .

Signal the rigger with thumbs up for contact . . .

The rigger acknowledged his signal and Digger pressed the starter button. Instantly the powerful engine burst into life.

Chocks away!

He waved his hand from the cockpit and the little bird of an aircraft leaped forward along the runway and into the air. He was just seconds ahead of the attacking enemy planes.

Digger soared to twenty thousand feet, turned on his tail and looked down at the German bombers below him. Dorniers . . . 215s by the look of them. There must be thirty at least.

He searched the skies above and behind him for their escorts. Yes, there they were, Messerschmitts . . . hovering above their charges like flies round a swagman's hat.

He made altitude rapidly, at the same time swinging his aircraft around in order to be able to face the enemy head-on. As he performed these manoeuvres, Digger pushed back his cockpit cover. A wise pilot ensured a quick get-away. The clear perspex gave no protection against enemy fire. The only part of the aircraft which was bullet proof was the windscreen itself.

He tried out the Browning automatic machine guns. Wing-mounted, they fired straight ahead. His thumb on the firing button felt clumsy inside his gauntlets. Using his teeth, he removed both gloves, allowing them to fall at his feet.

As the sound of his own weapons died, Digger heard the rattle of guns from a flight of Defiants attacking the rear of the enemy formation. His colleagues must have turned back on reaching the necessary altitude and were attacking the bombers which were fixed upon their course towards Manston.

Had they not seen the Messerschmitts?

Digger had taken to the air to save the Hurricane from the bombing, nothing more. Without the-back up of a full flight of aircraft, he could not use the tactics they had rehearsed so tenaciously all these months. If he got in amongst the enemy by himself, he might interfere with his colleagues' strategy and do more harm than good. He flew higher and stood off to observe the activity below him.

The main group of bombers flew straight across the airfield without dropping any bombs. Obviously they were destined for somewhere further on along the coast . . . Ford . . . Tangmere? As they cleared the area, the first of the Defiants swooped down on to the tail of the bomber formation and a lucky hit knocked one of the Dorniers out of the sky, its full load of bombs exploding in a fireball.

The Messerschmitts, alerted now, swarmed all over the British fighters and a fierce battle commenced. Digger saw his chance. With the

Defiants holding the attention of the German escorts, he could swoop in and take a pot shot at one of the bombers on the flank of the formation. This he did. Coming in sideways and taking the pilot by surprise, he loosed off his guns and had the satisfaction of seeing a great section of the bomber's fuselage ripped away. He dived under the aircraft and came up from below with all guns blazing, the shells pouring into the belly of the Dornier. As he spun away, gaining height ready for his next victim, the bomber slewed over, a pall of black smoke marking its passage earthwards. Three more of the bombers were damaged before the German escorts realised that there was a rogue Hurricane operating outwith the British attack.

The Germans had had little opportunity to gain the measure of this new British fighter. The Hurricane could outmanoeuvre, out-gun and out-run any of the German fighters. Stunned by the ferocity of the Australian pilot's onslaught, three of the Messerschmitts peeled off from the attack upon the Defiants which were attempting, against fearful odds, to make some inroads into the bomber formation. As Digger came in for yet another attack, he concentrated on his target and for a moment neglected to keep looking out for fighters. It was in that instant that the German bullets struck.

Crack! To his horror, Digger saw a section of his port wing disintegrate. The Hurricane balked for an instant and righted itself. Amazingly stable little craft, was his immediate thought. Crack! Again a cannon shell found its target and the Hurricane shuddered.

Recovering from this second impact Digger looked up to see a German fighter coming straight towards him. As they neared collision point, the Messerschmitt veered away to the left while Digger pulled to the right with all guns blazing. The German's machine-gun bullets showered the nose of the Hurricane. If Digger's shells reached their target, he was never to know. The German pilot, whether by accident or design, had found the most vulnerable part of the British fighter.

In order to obtain maximum aerodynamic performance and keep the weight in prime position, it had been found necessary to situate the gas tank right behind the engine and below the pilot's seat. When bullets exploded in the fuel tank, the cockpit instantly became an inferno.

For a few seconds, Digger froze in panic, watching in terrible fascination as the skin shrivelled and peeled back from his hands while they continued to grasp the steering column, seemingly unable to let go. As the flames shot towards him, he threw back his head to avoid the searing heat and heard his own voice crying, 'Dear God . . . save me!'

One damaged hand groped for the release button on his harness. Somehow he managed to break it free. With a movement born of instinct alone, he turned the aircraft into a wheeling dive and rolled out of the cockpit as the burning fuselage fell away behind him.

The shock of cold air rushing up to meet him after the intense heat which had been generated in the cockpit was sufficient to render the pilot unconscious. He must have tumbled over and over through the thin air for some seconds before he became aware of approaching aircraft and was again fully conscious. As he fell, his hand had automatically come to rest on the handle of his rip cord.

He pulled.

Relief flooded over him when he felt the parachute fly out behind. He reached for the shrouds and looked upwards as the silk canopy mushroomed overhead.

Digger stared in disbelief at the bloody pulps of raw torn flesh which only seconds before had been his hands. Mercifully, numbed by shock and cold, he felt no pain.

The parachute had drawn him up sharply so that his descent was now much slower. As the drone of engines grew louder he turned his head to watch the two aircraft which were following him down.

Single-engined . . . fighters . . . enemy planes for sure.

He was vaguely aware of a voice, praying loudly, ' "The Lord is my shepherd I shall not want," ' and realised it was his own.

There had been reports of German fighters firing upon helpless pilots as they parachuted to safety. Steeling himself for the final *coup de grâce*, Digger closed his eyes and waited.

The two aircraft overshot him and, surprised to be still alive, he opened his eyes again in time to distinguish the RAF roundels on the fuselage of one of the fighters. As they disappeared into the distance, the pilots waggled their wings in recognition. At least his descent would not go unrecorded. With luck someone would be sent out to look for him.

The ground below was becoming more distinct now. Digger could see that, if he was lucky, he was going to land on the gently sloping green turf of the chalk downland which on this part of the coast fell directly into the sea as a series of vertical cliffs: the Seven Sisters. He must have followed the bomber squadron along the coast as far as Eastbourne, nearly to Brighton, before losing control of his aircraft.

He could pick out the road running across the cliffs. A fence of barbed wire had been laid along its edge to repel invaders. He must certainly try to avoid that.

On the tightly cropped turf a flock of sheep grazed unconcerned, incongruous amongst the bristling defences.

With perhaps two hundred feet to go, Digger discovered that the evening breeze had already got up and, having reversed direction, was blowing back out to sea. He was alarmed to find that he was being dragged slowly but inexorably towards the cliff edge.

Desperately, he attempted to spill air from the parachute in hopes of landing more swiftly, but immediately he changed his mind, realising that should he land right on the cliff edge he was unlikely to have sufficient strength in his arms to release the parachute before it carried him over. Instinctively, his hand went down, seeking the knife which he no longer carried in his boot. It was only now that he became aware that the blast had torn away all his clothing below the waist . . . trousers, boots and stockings had completely disappeared.

In that instant, a stronger gust of wind caught the 'chute and he found he was looking down at the boiling surf below the cliff. Now his desperate movements were aimed at guiding his descent further from the shore. If only he could reach deeper water, away from the rocks . . .

Frantically he tugged at the shrouds and swung his legs in order to gain distance from the cliff.

When at last he sank into the waves, his last action before lapsing once more into unconsciousness was to turn the release catch on his parachute harness. The parachute drifted away towards the shore, but remained on the surface of the waves, providing a marker for the coast-guard who from his lookout station on the cliff above had watched the flier's descent and was even now directing rescuers to the position.

The cold salt water took away the pain which had begun to engulf him in those final moments of the descent. As he regained consciousness Digger was aware only of a feeling of extreme relief. His whole body felt numb. He floated on the water, his Mae West keeping him facing upwards so that he could see the edges of the fluffy white clouds turn to pink in the rays of the setting sun.

Now he began to be concerned about something else which, to his exhausted, befuddled mind, was even more worrying than his present predicament. Distressed at the all but naked condition of his body, he prayed that there would be no females present when he was landed ashore.

Digger was aroused from his stupor by the sound of a marine engine, put-putting as it approached slowly, searching for the downed pilot.

He opened his eyes to see the hull of a small fishing trawler drawing towards him sideways. A pair of faces peered at him over the side of the boat. One, wearing a peaked cap much faded by salt and weather, was clearly the skipper. The other held a boathook which he swung down towards the water in dangerous fashion.

It was clear that the fishermen were undecided about what they were going to do with their unusual catch.

'What d'yer think it is?' drawled one. 'Theirs or ours?'

'Dunno,' said another, regarding the naked torso, a look of disbelief on his face. 'Looks like a bleedin' mermaid t' me.'

The Australian, incensed at the delay in hauling him out of the water, felt a rush of adrenaline as he shouted angrily, 'Never mind who I am . . . pull me out, you fucking bastards!'

The two seamen exchanged glances.

'Must be one of ours,' the skipper decided.

The other agreed and reached for the collar of Digger's flying jacket with his boathook.

With considerable difficulty the two fishermen hauled the Australian over the gunwale and laid him on the deck. All compassion now that they had established his allegiances, they regarded his injuries with horror. Sprawled as he was amongst the entrails of the catch that they had been cleaning when the emergency call came over the radio, he looked as cold and bloody as the fish themselves.

The skipper went forward to the cabin and returned with a blanket. They laid him on it and wrapped him up tight.

It was time to start the engine and get away before the little boat drifted on to the rocks. While the skipper attended to his craft, his mate brewed tea in the galley and brought it to Digger who was by now beginning to thaw out. The flow of blood to the damaged parts of his body brought with it a pain as great as anything he had experienced in his entire life.

The skipper shouted down from his place in the wheelhouse, 'Give him a shot of rum, Fred. It'll warm him up and maybe dull the pain a bit.'

The mate poured a liberal quantity of spirit into the mug and propped the Australian's head and shoulders against the bulwark so that he could swallow the potent mixture. Digger gulped down the steaming liquid, feeling its warming balm travelling throughout his tortured body.

The mate disappeared in search of a second blanket. Digger, shaking from shock and fatigue, could feel tears trickling down his cheeks, stinging the seared flesh. Ashamed that he was powerless to stop the flow, he appealed to the mate on his return. 'You'll fetch Steve, won't you? When we get in . . . you'll send for Steve?'

'Not to worry, young feller,' the mate replied, kindly, 'just you get some rest. It will be another half hour before we can put you ashore.'

'Westcliff?'

'Bless you, no . . . Brighton's the best we can do with this tide. They'll take good care of you there.'

Digger did not want to die alone, among strangers.

'Can't you get me back to Margate?' he pleaded. 'Tell them at Manston . . . Steve'll come if you only say . . .'

The effects of his burns and the trauma of his descent and rescue at last overwhelmed him. In a haze of pain and alcohol, Digger drifted into unconsciousness.

Chapter Ten

For a few moments after the bomb dropped there was complete silence in the control room. The first indication that anyone had been left alive was the plaintive cry from a female voice.

'Damn! That was my last pair of silk stockings.'

The response, given by a disembodied voice from somewhere beneath the plotting table, was anything but comforting.

'Never mind, dear, winter's coming and lisle is very fashionable!'

As the staff began to extricate themselves from the wreckage, their individual groans and murmurings became one excited babble . . . a collective expression of relief that they and their companions had survived the explosion. For although a few huge blocks of plaster had fallen from the ceiling, the main structure of the reinforced room appeared to have held up against the blast. Only one wall had suffered substantial damage. Here, however, the concrete had shattered and fallen to create a pile of debris which had filled a corner and blocked the only door by which they might have been able to leave the bunker.

The CO attempted to make a move, cautiously at first, feeling his body for broken bones. To his surprise, he discovered that apart from a few cuts and bruises he was unscathed, so pushing away the lumps of plaster and piles of paper and other unrecognisable detritus which lay all about him, he struggled to his feet.

The low-voltage emergency lighting lent an eerie atmosphere to the place, and as others of the dust-covered staff began to move about, they seemed like ghostly apparitions wavering in the gloom.

Aware of the danger of sharp edges from broken furniture and glass from partitions and light fitments, Calcutt called out, 'Everyone keep still for a moment until we can see properly what we're doing.

Just remain where you are. Where's the Watchkeeper?'

'Over here, sir,' called out the WAAF Lieutenant responsible for the co-ordination of operations.

'OK, Lieutenant . . . take a roll call. Has anyone seen the Adjutant?'

'He's here, sir,' sang out a female voice, shrill with fear and shock. 'He seems to be trapped.'

'All right, lassie, keep a hold on yourself,' warned Calcutt in measured tones. He did not want any of these young women starting a panic.

He groped around under the sturdy wooden desk which had taken the brunt of the falling debris on his side of the room, and discovered the torch he was looking for. Its powerful beam scanned the faces of those around him.

He was relieved to hear so many of the girls calling their names in response to their officer's enquiry. At least a dozen female voices had answered so far.

'That the lot, Page?' he asked the Watchkeeper. 'Are any of your girls unaccounted for?'

There was a catch in the woman's voice as she answered, 'Just Dryden and Walters, sir. They were standing over there.'

She pointed to the mangled heap of concrete blocks and twisted metal on the far side of the room. 'They must be under that lot.'

'Thank you, Lieutenant.' Calcutt tried to keep his response matter-of-fact. 'We'll attend to them in a moment. First, let's see whether we can free the Adjutant.'

He swept the torch round until it picked out his second-in-command, spread-eagled on the floor almost entirely covered by debris. Working by the light of the torch, some of the girls tried to extricate him from beneath the loose material, but it soon became clear that Stumpy was pinned by one arm beneath a steel filing cabinet.

Stunned by the falling cabinet, the Adjutant showed no sign of life until Calcutt's torch was directed on to his face. Then Stumpy Miles stirred, opened his eyes and attempted to rise, but finding his arm pinned down sank back, unable to move the trapped limb for himself.

The aircraftswoman next to him tried to lift the filing cabinet but could not shift it. Calcutt made a passage for himself through the debris in order to help her. He moved a few pieces of masonry out of the way and got a grip on the lower edge of the cabinet.

'As I lift, you pull his arm clear . . . carefully now. We don't want to hurt him unnecessarily.'

A second WAAF moved over to Calcutt carrying a pile of ledgers.

'These'll take the weight as you get some purchase on her,' the girl explained.

Calcutt heaved on the steel cabinet, raising it a few inches, sufficient for the WAAF to push in one of the books. Grateful for her presence of mind, he released his grip and rested his arms before trying once again. This time he raised the cabinet several more inches and the girl managed to force in two more volumes.

'That should be it,' Calcutt decided, 'see if you can move his arm now.'

The first WAAF grasped hold of Miles's arm and applied what she considered to be firm but gentle pressure. All three of them heard a distinct twang. There was a sudden slackening of resistance in the trapped arm and the girl lost her footing. She sat down heavily on a pile of concrete and stared in horror at the result of her efforts. Stumpy's arm was free right enough, but everything below the elbow was missing! His dust-whitened sleeve lay flat and lifeless where his hand and forearm should have been.

The WAAF stared in disbelief at what she had done and keeled over in a dead faint.

Miles, who had regained his composure remarkably quickly, chuckled. 'Oh, cripes, she thought it was the real one!'

The girl's eyelids began to quiver and someone produced a bottle of smelling salts with which to revive her. When they told her of her mistake she went hot with embarrassment, only the fine white powder covering her face disguising her blushes.

The incident had relieved the tension somewhat and once Calcutt had retrieved the missing appendage from beneath the filing cabinet, everyone began to breathe a little more easily.

'Stumpy, is there any way to improve the lighting in here?' the CO demanded.

The operations room was the Adjutant's domain. He was supposed to know exactly how everything functioned.

'These lights are provided by batteries,' he explained. 'There is a petrol-driven generator only . . .' he lowered his voice to prevent the girls from overhearing '. . . if we start it, we shall be using up the air at an inordinate rate. The intake is over by the door, underneath that lot.' His glance travelled to the damaged wall. Both the door itself, and the air vent, were covered by piles of heavy concrete blocks.

'We have to find out if those two girls are still alive,' insisted Calcutt.

'Get the generator going. We'll turn it off again as soon as we have freed them.'

'I'll need help,' the Adjutant replied, holding up his stump. By the light of Calcutt's torch he addressed the WAAF who had extricated him. 'Aircraftswoman, give me a hand, will you?'

It was an unintentional gaffe, but once again it brought an amused titter from the other girls.

The women were all beginning to shuffle around more easily, each of them managing to clear a space in which to make herself a little more comfortable. Someone had discovered the First Aid box and was attending to the numerous minor injuries which they had sustained.

'Just stay still for a few minutes longer,' the CO urged them. 'Once we have some decent light we'll be able to start clearing up properly . . . see what we're doing.'

Under the Adjutant's instruction, his assistant had the generator running in a matter of minutes. At once the whole scene was flooded with bright light.

Calcutt rather wished he had left things as they were.

A tiny foot, shoeless and with only the tattered remnants of a regulation lisle stocking as covering, protruded from beneath the collapsed wall. Of the second girl there was no sign.

Picking his way carefully to the spot, Calcutt knelt down, removed some of the debris and uncovered the WAAf's arm. He felt for a pulse. Nothing.

He looked up as Flight Lieutenant Page joined him.

'I'm sorry,' he said, shaking his head.

The Lieutenant began to pull away more of the wreckage.

'Hazel must be under here too,' she declared, frantically. 'They were standing close together . . . she might still be alive.'

He feared her efforts would prove fruitless, but he was powerless to prevent her from looking. Soon others began to help, passing the lumps of concrete from hand to hand as Calcutt and Page worked.

At last, the dead WAAF could be dragged clear of the wreckage and two of the women helped Calcutt to lift her and carry her limp body away from the site. Someone found an overcoat with which to cover her. With little hope of finding the second girl alive, they returned to their task.

In a few minutes more, a corner of blue serge skirt was uncovered. Urged on by the thought that their comrade might still be alive, they made even greater efforts. In minutes they had removed the remaining debris from Aircraftswoman Hazel Marchant's body.

This time it was the WAAF officer who bent down with her ear to the casualty's chest.

There was a slight scuffle behind them and Calcutt turned swiftly to admonish those causing the disturbance.

'Quiet . . . we're trying to find out if she's still breathing.'

He looked enquiringly at Page, but the woman gave no sign either way. She grabbed at the girl's wrist and felt anxiously for a pulse. There . . . was that a flutter? Her fingers were busy with the uniform tie, loosening it and undoing the buttons beneath.

Calcutt gently moved her aside and placed two fingers on the spot where he should feel a carotid pulse.

Surely there was something? He too tried the wrist now. Yes, the girl was definitely still alive.

He pulled down her lower jaw and removed dust and debris from the inside of her mouth. Making sure her tongue was well down and her airway clear, he put his mouth to hers and breathed out, filling her lungs. She spluttered, coughed, and a trickle of saliva dribbled from the corner of her mouth. He wiped away the moisture with the clean handkerchief he had placed in his tunic pocket that morning, and tried again. Now she was breathing more easily, the coughing became more insistent.

'Do we have anything to give her to drink?' He looked round, helplessly.

One of the girls remembered the thermos flask from which she had poured their last round of tea before the bombing began. She dug it out and shook it.

'Sounds OK,' she declared, not hearing the expected rattle of broken glass. 'I'll see if there's any left.'

'Should we give her anything to drink?' enquired Page, anxiously. 'There may be internal injuries.'

'Just a little moisture,' Calcutt assured her, 'to make sure the throat is clear of dust. She seems to be breathing better already.'

As though to confirm this the girl's eyelids fluttered and her eyes opened. She gazed uncomprehendingly into the face of her Commanding Officer.

'Hazel . . . can you hear me, Hazel?' asked Lieutenant Page.

The girl seemed unable to understand what was going on. She stared about her, clearly frightened by the claustrophobic place in which she found herself.

'Answer me, Aircraftswoman Hazel Marchant,' ordered Page, desperate to elicit some response.

The girl raised a limp hand to her ear, her eyes troubled.

'I think she's deaf, ma'am,' said one of the other girls. 'P'raps it was the blast.'

'Yes, that's probably it,' decided Calcutt. He tested the girl's pulse again and seemed satisfied with what he found.

'Have we got anything to cover her with?' he asked, removing his tunic and rolling it into a pillow which he placed carefully beneath the WAAf's head.

'Here, sir.' Miles had slipped out of his own tunic, and handed it now to his CO. In shirt sleeves, the stump of his amputated forearm was exposed for all to see. The girl who had been helping him with the generator searched the area where they had uncovered the Adjutant, finding his prosthesis where Calcutt had placed it for safety. She brought it to him, holding it at arm's length by the tips of her fingers.

'Yours I believe, Adj,' grinned Calcutt, noting the manner with which the WAAF carried it.

Stumpy took the hand from her and examined it carefully.

'It looks OK,' he said at last, 'except for this broken strap . . . and a fastening has gone here. Thanks, m'dear,' he said to the girl. 'I reckon a decent needlewoman could soon put that to rights.'

The girl smiled and took it back, handling it less cautiously now.

'I've got a needle and thread in my pocket,' she said. 'I'll have a go at it while we're waiting, if you like?'

'Thanks,' said Miles. 'Could you work by the light of the torch, do you think? We really should turn off the generator now.'

He exchanged looks with Calcutt, still busily tending the injured girl. She appeared to breathe more easily when raised up, so he was supporting her in his arms to make her more comfortable.

Calcutt nodded his agreement and Stumpy Miles used his one hand to press the generator's off button. The emergency battery now provided the only light once again, but Stumpy held the torch for the WAAF as she worked. The other girls settled themselves as comfortably as they could and prepared to wait for rescue.

After a few moments he said, 'We can't sit here like this without my knowing your name. I'm Derek Miles.'

'Yes, I know, sir,' she replied, keeping her eyes on her sewing.

'Well?'

'Aircraftswoman second class, Audrey Dyer,' she answered, almost in a whisper.

'May I call you Audrey?'

The girl nodded, looking a trifle anxiously in the direction of Lieutenant Page. If the officer had seen or heard anything of which she disapproved, she gave no sign. Audrey smiled at him, her perfect white teeth glinting in the torch's beam.

'I suppose there'll be a young man outside, waiting anxiously to see you brought out of here?' he enquired.

'Not really,' she said. 'I haven't been on the base very long.'

'But you'll have seen the sights of Margate by now?' he asked, suddenly inspired.

'I used to go there before the war with my mum and dad . . . by steamer from Tower Bridge.'

'It's a bit different now,' he told her. 'There's soldiers camping in the amusement park, and part of the pier has been removed so it can't be used by the enemy, but there are a few cafés and pubs still open. Will you come with me, for a drink, when we get out of here?'

'Oh, I don't know,' she said shyly.

'Go on. I shall have to pay you back for doing all this work.'

'It's just a little bit of sewing,' she murmured.

'But the artificial hand . . . I know you don't really like it.'

'Oh, it's all right, now I've got used to it.'

By then she was manipulating Stumpy's prosthesis as though it was any piece of aeroplane she might have been given to repair. She could even look at the stump of his forearm now, without feeling sick.

At last she finished sewing.

'The fastening is a bit bent,' she said, 'but I think it will hold for the time being. Perhaps you can get someone to fix it in the engineering shop.'

'Yes,' he replied, 'that would be an idea.'

'Shall we try it?' she asked.

'You don't mind helping me?'

'Of course not.'

He stripped off his shirt and held out the stump while the girl fixed the prosthesis as though she had been doing it all her life.

The gentle touch of her fingers on his skin as she adjusted the harness straps over his bare shoulder made him quiver with excitement. She was arousing in him emotions he had rarely experienced before.

'There, how's that?' she asked, when finished.

'Perfect,' he said. 'Thank you very much.'

They sat together side by side without speaking, oblivious to the whispered conversations going on around them.

'Look,' he said, a trifle awkwardly, 'I really should conserve the battery in this torch. I'll turn it out for a while.'

He did so.

In the darkness he groped for her hand with his own good one and held it.

Audrey trembled a little.

'Don't be frightened,' he whispered, 'they'll come soon, I'm sure.'

'I'm not frightened,' she replied . . . and nor was she. Not with the Station Adjutant to protect her.

They had exposed the door to the basement room by the time that Stephen returned to the control tower. A passing aircraftsman had been persuaded to take charge of Shep, for the dog's activities had become more and more frenzied as the men had worked their way closer to where he knew his master to be. In his eagerness he had hampered them.

As the Morris drew up, the dog tore himself from the airman's grasp, and greeted Stephen so enthusiastically that the doctor was almost knocked off his feet.

'Sorry, sir,' the young man said, 'I just couldn't hold him.'

'That's all right,' Stephen answered, holding the car door open. 'Get in, Shep,' he ordered, and the dog meekly obeyed, settling on the rear seat with a forlorn expression. 'Stay there, old man,' said Stephen, rubbing the dog's ears. 'We'll be seeing him very soon now.'

He turned to the airman.

'Cut along, aircraftsman,' he said. 'Sergeant Ross'll find you something more useful to do.'

The airman saluted and hurried away to where the repair crews were still working frantically to make the runway safe.

One of the ARP men appeared at his side.

'Mr Tuffnell asks if you'll come now, sir. They're about to open the door.'

The sound of a heavy implement crashing into the steel door could be heard even as Stephen descended into the gloom. Tuffnell was standing back while two of his men used a large wooden post as a battering ram.

'Blast seems to have distorted the frame,' he explained. 'Either that, or there's something blocking the doorway on the other side.'

The implication of his words was not lost on Stephen. If the doorway was blocked, those inside would surely have made an effort to clear it and make their escape . . . unless they were all dead.

'Stop that racket,' he ordered suddenly. 'The pounding must have been heard inside. If there is anyone alive in there, they may be trying to attract our attention.'

The men set down their battering ram and Stephen, standing close behind the door, yelled, 'Hello in there . . . can you hear me?'

Silence hung heavily in the narrow passage. His heart sank.

'Wait a minute!' Tuffnell had his ear against the steel door. 'Try calling again.'

'Can you hear me?' Stephen repeated.

'There . . . did you hear that?' Tuffnell demanded. 'I'm sure I heard something. There's someone alive in there.'

Turning to one of his men, he said, 'There's only one thing for it. Bring the oxyacetylene gear down here, we'll have to cut through the door.'

The delay seemed endless. Stephen retreated to the outside and waited in the car with Shep until he saw the men manhandling a section of the heavy steel door out through the passage they had made. Tuffnell came over to him.

'There seems to be more than one of them alive,' he said. 'It's as we thought . . . a collapse inside the room itself. The men are trying to clear it now.'

'How much longer?' Stephen was concerned at the lack of air in the confined space. With several of them still alive, there could be little oxygen left by now.

Even as he asked, they heard a shout from down below and rushed to the tunnel, leaving the car door open. Shep, released from his prison, was there ahead of them. He darted below ground and his excited yelps when he found his master could be heard all over the field.

Stephen watched as the rescue men helped the dazed but otherwise unhurt WAAFs out into the daylight. He was relieved to see Derek Miles's smiling face as he assisted one of the WAAFs over the piles of rubble.

'Anyone else?' the doctor asked anxiously, expecting to see Digger Sheen following on behind.

'The skipper's down below with one of the girls who's badly hurt,' said Derek. 'There's one fatal casualty.'

Stephen didn't wait to hear him explain it was one of the WAAFs who had died. Fearing the worst had befallen his friend, he negotiated the tunnel and crawled through the opening which the rescue workers had made. The rubble had been cleared to one side.

He found Calcutt sitting there, still holding the injured girl who was conscious and moaning quietly.

Not allowing his eyes to wander in the direction of the swathed bundle in the corner, Stephen set about his examination of the patient. Heart and lungs seemed OK, but she had sustained several broken ribs. The crushed thorax indicated the possibility of internal bleeding.

One arm hung limply down and when he moved it she cried out in pain. He made a temporary sling to immobilise it, then felt her legs for any further breaks. Apart from a few grazes and some severe bruising, she appeared to be otherwise unhurt. He called for a stretcher and helped Calcutt to his feet. The CO had become cramped, holding on to the girl for so long. As he tried to put weight on his right leg it gave way under him. He rubbed at it vigorously. 'It's gone dead. She was no lightweight, that lass,' he explained, and yelped as the blood began to flow again into his numbed muscles.

'You're not injured?' asked Stephen.

'No, the only other casualty is over there.' He nodded towards the body in the corner.

Stephen moved over to it and hesitated before pulling back the covering.

A woman in her early-twenties . . . he thought he had seen her about the camp but did not know her name. He looked up enquiringly at Calcutt.

'She was one of the SD clerks,' the CO said, and Stephen remembered where he had seen here. Like so many of the girls who spent many hours every day poring over the brightly lit plot table, she had come to him suffering from ops eye, a condition in which the eyes puffed up and the whites became red. Vision was blurred, and the sufferer became lethargic and unable to concentrate. Stephen felt absurdly relieved that her eyes had recovered during the sick leave he had ordered, and had not yet had time to revert. In death her parents would see only the lovely young face to which they were accustomed.

'I must get back to the dispensary,' he told Calcutt, who was having some difficulty avoiding Shep's eager attentions.

'OK, old fella,' he said, 'there's no need to overdo it . . . I'm all in one piece.'

'It was Shep who insisted you were still alive,' Stephen pointed out, ' and it was he who began digging a tunnel to the door. Without him we might not have found you alive.'

'In that case,' the CO said as he cuffed the dog affectionately, 'we'd better order a special little something from the cookhouse.'

'What cookhouse?'

'How bad's the damage?' Calcutt demanded.

'Bad enough,' said Stephen. 'Best come and see for yourself.'

Out in the open, the CO looked about him in a dazed manner, unable to comprehend the extent of the damage to his station. Stephen drove cautiously to the Camp Office, avoiding the craters and debris left by the bombing. He pointed out the most significant areas of damage and explained the action he had put in train to set things to rights. They had almost arrived at the command post when he remembered the Wing Commander sent from Group to take over in Calcutt's absence.

'I was the only officer still functioning,' he explained, 'and had no idea what we were going to find once we had dug you out of the ops room, so I had the WO send for help. The Wing Commander is waiting in your office.'

'You don't know his name?'

'No, sir, I never thought to ask.'

'Always best to know who you're talking to, Doc.'

As Stephen looked a trifle crestfallen, Calcutt added hastily, 'You did right, boy. In fact, a great deal better than one might have expected of any Sawbones!'

'I thought that Flight Lieutenant Sheen was in the ops room with you, sir?' Stephen ventured. There had been no opportunity before this to mention what had been troubling him from the moment he had examined the dead WAAF in the bunker.

'He was,' replied Calcutt, 'but when the hostiles were getting too close for comfort, I had him take up the new Hurricane . . . against my better judgement, I might add, in view of his last escapade. I could hardly refuse him,' he explained, seeing Stephen's pained expression. 'I couldn't leave that beautiful kite sitting on the ground, just waiting to be destroyed.'

'No, I suppose not,' Stephen replied. 'I just hope he remembers where the brakes are!'

Once Stephen had dropped off the CO and his dog, he made his way back to the dispensary where his team of medical orderlies and volunteers seemed to have dealt successfully with most of the minor casualties.

'Dr Lewis went in the ambulance with the aircraftswoman they brought out of the ops room,' Devlin told him. 'He said he hoped to see you at the hospital as soon as you were free to leave the field.'

'I'll get along there right away,' Stephen confirmed. Then, noticing that the girls who had been working with Devlin were waiting for him to dismiss them, said, 'Thank you for your help, ladies. All the First Aid training in the world could not have prepared you for what has happened today. You did splendidly.'

He was rewarded with tired smiles and a warm feeling of comradeship. Not waiting even to drink the cup of tea he was offered, Stephen returned to his car.

'I'll be at the hospital if anyone wants me,' he told Devlin. Automatically glancing at the back seat to make sure that Shep was not intending to accompany him, he let in the gear and pulled away.

They had been working continuously in the theatre for a couple of hours and Stephen was beginning to anticipate a shower, a drink and an hour's rest before dinner in the Mess, when word came through that an ambulance was on its way from Brighton with a downed airman suffering from severe burns.

While the theatre sister prepared to receive the casualty, Stephen and David Lewis went out to wait for the ambulance. No doubt the flyer had been some time in transit and burns cases required immediate attention if there was to be any hope of a reasonable recovery.

In the event, David Lewis was alone when the ambulance arrived. He recognised the burned pilot immediately. Despite the huge blisters on his lips and forehead and the complete absence of either eyebrows or hair, Digger's massive frame was unmistakable. Ignoring the grotesque visage for the moment, Lewis examined the pilot's legs just to make absolutely sure. Yes, there was Stephen Beaton's handiwork right enough.

Considering the extent of those earlier injuries, the leg didn't look at all bad. Fortunately it had not sustained any additional damage.

Whereas the pilot's hands and arms looked – and smelt – like a poorly butchered joint of underdone meat. The ambulance men had wisely covered both arms with sterile cloths and left the injuries alone.

'We'd have taken him to Brighton General,' one of the men said, 'but he kept on about Margate, and someone called Steve. It don't look

THE POPPY ORCHARD

like the poor devil stands much of a chance anyway, so we thought we'd humour him.'

'You did the right thing,' said David Lewis. 'This young man is well known to us here. If anyone can save him, Steve Beaton will.'

He assisted the ambulance men to get the casualty into the theatre ante-room and went to find Stephen.

'Our patient has arrived,' he said. 'Better prepare yourself for a shock.'

'Why, is it that bad?' Stephen had become almost inured to the ghastly effects of burning aviation spirit.

'It's bad,' Dr Lewis answered, 'but what's more important . . .' he hesitated, aware of the bond of friendship which Stephen had formed with the Australian '. . . it's Digger Sheen.'

Without a word, Stephen pushed past him and ran the length of the corridor, the tails of his white coat fluttering behind him.

At the sound of the swing door opening, Digger roused himself from his morphine-induced stupor sufficiently to acknowledge Stephen's presence.

'Hi there, Doc,' he whispered. 'Here we are again.'

'Good grief!' said Stephen. 'What does the other feller look like?'

'Dunno, mate . . . never even saw 'im.'

Satisfied that he was at last in safe hands, the flier relaxed and dozed off.

Stephen examined all the burns intently. The facial injuries, although extensive, were at the worst second degree. The lowest lying tissues had not been affected and the top layers of epidermis would regenerate satis-factorily. There would be scars, no doubt, but with luck the overall effect would not be too bad.

The hands were another matter entirely. Stephen contemplated the charred flesh, noting that in places all skin had been removed and the bone itself was visible.

David Lewis had come to stand beside him.

'What do you think?' he asked. 'Amputation?'

Stephen had already asked himself this question but when voiced, it angered him so much that he turned on his colleague fiercely.

'Certainly not. I'm going to go for a repair!'

Unmoved by Stephen's outburst, Lewis took up a pair of scissors. 'Better get the rest of his clothes off then,' he said, and began the laborious task of cutting up the pilot's leather jacket so that it could be removed, piece by piece, without disturbing the wounded flesh.

'What kind of anaesthetic?' asked Lewis. 'His mouth is in a bad state.'

Stephen could see the difficulty of using a mask and decided upon local injections of Novocaine as the best solution.

Lewis searched for an unburned area of skin and eventually found it on the upper right arm. He wound around it a piece of rubber tubing and constricted the blood flow sufficiently to show him a vein suitable for inserting the hypodermic needle.

Stephen painstakingly removed every scrap of destroyed flesh, laying open the wounds and cleaning them thoroughly. He tied off the severed ends of blood vessels and carefully reconnected the cut ends of ligaments to their attachments, using the finest of sutures. His researches had shown that when ligaments were repaired immediately, there was a greater chance of reasonable movement in the fingers. The worst problems arose from the retraction of these delicate structures. If neglected in the early stages, the fingers curled up to form a claw which was almost impossible to straighten.

Once he had finished with these repairs, Stephen decided against the use of tannic acid on the open wounds. The widely recognised treatment resulted in the formation of a tough, black waterproof coating which prevented the escape of body fluids but left terrible scarring and limited the success of any grafting at a future date. Instead he laid paraffin-soaked gauze dressings over the damaged skin, ensuring that there would be no infection by bacteria. Finally he placed both hands in splints to prevent the anticipated retraction.

In addition to the facial burns which Stephen dealt with by washing the affected areas clean and covering them with sterile gauze, there was a deep gash on Digger's left cheek which stretched from ear to chin. With so much damage to the skin from scorching, he felt obliged to use his butterfly plasters technique to bring the lips of the wound together.

When all was done, the two doctors stood back to view their patient with some satisfaction.

'What's the prognosis?' enquired Lewis. 'I must admit that when they brought him in I thought we might be just tidying him up ready for his coffin. But now . . .'

'He has a good chance of recovery,' said Stephen, 'but whether he will thank us for making it possible . . . that's another matter.'

The older man nodded, sadly. They had seen so many pilots seriously disfigured in the past few weeks. The mental torments these patients must undergo would be with them long after their physical injuries healed.

'There is one more thing I can do for him,' Stephen decided without hesitation. 'I shall get on to McIndoe at East Grinstead right away. Nothing but the best for Digger.'

'Shouldn't you go through central clearing?' asked Lewis warily.

'Yes, but there's no time for red tape now. We can complete the paperwork later. For now, he goes to East Grinstead. We'll take on the powers that be afterwards.'

Chapter Eleven

Colin's days were now filled with pain, a terrible unrelenting agony which was exacerbated by a constant, raging thirst and relieved only by intervals of morphine-induced oblivion. He slipped in and out of consciousness, indifferent to his whereabouts and unable to measure the passage of time.

He was aware of soft-footed figures in white, who drifted from time to time into his blurred line of vision and spoke to him in hushed tones. Sometimes a group of them would hover at the end of his bed and whisper to each other before dispersing about their duties.

As the days passed, he became increasingly aware of another figure, also in white but sturdier in build, and with a deeper voice. He it was who inspected Colin's dressings, gave murmured instructions to his acolytes and whose soft cool touch was all that confirmed to the Australian that he was still a living, feeling human being.

As the pilot's wounds began to heal and the doses of morphine could be reduced, he gradually emerged into the land of the living with an aching head and an overwhelming desire to sleep, never to wake up.

At last the day arrived when Colin was fully awake when the time came for Doctor's rounds. Through slitted eyes, still puffy, stiff and sore from their singeing, he watched the surgeon approach . . . a good-looking fellow with thick dark hair, centrally parted and plastered close to his head with Brylcreem. Horn-rimmed spectacles gave him a mature, serious expression but his appearance was that of a man in his late-thirties, no more.

His broad shoulders and huge hands suggested a rugby football player rather than a surgeon – an impression which was reinforced by the flat

Colonial speech of a New Zealander. Colin wondered vaguely if he had ever played for the All Blacks.

'Ah, I see our *sleeping beauty* is awake at last, Sister. Good morning, Flying Officer Sheen, my name is McIndoe – Archie to my friends, of whom I trust you are one, even if this is the first proper communication we have enjoyed.'

His boyish grin lit up the rather heavy features. It was impossible not to take an instant liking to the man.

'Good morning, sir,' Colin responded, surprised to hear his own croaking utterance.

'Throat still a bit sore, I expect,' said McIndoe. 'Open up . . . let's have a look-see.'

Dutifully Colin opened wide and McIndoe shone his torch around inside the buccal cavity.

'Humph. You must have been singing as you fried . . . you were badly scorched in there. However, that will all heal up very nicely, given time. Now that you have returned to us in mind as well as in body, may I urge you to use sign language whenever possible, and give your voice a chance to recover.'

Colin could think of no emergency which would be pressing enough to cause him to use his aching vocal chords ever again, so rather than reply, he nodded sagely.

The surgeon began to remove the bandages covering Colin's arms and it was then that he recognised these as the gentle hands which had tended him so carefully during those terrible preceding days.

When at last his forearms were exposed, Colin gazed at them in horror. From elbow to wrists they were covered with pus-filled boils resulting from the massive disturbance of the blood caused by the excessive heat to which it had been subjected. From wrist to finger tips his hands looked as though they must belong to someone else. A Red Indian perhaps.

'Looks pretty awful, don't you think?' asked McIndoe, cheerfully. 'You may not believe this at the moment, but I can assure you that you are one very lucky young man. Whoever sewed up those hands in the first place made a very good job of them. It's what counts, y'know, getting in the basics in good time.'

Digger had only the vaguest memory of what had happened to him before he had arrived in this place. Steve Beaton had figured largely at one point, he felt sure, but it was all very hazy. Maybe he had simply been delirious. He remembered asking to be taken to Margate . . . almost crying in his attempts to persuade the ambulance men . . .

McIndoe examined the Australian's face carefully. The pustules were beginning to burst of their own accord and he was pleased to see pink skin appearing beneath the flaking tissue. The most important thing at this stage was to have as much of the skin surface as possible closed over to prevent infection. He examined the gash which Stephen had repaired in his own fashion and remarked to the RAF nurse at his side, 'You know, Sister, that fellow at Margate is a pretty neat surgeon. I thought only the favoured few knew about this kind of closing technique.'

Sister lifted back the bed covers so that the surgeon could make his routine reflex tests on the patient's legs. Stephen's handiwork of the previous spring was exposed. 'These are fairly recent wounds,' McIndoe remarked, running his finger along the thin white line which was all that remained of the tear in Colin's thigh. The lower leg showed more extensive damage and McIndoe noted the hollow pits where tissue had not regenerated. 'And as you can see,' he continued, 'a similar method was used to close them. I would suspect both operations to be the work of one man.'

Once more addressing his patient, he observed, 'You're quite a glutton for punishment, aren't you, feller? Just how many aircraft have you managed to prang in a very short lifetime?'

This casual remark reminded Colin that he had indeed taken down two expensive machines, and he began to worry for the first time about the CO's reaction to the loss of his precious Hurricane. Had the kindly surgeon realised the anguish his words would arouse in his patient, he would have been mortified. As it was, Colin remained silent, reserving his concern for the long hours of solitude during the sleepless nights which were to follow.

But from that morning on, Colin Sheen began to take an interest in the new world into which he had been transported. He soon realised that in the company of the blind, the one-eyed man is king. In his case, he was mobile, if unable to handle anything, while most of his companions in the ward were bedridden.

He devised a system for getting in and out of bed when Sister was absent from the ward, by flipping back his covers with his feet, and swinging his legs over the side of the bed. He could fetch and carry for his fellow patients so long as they had no objection to his holding everything in his mouth. He was reminded of old Shep, and thought fondly of the friendly hound with his viciously wagging tail. The recollection made him feel quite homesick for Manston.

In a ward full of burns victims it was policy to exclude every kind of looking glass. Only when patients were beginning to resume a reasonable appearance were they allowed to shave themselves, and going to the bathroom to wash was strictly against the rules.

Colin soon became obsessed with a desire to see his own face in a mirror. He had a pretty good idea what he must look like from observing his companions, but he would not rest until he discovered the truth about his own appearance.

Every morning he pleaded with Sister: 'Aw, c'mon, Brighteyes, just let me hop along to the bathroom for a sec . . . it won't take a minute.'

'You will be permitted to look in a mirror, Pilot Officer Sheen, when I say so and not before!' was her customary reply.

Between two and three each afternoon the patients were expected to rest before visitors were allowed entry. It was a time when the nurses too could afford a moment to read a newspaper, or to have a chat with their friends over a cup of tea.

Attention was at a low ebb for just one hour.

It was this time that Digger chose to slip out of the ward. Once outside, he paused, trying to get his bearings. From Sister's office at the far end of the corridor came the sound of women's voices, the occasional spontaneous burst of laughter and the rattle of spoons in china cups. Turning in the opposite direction, he went in search of the nearest bathroom.

He found it easily enough, and was relieved to discover that entry was by a swing door. He had been wondering how he might manage to turn an ordinary knob. Pressing his shoulder to the door, he entered the clinically white, echoing vault where every slight sound reverberated off the hard porcelain tiles which covered the walls from floor to ceiling and from the equally hard quarry-tiled floor.

He padded in his bare feet to a large mirror which stretched the length of a run of wash basins, and stared at his reflection in the glass.

A monster far more horrifying than anything which Hollywood could have devised stared back at him. With a primeval cry of despair Digger sank down on a stool beside the slipper bath and, unable to bury his head in his hands, lowered his chin on to his chest and sobbed. Hot tears stung his delicate, newly formed skin as they rolled down his scarred and puckered cheeks and soaked into the clean white bandages on his mutilated hands.

It was thus that Sister found him a few moments later.

'Serves you right, you silly man,' she cried on seeing his distress. 'My patients get to look in the mirror when I say and not before!'

Her words sounded harsh, but she too was weeping as she gently coaxed him to his feet and led him back to the ward.

The raid on Manston was the last for a while. The runway was quickly restored, and in view of the importance of the base as a first line of defence, much-needed improvements were introduced to the runway and to the system of lighting for aircraft returning after dark.

None of which prevented Calcutt from expressing his disdain for those in high places.

'They have to wait for Gerry to smash the place up before they make a move . . . the bastards did us a favour tearing up the field the way they did.'

Stephen and Derek Miles exchanged glances.

The loss of several good pilots and innumerable machines weighed heavily on the CO. His inability to take any part in the clearing up activities which had followed the raid still troubled him. As Station Commander it was his job to take control when things went wrong. His involuntary imprisonment below ground had left him feeling totally emasculated. He found it impossible to accept that there had been absolutely nothing he could have done in order to take command of the situation. While acknowledging the MO's part in getting the base back into service as quickly as possible, he could not accept his own ineffectiveness. In his eyes he had committed a serious offence, rather like falling asleep when on guard duty. He agonised over ways in which he might have freed himself from the bunker earlier, and dismissed Derek's logic when the Adjutant tried to reason with him.

The loss of so many of the ground staff, many of them WAAFs, also bothered him.

'Those stupid idiots at the War Office! What do they mean, sending women to a place like this? Don't they realise how dangerous it is?'

'This is total war,' Stephen observed. 'Far more women are being killed in their own homes as a result of the bombing – and at least our girls are making a fight of it. They're not just having to sit there and take whatever Gerry decides to throw at them.'

Derek thought of Audrey. How level-headed she had been after the bomb dropped – until she thought she had pulled his arm off! He smiled to himself and patted his top pocket where he kept her photograph.

Despite all of Manston's misfortunes, Derek Miles went about these days with a constant smile on his face which led his colleagues to suspect that there was something he was not telling them. Even the CO's gloom could do nothing to squash his exuberance. At last, unable to contain his good fortune any longer, he decided to confide in Stephen.

He chose one of those warm evenings in late-September to unburden himself to the doctor. There had been a flap on for most of the day, with enemy reconnaissance planes disturbing the peace every hour or so. The skies were clear at last and it had begun to look as though they might be in for a quiet night after all.

'There's something I've been wanting to ask you,' Derek began, digging deep into his pouch and spending an inordinate amount of time tamping tobacco into the bowl of his pipe.

Stephen waited patiently for a few moments but as the silence deepened he felt unable to contain his curiosity any longer.

'What is it, Derek?'

'Well, the fact is . . . um . . . I'm thinking of getting married . . . quite soon . . . and I wondered if you'd be willing to be my best man?'

'Right, fine.' Stunned by his friend's announcement, for a moment, Stephen was lost for words. 'Well, congratulations, old man. I hope you'll both be very happy! Do I know the poor unfortunate young woman?' he asked, the suspicion of a twinkle in his eye.

'She's one of the girls who was trapped with me in the control room,' Stumpy replied sheepishly. 'Audrey Dyer . . . perhaps you know her?'

Stephen recalled a rather dumpy girl with good teeth and a cheerful disposition. Nothing remarkable in her looks, but a nice, friendly face.

'Yes,' he said, 'I think I know who you mean. Well, this is something which calls for a celebration. I'll fetch us a drink. What'll it be . . . whisky?'

'Oh, right, thanks. Yes, Scotch'll do fine. Er, Steve, I'd be grateful if you wouldn't say anything just yet . . . to the others, I mean. We have to go and see the CO first and then there's the arrangements to make. We thought we might ask old Dobbie to do the honours. You know, pretty little country church and all that. Audrey is a bit of a romantic.'

Stephen hurried into the Mess to fetch the drinks. 'Well, fancy that,' he said to himself. 'Old Stumpy, of all people. Who'd have thought it!'

'There's a civilian lady at the gate, sir, says she has come to see you on urgent Ministry business.' Pritchard's voice betrayed nothing as he regarded the attractive young woman before him with the eye of a connoisseur.

'Have an escort bring her along to the dispensary,' Stephen ordered over the telephone. He was still only halfway through the morning's routine aches and pains, sore throats and calloused toes. What were the Ministry foisting on him now? he wondered.

The overlap between civilian and Service medicine seemed to be more blurred every day in this part of the country, where everyone was in the Front Line. Only yesterday he had been obliged to assist Lewis with a particularly tricky obstetrics case. Still, he supposed it was good to keep in practice. One never knew what kind of surgery one would be involved in once the war was over.

He heard the jeep pull up outside, and the flutter of excitement in the front office which heralded the arrival of the Lady from the Ministry.

The telephone rang again on his desk. Devlin's voice stated, blandly, 'The Ministry of Agriculture vet, sir, come about the sheep.'

A flock of sheep had been introduced on to the base to lend some authenticity to the camouflage applied to the new hangars which had replaced those destroyed earlier in the year. These resembled giant Nissen huts and had been sunk beneath mounds of soil and covered in living turf. From the air they resembled the rolling downland over towards Dover. Real live animals grazing completed a picture of rural tranquillity.

No one supposed for one moment that German High Command was fooled by this, but there was always the chance that an inexperienced pilot might lose his bearings and mistake Manston for a piece of Kent countryside. The sheep had seemed like a good idea at the time, but no one had bothered to mention to the CO that the wire fencing which could contain these persistent wanderers had not yet been invented. Sheep trespassing on the runway were a constant hazard to ground traffic, although even they had the sense to keep clear of aircraft landing and taking off. The occasional woolly casualty introduced a welcome addition to the rather frugal menu in the Officers' Mess, however, and for this reason alone the sheep continued to be tolerated.

There was a tap on the door and at Stephen's command Devlin threw it open to reveal Ellen McDougal standing smiling in the doorway.

'I really have come about the sheep!' she insisted, enjoying Stephen's confusion. 'It seemed too good an opportunity to miss.'

'Ellen!' he exclaimed, getting to his feet and coming to greet her. 'What a marvellous surprise.'

THE POPPY ORCHARD

'I waited patiently for your call,' she said, still laughing, 'but in the end the mountain was forced to come to Mohammed.'

'I really did mean to get in touch,' he insisted. 'It's just that things have been pretty hectic around here lately.'

'And for me too.'

He grabbed her by the shoulders and held her away so that he could take a good look at her.

'My, but you're a sight for sore eyes,' he declared, and kissed her firmly on the lips.

'I'll bet you say that to all the Ministry vets!'

'Only the ones wearing tweeds and squashy felt hats,' he laughed, as Ellen self-consciously smoothed her thick woollen skirt and straightened her misshapen hat.

'I have to wear sensible clothes when dealing with sick pigs . . . and randy airforce officers,' she responded.

'You look wonderful,' he insisted. 'Everyone around here is so pale and zombie-like, it's refreshing to see rosy cheeks and bright eyes for a change.'

'You'll be feeling my nose next to see if it's wet enough,' she chided. 'By the way, how did your canine patient get on?'

'Oh, the dog's fine now . . . you'll no doubt see for yourself. I'm surprised you haven't met him already. It's not like Shep to miss greeting such a distinguished visitor.'

As though on cue, they heard the sound of scratching at the door and when Stephen opened it there was Shep, ears pricked, tongue lolling, panting as though he had come racing at the double.

'Word must have got to him.' Stephen grinned. 'Shep . . . this is Ellen. Treat her gently, she's a special friend.'

The dog sniffed Ellen excitedly, finding her exclusive mixture of scents, farmyard and feminine toiletries, particularly interesting.

She crouched down and ran her fingers over the dog's flanks, tracing the wounds which Stephen had treated. In response, Shep stretched out and rolled on his back almost as though he knew that she wanted to examine his scars.

'You old hypochondriac, you!' laughed Stephen. 'Just because it's a lady vet.'

Shep licked Ellen's hand and sat down close beside her, leaning his entire weight against her legs. No higher mark of friendship could he bestow upon anyone.

Stephen suggested that they go over to the Mess for coffee. As they walked, Shep with his nose the regulation three inches behind Ellen's knees, she explained that she had come to examine the flock for signs of scrapie.

'The Ministry are clamping down on all diseases likely to inhibit meat production,' she explained. 'The next big move is to test every dairy herd for TB. There has been an enormous increase in the numbers of tuberculosis patients amongst the human population, as you must know, and they believe that unpasteurised milk may be the means of the disease spreading.'

'A bit more propaganda, I suspect,' said Stephen. 'You know as well as I do that it's lack of fresh air, and too many bodies crowded together in closely confined quarters, which are the real cause of tuberculosis epidemics.'

'Well, whatever the cause,' Ellen insisted, 'the plan is to have all dairy cattle attested. If a farmer wants to be registered as a milk producer, he has to have his animals tested. Any herd with infected cattle will have to be destroyed.'

'Some farmers may not take kindly to the slaughter of animals they have reared through several generations,' Stephen warned. 'Perhaps you should take a bodyguard with you.'

'Is that an offer?' she joked.

'I'm being serious.'

'I know you are,' Ellen told him. 'Actually, they send along a burly Police Sergeant just to make sure I get the job done without interference.'

'It can't be very pleasant.'

'It's not. . . but then, what jobs are these days?'

They had reached the Mess now and as Stephen pushed open the door and stood back for Ellen to enter, a hush fell over the assembled company. Suddenly a dozen young men sprang to their feet and instantaneously offered tea, chairs, a place by the stove – it was chilly today with a real nip of autumn in the air. Stephen waved them all aside and found a pair of armchairs, hastily vacated by some very junior flying officers.

'Sit here and I'll see if I can rustle up some tea,' he said. At the counter he overheard, 'Get the Doc . . . lucky old bastard!'

He turned on the speaker. 'She's my cousin, actually,' Stephen explained, and when they looked sceptical, 'why don't you come over and I'll introduce you?'

It took until the tea was ready for all the pilots to introduce themselves. Ellen accepted their obvious admiration as one used to causing a stir and held court in regal fashion.

'Are you here for long, Miss McDougal?' The younger men hung back when Stumpy Miles emerged from behind his newspaper to introduce himself.

'I'm staying in Canterbury, actually,' she answered, 'but I shall be working in this area for a week or two.'

'Perhaps your cousin would like to come to the shindig on Saturday?' he suggested to Stephen. And then to Ellen, 'I'm getting married, you see.'

'Oh, I don't think . . .'

'No, really, we'd love to have you come,' he insisted. 'The skipper has had so many of the girls shipped out just recently we're going to be short of dancing partners.'

'It's very kind of you.' She appealed to Stephen with her eyes for some indication as to how she should respond.

'Yes, Ellen, why don't you come?' he urged. 'It should be fun.'

'Well, thank you very much,' she conceded. 'I'd love to.'

Stephen gave Derek a glance loaded with meaning. Introductions were over and he wanted to talk to Ellen himself.

The Adjutant dismissed the crowd of eager young men with, 'Push off you lot, give the Doc a chance.' They all disappeared as though by magic, while Stumpy Miles cleared his throat noisily and retired behind his newspaper once again.

'You have to forgive the lads,' Stephen explained to Ellen. 'Most of them haven't seen a real woman for several weeks. We have been standing to constantly ever since the raids started on London.'

'What about these gorgeous WAAFs I'm always hearing about?' she asked, archly. 'Seems to me that there should be more than enough pretty girls about to keep the men happy.'

'It's not the same,' he replied, laughing. 'The uniform renders everyone asexual, if you know what I mean! Witness the distinct change in male attitudes when the girls turn out in civvies for dances. They treat aircraftswomen they work shoulder to shoulder with all week as though they were meeting them for the first time . . . but, joking apart, the CO has had as many of the WAAFs as can be spared shifted out. We lost rather a lot in the bombing back in August. He's never really got over it.'

Ellen became suddenly very serious.

'I sometimes wonder if I shouldn't become more involved?' she suggested. 'Put on a uniform of some kind.'

'Nonsense,' he replied, 'what you do is absolutely essential and there can't be too many people with your knowledge and experience.'

'I suppose you're right,' she agreed, 'but it is rather unpleasant to have to face the accusing looks I get sometimes from fellow passengers on trains and buses. I can't really turn round to them and say, "look here, I'm a Ministry vet doing essential war work," can I?'

'Perhaps you should wear the new Land Army uniform,' he suggested, grinning.

'Absolutely not,' she retaliated. 'You won't catch me wearing winceyette bloomers, especially when they're a pale shade of khaki!'

There had been a larger than usual number of emergency cases at Margate Hospital in the week leading up to Derek and Audrey's wedding. Although Dr Lewis had tried to manage without calling upon Stephen unnecessarily, there were several occasions that week when his surgical skills were required and on Saturday morning Lewis had called him in to take a look at a patient brought in from a fishing boat which had struck a mine, killing all but the skipper of the vessel.

The man had suffered a ruptured spleen which Stephen had been forced to remove. It would have been a tricky operation at any time but in this case the patient was already severely shocked and had suffered burns to his face and back.

They had rigged up a special sling to avoid further irritation to the burns on the man's back, his spleen operation making it essential for him to lie face up to ensure good drainage away from the site of the wound. Having adjusted the supporting apparatus and reconnected the drainage tubes, Stephen felt confident that he could leave his patient in Matron's capable hands.

He smiled to himself, recalling his discussion with the Prof last year. He had been so concerned at that time that he was getting no practice in surgery, he couldn't see how he could qualify for Registration. These days he was expected to turn his hand to anything, and in this case several problems at once!

When he removed his white coat to reveal his best uniform, Lewis appeared suitably impressed.

'You're looking particularly sharp this morning,' he observed. 'Going somewhere special?'

'I'm supposed to be best man at a wedding,' Stephen explained, glancing at his watch. 'I'm going to be late!' he cried in dismay. So absorbed had he been in his work that the time had simply flown by. It was already one-thirty and the kick-off was at two o'clock.

'Well, drive carefully,' warned Lewis. 'It's a wedding you're supposed to be going to, not your own funeral!'

'Anyone seen the Doc?' demanded Derek Miles, coming into the Mess to a chorus of wolf whistles. He was wearing his No.1 Service dress with a row of fresh-looking medal ribbons brightening up the otherwise sombre blue-grey of the RAF uniform.

'He had a call to the hospital just after breakfast,' offered one of the younger pilot officers. 'He said to tell you, if he was held up, not to wait for him . . . he would see you at the church.'

Derek studied his watch with a pained expression. Just after thirteen hundred hours. It would take about fifteen minutes to get to the village.

'I'll give him another ten minutes,' he said. 'Anyone able to give me a lift if he doesn't come by then?'

The CO appeared at that moment, also splendidly attired. 'You can come with me, if you like,' he suggested. 'But I do have to call in at the base on the way over.'

When one-fifteen arrived and Stephen still had not appeared, they decided to leave without him. At the base, Calcutt went into his office to telephone Headquarters and found himself involved in an argument with Higher Command concerning his replacement fighters.

'How can I be expected to keep up any kind of a defence with half a dozen Defiants which have been shown to be ineffective against Messerschmitts, three Bristols which should be in a museum somewhere, and a couple of Westland trainers? Oh, yes, I forgot. And I had to go cap in hand to the Fleet Air Arm this week. Westgate have let me have the loan of a pair of Swordfish! Do they expect me to fight this bloody war with my bare hands?'

He had been rattling away so fast that the person on the other end of the line could not get a word in edgeways.

'What's that?' Calcutt paused at last. 'When? . . . Well, yes, I think we can manage that. I'll alert the maintenance crew. Of course . . . the sooner we have them ready to fly, the greater chance we'll have of using them to good effect before they're destroyed on the ground. Can't you spare a few fitters to help us out? . . . Well, do your best, eh? Thanks.'

'What's up?' demanded Stumpy as the CO replaced the receiver and grinned up at him.

'A squadron of new Spitfires, ready for delivery.'

'For us?' Stumpy was incredulous.

'For us. Only trouble is, they'll be delivered by road tomorrow, and assembly has to be completed when they arrive. It'll take every mechanic we have to get them ready to fly before there's another raid.'

'It's a pity you turned down those WAAF fitters you were offered,' observed Derek.

'Yes,' agreed Calcutt, thoughtfully, 'but you've given me an idea.' He examined his watch. 'Come on, we're going to be late.'

Audrey was determined to make the most of her day and that included a traditional wedding dress.

She had scoured the whole of Canterbury looking for suitable material and had done some tough bargaining with a market trader for a bolt of white brocade which had been damaged in the bombing and sold off as defective stock. With her mother's wedding veil, and a hairband of wax orange blossom flowers, the simple gown looked quite lovely.

Mrs Dobbie, aware of the difficulty of finding flowers in a country-side dedicated to the production of vegetables, had offered to pick a bunch of her white roses for the bride. The simple bouquet was exactly right for the white dress and set it off to perfection. With her fresh complexion and dark brown hair carefully curled, while no one could call her beautiful, on her wedding day Audrey Dyer was as handsome a bride as had ever walked down the aisle of Manston Parish Church.

Stephen recognised the tiny dark red Austin Ruby, bearing the insignia of the Ministry of Agriculture and Fisheries, as soon as he drew up beside the war memorial. Good, Ellen had come after all. She had seemed a little reluctant to gatecrash someone's wedding, as she put it, but obviously she had changed her mind.

While he dithered in the centre of the road, a familiar figure tapped on the window. 'We're using the site of the Malt Shovel for parking.' Fred, the CO's driver, indicated the empty space across the road where the pub used to stand.

The blackened shell of the building had been demolished and the ground cleared a week or so before. The levelled plot now served as a car park for the village hall which, when not in use for Brownies and Women's Institute teas, was transformed nightly by the landlord into the village local.

Stephen lifted the bonnet of the Morris and hurriedly detached the distributor cap. If Fred was already here, it must mean that the bride had already arrived! The CO had agreed that the station's Humber should be used for the wedding and Fred had spent all the previous day washing and polishing all those parts not covered in dull camouflage paint.

Stephen passed the Humber now, on his way towards the church. On the rear seat, looking somewhat distressed and with a rather bemused, bald-headed little gentleman beside her, sat the bride. He gave Audrey a cheerful wave and received a watery smile for his pains.

At the lych-gate Mr Dobbie, resplendent in his special marriage vestments, waited anxiously. Stephen's heart missed a beat when he recognised the neat little figure standing at his side. It was Grace.

She had discarded her uniform for the occasion and looked cool and summery in a full-skirted flowery cotton dress.

'Grace, how nice to see you,' Stephen cried, rather breathlessly. He turned to the Vicar. 'I thought I was going to be late.'

'There can't be a wedding without a groom,' observed Grace dryly. 'Unless proxy weddings are in order these days?'

'I'm sure they'll be here soon,' said Mr Dobbie. 'Someone said that Derek was with Wing Commander Calcutt. They've obviously been held up at the station.'

'I feel sorry for the bride,' observed Grace, glancing over at the Humber. 'It's so humiliating to be kept waiting at the altar, as it were.'

'I'm sure that the delay is unavoidable,' Stephen soothed.

As though to prove him correct, at that moment the CO's own little red MG swept around the war memorial and slotted in behind the Humber.

Derek leaped out almost before the car had stopped and darted across to join Stephen without even a glance in the direction of his bride-to-be.

'Oh, Lord,' he exclaimed, 'what a rotten start! I should have waited for you after all. The CO had to make a phone call and it went on a bit.'

He did not attempt to elaborate as Stephen hurried him along the path and into the vestibule, leaving Dobbie to greet the bride and her father.

Inside the porch, a pimply Flight Lieutenant handed them each a hymn book and in a stage whisper that could be heard the length of the nave, indicated to Stephen where Ellen was seated.

'Your young lady is over there, sir, by the Memorial Chapel.'

Stephen glanced among the sea of faces and caught sight of his cousin waving to attract his attention. He turned back to Derek and was startled to find Grace close behind. It was clear that she too had followed the young officer's direction and was summing up the fair Australian with an enigmatic smile on her face.

Stephen, in an attempt to hide his confusion, urged Derek to proceed to the front pew where they took up their allotted places, while Grace slipped into a rear pew beside her aunt.

At the same moment, the organ began to play.

Chapter Twelve

For the wedding breakfast Derek had arranged to take over the village hall. Mr Clark, the landlord of the Malt Shovel, had been only too pleased to be asked to do the catering, especially since the RAF chef from the base had managed to help him out with some of the major ingredients. Corned beef and egg sandwiches – the local poultry farmer had been persuaded to increase Manston's allocation for the occasion – and pilchards with fresh green salad. It constituted a feast at a time when food rations were becoming more and more restricted, even for service personnel.

Mrs Clark had done her best to make the sombre hall look festive with vases of wild flowers gathered from the hedgerows and paper streamers saved from some Christmas long ago. The centre piece of the decorations was the wedding cake. One had to examine it very closely to discern that the elaborate white icing was only a cardboard covering. When the time came for the cake to be cut, the ceremony was simulated, the bride and groom placing the knife in a pre-prepared slot and making a cutting motion as the cameras clicked. Afterwards, Mrs Clark whisked away the marvellous edifice and executed the cutting of the real single-tier cake in the tiny kitchen behind the stage.

Everyone had chipped in with drink for the occasion. The Officers' Mess had surrendered several bottles of precious Scotch, while the parents of both bride and groom had arrived with carrier bags filled with a variety of bottles: wine from the cellar of Streatley Manor, home of Colonel and Mrs Miles, and stout from the cellar of the Nag's Head, Balham, Albert Dyer's local, the only building in the street to have escaped the raids.

Mrs Dobbie had contributed six bottles of her own elderberry wine of 1939 vintage, just ready for drinking, while Mr Clark's contribution was a barrel of cider, made using his own ancient apple press which, stored in the cellar of the Malt Shovel, alongside the beer, had miraculously escaped the conflagration and was at this time of the year in regular use. The one thing which was not rationed on this occasion was the goodwill of those gathered to wish Derek and Audrey happiness on their wedding day.

Nor was there any shortage of speeches.

To Stephen, as best man, fell the task of reading out the messages of congratulation from those unable to be there on the day. There were letters and cards from absent relatives on both sides, and several telegrams from RAF colleagues posted elsewhere in recent weeks.

Stephen was taken completely by surprise when he tore open one small yellow envelope and read:

CONGRATULATIONS MATE STOP WISH I COULD HAVE BEEN WITH YOU TODAY STOP DRINK A COUPLE OF BEERS FOR ME STOP DIGGER

Stephen's voice faltered. It was not that they had forgotten Colin Sheen, fighting his own particular battle alone in strange surroundings. There had simply been too much going on, during these past days, to be able to leave the base and pay him a visit. He really had intended to go and see the poor old chap . . .

He wondered how Digger had heard about the wedding and assumed that Derek had written to him.

The toast to the bride was given by Audrey's father.

He rose to his feet uncertainly, and the noisy guests were suddenly hushed, all attention.

Albert Dyer was out of his depth among the public schoolboys and university graduates who constituted the Officers of Manston's No. 11 Squadron, Fighter Command. His South London accent might have been more at home in the NCOs' Mess. He began nervously, voice strained and tight, so that someone at the back of the hall called out cheerily, 'Speak up!'

He cleared his throat and began again. His sentiments were those of any father for his daughter.

'The missus and me, we're very proud of our girl. She got a scholarship to Grammar School, y'know, and we thought that when she got her School Certificate she'd be able to work in a bank, say, or one of them posh shops in the city. Then the war come, and before we knew it she was in the RAF and doing a really important job with you people. Well, now she can hold up her head with the rest of you and when this little lot is all over I hope that she and Derek here,' he glanced across at his new son-in-law with a friendly smile, 'will be able to set up a nice little place together and have a family. What more can any of us hope for?'

His wife nudged him. He had left out the most important bit.

'Oh, yes,' he concluded. 'I'd like to thank all the kind friends who have contributed to this feast. I understand that the whole village as well as the air base has chipped in, one way or another. That just shows how highly everyone regards Derek and my little girl. It's very kind of you all. Thank you.'

He sat down to hearty applause, stimulated by liberal supplies of Mr Clark's scrumpy.

There had been a raised eyebrow or two between some of the more snobbish guests present. Did old Stumpy appreciate what sort of a situation he was marrying into? Weren't Audrey's parents a bit . . . well . . . working-class? Just look at the woman's outfit . . . I know there's a war on, but really!

During the dancing that followed, Stephen overheard one or two such remarks which angered him. Turning roundly on one commentator, he snapped, 'She was good enough to be working in the plot room with him, wasn't she? Nearly got herself killed doing it. Remember, you people rely on girls like Audrey to get you home.'

Shamefaced, the speakers turned away with a mumbled apology, while Ellen, who had been dancing with him at the time, applauded Stephen's intervention.

'That needed saying,' she told him. 'Mrs Dyer has been telling me that their house was bombed two nights ago . . . they were both buried in the rubble for several hours. They lost everything. He's wearing a borrowed suit and she had to find something at the WVS centre.'

Stephen glanced across to where Mary Dobbie stood deep in conversation with Audrey's mother. He took in the long navy dust coat which hung just a little too snugly around the broad hips, and the unfashionable black straw hat with weary-looking silk roses on the brim. Only then did he register the tired shadows beneath the woman's eyes and the slight flush on cheeks which still bore the bruises and scars of her ordeal.

Until now Stephen had seen nothing exceptional in Stumpy's choice of a bride. There was quite a difference in age, of course, and Stumpy was an officer while Audrey was not, but it hadn't occurred to him until now that there could be any other barrier to the union. Over Ellen's shoulder, as they danced, he spotted Derek's father, attempting to put Albert Dyer at his ease by exchanging tales of exploits in earlier wars.

Colonel Miles was a tall willowy figure who even in his late-seventies retained the straight back and squared shoulders of the professional soldier. He bent his head to catch Albert's words and laughed heartily at the anecdote. No problem there that Stephen could see.

As he steered Ellen around the floor to the music of the station's own amateur quartet of drums, double bass, fiddle and saxophone, Stephen picked out the lady in pink chiffon who had been introduced to him as Charlotte Miles, Derek's mother. She was standing beside the buffet table, deep in conversation with Grace Dobbie.

'Strange woman,' Ellen observed, as though reading his thoughts. 'If she's Derek's natural mother she must be nearer sixty than forty. Either she's married to a much older man, or she's wearing extraordinarily well!'

Stephen wondered if Mrs Miles's youthful appearance might be due to some expert plastic surgery as well as the kind of expensive beauty treatments apparently enjoyed by American women. Funny, Stumpy had never mentioned that his mother was American . . .

'You know, I really ought to be circulating more than this,' Stephen said suddenly. 'Do you mind if I hand you over to this harmless young chap? I guarantee he won't step on your feet too often!'

He grabbed a passing Flight Lieutenant.

'Wacko, would you be kind enough to take over from me here . . . duty calls!'

Wacko, only too happy to oblige, gathered Ellen in his arms and whisked her away, leaving her no chance to protest.

Stephen crossed the floor to join Stumpy's mother and her companion.

'I do hope you're enjoying yourself, Mrs Miles,' he interrupted their conversation.

'A nice little wedding,' the woman condescended, then added in a derisive tone, 'considering . . .' She did not elaborate and Stephen deliberately misinterpreted her meaning.

'We all have to do the best we can in the circumstances,' he told her. 'At least we can thank Gerry for giving us a raid-free afternoon.'

'I gather that things have hotted up considerably since I was last here,' Grace put in. 'The boys have been telling me about the damage done to the base.'

'All cleared up now,' said Stephen, consciously avoiding any reference to the severe casualties. There were too many familiar faces missing today.

It had taken some persuasion on her husband's part to get Mrs Miles to attend her son's wedding. Having waited so many years to see him settled, she could not help being disappointed at such an unsuitable match.

'It really is time we were going,' she said now, glancing pointedly at the tiny gold watch on her thin wrist. Clucking in an irritated fashion, she went off in search of her husband.

'She sounds like some old hen calling her chicks,' Stephen couldn't resist remarking.

'I must say, she doesn't seem too happy about her new daughter-in-law,' Grace observed. 'It's such a pity. Audrey seems absolutely right for Derek.'

Their attention was drawn towards the bride and groom who were, at that moment, receiving some ribald banter from Squeaky Piper and what remained of B flight.

Watching the tight-knit little group surrounding Stumpy and his radiant bride, Grace found herself forced to comment, 'Colin is very conspicuous by his absence. It's such a shame he can't be here.'

Stephen had noticed before that she never referred to the Australian as Digger. Her use of his Christian name seemed to place her relationship with him in a category a little more intimate than mere friendship. Stephen had hoped that their attachment had been restricted to Digger's time in the Margate hospital. Was it possible that Grace had continued to keep in touch with him?

'I've been meaning to go and see him,' Stephen admitted lamely. 'There just hasn't been a time when I could get away for long enough . . .'

'It's no more than a couple of hours' drive to East Grinstead,' Grace pointed out. 'He's been asking about you.'

'Have you been there yourself?' Stephen asked.

'No . . . he won't allow me to see him yet. Says he's not a pretty sight and I should wait until he's more presentable. I have been writing, though, and he gets one of the nurses to reply for him.'

'East Grinstead . . . isn't that where Archie McIndoe is working?' Mrs Miles had rejoined them, her search for her husband unrewarded. 'Such a talented man . . . a wonderful plastic surgeon, you know.'

Realising suddenly that she might have let a cat out of the bag, she covered her confusion by adding, 'Some of my elderly friends were treated by him States-side before the war.'

So Stephen had been right, it was a plastic surgery job she'd had done. His glance assessed her neck and the line of her jaw. Almost invisible, but there, if you knew what you were looking for, were the tell-tale white lines indicating the passage of the surgeon's knife. It was a job anyone could be proud of. Digger was certainly in good hands if that was an example of McIndoe's work.

'It's a lovely part of the country . . . East Grinstead,' ventured Grace, attempting to include Mrs Miles in their conversation. 'Much nicer than where we are. The Royal Masonic is housed in a ghastly mausoleum out in the sticks in Berkshire. Actually, I thought I might apply for a transfer to McIndoe's burns unit myself.'

Torn between his wish to see Grace move to somewhere within reasonable distance of Manston and the knowledge that such a transfer could bring her daily into contact with one whom he must regard as his rival for her affections, Stephen was at a loss to comment.

Mrs Miles quickly filled the vacuum.

'Oh, my dear, you must . . . such a worthwhile job, putting our poor burned boys to rights.' She spotted her husband at last, no longer in the clutches of that awful little man. 'Ah, it looks as though things may be moving at last . . . Geoffrey . . . Geoffrey!'

It crossed Stephen's mind that had she had an umbrella, she would have gone off waving it.

'I've had quite a chat with your Australian girlfriend,' Grace said, watching the bridegroom's mother depart in a mist of swirling pink and Chanel No.5.

'Not a girlfriend exactly,' Stephen was quick to put her straight, 'more like a cousin actually . . . she's my grandmother's step-grand-daughter, if that makes any sense?'

'But you have seen quite a lot of each other?' Was Grace playing games with him? To his sensitive ear, the question seemed loaded with meaning, and she had that teasing little smile playing about her lips. God, she was beautiful today!

'I spent some time with her people in Western Australia a few years ago. We were young kids at the time . . . she was all moonlight and roses. You know how girls are at that age!'

Grace was quick to notice the guilty flush when Stephen dismissed his relationship with Ellen.

'And since she's been over here?' Grace pursued the subject relentlessly.

'My mother has promised Ellen's father to keep an eye on her . . .

we've met in Glasgow from time to time.' If he was conscious of any hint of disloyalty in his words Stephen thrust this aside. His infatuation with Grace was such that nothing must be allowed to stand in the way of his relationship with her.

'If this hospital of yours is out in the sticks,' he hurriedly changed the subject, 'where do your patients come from?'

'From airfields all over Southern England,' she replied, 'and of course now that the raids on London are so bad, we receive quite a lot of civilians. They make an awful fuss about being taken so far from home. It's difficult for relatives to visit them and what with worrying about their homes and their families, they can be pretty miserable to work with. That upsets the nursing staff generally and it's all pretty depressing. I really think a transfer to an all-Service unit would be an improvement.'

'Well,' said Stephen, hopefully, 'if you do go to East Grinstead, there'll be a better chance for us to get together . . . I'll certainly find time to visit Digger very soon.'

Their conversation was interrupted by Group Captain Calcutt.

'Sorry to talk shop, Doc,' he gave Grace an apologetic smile, 'but I'm calling a meeting of all pilots not scheduled for normal flying duties at twenty-two hundred hours. I'd like you to be there.'

'What's up?' demanded Stephen.

The CO placed his index finger against the side of his nose and said in a loud stage whisper, 'Walls have ears.' He was grinning as he spoke so Grace could hardly take offence. When in the next breath Calcutt offered her his arm, demanding that she dance the quickstep with him, she accepted readily. They whirled away into the crowd, leaving Stephen wishing he had thought of asking her himself while he had the chance.

'A formidable lady, that,' Ellen observed, joining him the instant he was free. 'She'll need all the courage she's got when she marries her pilot. I understand he was very badly burned?'

Stephen stared at her in disbelief. 'What do you mean, *marries*? I didn't know she was getting married!'

'She was telling me about her fiancé . . . Colin, is it? I gather he was badly injured during the raid on Manston.'

Stephen swallowed hard before answering.

'Grace never said that they were engaged . . . I wonder why Digger never mentioned it himself?'

There was a flurry of activity at the far end of the hall. The happy couple were on their way at last.

Outside in the gathering gloom Stumpy Miles pecked his new

mother-in-law on the cheek, avoiding the bruising which had become more obvious as the evening wore on.

'You take good care of yourselves,' he said, solicitously. 'A few days in Torquay will do you both good, and Audrey will be able to enjoy her honeymoon all the more for knowing you're safe.'

'Don't you worry about us, son.' Mr Dyer enjoyed using the term for Audrey's husband. 'The Mrs and me'll be fine. When we get settled in a new place, you will come and stay with us, won't you?'

'Of course we will.' Audrey kissed her dad, giving him a big hug.

Charlotte Miles, making the minimum of effort to disguise her disappointment in her new daughter-in-law, allowed Audrey to brush her heavily pancaked cheek with lips from which the lipstick had long-since vanished, and shuddered ever so slightly. Passing on to her son, she hugged him tightly, making the contrast in her feelings for the pair very clear.

Audrey turned to her father-in-law.

'I'm so pleased you decided to become a part of our family,' he told her, catching her in his arms and kissing her soundly on the lips. He caught sight of his wife's disapproving glare and deliberately kissed Audrey a second time.

The Humber drove off into the night, a string of tins and a pair of old boots trailing behind. Fred was to take them as far as Eastbourne where they were to spend the night before carrying on to Ilfracombe by rail. To two people who had seen little else but the plot table for the past three weeks, seven days of freedom seemed to stretch ahead into infinity. Audrey snuggled into his shoulder and Derek used his one good hand to stroke her hair back from where it had fallen into her eyes in those last few moments before their departure.

'Happy?' he asked.

'Deliriously,' she replied.

He pulled down the blind behind Fred's head before taking her in his arms.

Outside the village hall, Mr and Mrs Dyer stood gazing forlornly down the road after the departing vehicle.

'I 'ope she knows what she's doin',' murmured Queenie. 'What's a bloke with only one 'and goin' to do to make a living in peacetime?' She remembered the city streets of the 1930s when mutilated war veterans sold bootlaces and matches in order to scrape a living.

THE POPPY ORCHARD

Albert laughed at her concern. 'Don't you worry, Queenie . . . that Derek has managed well enough so far, and the Colonel will see them orl right, just you wait and see.'

Overhearing this exchange Stephen, his thoughts once more upon Grace and the startling news of her engagement, wondered how it was that women instinctively turned to those men who needed their support and seemed quite heedless of their infirmities. Recalling the terrible state of Digger's hands and the ghastly scars on his face which he must inevitably bear for the rest of his life, Stephen found it incredible that a beautiful young woman like Grace could even contemplate such a union.

'Well, I must be on my way,' Ellen interrupted his thoughts. 'I have to drive over to Burwash in the morning to talk to a few sheep.'

Stephen turned. An expression of hurt and bewilderment lingered in his eyes.

'Maybe I should have kept my mouth shut about Grace and her flier?' Ellen watched his face carefully as he struggled with his emotions.

'Eh? Oh . . . no . . . I was just surprised that Digger had said nothing to me,' he told her. 'I thought we were friends enough for him to have shared such important news.' He paused, still marvelling that Grace could contemplate marriage to a man so severely injured. 'I hope she's not marrying him out of pity.'

'I think there's more to it than that,' said Ellen. 'It sounded to me as though she was marrying him despite, not because of, his injuries.'

Not wishing to continue this discussion a moment longer, Stephen asked her, 'Where will you be going to after Canterbury?'

'Back to Aberdeen for a short while,' she replied. 'After that, who knows?'

'Will you be able to call in on the folks in Glasgow?' This was safer ground for them both. 'I've had plenty of letters, of course, but I haven't had a chance to get home since Christmas.'

'Aunt Annie knows I'm due to travel North any day . . . I think she's expecting me to stay a night or two. She'll be pleased to hear that I've managed to get over to see you, at last.'

Not having heard from Stephen himself for so long, Annie had extracted a promise from Ellen that she would look him up if she possibly could and report back as soon as possible. Talking to the pilots today, Ellen had understood more clearly the ordeal they had all endured during the past weeks and realised that Stephen had had a large part to play in the process of keeping the station's personnel fit for operations. He really did look exhausted.

'Can't you take a few days off yourself?' she asked. 'It would be rather nice if we were to travel North together.'

Stephen was due for leave.

He had been dreaming of persuading Grace to spend some time with him, up in London perhaps . . . he'd have to forget about that now. Perhaps he should go home and check up on his parents.

'Look,' he said impulsively, 'let me know when you're ready to travel and I'll see if I can join you.'

Ellen, more sensitive to the situation than Stephen could possibly have imagined, understood that her company would be only second best in his estimation, but where her cousin was concerned she knew no pride.

'Right,' she said, stepping into her car. 'I'll give you a ring just as soon as I know when I'm leaving.'

He stooped to kiss her goodbye through the open window. It was just a brotherly peck on the cheek.

Ellen, disappointed and struggling to hold back her tears, managed to drive well out of the village on the Canterbury Road before she was obliged to pull over and give vent to her emotions.

The day had been a disaster . . . she wished she had never agreed to come! Angry with herself for being unable to prevent the flow of tears, and furious with Stephen for being so blind to her affections, her uninhibited sobbing attracted the attention of a pair of horses who emerged from the gloom to gaze intently at her from the far side of the fence.

She reached through the open window and fondled the soft nose which was thrust into her palm.

'It's times like this when one finds out who one's true friends are,' she told the horse, ruefully.

Ellen climbed out of the car and reached for some apples which were hanging from a branch, just out of the animals' reach. She fed them both, patting each silky neck in turn and wiping her damp cheeks on the back of her hand. When their soft snuffling and delighted whinnies had calmed her sufficiently, she climbed back into the car and started the engine. With a little wave of a white hand in the darkness she drove off into the night.

Stephen watched the car out of sight. He had been unable to avoid the hurt in Ellen's eyes and cursed himself for an unfeeling wretch. Well, it was too late to make amends now. He turned to where the Group

Captain was gathering up some of his men for a lift back to camp.

What was this about a meeting in the briefing room? he wondered, forcing himself to think of less personal problems. He glanced at his watch, realising suddenly just how late it was. Fifteen minutes was all the time he had to get back to camp.

With the heavy blackout curtains securely closed, the fug in the smoke-filled briefing room was almost unbearable. There was plenty of coughing and many uncomplimentary remarks about old socks when Stephen produced his pipe and lit up.

'Good heavens, Doc . . . can't you find a better use than that for used dressings?' one wit enquired. A number of coarse suggestions followed and, amidst the general banter, the appearance of Group Captain Calcutt, accompanied by the Flight Engineer, WO1 Tony Poulson, went almost unheeded. Only when the Deputy Adjutant hammered on the table did silence reign at last.

'Good evening, gentlemen.' The CO was positively beaming. Could he actually have some good news for once?

'I have been informed by Fighter Command that No. 11 Group is to receive a squadron of Spitfires to replace the Defiants lost in the past few weeks.'

A frisson of excitement followed these words.

'If it was to be Spits after all, why send us a Hurricane to practise on? Typical War Office botch-up if you ask me . . . About time too . . .'

'The aircraft will arrive in batches of three, by transporter, during the next four days. They come minus wings and other essential bits and pieces, which means that the fitters will be working all out to get each batch ready for test flying before the next three arrive. I want these kites ready for combat and all of you prepared for flying them as soon as possible. The Adjutant will distribute manuals which I want you all to study. Once the first three aircraft are ready to be tested, you will go up for trials, beginning with A flight.' A few chortles followed this rather obvious decision.

'I have brought Warrant Officer Poulson along this evening to run over some of the finer points of the new Mark IIA Spitfire,' Calcutt continued. 'A few of you have already had the privilege of flying Spits, I know, but the new machines have a few refinements that even *you* will want to know about. Once Mr Poulson has had his say, I'd like an open discussion so that we can pool all the knowledge we have.'

There was a general buzz of conversation while WO1 Poulson set up his epidiascope.

Stephen, pleased to be included in the briefing, wondered nevertheless what his part in the operation might be. He had not long to wait.

Calcutt cleared his throat and gained instant attention.

'We've all been pretty stretched these past weeks,' he began, noting the shadowed eyes and parchment-coloured faces of some of his men; all of them looked old before their time. 'This change over of machines gives us an opportunity to take stock.' He glanced in Stephen's direction. 'I want every pilot to take a full medical examination, Doc. My new aircraft are too precious to be placed in the hands of the halt and the lame.' There was a titter of nervous laughter. The one thing every pilot dreaded was to be grounded for medical reasons. Nervous exhaustion was the most common explanation given, but it displayed itself in many different ways. Hypertension, bad temper and over reaction to minor incidents, the appearance of strange rashes and apparently unaccountable stomach pains, were the symptoms for which Stephen would be looking.

His glance met Calcutt's and he nodded briefly.

'I'll post a schedule of appointments in the Mess,' he agreed and rose to go.

'Feel free to stay and listen,' said Calcutt, knowing of Stephen's interest in flying. 'You never know . . . we could be that short of pilots, ones of these days!'

'Heaven forbid!' cried Squeaky Piper to a chorus of derisive comments. Stephen laughed with them. The tension was broken. Now they were able to concentrate fully on the description of the new aircraft given by the Flight Engineer.

The meeting broke up around midnight.

Calcutt turned to Mr Poulson with a weary grin.

'What do you think, Tony? Can we be operational by the end of the week?'

'Only if I can get some extra help,' was the reply.

'Ah, yes,' said Calcutt, thoughtfully. 'I have been giving that some thought. A week or two ago I was offered some WAAF fitters, but in view of the activity at the time, I refused them. How do you feel about working with women?'

'Do they know what they're doing?' asked Poulson, doubtfully.

'I'm told that they do,' Calcutt replied.

'I don't want to be in a position where I'm spending my time showing a bunch of cack-handed females how to hold a screwdriver, when I could be getting on with the job myself.' Poulson was not an unreasonable man. His own daughters had shown some aptitude with mechanical things as they grew up. One of his girls was a driver in the ATS and she was capable of stripping down the engine of a five-ton vehicle, so why not a Spitfire?

'OK,' he said decisively, 'I'll give it a whirl.'

'Good lad.' Calcutt clapped a hand on the Warrant Officer's shoulder. They were much of an age, and both had seen service in the early days of the RAF. Each in charge of his particular sphere of operations on the base, they shared a mutual respect which was to the great benefit of the entire company. Calcutt knew that Poulson would make every effort to use these new workers to the best of their ability. Should the WAAFs prove inadequate for the task, the CO also knew that Poulson would not hesitate to demand more suitable staff.

Chapter Thirteen

The following day began with the arrival of the first of the transporters and its precious load.

With WO1 Poulson supervising the work, every available hand was set to assist in the unloading of the fuselage and wings of the Spitfire.

The work was slow. At every stage checks must be made to ensure that each man had completed his particular task satisfactorily. Since this was the responsibility of the senior engineer it meant that there were frequent pauses while one thing or another was put right. The possibility that the first three aircraft could be made ready before the next consignment arrived, seemed very remote.

In the middle of the afternoon a lorry drew up at the main gate. The sentry was not particularly surprised to find that the driver was a WAAF, although they had seen few enough of the female branch of the Service since the big raid when so many girls had been casualties.

Beside the driver sat a senior NCO, obviously in charge of the vehicle. He examined her papers and directed the lorry to Group Headquarters.

Pritchard looked up in some surprise as Bertha Dorkins placed a bundle of documents before him. Her rank of WO1 commanded his respect. He leaped to his feet as though stung by a bee.

'Contingent of aircraft mechanics from Headquarters, Southern Command,' she explained. 'Reporting for duty.'

'One moment, ma'am.' Pritchard rang through to the Assistant Adjutant.

'Your mechanics have arrived, sir,' he reported, adding in disbelief, 'they're WAAFs.'

'Oh, good show.' Charlie Percival was relieved. 'Get hold of Mr

Poulson, will you? Ask him to come and collect his people.'

Percival knew that the CO would be pleased. He had been like a bear with a sore head all morning.

The work of assembling the new fighters had gone slowly and Calcutt was constantly on the alert for any sign of enemy activity. He felt it unlikely that they would go unmolested for a whole week and was anxious to get the aircraft into a position to defend themselves as soon as possible. Half-built fighters would be no use against enemy dive bombers.

WOI Poulson arrived in minutes, looking hot and dishevelled. He introduced himself to the tall dark woman in charge of the WAAF mechanics. Unsympathetic critics might describe her features as a trifle horsey. Her bearing was that of one used to giving orders and expecting to be obeyed.

'WOI Bertha Dorkins.' She saluted smartly.

'Welcome to Manston.' He shook hands with her, noting her firm grip. No problem there with handling the heavy spanners and wrenches of their trade. 'I'll just direct your transport to the WAAF accommodation block,' Poulson told her, 'then we'll get over to the hangar right away and I'll explain what's wanted. Can you have your people ready to begin work in the morning?'

'I understood that this was an emergency detail,' she replied. 'My girls can be on the job in half an hour. Give them a chance to unload their gear and they'll be ready for action.' She spoke with the precision and rapidity of machine-gun fire. Poulson could just imagine her on the hockey field of some girls' public school, directing the play.

As they approached the lorry, she rattled the tailboard and a junior NCO leaped out at her command.

'Fraser, WOI Poulson will direct you to your quarters. Have the girls settle themselves in. Report to that hangar over there –' pointing in the direction which Poulson had indicated – 'at . . .' she consulted her watch '. . . sixteen hundred hours, precisely.'

The Corporal saluted smartly. 'Yes, Ma'am,' she replied, and jumped up into the cab beside the driver.

Poulson was impressed. Bertha Dorkins knew her Spitfires. As they walked around the first of the aircraft, now nearing completion, she recited the components, assembly procedures and faults to look for, and without pausing for breath took the spanner out of one young lad's hand and gave a yank on a particularly stiff nut.

'Wouldn't want that one to come loose at fifteen thousand feet now, would we, sonny?' She handed back the tool and continued with what she had been saying.

'My girls have spent six weeks in the Vickers factory at Weybridge,' she explained. 'Some of them have had no other experience since basic training, but they do know Spits. I think you'll find that your kites are safe in our hands.'

Poulson could believe it. Whether or not the rest of his team of hardened veterans would agree with him, only time would tell. To keep relationships on an even keel, until such time as the men had become used to their female counterparts, he suggested quietly, 'It might be as well to deal with my men through me, Miss Dorkins. The younger fellows take orders from anyone, but some of the older types might resent being corrected by a woman, even if she does know what she's doing.'

Dorkins appraised him thoroughly. Yes, she decided, he was quite sincere. She had taken him for a man with the common sense to accept women as equals. For a moment there she had suspected him of prejudice, but now she saw that he was simply warning her that some of the men might not be so accepting of her girls as he. Well, she thought, we'll soon put them straight on that score.

To Poulson she replied, 'Oh, just as you say, Mr Poulson . . . in the same way, instructions to my mechanics go through me, OK?'

He nodded, at a loss to find any adequate argument against her suggestion. This was not going to be as easy as the CO had suggested.

When the Women's Auxiliary Air Force was founded in 1939 it had been with the intention of recruiting women to perform those tasks seen at the time as women's work. By engaging women in clerical, cooking, parachute packing, medical orderly and cleaning duties, it would be possible to release more men for fighting.

There were, however, those in the War Office far-sighted enough to appreciate the particular skills of women which could be brought to bear in other areas. RADAR operators required a high level of concentration and an aptitude for carrying out repetitive tasks with precision. Plot room operatives needed to be well organised and unflappable. In both of these situations women were found to excel.

Only later was it realised that WAAFs could maintain heavy vehicles as well as drive them. Not only were they able to operate radio equipment, they could install and repair it and, when adequately trained, they were also shown to be quite capable of mastering the skills of aircraft fitters and maintenance mechanics.

Bertha Dorkins, a one-time teacher of Physical Education, had anticipated a career in that field when she joined the WAAF. It was her outstanding mechanical aptitude, however, which had most interested the Appointments Board, and her natural ability to take command which had seen her rapid promotion to her present rank. In eighteen months she had reached a level it had taken Brian Poulson ten years to achieve.

When, half an hour later, Corporal Janet Fraser entered the hangar with half a dozen aircraftswomen at her heels, they were greeted with wolf whistles which were quickly hushed by a fierce look from Bertha and a heavy frown from Poulson.

Females did not normally look their best in the shapeless white overalls provided by the War Department. Corporal Janet Fraser, on the other hand, looked as if she had just stepped off the cover of *Vogue* magazine. Her chestnut brown hair was twisted into a neat bun and secured by combs above her dainty ears. Her wide-set, velvety brown eyes were set off by a flimsy scarf of orange chiffon which was tucked neatly inside her collar to prevent the harsh twill rubbing against her delicate skin. A handkerchief of similar hue enlivened the plain white of her breast pocket. These little additions, which made all the difference to a girl's attitude to her work, were ignored by her superiors during working hours. When on parade, Janet, like all her comrades, wore immaculate Service Dress and there was no question of tarting that up!

The second Spitfire was already aligned ready for the assembly of its wings which had to be bolted into position on either side of the fuselage. At a signal from Poulson the men stood back and Bertha's girls set to work. In seconds Fraser had assessed what needed to be done and had allocated the various tasks to her team. With astonishing precision they demonstrated how to assemble an aircraft with minimum effort and in record time. The men did not hesitate to show their appreciation of these skills and watched with growing admiration as the work progressed. Poulson himself was totally absorbed in the display for a few moments. Then, because there was plenty more work to be done, he rallied his own workers to begin assembling the third machine.

Now it became a competition to see which group could finish first. Realising that this might result in corner cutting and carelessness, the two leaders conferred once again.

'I think we would work more effectively by mixing up the men and women,' suggested Bertha. 'My girls are obviously more practised with the fiddly bits, but your fellows have the required heave-ho. What do you say?'

Poulson winced at her manner of expressing herself but, now that his men had been convinced that the girls knew what they were doing, he saw no reason why they should not try it out. During a pause for tea and sandwiches he put the suggestion to his men. To his relief they seemed more than willing to join forces with the girls.

The ice thus broken, the work continued into the early hours with no more than a grunt or a nod of the head passing for discussion. When at last the third aircraft was completed except for its final engine check, Poulson called them off.

'Right, everyone, time to hit the sack. The next consignment should be arriving mid-morning. Reveille for you people will be oh-eight hundred hours.' He turned to Bertha. 'Come along, I'll walk you to your quarters.'

Janet wiped her hand across a damp forehead and absently thrust an escaped lock of hair behind her ear, leaving a smear of grease wherever her fingers had touched.

The eighteen-year-old recruit who had been standing by to hand up her tools all morning, had allowed his attention to wander. He was a willing enough lad, but lacking both skill and experience he had been delegated to the role of general runabout. Smitten by the glamorous corporal, he had attached himself to her in the hope that he might go unnoticed by the sharp eyes of Mr Poulson and be given some less agreeable task.

'Number three spanner, Bob,' she called down to him. 'Hurry up! I can't hold on to this section forever.' The metal cover plate was an awkward shape and heavy, she could feel it moving beneath her fingers.

The boy fiddled about in the tool case, desperately trying to remember which was a number three.

'Damn!' The plate slipped from her fingers and as Janet made to grab at it with her other hand, the sharp edge cut across her palm, leaving a deep gash. The metal clattered on to the concrete at Bob's feet. He stared at it for a few seconds then looked up to see Janet gazing horrified at the blood oozing between her fingers.

'Help me down, you idiot!' she yelled at him.

As he moved forward to do so, Poulson thrust him aside and held out his arms so that the girl could slide off the wing into them. One look at the injury was sufficient to tell him that this was no Band-Aid job. As he looked around for something to staunch the bleeding, the girl herself obliged by tearing the scarf from her neck and winding it around the palm of her hand.

Poulson called to his second in command.

'Take over here for a short while, Corporal. I'm escorting a casualty to the dispensary. If Miss Dorkins arrives before I get back, tell her Corporal Fraser has had an accident. Nothing too serious,' he added, conscious of the manner in which such events could become dramatised.

Outside he helped Janet into a waiting jeep and drove her himself to have her hand attended to.

Stephen studied the wound intently, using his magnifying glass to ensure that no metallic fragments had been left behind.

'Can't be too careful with this sort of thing,' he explained. 'One foreign body can cause a whole lot of problems.' He used tweezers to extract a fine sliver of steel which he dropped with a tinny sound into the dish at his side. 'They don't take time to smooth the edges these days, do they?' he remarked lightly, glancing up at his patient to see how she was faring. He was amused to see smudges of grease on the wide unfurrowed brow. Strangely the dirty marks seemed to enhance rather than detract from her appearance. Even grey with shock, she really was a very pretty girl.

He bent to his task of seeking out each of the severed tendons and nerves. Absolute concentration was necessary if he was to ensure that she regained full use of her injured hand.

The damage was extensive and as each torn tendon required two sutures – one to draw the cut ends together and the second to secure the elastic tissue sufficiently for healing to occur – Stephen found the operation took longer than he had anticipated. Finished at last, he wiped the palm of her hand gently with gauze soaked in turpentine then, accepting a small paper sachet from his orderly, tore it open with his teeth and shook the powdery contents into the open wound.

Janet flinched.

'OK,' he said, gently, aware that the effect of the local anaesthetic must be wearing off. 'That's Sulphanilamide . . . a precious consignment from our American cousins. It should ensure that there is no sepsis.'

He smiled his broad smile and Janet Fraser, sick and faint though she might be, was not unaware of her own heightened response to the handsome, red-headed Scottish doctor.

'I'll give you a second injection of Novocaine before I close the wound,' he explained. 'You won't feel a thing, I assure you.'

True enough, she hadn't felt much so far. She steeled herself for the second needle and waited for the blessed numbness to return to her fingers. Janet was in no doubt about the pain which this stupid little accident was going to cause her later. Thank goodness the aircraft she had been working on was the last of the twelve delivered that week. Manston had its new squadron of Spitfires and she and her colleagues would soon be on their way.

It was a pity really. Her unit had made friends amongst the engineers here. Once their initial suspicions had been proved to be unfounded, the men had come to accept them as equals.

She felt nothing at all as Stephen worked behind the screen of towels arranged over her upper arm to prevent her from seeing what was going on. She wondered if the injury would keep her here at Manston even when the others had left. Surely not? Anyone could remove a few stitches . . .

Janet had kept her eyes tight closed during the operation but now, as the work was coming to an end, she opened them. She was startled to see herself and the medical team clearly in the huge stainless steel reflector positioned above the operating table. Her left hand was swathed in bandages which the doctor was fastening with a neat row of safety pins. All she could see of him was the top of his head, his hair neatly cropped, Service fashion. There was just the hint of a curl there nevertheless. She pictured him with it just an inch longer and without the Brylcreem which darkened it to a dullish auburn.

Someone switched off the light and Janet saw spots before her eyes for a few seconds.

Stephen put his arm behind her shoulders and gently eased her into a sitting position.

'There you are . . . all done.'

She might have been three years old, she thought, just a trifle resentfully. He steadied her as she slid off the table and helped her to a wheelchair placed close by.

'I don't need that,' Janet complained. 'I can walk perfectly well.'

To prove her point she shrugged off Stephen's supporting arm and began to make for the door. She felt her legs buckle under her as the doctor resumed his hold.

'You've had a bad shock,' he insisted, planting her firmly in the chair. 'Devlin will take you along to the recovery room so that you can have a wee rest before returning to your quarters.' Forestalling her protest, he continued, 'I shall want to check you over again before you leave, so no bunking off before I say so . . . understand?'

She nodded. That short experience of being on her feet had convinced her that she was more shaky than she had imagined. Besides which, she rather relished the thought that she would be seeing more of the dishy doctor before she was dismissed.

It was two hours or more before Stephen was free to take another look at his patient in the recovery room. When he stepped in she appeared to be sleeping. Not wishing to disturb her he would have withdrawn, but suddenly she opened her eyes and for a moment her confusion was evident.

'Hello,' he said, grinning at her and exposing a row of perfect white teeth. 'Had a good sleep?' He checked her pulse and felt under her jaw for any swelling or other indication of infection. So far, so good. He examined her further. Armpits, groin, no swelling there either. Maybe she was going to be lucky . . .

'Unfortunately,' he explained, 'a cut from equipment just arrived from the factory is more likely to become infected than one from a machine that has been exposed to the elements for a time . . . there's so much loose material involved, dust and metal fragments. We'll have to keep a close watch on things for the next few days.'

'We're going to be transferred now that the new aircraft have been assembled,' she told him.

'I think it would be best for you to remain at Manston until I'm quite certain you're OK. There's no knowing what situation your unit will find itself in next . . . anyway, you can't work so you might as well convalesce here as anywhere.'

Concerned that she might become detached from her friends, Janet began to protest, then hesitated. Finally she decided to see what the fates might bring. He really was a smashing guy. She could do far worse for medical attention . . . and who knew what her extended stay at Manston might lead to?

'Pretty unusual isn't it . . . for a girl to be so interested in mechanical matters?' Stephen asked innocently. Had the question been directed at Bertha Dorkins he would have received a very sharp retort about male chauvinism. As it was, Janet simply nodded and explained, 'My brother's a racing driver. You may have heard of him . . . Andrew Fraser?'

How could anyone not have heard of the young Scot who had won

MARY WITHALL

the Monte Carlo Rally on two occasions, not to mention countless successes at Brooklands and an attempt on the world speed record set by Malcolm Campbell just before the war. Stephen viewed his patient with greater interest.

'I was born with a spanner in my mouth in place of a silver spoon,' laughed Janet. 'Gender has no significance in our family . . . when there's work to be done on one of the racing machines, we all set to.'

'All?'

'My two brothers, my mother and my father. My mother was flying aircraft when they were made of matchsticks and linen, joined together with string and spit!'

Stephen found it hard to visualise such a family. What he *was* certain of was that the Frasers had plenty of money to indulge their sporting activities. Ordinary people could scarcely afford to drive a car in the 1920s, let alone own an aeroplane.

'Where do you come from?' he enquired of his fellow Scot.

'Cairndow on Loch Fyne. Do you know it?'

'I used to pass through it on my way to and from my grandmother's home at Connel,' he told her. 'It's a very small place. Is your house in the village?'

'Oh, no, quite a way outside.' She offered no further details and he did not pursue it.

'Well, I think you're ready to return to your own quarters,' he said. 'I'll have a word with the CO about delaying your transfer. Pop in tomorrow so that Devlin can check on the dressing and if there's any sign at all of reddening of the surrounding skin, or if there is any undue throbbing, come back at once. I shall be away from the base tomorrow but I'll leave instructions for the orderly . . . just in case.' He wrote a prescription and handed it to her. 'Give that to Devlin as you go out . . . it's for pain killers. You may have trouble sleeping.'

'After this week, I believe I could sleep forever, pain or no pain,' she replied.

Stephen knew that they had been working flat out to get the Spitfires assembled. It was probably exhaustion which had contributed to Janet's accident. He would have a word with Calcutt. There came a time when excessive zeal could bring its own dangers.

Stephen drove into the ancient town of East Grinstead from the south. He was struck by the chocolate-box array of Tudor buildings, narrow cobbled streets and the medieval hospital, now a prestigious public school. Used to the massive red granite constructions of cities North of the Border, he found it all unbelievably quaint. This town was like something constructed from a child's set of bricks.

His enquiries led him to a right-hand turn halfway along the High Street. Half a mile along the road to Tunbridge Wells he found the Queen Victoria Hospital and turned in between red brick pillars which must once have supported a pair of wrought-iron gates, now gone, probably to be melted down for the war effort.

Half expecting yet another ancient building, he was pleasantly surprised to find that the hospital, built during the 1930s, was very similar in outward appearance to Doune House where he lived with his fellow officers at Westgate on Sea.

In the absence of petrol for domestic purposes, the visitors' car park was nearly empty. Stephen pulled in beside a rather handsome green Bentley and switched off his engine.

Following the crowd of visitors, many of whom had dismounted from a single-decker bus which he had followed along the road, he entered the building and, after making enquiries at the desk, was directed to a bright airy ward.

The atmosphere was more akin to a day-room than the pristine kind of hospital ward to which he was accustomed. The patients seemed to be everywhere but in their beds. Stephen was rather taken aback by the laxity of the Ward Sister's discipline. He was accustomed to seeing patients neatly tucked in, with never a crease in a counterpane and only the single statutory dent per pillow.

He looked around for a familiar face but it was the voice which led him to the right place. Digger, seated with two others in easy chairs placed beside an open window, was ribbing one of the boys whose visitor was a particularly attractive WRNS officer. As Stephen approached he was singing raucously, "'A life on the ocean wave . . .'" He stopped abruptly when he caught sight of Stephen.

'Well now, if it isn't me old mate. Hiya, Doc! Let you out at last, have they?'

Stephen knew what to expect but nevertheless the sight which greeted him was a devastating one. It was no wonder Digger had refused to see Grace.

The skin across his brow and down one side of his face was bright pink in the centre, yellowing towards the puckered edges of the burned areas. The boils of the early days were healed but they had left deeply pitted scars. Part of his nose had been destroyed so that one nostril appeared half an inch higher than the other, giving the Australian a tragi-comic expression. Stephen thought fleetingly of that broad welcoming smile which had greeted him on the day of his arrival at Manston. This hideous mask was a travesty of the original.

Catching his expression and recognising it as one filled with horror and sympathy, the much-practised Digger forestalled any comment by holding up his bandaged hands.

'If you think that's a sight, mate, you should see these!'

Digger's companions melted away, leaving the two friends alone to adjust to this new situation. Stephen could see that Digger was tense and tried to lead the conversation away from his injuries.

'The wedding went off well,' he told him. 'Who'd have thought old Stumpy would be the one to take the plunge?'

'What's the girl like?' Digger asked. 'Should I know her?'

'She was one of the WAAF operators in the ops room. You must have worked with her every day.'

'In uniform they all look alike to me,' the Australian commented. 'It's like the nurses here. It was days before I could distinguish one from another . . .'

His mind was obviously wandering among his most recent experiences. Stephen drew him back to the wedding.

'We got your telegram,' he said. 'I picked it out of a bunch of messages. It gave me quite a shock to see it had come from you.'

'Like a voice from the dead?' Digger demanded.

Stephen could have bitten off his tongue. He tried another tack.

'Grace was telling me that she had been writing,' he said. 'What's all this I hear about an engagement? You're a dark horse!'

Digger was silent for a few moments.

'That was before . . .' He tailed off. Then, suddenly brightening as though he had thrust all thought of Grace from him, he continued with, 'I'll bet the Old Man was mad about the precious Hurricane I pranged?'

'Not any more . . . he's got some new Spits now, a whole squadron.' Stephen told him about the new arrivals, and about the excitement caused by the introduction of female mechanics on the base.

'I can just imagine WO1 Poulson's face when confronted with half a dozen girls instead of real mechanics!'

'Surprisingly, Poulson was OK about it,' Stephen explained. 'It was the other fitters who made a bit of a fuss at first. The WAAF sergeant soon put them straight, however . . . like lambs, they were, by the end of the week.'

He went on to describe in detail Big Bertha, as the WO1 had come to be known, and some of the funnier exchanges which had gone the rounds of the camp while the WAAF mechanics were at work. So deep in their conversation were they that they did not notice the approach of the white-coated figure who sank into the vacant chair beside them.

'Sorry to interrupt, Colin,' he said, 'but I thought you should know . . . it's on for tomorrow. Usual drill. No breakfast, in the theatre by about ten. OK?'

The Australian nodded, his eyes betraying his anxiety while his excuse for a smile suggested only nonchalance.

'This is my mate, Doc. Steve Beaton . . . from Manston. You and he should have a lot in common. He's the doc who patched me up before I came here.'

The plastic surgeon regarded Digger's visitor with renewed interest.

'McIndoe,' he introduced himself, 'or Archie to my friends . . . and to these goons.' He grinned as he indicated the mutilated patients all about him.

Stephen shook his hand.

'I'm very pleased to meet you,' he said. 'You've probably forgotten, but I wrote to your boss some time ago concerning the initial treatment of burns in aircraft accidents.'

'Beaton . . . of course, I remember. You've been directing quite a few patients my way in recent weeks.'

'Yes, including this reprobate. I must apologise for landing him on your patch!'

All three of them laughed as McIndoe took his leave.

Stephen noticed that the appearance of Archie McIndoe had had a profound effect upon Digger. He seemed completely relaxed by the time the bell went for the end of visiting hour.

As Stephen rose to go, Digger waved one bandaged paw in lieu of a handshake.

'Thanks for coming,' he said.

'What shall I tell Grace if I see her?' Stephen felt obliged to raise the subject. 'Will you talk to her if she manages to come over?'

'There's really no point just now,' Digger replied, blankly. 'Just tell her I'm OK and I'll look her up once they discharge me. You never know what I'll look like by then . . . they perform some pretty remarkable miracles in this place you know.'

'I'll come again,' Stephen promised. 'Maybe I'll bring a couple of the boys with me. Squeaky Piper was saying only the other day how much he misses your Antipodean twang!'

'That'll be great,' said Digger, the lack of enthusiasm in his voice belying his words.

As Stephen passed the reception desk the porter called him over.

'Flight Lieutenant Beaton, sir?'

'Yes?' Stephen was a little surprised to be addressed in this way.

'Mr McIndoe wondered if he might have a word before you left the premises, sir.'

Mystified, Stephen assented.

'Just along the corridor to the right.' The porter pointed in the direction he should take and Stephen, finding the correct door, tapped lightly.

'Come in!'

He pushed open the door and stepped into the unimposing room which was Archie McIndoe's private sanctum.

'Oh, come along in, Beaton,' the surgeon cried, pleasantly. 'It's good of you to spare me a few moments . . . please, do sit down. Can I get you a drink?' He indicated a small side table with a few bottles and glasses on display.

'No, thanks, I have to drive back to Manston directly.'

'I was very impressed with the way you tackled young Sheen's injuries,' McIndoe told him. 'It's largely due to your initial treatment that I've been able to save his hands, you know.'

'What's the prognosis now?' Stephen asked, relieved to hear that his efforts had clearly satisfied the specialist.

'Several more grafts, I'm afraid, but a good chance of eighty per cent flexibility on the right hand. Maybe a little less on the other. He'll never be a watchmaker, but for normal usage they should do well enough.'

'What about his face?'

'Oh, a much happier prognosis there.' McIndoe assured him. 'I plan to rebuild the nose so he doesn't look quite so lopsided, and those initial grafts will slough off soon. The second round will make him much more presentable . . . almost back to normal, I should think. Just an interesting ruggedness. The kind of thing the women go for in a big way.'

'Have you told him that? He seems to be particularly despondent about the future.'

McIndoe looked up, sharply.

'Do you think so? Of course, you know him better than I . . . he always seems so cheerful, talking to the nurses and to myself.'

'He has a fiancée whom he will not allow to visit him.'

'I didn't know that.' McIndoe looked thoughtful. 'That's a pity. Still, the longer he keeps her waiting, the less of a shock it will be.'

Remembering his own reaction to Digger's appearance, Stephen doubted that Grace would be less dismayed than he had been himself . . . and he had known what to expect.

'Anyway,' McIndoe continued, 'it wasn't to talk about Sheen that I asked you in here. What are your own plans for the future?'

'Can any of us make plans at such a time?' Stephen asked. 'I haven't really given a lot of thought to any particular specialism. Just a regular run of the mill sawbones, that's me.'

'I don't think so,' McIndoe assured him. 'You should certainly consider plastic surgery. You have a natural talent for the painstaking work involved. There's a great deal of satisfaction to be had from successfully rebuilding a badly burned face . . . giving a mutilated victim of bombing a reason for living.'

'Well, I'll certainly give it some thought,' Stephen replied, rather flattered by the great man's opinion of him. 'Unfortunately I haven't had an opportunity to take my Fellowship exams yet. When I do, I'll consider plastic surgery as a specialism.'

McIndoe nodded, then began fingering papers which lay on the desk in front of him. Stephen, recognising the signal, knew it was time for him to go.

'I'll try to come and see Colin Sheen again, soon,' he said, reaching for his cap and gloves.

'I'd be grateful if you would,' said McIndoe, rising to accompany him to the door. 'He needs to feel that he's still a part of the Old Firm . . . it will give him an incentive to get back into the fight.'

'You think he will fly again?' asked Stephen, doubtfully.

'I suspect that nothing will stop him.' McIndoe grinned. 'These boys are tougher than you might think.'

Stephen remembered Digger's anxiety to get back into harness after his previous injury and knew that the surgeon was right.

McIndoe shook him by the hand.

'You have a talent given to few men,' he said. 'Be sure to use it wisely.'

'Thank you, sir,' Stephen replied. 'Once this is all over, I'll give your suggestion some serious thought.'

Chapter Fourteen

As 1940 drew to a close Stephen became increasingly aware of a general downturn in fitness, both physical and mental, amongst his charges.

The almost continuous enemy attacks upon Fighter Command's bases, designed to bring the RAF to its knees, had been switched to London and provincial cities across the country. Daytime bombing raids were followed by night attacks, when the fighters for the most part were rendered impotent and the Air Ministry had to rely upon the anti-aircraft guns of the army to protect both airfields and civilian targets. There was little respite at Manston either day or night, the fighter squadrons being kept on the alert during daylight hours and the personnel getting little sleep because of night raids.

Everyone was tired, tempers were frayed and accidents threatened to take a heavier toll than the enemy, of both pilots and aircraft. It was with some relief therefore that Stephen found himself summoned to the CO's office late in December to be told that the entire Group, including ground staff, was ordered to Prestwick for some well-earned rest.

'You'll be spending Hogmanay in your home territory, you lucky bastard,' observed Stumpy Miles ruefully. He had left Audrey weeping that morning because he was unlikely to be with her for Christmas. Stephen had pronounced her pregnant a few weeks after the wedding and she had been forced to resign from the WAAF shortly afterwards. The couple now occupied a tiny flat in Westgate where Stumpy spent what little free time he had.

'Well, you might get a few days' leave over Christmas,' suggested Stephen, trying hard to suppress his own elation. 'In any case, what's to prevent you getting quarters for Audrey up in Ayrshire?'

'I'm told there will be no facilities for wives close to the airfield and

Audrey feels she'll be too lonely, stuck miles away in a strange place and me not on hand when it's time for the baby . . .'

'She's not planning to go to her parents in Balham, surely?' Stephen demanded. 'That would be asking for trouble.'

'Until we can find something more suitable, I'm afraid there's no alternative,' Stumpy replied.

Stephen hesitated to mention the idea which had been forming in his mind as his friend spoke. Prestwick was not all that far from Glasgow . . . maybe his mother could be persuaded to help.

'Look,' he said, 'I might be able to work something out for you. Will you leave it with me until I can make a phone call?'

'OK,' Stumpy agreed, 'but time's rather short. I'll need to know by the end of the day, because we have to get out of our flat by Thursday at the latest.'

'Why the rush?'

'The landlord has already got another tenant . . . the wife of the new CO.'

'I'll get back to you as soon as I can.'

Stephen put his head around the door to the CO's office. 'Can you spare a moment, Harry?'

'Oh, hello, Doc.' Calcutt straightened up from the pile of papers before him and stretched his arms above his head. 'I can't say that I'm sorry to be getting out of here.' He smiled wryly. 'The only trouble is, I have to account for every last nut and bolt to the next feller. Come in and take a pew. What's the problem?'

'I wondered how we lesser mortals would be travelling?' Stephen explained. 'Stumpy tells me that we're taking our Spitfires with us. I suppose that means most of the aircrew will be flying up in their own machines?'

'That was the idea, yes.' Calcutt grinned. He suspected that he knew what was coming next.

'I just wondered . . . would there be a machine for me?'

'As it happens we have to shift a couple of trainers,' the CO replied. 'How would it be if you and I were to share one? We'd be two old *has beens* together, eh?'

At twenty-six Stephen had to admit he did sometimes feel like an old man amongst the young pilots who were constantly being brought in to replace the experienced men killed or injured in the battle. He felt that *has been* was a bit strong, nevertheless.

'Oh, OK. Well, thank you, sir,' was his rather disappointed reply.

He had had little opportunity to fly anything at all since he joined the Group.

'Don't worry, Steve.' Calcutt grinned. 'I'll let you do the driving. Make sure the bulk of your gear goes on one of the transports this afternoon. We'll be taking off at first light on Thursday.'

Heartened by Calcutt's display of generosity, Stephen saluted smartly, much to his Station Commander's surprise, and consequently nearly tripped over Shep who had quietly sneaked in whilst they had been speaking.

'Sorry, old chap,' he said, bending to ruffle the dog's ears. He glanced back to where Calcutt stood observing them both from his position behind the desk. 'How's Shep going to get to Scotland?' he enquired.

'Oh,' the CO replied, non-comittally, 'I'm sure we'll think of something.'

'Mum?'

'Stevie? . . . Oh, my goodness, it's so good to hear from you.' Annie cursed silently as the surgery bell rang. 'Hang on a minute while I see who's at the door . . . Mrs Brown! Mrs Brown . . . see who that is, will you . . . I'm on the phone.'

The housekeeper swept past her and as Annie gave attention to her caller, a murmur of voices suggested that Stuart's surgery was going to be a full one this morning.

'Sounds as though things are much the same as usual up there,' he laughed, glad to be reunited with the familiar activities of his parents' home life even if only by a telephone call.

Annie, troubled as usual by any exceptional communication with her son, wondered what had prompted him to telephone so early in the working day. His calls were usually made in the evening when things were quiet.

'Good news.' He heard her sigh of relief across the wires. 'I'm coming home . . . well, almost.' He could not give details in such a public way. They were constantly warned against giving any scrap of military information to the enemy. 'One of my pals has a pregnant wife whom he doesn't want to leave in London, and for whom there will be no accommodation where we're going. I wondered if you and Dad could give her a room for a short while . . . just until they can find a suitable place for her to stay?'

Annie hesitated for a moment only. Stephen made few demands

upon their hospitality . . . she might even welcome some companionship during the long winter nights when Stuart was on duty . . . anyway, it wouldn't be for long . . .

'I'll be happy to take her in,' she replied, 'just so long as she understands that both your father and myself are often out and about engaged in our war work . . . my latest is fire-watching on the roof of the City Hall. She might well be alone in the house some nights.'

'Oh, Audrey would have no problem with that,' Stephen dismissed his mother's reservations. 'She was a WAAF, here on the field, until only a month or two ago.'

'Well then, all right, dear. When will she be arriving? I'll try to meet her at the station.'

'I'll let you know later on today. It will be some time this week anyway.'

'Oh . . . right.' Annie was a little taken aback at the short notice. Still, that was wartime for you. Everything happened at once or not at all.

'And, Mum . . . thanks.'

'Does this mean we'll be seeing you too, soon?' Annie held her breath. It had been nearly a year since his last visit.

'I hope so . . . give my love to Dad. Goodbye for now.'

'Goodbye, dear.'

She put down the phone, her mind already forming plans to accommodate this unexpected visitor. She hurried back to the kitchen.

'Mrs Brown, we are to have a guest staying for a while. Will you give me a hand to get the room ready?'

Fred had said that he knew just the person to take over the old Morris.

'Twenty quid?' he had suggested. 'The prices are improving on small cars like this but she's getting on a bit.'

Stephen was well aware that a small car, economical on petrol, would sell for twenty-five pounds at today's prices, but who was he to prevent Fred from taking his cut? Someone in the incoming contingent would surely be prepared to pay that price for a reliable runabout.

'Oh, all right,' he agreed. 'You can have the car this evening. I'll need to use it this afternoon to pop round to the Vicarage to say goodbye to the Dobbies.'

It had been some time since Andrew Dobbie had joined them all in the Mess for dinner. Stephen was rather taken aback to see just what a toll the last few stressful weeks had taken of the elderly Vicar and his wife.

Dobbie, never a stout gentleman, had lost a lot of weight. His face was thin and drained of all colour. Mary's complexion on the other hand lacked nothing of its old rosiness and unlike her husband's her features had suffered little alteration. As she came forward to greet him, however, he studied her painful movements with a sinking heart. Her arthritis was undoubtedly much worse than when he had seen her last.

'Oh, do come in, Stephen,' Dobbie greeted him cheerfully from the depths of his armchair. 'We heard that the Group was moving out this week. My goodness but we shall miss you all.'

He fell silent for a few minutes, regretting the ending of an association which both of them had enjoyed so much.

'I can only stay a few moments.' Stephen refused the seat Mary offered. 'I felt that I must drop in to say goodbye. You have both been so kind . . .' he trailed off, not wishing to prolong the pain of parting.

'It's been a pleasure to know you, my boy,' the old man told him warmly. 'You will keep in touch?'

'Of course,' Stephen said, taking Mary's withered hand gently in his own. Bending forward, he kissed her lightly on the cheek.

'The least we can do is wave you on your way,' declared the Vicar, getting to his feet and wrapping his bulky woollen sweater tightly around him.

As the old people followed Stephen to the gate, he paused to admire the garden, still trim despite the lateness of the season.

'The roses are nearly all dead,' Mary lamented. 'Grace should have come to cut them before this. They'll all be gone by the time she gets here . . .'

'I'm quite sure she won't mind, my dear,' said her husband, gently. 'It's very cold out here, Mary, perhaps you should be by the fire. I'm sure Stephen will forgive you.'

Wordlessly she lifted her face for his farewell kiss.

'If you're going to Scotland, no doubt you will manage to get home for a while?' Was this by nature of a gentle reprimand? he wondered. 'Give my love to your mother,' she said and turned to go in.

Both men followed her painful progress, neither speaking until she was out of hearing.

'The time is coming when she will need someone with her at all times,' Stephen advised. 'If you are to go on working as you are now, you will really have to consider hiring someone to live in and lend a hand with the house.'

'Grace would come like a shot in normal circumstances,' Dobbie told him, 'but I don't like to trouble her with it at the present time. Did you know she has transferred to the hospital in East Grinstead? She's helping to nurse in the burns unit.'

'Really?' This was news to Stephen. The last time he had seen Digger, the poor old chap was pretty fed up. There had been no talk then of Grace's joining him. Perhaps her presence on the scene would give him the lift he needed.

Stephen had agonised for a long time over his friend's betrothal to the girl he himself had set his heart on marrying. Despite his terrible injuries, there was no doubt in Stephen's mind that Digger was the luckier of the two.

'It seems that plans for a wedding have been postponed indefinitely,' Dobbie told him. 'Not Grace's idea, you understand. It's Colin who has had a change of heart, although I suspect he thinks it is in Grace's best interests to cancel the engagement.'

Stephen could understand his friend's reluctance to tie the beautiful Grace to himself for life, but if he thought she would be deterred by his rejection, he had another think coming. As Stephen himself was only too aware, Grace was a woman with a mind of her own. If she was determined to marry her Australian, nothing in the world would stop her.

'Grace may come across a victim of the bombing only too happy to get a job in the country,' Stephen suggested, thinking again of Mary Dobbie. 'Perhaps you should ask her to look out for someone suitable?'

'Yes,' the Vicar agreed, somewhat reluctantly, 'I suppose that might be an idea. Well, anyway, you must have a lot to do before you can get away. Come and see us again if you have the chance.'

Stephen's lasting impression of the village of Manston, as he reversed the Morris into the road and circled around the war memorial, was of his old friend bending to pluck one final late rosebud from the bush beside the wrought-iron gate.

The Westland Trainer stood dark against the wintry sun as Stephen approached her on foot, across the tarmac. The previous evening the incoming pilots had joined No. 11 Group in their farewell party and Stephen, who should have known better, was no less hung over than his messmates. His head throbbed and his vision was somewhat blurred. He prayed that the rush of cold air in the open cockpit would soon put paid to all the cobwebs.

He turned at the sound of an approaching car and was surprised to see that it was his old Morris with Fred at the wheel. The CO, already dressed in his flying suit, jumped clear as the vehicle came to a halt.

'OK, Doc,' he called, 'climb aboard and get her revved up, will you?'

He busied himself with stashing a few personal items in the minute locker provided and as Stephen gave his attention to preparations for take-off, climbed into the rear seat.

'Don't forget we're neither of us lightweights. Given her plenty of gun for the lift-off.'

Calcutt's warning came to Stephen by way of his earphones, rather unnecessarily, he thought. He hoped the CO wasn't going to be a back-seat driver all the way to Scotland.

He felt Calcutt settle himself rather heavily into the rear cockpit. The flimsy superstructure seemed to creak a bit under the strain. Stephen hadn't realised the Old Man had put on quite so much weight. He adjusted the throttle for take-off and as the engine roared into life, the ground staff withdrew the chocks.

Remembering the CO's veiled warning, he taxied to the far end of the runway, giving himself plenty of room for the take-off. The aircraft felt sluggish as she gained speed and Stephen could feel himself willing her to get off the ground as the perimeter fence loomed before them. With a final burst of power he pulled back on the stick and the little plane leaped into the air, passing the control tower within a hair's breadth of the observation windows.

'Crikey!' Calcutt's voice came over the radio. 'That was a bit close. Well done, Steve.'

At least it wasn't a reprimand, he thought, finding it astonishing that the aeroplane, designed to carry two people, should have had so much trouble getting off the ground. He just hoped that there had not been any corners cut on its maintenance.

Their route was across country to pick up the River Severn and then northwards following the Welsh border. Attacks by the enemy were unlikely, but it was Calcutt's responsibility to keep an eye open for other aircraft as well as to act as navigator. When Stephen heard the distinct sounds of snoring coming over the intercom he heaved a sigh of relief and settled back to enjoy the flight without having to feel that his boss was monitoring every move he made. Landmarks were plentiful. It was a clear day and Stephen was happy to navigate himself.

Approaching Manchester, Stephen heard a snort as Calcutt awoke.

This was followed immediately by an unprintable expletive.

'Great heavens, Shep, couldn't you wait just a few more minutes!'

Startled, Stephen glanced back over his shoulder to see a pair of very familiar, sharply pointed sable ears poking above the cowling of the rear cockpit.

'Bloody dog's puked all over my feet,' complained Calcutt, and then to the dog, 'You might have told me you got airsick, you useless hound!'

At the absurdity of this remark Stephen burst out laughing, whereupon Shep, recognising his voice, put both paws on the coping and lifted his great muzzle to the wind in order to savour the familiar scent of his friend the doctor.

'We'll be coming in to land in a few minutes,' warned Stephen. 'What do you want to do?'

Struggling to get the dog back down under his feet, Calcutt shouted, 'You get out when we land and see to the paperwork while they're refuelling. I'll stay put. No need to mention who I am . . . just a passenger, OK?'

Fortunately for Calcutt, the formalities took only a few minutes and within half an hour the Westland had taken to the air for the final stage of its journey. A cock and bull story from Stephen about his passenger being too incapacitated to leave the aircraft without assistance seemed to satisfy regulations concerning disembarkation during refuelling, and while Stephen made his way to the administration block, Calcutt kept a very low profile. In the blustery wind the mechanics appeared not to notice the occasional canine whimpers emitted from the rear cockpit.

On this occasion, fully aware of the allowances he needed to make for the additional weight on board, Stephen was able to take off without undue attention being drawn to the small aircraft. As they soared into a bank of cloud lying to the west of the Cumbrian hills, Calcutt was heard to say to his dog, 'You needn't think you're getting any supper tonight, you mangy beast . . . you've cost me a fortune in cleaning bills and ruined a good pair of flying boots!'

Stephen grinned happily to himself. It was a story which would be worth a pint or two in the Mess for weeks to come.

This late in the year daylight faded around three o'clock and it was nearly dusk when the little trainer landed on a temporary airstrip a few miles from Prestwick. In the gloom, no one observed the huge hound which leaped nimbly out on to the wing and down to the ground, disappearing into the gloom at his master's heels. The mystery of how Shep had arrived at their new station kept tongues wagging for a long time and when at last the truth filtered out, the story was added to the list of exploits which was to make the CO's dog a legend in his lifetime.

The telephone rang incessantly.

Why was it they always left her to answer it? Ellen wondered, gazing around at her three colleagues, who were studiously concentrating on their microscopes.

'Agricultural Research Unit, Ellen McDougal speaking.'

She recognised the voice immediately.

'Malcolm?' She turned her back on the others and lowered her voice so that they might not overhear. 'I've told you before not to call me here!'

'I know.' There was a pause, then the disembodied voice continued. 'You must meet me tonight. Look, I can't say much over the phone but it really is terribly urgent . . .'

She had met him earlier in the year, at a dance aboard a naval destroyer which had berthed in the harbour while running repairs were carried out to her superstructure. Grateful for the welcome given to his crew by the locals, the skipper had invited a group of townspeople to a farewell celebration on board. Ellen had gone along with other members of the University Faculty.

The wardroom of one of His Majesty's destroyers was cramped enough in normal circumstances. With an additional thirty or more visitors on board, there was barely room to stand shoulder to shoulder. Ellen soon became separated from her two colleagues and found herself thrust into the arms, quite literally, of a Naval officer holding two glasses of pink gin at shoulder height to avoid collision.

'Oh, I'm terribly sorry,' she said, attempting rather unsuccessfully to mop up that part of the drink which had slopped down his lapel. 'It really is very crowded in here, isn't it?'

'Quite impossible,' he agreed, smiling broadly at the gorgeous creature whom Providence had thrust in his path. 'There's no way I'm going to get these drinks to the other side of the cabin,' he decided. 'How about sharing them?'

'Don't you have someone waiting?' she demanded, accepting the glass anyway.

'I was only attending to the Provost's wife,' he explained. 'I'm sure someone else will look after her.'

Too thirsty to experience much guilt, Ellen downed the gin and began to feel better.

'Ever been aboard a naval ship before, Miss . . . ?'

'McDougal . . . Ellen McDougal.' She put out her hand for him to shake. 'No, it's my first and likely to be my only visit,' she laughed, as someone pushed past her, thrusting her against him once more.

'You're not a local lassie,' the officer commented, intrigued by the colonial twang in Ellen's speech.

'No . . . I'm from Australia,' she replied, smiling.

She found him attractive, in a rugged sort of way.

He was dark-skinned, almost swarthy, with a shock of black hair prematurely tinged with grey at the temples. Dark, bushy eyebrows emphasised his eyes which were black as shining coals. A fan of lines at their corners, where they had been screwed up against the glare, indicated long periods of exposure to the elements. Stocky in build, his broad shoulders made him appear rather shorter than his six feet. He wore the No.1 dress uniform of a full Lieutenant in the RNVR. 'Malcolm McGregor,' he introduced himself.

'If you'll forgive my saying so, you don't sound like a Scotsman either,' she challenged him in turn.

'That's because I was born and brought up in Cornwall,' he told her. 'My father was Scottish, though. He moved south in 1913, looking for work in the tin mines.'

'My father and grandfather were crofters in Argyll,' Ellen told him. 'They emigrated in 1911 and started a sheep farm in Western Australia.'

'*Touché*,' he said with a laugh. 'I say, you do look awfully hot. Shall we go out on deck for a spell . . . get a breath of fresh air? At least we'll be able to hear ourselves speak.'

How could she refuse? If she stayed where she was a moment longer she felt she would melt away.

He held back the heavy curtain for her to pass through to the companion way and grasped her elbow firmly for a moment while her eyes adjusted to the darkness.

They leaned on the rail and gazed across the harbour towards the open sea. The town lay in its total blackout, a velvety shadow at their backs, while in the distance they watched silvery waves breaking silently across the boom at the harbour entrance. Safe from attack by enemy submarines a little fleet of ships, huddled together within the inner basin, were black silhouettes against the night sky. The only light from their decks came from the occasional glow of a cigarette where some lookout, supposing himself unobserved, was sneaking an illicit smoke. The moon would soon be up. Already some stars had appeared in the heavens and Malcolm pointed out those she was most likely to recognise.

'Look, there's Orion . . . and the Plough . . . and see that one just standing off a little to the left? That's the North Star. I can't tell you how many times I've had to rely on her appearance to get me home.'

He had placed an arm about Ellen's shoulders to guide her as they studied the heavens. She was acutely aware of his nearness but finding the sensation not at all unpleasant, relaxed within his grasp, enjoying the feel of the fine wool cloth of his uniform jacket on her bare arms.

'I haven't had a lot of time to study the stars since I've been over here,' she told him, 'but I used to be able to recognise the constellations in the Southern hemisphere. One of the sights I miss most is the Southern Cross, twinkling up there in a cloudless sky.'

'I've never been south of the equator,' Malcolm confessed. 'You're probably a much more travelled sailor than I am!'

'If you can call six weeks as a passenger on board an ocean liner, being a sailor . . . I suppose you could say that,' laughed Ellen. 'I loved the voyage. It was in peacetime, of course. The thought of submarines lurking beneath the waves and dive bombers overhead never even crossed our minds.'

'Yes, well, it's not much fun going to sea these days, that I can tell you,' he agreed.

He leaned far out over the rail and pointed down the steep side of the ship's hull.

'That's my bus . . . down there.'

Tucked in beneath the bows of the destroyer, she could just make out the outline of a small fishing boat of the kind she was familiar with, coming and going daily from the harbour.

'What, that? It's a fishing boat,' she exclaimed, unnecessarily.

'But she's all mine,' he told her proudly. 'My very own command. Not bad for a Lieutenant with less than nine months' service eh?'

'I don't understand,' said Ellen. 'What kind of a battleship do you call that?'

'Special operations vessel.'

He turned her towards him and gazed into her clear grey eyes for a minute. 'I say, you really are an Australian, aren't you . . . you're not some dastardly German spy or something?'

She laughed despite herself.

'Don't be daft,' she cried. 'I only wondered what a Naval officer could be doing in command of such a small boat.'

'Oh, this and that,' he told her. 'Sometimes we fish a few airmen out of the drink . . . and other things.'

She thought of Stephen's pals down at Manston, remembering how much they relied upon the Air Sea Rescue Service.

'I thought you people had fast motor boats for that job,' she suggested. 'They do down on the Kent coast.'

'Ah . . . well . . . as I said, we do sometimes have other duties.'

It was obvious he was going to tell her no more. If what he did was so very secret, it was probably best if she knew nothing about it anyway.

They switched the conversation to their own backgrounds, she telling him about Kerrera station and he describing his boyhood on the River Tamar, where he had sailed a succession of dinghies and yachts pretty well from the time he could walk.

When the party began to break up, they found their way back to the wardroom, where they took their leave of the skipper.

Commander Salter shook Malcolm by the hand and gave him a meaningful glance which was tinged, Ellen thought, with admiration . . . or was it compassion?

'Good luck, old feller,' he said. 'Let us know when you get back. We'll down a couple of pink gins together next time you're in Rosyth. Goodnight, Miss McDougal, it was good of you to come.'

He held her hand briefly, looking from one to the other and smiling. They made a handsome enough couple, but he hoped she wouldn't get too attached. Blokes like McGregor could expect a pretty short span.

'Are you leaving soon, too?' Ellen asked as Malcolm steered her down the gangway and on to the dockside.

'On the morning tide,' he answered, curtly, returning a salute from the rating standing guard at the foot of the steps. His exchange with the Commander seemed to have altered his mood. He had suddenly become detached from her and Ellen assumed his mind was on his forthcoming trip.

She stopped when they were abreast of the little fishing smack which he had pointed out to her. It was a forty-footer with a tall wheelhouse two-thirds of the way along its length. The deck was strewn with the usual fishing gear; stacked, she noticed, in better order than many such vessels she had visited.

Ellen had been aboard a few trawlers since taking up her post with the Ministry of Agriculture and Fisheries. One thing she had found quite nauseating was the overpowering smell of fish. One could normally detect it while still yards away from the mooring. Malcolm's boat did not strike her in this way. She found herself commenting on the fact.

'You must have a very houseproud crew,' she observed as she stood beside him, noting with amusement his own obvious pride in his strange command.

'How do you mean?' he asked, his mind elsewhere.

'I can't smell any fish,' she said. 'I might even find myself able to take a trip to sea in this trawler. They usually make me sick.'

'Good Lord,' he said, staring at her in surprise. 'You're right . . . there ought to be a smell . . .'

'Well, I must be going,' she said brightly, catching sight of the two girls she had started out with. 'There're my friends . . . I'd best join them.' She waved and the two young women stopped, waiting for her to catch them up.

'I would see you to your digs,' he began, 'but I have a few things to attend to before we sail.'

'No need,' she replied, brightly. 'I'll be fine with the girls.'

'May I give you a call when I get back?'

'By all means,' Ellen replied, eyes shining in the starlight.

She had been mooning for long enough over Stephen, worrying about his apparent lack of feeling for her. Perhaps it was time for her to branch out a bit.

Malcolm watched her join her friends and waved as she turned at the corner. Leaping on to the deck of the trawler, he called out to the deck hand on duty.

'Able Seaman!'

'Sir?'

'Get down to the fish market as soon as it opens and buy a couple of crams of herring.'

'Oh, cripes,' the rating muttered, 'not bloody herrings again.' They seemed to get nothing else for breakfast but kippers and roll mops these days.

'When you get them on board,' Malcolm continued, 'I want both cases put down in the bilges and left to rot . . . understand?'

'Aye, aye, sir!'

No, he did not understand. What was the Old Man thinking of? In no time at all the ship would stink like a real fishing smack. He felt sick already!

All that had happened months ago, since when Ellen had been wined and dined frequently by her new boyfriend.

Malcolm was good company and she enjoyed their outings together. His calls were often unexpected and his suggestions for their entertainment generally came as a surprise: a walk in the hills, a trip in his vintage Bentley, a *ceilidh* in some little village in the mountains . . . always different, always enjoyable.

As though by some unspoken mutual consent their relationship remained Platonic in nature. Ellen continued to feel bruised from her treatment at Stephen's hands but nevertheless still carried a torch for him. Although she was happy to go out with Malcolm and even indulge in a little harmless petting when they had had a few drinks, she knew in her heart that she could never love him as she loved Stephen.

This evening she had been waiting half an hour already in the little tea shop where they had gone on their first outing together. Thinking he must be unavoidably detained, she was on the point of leaving when he burst into the shop, water streaming from his black oilskin coat. He took off his cap and hung up his sodden things on the stand before coming to her table.

'It's raining buckets out there,' he said cheerily, giving her a salutatory kiss on the forehead before sitting down in the opposite chair. 'Sorry about the phone call this afternoon. This really is a flying visit. I'm sailing again in a few hours.'

He gave an order to the waitress who hovered nearby.

'I had to let you know that I'm to get some leave at Christmas after all. I wondered if we might spend a few days together?'

'I don't know . . .' she hesitated, not liking to disappoint him. 'My aunt was rather expecting me, I think.'

'I thought that was for Hogmanay? I shall be back at sea by then.'

'I'm not sure . . .'

They both knew what was bothering her.

'Two coffees, two teacakes . . . no butter, only marge today.'

The waitress plonked the tray on the table and began to unload it.

They did not speak while the woman worked. When she had gone, Ellen looked up to find Malcolm watching her, anxiously.

'Look, if it makes you feel any better, I'll take separate rooms. I just want to spend the time with you, that's all. There's no need for anything else . . . unless you want it.'

'Oh, Malcolm, you're far too good to me,' Ellen told him, sincerely. 'I must seem like a terrible prude to you. It's not that I don't want to be with you . . .'

'But you're saving yourself for another, is that it?'

There was a note of bitterness in his voice. Until this moment they had scrupulously avoided discussing the other people in their lives. The future was too uncertain; happiness was for grabbing while it was available. Who knew what the next months, weeks, even tomorrow, might bring?

Ellen knew that she was being unfair to him. Although they never spoke of his mysterious missions, she was aware that what he did was highly dangerous. How could she deny him, when this might be his last opportunity?

'I want to go with you,' she said, suddenly making up her mind.

'And, Malcolm, one room will be enough.'

He lifted her hand and brushed the tips of her fingers with his lips.

'I love you, Ellen,' he whispered.

She could not answer him.

In the last weeks, coming up to Christmas, Ellen found herself busy visiting hill farmers in the Sutherland hinterland. In such a remote area, she was obliged to find accommodation with some of her clients and unable to get near a post office or even a telephone for several days. It was Christmas Eve when she at last drew into the University compound and parked her Ministry van.

She lifted a box of files and her instrument case from the car and made her way into the building. At the reception desk, the porter called to her.

'Miss McDougal, there's a couple of messages for you. I thought you'd want them right away.'

He handed over an envelope addressed in Annie's handwriting and another which was marked OHMS. Something from the Ministry, she supposed.

'Oh, and there was a call from a gentleman two or three days ago . . . he wanted you to ring him back but I told him you would be away until Christmas. He left this number to contact . . .'

She took the slip of paper, expecting it to be the number for Malcolm's landlady in Aberdeen. When she glanced at the figures, she knew at once it was not the number she was familiar with.

'Thanks, Angus,' she said, taking the paper and her letters to the booth. 'I'd better make this call right away.

'Operator, can you give me a Rosyth number, please?' she rattled off the figure written on the paper.

'Commander Salter,' a clipped, precise voice answered. She recognised it as belonging to the skipper of the destroyer she had last seen in Aberdeen Harbour.

'Oh, I thought I would be speaking to Lieutenant McGregor,' she stammered. 'I'm sorry to have bothered you.'

'No, hang on a minute . . . is that Miss McDougal by any chance?'

'It is.'

'Malcolm left a message for you. He asked me to pass it on. The thing is . . .' There was an embarrassed pause. 'Well, he asked me to say he's sorry about having to cancel your Christmas arrangements but he has a pressing engagement elsewhere.' There was another long pause then he repeated, 'Sorry!'

Ellen did not know what she replied. In a daze she put the handset back in its cradle and grabbed the shelf for support. Her legs had gone to jelly and she thought she was going to faint. For days she had been trying to adjust to the notion that she was about to burn her bridges where Stephen was concerned. She had just about come to terms with her decision and now, quite suddenly, all that mental preparation had gone for naught. She didn't know whether to feel angry, disappointed or relieved.

Angus was hovering nearby, possibly expecting her call to be some bad news . . .

'Are you all right, miss?' he asked anxiously. Ellen had gone very white. 'Just you come and sit down, lassie,' he insisted. 'I'll fetch you a wee glass of water.'

He returned in a few moments, bringing with him one of the girls from the lab.

'What's the matter, Ellen?' she asked, running to her side. 'Angus said he thought you might have had some bad news.'

'No, not really.' Ellen looked up and gave her friend a weak smile. 'A little disappointment, that's all. Some holiday arrangements have been cancelled at the last minute.'

'Oh, bad luck,' said the girl. Then, 'If you're at a loose end, you can always join Brenda and me at our digs . . . we've a bit of a party laid on for tomorrow evening.'

'That's very kind of you,' Ellen told her, quickly recovering her composure, 'but I think I'll have to revert to my original plan and go to my aunt's place in Glasgow.'

Ellen had quite forgotten the letters which Angus had thrust into her hand on her arrival. It was not until later, when she had finished packing her small suitcase and sat waiting for her taxi to arrive, that she remembered them.

We have seen a bit more of Stephen since his unit was posted to the West Coast. You will perhaps know that his friend's wife, Audrey Miles, is a house guest at present. We have heard nothing of the boy's chances of getting leave over the holiday so it would be wonderful if you could get down here. Audrey misses her Derek so dreadfully, I'm sure your presence will go a long way towards cheering her up . . .

Ellen put down Annie's letter and went to the window. Still no sign of the wretched taxi. They would be busy because it was Christmas Eve.

All the better if Stephen were not going to be there, she decided. She was not quite ready to meet him again, not just yet.

She tore open the second envelope.

You are directed to take up your new posting on 8 January, 1941. Report to the Administrative Offices, address as shown above, where arrangements will have been made to billet you for the duration of your posting.

Ellen had spent the last year attempting to get herself a permanent transfer to the South East of England. It was ironic to think that now her new appointment had come through, Stephen had transferred to Ayrshire. Perhaps it was just as well, under the circumstances.

The last month of 1940 and the early weeks of 1941 were marked by some of the harshest winter weather on record. For Calcutt's command it meant at first a welcome rest, but this was followed by week upon week of inactivity and an air of boredom descended upon the camp.

There were no specially constructed 1930s Officers' Quarters here. The temporary airstrip and its surrounding buildings had been thrown up earlier in the year. Accommodation consisted of Nissen huts and wooden buildings from the First World War. Many of the ground crew were housed in tents and so primitive were the arrangements that the WAAF contingent had to be farmed out to civilian houses in the vicinity, collected and returned to their billets at the end of every shift by lorry.

Heating was by a single iron stove situated centrally in each of the huts and even the officers were obliged to sleep two to a small cubicle-like room.

Stephen shared with Derek Miles.

Stumpy, eternally grateful to the doctor for arranging for Audrey to stay in Glasgow with his parents, did everything he could to ensure that the medical facilities at least were as Stephen would wish them. In these difficult conditions their friendship blossomed.

With so little work on hand, it was possible to get leave most week-ends and both of them travelled in to the city on a regular basis. While Derek enjoyed the company of his wife, Stephen pursued his studies in the University Library, having established that he could take his final examinations in surgery towards the end of March.

Audrey had settled in remarkably well in the tall terraced house on the Great Western Road. There had been a little difficulty at first between Mrs Brown and the Englishwoman, largely due to their inability to communicate readily. Audrey found it hard to understand Maggie's broad Glaswegian accent and asked so often for the housekeeper to repeat what she had said, that Mrs Brown was overheard to say to the cat on one occasion, 'Is yon Sasunnach deif or what? She canna understand the King's English!'

Anxious not to intrude any more than was absolutely necessary upon the privacy of Dr Beaton and his wife, Audrey spent a great deal of time in her room or, on dry days, walking in the Botanic Gardens.

From the start, she had undertaken to keep her own room clean and to see to her own laundry. She made sure that she used the kitchen only when Mrs Brown was out of the house and hesitated to offer any assistance with other household duties, not wishing to antagonise Maggie or cause any kind of an upset in the established arrangements.

Stuart had made an appointment for her to see the obstetrician at the maternity hospital and she was to have her baby there when the time came. It had been a great comfort to Derek to know that should there be any problems with the pregnancy, there would be a doctor on hand to take care of his wife. While Stuart did not take an officious interest in Audrey's pregnancy, he did keep an eye on her and encouraged her to speak up if anything was bothering her. She seemed to be a very healthy young woman and so far had had no reason to trouble him with her condition.

Annie, busy with her duties on behalf of the City Council, had had little opportunity to get to know her visitor properly. Audrey rose late so as to keep out of the Beatons' way when they were preparing for the day ahead, and retired early, protesting that she felt she needed plenty of rest. When the three of them met for the evening meal, they exchanged pleasantries and there was a cordial enough atmosphere but Stuart and Annie were concerned to discuss matters of mutual interest from their day's activities and, inevitably, Audrey's participation in these conversations was rather limited.

'Will Stephen be getting leave during the festivities?' Stuart asked one evening when, the meal finished, Audrey and Annie were collecting the dirty dishes.

'I don't know . . . have you heard anything, Audrey?' Annie enquired.

'It seems that they had to decide whether they would take their leave at Christmas or New Year, and Stephen and Derek have both chosen New Year.'

Audrey had been disappointed to learn that she and Derek would not be together on Christmas Day. It had always been a very special time at home and she knew that she was going to miss all the little rituals which her parents had built in to their celebrations over the years. That she would be obliged to spend the day without her husband and in the company of strangers, no matter how thoughtful and caring, filled her with dismay.

'I believe that Ellen is hoping to join us for Hogmanay,' said Annie excitedly. 'With the boys home as well, we shall have quite a party.'

'Ellen? Isn't she the Australian girl who came to our wedding?' Audrey remembered Stephen's cousin. She had caused quite a stir amongst the young pilots at Manston that day. Ellen was a lively spark, likely to brighten up any gathering. It would be a change to have a woman of her own age around for a day or two.

'Yes, that's her,' Annie agreed. 'It rather depends on her work, of course,' she went on. 'She's a veterinary surgeon with the Ministry, you know. She ought to be able to take a few days' leave, but like doctors, vets are invariably called out at all the most awkward times. Let's hope she really can get away for a day or two.'

'I imagine that Christmas is more important than New Year to Audrey,' Stuart suggested. 'We'll have to do something extra special to mark the day, Annie. We can't let our English visitor think that the Scots don't know how to do the job properly.'

'It's not that we don't celebrate Christmas,' Annie explained, hurriedly. 'It has always been a great time for the children, with presents on Christmas morning and so on, but we Calvinists were brought up to observe the religious aspects of Christmas with sobriety and tend to reserve the extremes of gluttony and merrymaking for the New Year!'

'I wonder . . .' Audrey hesitated, shyly. 'Would you allow me to organise Christmas for you? Then we could have the best of both worlds.'

'That would be a lovely idea,' cried Annie, delighted that at last their visitor was taking a real interest in things.

She had been worried that Audrey had been so distant with them, always polite and agreeable but not integrating in any way. The only time she had really shown any sign of exuberance had been on the one or two occasions Derek had come to join her. In his presence, and with the Beatons gathered around the table, she had sparkled, joining in with the witty conversation of the two younger men and recalling anecdotes about life in the WAAF which had them all reeling with laughter. As soon as Derek departed, however, she'd immediately crept back into her shell.

'It will be very quiet, of course,' said Annie. 'Just the three of us. Mrs Brown will be going out to Bearsden to visit her mother so we shan't see her on Christmas Day.'

'Oh, that doesn't matter,' said Audrey cheerfully, 'there was always just the three of us at home.'

She finished on a wistful note and Annie and Stuart exchanged glances. They had not realised just how homesick the poor girl had been.

'I shall really look forward to Christmas this year,' Stuart declared. 'When we were kids it was always rather a dull day: two trips to church, a huge meal and carol singing round the piano.'

'Just you make sure that none of your patients does a wobbly on us,' laughed Annie. 'Audrey and I are relying on you to be Father Christmas!'

The two women retired to the kitchen to do the washing up and Stuart relaxed with his pipe and the evening paper. Above the rattle of crockery and the clash of pans he heard their animated conversation and smiled contentedly to himself. Annie had been needing something to get her thoughts away from the daily grind. Her duties as an Air Raid Warden had been placed on the back burner while the enemy concentrated his activities in the South and East of Britain, but her work in the field of social services had increased as the casualty lists had lengthened. Many of the Clydebank men had joined the Navy and the Merchant Service, both of which had suffered greatly in this first year of the war. It had been Annie's task to see to it that the families of those killed and injured were taken care of properly and not a day passed that she did not have some harrowing tale to tell him. He had hoped that the introduction of another woman to the household might help to take her mind off her problems, but until today Audrey had had little impact upon either of their lives.

As Christmas drew near, excitement began to mount in the Beaton household. Mrs Brown became involved in the preparations, assisting Audrey to collect the necessary ingredients to make a really impressive Christmas cake.

'I've been keeping back a few treats just for this,' she told the Englishwoman with a knowing wink, and brought out a tin of black treacle, a packet of sultanas and one of currants together with a handful of dried apricots.

On the day of the baking, Stuart suddenly appeared mid-morning.

'Look at this,' he said. 'Old Mrs Meldron was down to see her daughter in Luss last weekend and she's brought back some eggs. Wasn't that kind of her?' Carefully placing a small dish on the table he proudly revealed its contents: three large brown eggs.

Mrs Brown pounced upon them enthusiastically.

'Just what we wanted,' she exclaimed. 'I was expecting to have to do with milk for binding and grated carrots for moisture. A pity it's not six, though. My recipe calls for six.'

'Be thankful for small mercies,' said Audrey, cracking the precious eggs into a bowl and beating them vigorously.

Stuart had acquired a small Christmas tree on one of his trips into the countryside and Annie unearthed a lifetime's collection of tinsel and ornaments, so that when Christmas morning arrived, the house looked as festive and welcoming as anyone could have wished.

From the early-morning tea, served in bed, to the four-course dinner which Audrey and Mrs Brown had devised despite food rationing, the day was entirely within Audrey's control and she revelled in the cries of delight as each new extravagance was unveiled.

After breakfast, they had attended Morning Service in the United Reformed Church were Annie and Stuart had worshipped ever since they had first come to live on the Great Western Road, sixteen years ago.

Audrey was astonished at the number of people who had gathered around them as they left the church that morning. Apart from friends and neighbours, there were many of Stuart's patients, clients of Annie's, and several members of the volunteer services, never without their badges of rank and their tin helmets, even in church. Audrey, standing beside them on the gravel drive, was conscious of the goodwill surrounding her hosts. She did not envy them their popularity, however, for she had seen at first hand the toll that their efforts on behalf of the community had taken of their lives. Having witnessed the cost to them in terms of loss of privacy, she cherished her own anonymity.

This did not stop her sharing in the warm glow of belonging, however. These past few days had proved to her that the Beatons did not resent her presence among them at all, and she resolved to take a greater part in running the house from now on. There were numerous little ways in which she could be of help to Annie.

They arrived home to find a visitor squatting on the top step. When she stood to greet them, Audrey saw that it was a tall woman, effectively disguised by an all-enveloping tweed cloak and a felt cloche hat pulled down tightly over her ears. Even Annie appeared mystified until a thick woollen scarf was drawn back to reveal a pale face, drawn and pinched in the cold wind, which broke suddenly into its more familiar smile.

'Ellen,' gasped Annie, 'how lovely . . . we weren't expecting you till later in the week.'

'I'm sorry to spring this on you, Auntie,' gasped Ellen, her breath clouding in the crisp atmosphere. 'They decided to close down the laboratories for the whole of the holiday. I'm not due back until the second. Hello, Audrey, Aunt Annie mentioned in her letter that you were staying. How's Derek? Is he getting any leave at all?'

'Why are we all standing shivering on the doorstep?' demanded Stuart, thrusting his key into the lock and opening wide the door.

They piled into the cosy parlour where the Christmas tree glistened in a watery sunlight which filtered through heavily protected windows. Crossed strips of brown sticky tape were supposed to reduce the shattering of the glass when a bomb fell.

'Oh, how pretty you've made it,' cried Ellen. 'In Aberdeen they don't seem to make a great deal of Christmas.'

'No, I can just imagine . . . in Aberdeen!' Stuart laughed and all but Audrey joined in.

'The Granite City enjoys a reputation for strong Calvinistic attitudes,' Ellen explained. 'It'll be very different at Hogmany, I can assure you.'

Stuart agreed, recalling one party he had attended there as a student from which he had only fully recovered three days later.

'We can only offer you a scratch lunch, I'm afraid,' said Annie, 'our main dinner is planned for this evening.'

'That'll be fine, thank you,' said Ellen. 'I've been travelling since early this morning. It will be nice to have a rest before the feasting begins.'

Audrey's dinner was a tremendous success.

She refused all help in the kitchen until the time came for washing

MARY WITHALL

up, whereupon Ellen and she insisted that Annie and Stuart should stay where they were in the parlour while the girls worked.

'Would you care for a brandy?' Stuart asked as Annie settled herself on the sofa before the fire.

The flickering flames were reflected in the gleaming blackness of the ornate cast-iron fire surround. Annie had turned out the electric lighting and the room was illuminated by just two old oil lamps, brought with her from her mother's home on Eisdalsa. Their soft light picked up the polished brass of the fire-irons and reflected off the many pieces of antique porcelain placed strategically to catch the eye. The only other illumination came from tiny sparks of light reflected from the tinsel and glass ornaments which decorated the tree.

Stuart joined his wife on the couch and she snuggled against his shoulder, their bodies moulding into one. Content to sip their brandy in silence, Annie and Stuart reflected upon past Christmases, recalling parents and grandparents long departed, and all the years of their child-hood.

In the kitchen the two young women washed and dried, stacked china and polished saucepans.

'I'll bet you're looking forward to next week,' observed Ellen. 'It must be awful, only seeing Derek occasionally.' She had not yet steeled herself to ask if he would be coming alone.

'We're fortunate compared with so many people,' Audrey insisted. 'Some women have not seen their husbands for more than a year, and what about those men who are prisoners of war . . . who knows how long it will be before they're home again?'

'I imagine that weddings amongst aircrew and groundstaff are quite common in the RAF?' Ellen observed.

'Lots of people form friendships,' Audrey agreed, 'although marriage for most of them is out of the question. The boys who fly the fighter planes have such a short life expectancy, you see.'

She sounded casual, but it was obvious that Audrey had been deeply scarred by the continuous losses she had witnessed amongst the Company's personnel.

'What about Stephen, does he have a permanent girlfriend?' Ellen asked, suddenly. She had understood that Grace was beyond his reach but that did not mean there wasn't someone else.

Audrey was surprised at the harshness in the Australian girl's voice

234

when she asked about Stephen. What was it? Was she interested in him herself perhaps?

'There's no prospective Mrs Stephen Beaton, so far as I know,' she replied, lightly, 'though I know one or two girls on the station who swoon every time he crosses their path. He goes to the local dances and so on, but I wouldn't say there was anyone special.'

Changing tack she asked Ellen pointedly. 'Have you known him long yourself?'

'On and off, most of our lives. He came out to Australia to visit his grandma when he was only three years old and we sort of took a shine to each other. When we were little, we exchanged letters and cards every Christmas and then, while he was waiting to get into Medical School, he spent three months at Kerrera station . . . back in 1932, that was. Of course his gran – Anne McDougal – was dead by then but he stayed with his Aunt Mary and her daughter Flora, and we spent the best part of every day together. We had a great time!'

'Didn't he introduce you as his cousin?' Audrey found herself confused by their relationship.

'Yes, well, that's not strictly true,' Ellen answered. 'His Grandma, Anne McDougal, was my father's step-mother. She married her second husband, John McDougal, when they were both quite old. Before that her name was McGillivray – that was Aunt Annie's name before she was married. I grew up calling Mrs McDougal "Gran" of course. I never knew my real grandmother, she'd died years before I was born. So, you see, Stephen and I have no real blood ties. I suppose you could say, like the Hollywood stars, we're just good friends.' She gave a hollow little laugh.

'Something tells me you'd like to be more than "just good friends",' observed Audrey, smiling at her companion. 'Stephen must be blind if he can't see it.'

'He seemed very taken with Grace Dobbie when I saw him last,' Ellen confessed. 'Despite the fact that she's engaged to his best friend, Stephen seems to think the sun shines out of her eyes.'

Audrey had heard that Colin Sheen had broken off his engagement to Grace but she didn't want to upset Ellen further by telling her.

'Oh, well. Maybe now he's so far away from Manston, he'll find other things to concentrate on,' she suggested. 'You'll have a chance to work on him yourself at the end of the week. I hope you've got some suitable glad rags for partying?'

'You mean, he's coming on leave too?' Ellen asked, sounding dismayed.

'I would have thought you would have been pleased,' said Audrey.

'Not now . . . there's someone else, you see.'

'Whoops! And where's he going to be next weekend?'

'We were meant to be spending Christmas together,' Ellen explained, 'but he got called away for special duties at the last minute.'

'What's he, another vet?'

'No, he's a sailor. RNVR.'

'Are you going to marry him?'

'I doubt it . . . I really don't know. He's not asked me . . . yet.'

'And anyway, there's still Stephen,' Audrey concluded. She thought carefully for a minute before offering her next piece of advice.

'If I were you, when the boys are here at Hogmany, I'd let it slip that there's someone else in the offing. A little competition can do wonders in circumstances like this.'

Ellen continued polishing glasses with elaborate care, stopping momentarily to wipe away a tear.

'Oh, look here . . . no man as insensitive as Stephen Beaton is worth shedding tears over,' Audrey insisted. 'Come on, dry your eyes before Mrs Beaton sees you.'

Ellen managed a brave smile and finished putting away the glasses.

'I think it's about time we disturbed those two love birds in the parlour,' she said at last, a little more cheerfully.

Audrey looked surprised.

'Did you ever see two old fogeys so attached to each other?' Ellen demanded. 'Talk about Darby and Joan! I hope you and Derek are still cuddling up in front of the fire when you've been married as long as they have!'

Chapter Fifteen

'Will you be going home for New Year?'

Janet Fraser frequently found an excuse to report to the dispensary when she knew that Stephen would be there. Since her accident she had been a regular visitor, despite the fact that the injury to her hand had healed quickly, leaving only the faintest scar.

Stephen, nodding in answer to her question, waited patiently for her to tell him why she had come. With so little activity on the airfield, even routine maintenance jobs had dried up. He realised that one reason for the lengthening queues at sick parade was sheer boredom.

Janet was unusually reticent today. He had to prompt her to find out why she was here.

'I seem to have a little problem with my periods. I'm a few days late . . .' She blushed. It wasn't the sort of thing one wished to discuss with a doctor whom one rather fancied in a non-professional way.

'How many is a few days?' he asked.

'Well . . . about ten, actually.'

Stephen pursed his lips, sat back in his chair, placed the tips of his fingers together and gave her a long appraising stare.

'I hoped you might give me something to bring them on . . .' Her voice trailed into silence under his penetrating gaze.

'Not a lot I can do about it, I'm afraid,' said Stephen, casually. 'Are you usually quite regular?'

'Yes, as clockwork.'

'Then we'll just have to see, won't we?' He got to his feet and went to the basin. As he scrubbed his hands he told her to strip off and get on to the couch.

The examination was over in a few minutes. Really, he wondered, did these girls take him for an idiot? He knew, and she knew, that she was pregnant. Ten days indeed! Nearly two months would be his guess.

His first impression of Janet Fraser had been of a straightforward young woman with an extraordinary aptitude for things mechanical, but in all other ways a very attractive female. She was immensely popular with the boys and had most probably broken a few hearts during her stay amongst them.

Stephen himself had kept her at arm's length, regarding her as way out of his league. He had looked up her family background. He even knew where she lived now. Before the war he had often cycled past the imposing gates to the Frasers' estate on Loch Fyne. He rather envied her the spanking little open tourer which she kept on the station, but he was not going to allow the promise of a turn behind the wheel to get him ensnared.

'I'll need a urine sample,' he said casually, handing her a specimen jar. 'Just leave it with Devlin as you go out.'

Janet looked at him in surprise.

'Is that all?' she demanded.

'Until we get the result of the test, yes.' He made a note on her file and thrust it on top of the pile in his OUT basket.

'If it proves positive, we'll need to see about getting you a discharge.'

'Discharge?' she cried out, ignoring the thinness of the partition and the fact that the repulsive Devlin creature was probably listening behind the door.

'You won't be able to stay in the Service if you're pregnant,' Stephen told her, dismissively. 'Send in whoever's waiting out there, will you?'

Ignoring this request, she sat down on the chair in front of his desk and crossed her legs. Her tight uniform skirt receded to expose an expanse of comely thigh.

The front leg swung to and fro, invitingly.

'Surely you can help out a friend, Doctor?' she purred. 'I mean, we all enjoy a bit of fun now and again . . .'

He coloured slightly, remembering an evening he had spent in company with Janet's best friend. He'd been a little drunk at the time, he recalled. There'd been something to celebrate that day when, for the first time, more enemy than allied aircraft were shot down.

'Most of us have the sense to know when to stop,' he said sharply, regaining control of the situation.

He found himself unable to avoid Janet's steady gaze.

'I hope you're not suggesting that I arrange for you to have an abortion?' he blurted out when she still remained silent. 'That's something you'd need to talk about with some of your Maryhill tycoons!'

She had boasted to him of her brother's work in Glasgow's West End, where he had a very lucrative practice providing medical services for the wealthy which were way out of the reach of ordinary mortals.

'Oh, but I can't go there, Doctor,' she whimpered. 'Fergus would tell my parents and there'd be hell to pay. If you can't do it, at least give me a telephone number or something.'

'I won't be party to an abortion,' Stephen told her firmly. 'You'll have to get the fellow to marry you.'

'Can't do that, darling, don't you see?'

Stephen chose to ignore the 'darling'. 'He's already married?' he concluded.

Janet nodded, miserably.

'In any case . . . marriage would be out of the question. Daddy would never hear of it.'

'Well then, let's hope it's a false alarm. Come and see me when you get back from your leave. I should have the result of the test by then.'

A girl with Janet's privileged background would manage to pay her way out of her difficulty. She was not going to drag him into it. It was the other poor little devils Stephen felt sorry for, the young girls away from home on their own for the first time and easy prey for any chap in a uniform who showed an interest. No one blamed the pilots for having a good time while they had the chance, in some cases it was their first and last opportunity to experiment with sex, but it was a pity that they seemed to leave such a legacy of unhappiness behind them.

Two days later, as Stephen was leaving last-minute instructions for Devlin, Janet came again to his surgery.

'Look,' she said, all sweetness, 'I'm really sorry about the other day – everything's OK after all.'

'I'm very glad,' he replied. 'Just be more careful next time.'

'My dad's throwing a big Hogmanay shindig at the Marlborough Halls in Shawlands. How would you like to go? It should be lots of fun.'

'That would be rather difficult,' he told her. 'My mother has already invited quite a party for the evening, and I can hardly walk out on everyone. Thanks all the same.'

Apart from Derek and Audrey he had persuaded the sole remaining member of B flight, Arnold Piper, to share his leave.

But Janet was not prepared to take no for an answer.

'Bring them all along,' she insisted, 'the more the merrier.' She took from her bag an impressive-looking invitation, heavily embossed with lettering in black and gold. Janet scribbled something carelessly across the top, murmuring as she did so. 'There . . . that should do the trick. If anyone queries it, tell them to fetch me.'

Without waiting for his response she dropped the card on his desk and glided out in a cloud of expensive perfume. At the door she turned for a brief moment. 'I'll look forward to seeing you there.' It was more of a command than an invitation. Before he could say another word, she was gone.

Stephen picked up the card and read what she had written: 'Admit Flight Lieutenant Beaton and party', followed by her signature.

It was just possible that they might be looking for something to do . . . after the bells. Stephen thrust the invitation into his tunic pocket and resumed his preparations for departure.

Maggie Brown was determined that not one speck of the previous year's dust should be carried over into 1941. As she burnished brassware and polished the heavy mahogany furniture in the parlour she could hear the sounds of activity in the kitchen and pursed her lips in resignation. No doubt those two young women would leave the place in a terrible mess and she would still be clearing up long after she was due to go home to her own celebrations.

She had been relieved to find that the presence of Miss Ellen in the household had considerably cheered the other young woman. Maggie had some sympathy for the pregnant Audrey as she herself was having to manage without a husband at home. She understood what the poor thing must be going through. Maggie took what life had to offer on the chin, however, with never a murmur of self-pity. What a shame that Audrey had to be English!

Annie had been anxious to find something suitable for their Hogmanay dinner. Their combined ration cards could produce only half a leg of pork, hardly enough for six people, and then when Stevie had phoned to say he was bringing an additional friend, she knew it would not do.

Stuart had saved the day by bringing home the solution to her problem in the shape of a very large goose; a present from a grateful patient. There was just one problem with this generous gift. The goose was still complete . . . unplucked and undrawn.

'I don't know how you can do that,' declared Audrey, whose limited experience of cooking poultry had always begun with an oven-ready bird.

She turned away in disgust as Ellen thrust her hand into the bird's rear end and withdrew it grasping a bloody mixture of entrails.

'Started doing this as soon as I could stand on a chair beside my mother at the kitchen table,' Ellen told her. 'We can have as many as twenty men to feed at shearing time, and on any day of the year no fewer than eight of us sit down to dinner. We kill our own sheep and chickens. I've known Mum and me pluck and dress as many as six birds for one meal when we were really busy.'

Audrey shuddered at the thought and concentrated on preparing the potatoes. That was something she *had* had practice with . . . in the early days of her service in the WAAF she had peeled mountains of vegetables.

Ellen held the bird by its legs and plunged it, whole, into a pan of boiling water which she had left simmering on the stove.

'What's that for?' demanded Audrey.

'Helps with the plucking,' she explained. With a cloth wound tightly around her hand, she grasped the bird's legs, dangled it for a few moments over the pan to allow most of the water to drain and then swung it back on to the table, leaving a trail of water across Maggie Brown's polished tiles.

As Ellen squatted with the bird between her legs and plucked its feathers on to a sheet of newspaper spread at her feet, Audrey got on her knees to mop up the spilled water. After a few moments both girls, the floor, the table and every flat surface in the room was covered in soft white feathers. Audrey began to laugh.

'What's up?' demanded Ellen.

'I'm just imagining what Mrs Brown will say when she sees this.'

She tried to rise, but encumbered as she was by her swollen belly, sat back laughing. 'Someone will have to pull me up,' she gasped.

At that moment the doorbell rang insistently.

'Heavens . . . that can't be them already?' gasped Audrey.

They could hear the deep murmur of men's voices and Mrs Brown's higher pitched reply.

Footsteps approached from the hall and the door was flung open.

Disturbed by the sudden gust of air from outside, the feathers lifted and swirled around the room. Now, not only Audrey but Mrs Brown, Derek and Squadron Leader Arnold 'Squeaky' Piper were all enveloped by the downy cloud.

Derek, disregarding the mess, grasped his wife around the waist and hauled her to her feet. He hugged her to him and kissed her despite the fact that she was helpless with laughter. Ellen, seeing the expression of horror on Maggie's face, began to giggle uncontrollably as well, while Arnold Piper, looking totally bewildered, stood stiffly, like a snowman in a glass bottle, waiting for the feathers to settle all about him.

'I think,' said Mrs Brown, with a wooden expression and beginning methodically to remove feathers from Arnold's shoulders, 'that perhaps I should show the gentlemen where they will be sleeping, while you two ladies get this mess tidied up.'

Sheepishly the men followed her up the stairs carrying their cases. From the kitchen below, gales of laughter could still be heard as the two girls struggled to gather up the feathers into an old pillowcase.

When they had calmed down sufficiently to speak sensibly, Audrey asked, 'What shall we do with this lot?'

'At home we collected all the feathers and used them to stuff eiderdowns and bolsters,' Ellen told her. 'The trouble is, there aren't really enough here to do anything decent. She glanced across at her companion, thoughtfully. 'On the other hand, we might have just enough to make a tiny pillow for a baby's cot.'

Audrey was delighted. 'Oh, could we? I'd like that.'

'Let's hide them out of the way for now,' suggested Ellen, 'and perhaps tomorrow, when all the fuss is over, we can look out some ticking to make a suitable case.'

Ellen had expected Stephen to appear at any moment. When he did not come in to see them, she went looking for one of the others. Squeaky was the first to appear, Derek having disappeared upstairs with Audrey close on his heels.

'What happened to Stephen?' she demanded. 'Isn't he with you?'

'He had to see his Professor at the University,' Arnold told her. 'Something to do with these exams he's working for. He swore he'd be joining us in time for luncheon but he must have been held up.'

He glanced at his watch and Ellen gasped.

'Oh, my goodness! Just look at the time. Aunt Annie left a vegetable pie to be heated up for us to eat now, but we were so carried away with the goose I quite forgot to put it in the oven.'

She looked pleadingly at Mrs Brown. 'Do you have any suggestions, Maggie?'

'There are some sausages in the larder, and some cold potatoes left over from yesterday . . .'

'I'll tell you what,' said Derek, overhearing their discussion while still on his way down from the second landing, 'how will it be if Arnold and I go for some fish and chips while you girls tidy yourselves up? We'll leave the sausages for Steve.'

Mrs Brown's thinly disguised disapproval of the suggestion was quietly ignored. The men departed, the girls scurried off upstairs to repair the damage wrought by their exploits in the kitchen, and Maggie made her final rounds with the duster before leaving the whole bunch of them to do their worst with her spotless domain.

If she could manage to catch the early bus, she and wee Tommy would be at her mother's house at Bearsden in time for high tea.

'I wish I could say that my experience of surgery these last few months has been wide-ranging and testing,' Stephen confessed. 'The truth is that much of what I have been doing could be carried out by any reasonably competent medical orderly. In fact, I have just such a person standing in for me at the present time.'

The Professor reached into a drawer and withdrew a slim file from which he extracted a number of letters.

'That is not the opinion of those whom I have contacted at your suggestion,' he replied. 'Dr David Lewis of the Margate Cottage Hospital tells me that your conduct of routine operations satisfied everyone concerned, and that in a number of serious trauma cases your intervention undoubtedly saved the patient's life. He even provides detailed case histories of some of these incidents to substantiate his recommendation.'

The Professor shuffled the papers in his hand and continued, 'The report from your CO at RAF Blackpool Recruitment Centre, states that although you were not called upon to perform any important surgical operations, you were instrumental in reorganising the system for carrying out the basic medical testing for aircrew. He seems to have been impressed by your organisational abilities and your facility for co-operating with others. Both are qualities which one would look for in a surgeon.'

Stephen could not hide his surprise that the Wing Commander with whom he had enjoyed a rather stormy relationship had taken the trouble to reply at all, let alone in such glowing terms. Maybe he wasn't such a bad old stick after all.

Stephen realised he must have got a few people's backs up in those days when, as a very raw recruit, he was still smarting from being drafted into the Medical Service after expecting to become a pilot.

'The final communication,' the Professor continued without pause, 'was unsolicited, but carries no less weight because of that. It comes from the Burns Unit at the Queen Victoria Hospital, East Grinstead. It seems that the surgeon there has dealt with a number of patients who received their initial treatment at your hands. He not only recommends your Registration as a Member of the Royal College of Surgeons, but states that in his opinion you should specialise in the field of plastic surgery.'

The Professor paused to see what Stephen's reaction might be. The younger man seemed bemused. How did McIndoe know that he was applying for Membership at this time? He had mentioned it in passing to Digger, he remembered, and he might well have told Grace, but surely McIndoe didn't even know from which medical school Stephen had graduated?

'I have been making some enquiries about your Mr McIndoe,' the Professor continued. 'It seems that he is just about the most respected surgeon in his field . . . you have found yourself a very worthy sponsor. How do you feel about his suggestion?'

'I've only visited East Grinstead on a few occasions,' Stephen replied, 'but I must admit that the standard of work there is impressive. I suppose that I do have some aptitude for the delicate surgery involved but McIndoe would be a hard act to follow.'

Since his transfer to Prestwick, Stephen had had time to consider where his career might take him once the war was over. He had thought often of his father's conviction that in future surgery would be a matter of specialisation. The days of the country practitioner performing miracles on a kitchen table were long past. With modern methods of transport, the patients could be more easily brought to the appropriate surgeon for treatment, rather than the other way around.

'For your dissertation you will be required to prepare a number of related case studies from your own experience,' the Professor continued. 'Mr McIndoe offers you access to those files connected with your patients referred to his unit. Aware of the restraints upon your travelling to Sussex at this time, he has actually sent the material in anticipation of your agreeing to take anaplastics as your main discipline.' He reached again into his drawer and withdrew a bulging envelope which he handed across the desk to Stephen.

'You would be entering a relatively unknown area in which there is a great deal of work to be done . . . you could not choose a more appropriate field.'

The Professor had had his say. It was now up to Stephen to make up his mind.

He got to his feet, took up the package which the Professor held out to him and shook hands.

'With backing like this, I'd be a fool to refuse, wouldn't I? It looks as though I shall be spending my entire leave in the Library,' Stephen grinned.

'No harm in taking a few hours off this evening, though,' laughed the Professor. 'I intend doing so.'

Stephen took his leave, agreeing to present himself for examination in the spring. Taking the stairs two at a time, he hurried out into Byres Road and bent his head against a chill north-easterly wind as he struggled up the hill towards the University Library.

When it closed for the holiday at five o'clock, he was roused from his studies to the realisation that luncheon was long past and that his friends would be wondering where he had got to. Grabbing up a handful of books, he replaced them on the shelves. He collected two others which he needed to take with him and carried them to the counter.

By the time he arrived home, the entire company had already assembled and delicious smells were wafting from the kitchen where the goose was well under way. He burst into the drawing room to a chorus of greetings, his mother being the first to fling her arms around his neck and kiss him. His father got up from his chair and came over to shake his hand.

'How did you get on with the Prof?' he asked, eagerly.

'It's all fixed,' Stephen told him, and anticipated the next question before Stuart could ask it. 'Anaplastics. Would you believe, that fellow McIndoe actually sent in a recommendation, without being asked for one!'

'He must be impressed,' said Stuart, proudly. While his friends chivvied him about forgetting the time, Stephen greeted Audrey with a friendly peck on the cheek and looked about him, rather disappointed.

'I had hoped to find Ellen here,' he said to his mother. 'Couldn't she get away?'

'She's in the kitchen, dear. She'll be so pleased to see you.'

Throwing his overcoat carelessly into the nearest chair, Stephen strode out, calling, 'Come out, come out, wherever you are!'

At the sound of his voice, all Ellen's resolve left her. For hours she had been steeling herself for their first encounter and he hadn't appeared.

Throughout luncheon she had kept only half her attention on the conversation, expecting at any minute to hear him arriving. As the time had worn on her imagination had taken over . . . he'd met someone and was drinking in a bar somewhere or else having a jolly tête-à-tête over tea and cream cakes with his latest conquest. How could he treat his mother so casually? Annie had been waiting for him just as anxiously, poor woman. What a selfish beast he was!

Ellen had been basting the goose and as he entered the room she slid the heavy meat tin back into the oven so quickly that she caught her wrist on the red hot oven door, tipping the tray so that hot fat spilled on to the floor.

'Oh, damn!' she cried out, and stared down at the reddening area of skin.

'Here, stick it under the cold tap.'

Stephen led her to the sink and ran the cold water.

'It'll take away the pain and reduce the damage,' he said, forcing her burnt wrist under the flow. Then, when after a few seconds she tried to turn off the tap, 'No, keep it there until I tell you to stop.'

After a few more minutes, he turned off the water himself and examined the burn.

'How does it feel now?' he asked.

'Sore,' answered Ellen, an ungovernable rage mounting within her. She snatched her hand away and grabbed at a cloth, beginning to mop up the spilt fat.

'Here, I'll do that.' He attempted to take the cloth from her. 'You sit down, you've had a bit of a shock.'

'Oh . . . keep your doctoring for those who need it!' Ellen screamed at him. She threw the cloth down and ran out of the room, slamming the door behind her.

The goose was cooked to perfection.

Stuart leaned across and patted Ellen's hand. 'What a wife you'll make for someone,' he said, glancing pointedly in his son's direction.

Annie shot him a warning glance. The worst thing Stuart could do would be to urge Stephen towards marriage with anyone. He would probably do the opposite, just because his father had recommended it. What a stubborn, independent lot these Beatons were . . .

'If I were thirty years younger, and single,' Stuart added, forestalling any protest from Annie, 'I wouldn't hesitate to ask you myself.'

'And I would not hesitate to say yes.' Ellen leaned over and gave him a kiss to applause from all around the table.

Having regained her composure by lying down for a few moments on her bed, she had gone in search of Stuart and a bandage for her wrist. When she eventually appeared in the drawing room, she took her place on the couch between Squeaky and Derek, avoiding Stephen's questioning gaze. She had spent the remainder of the afternoon on the periphery of a number of different conversations. There were enough people talking for her to remain silent without attracting attention.

At dinner she had managed to seat herself next to Stuart while Stephen had been placed at the far end of the table, next to Annie.

'I don't know what I would have done without you girls today,' she said now. 'It's quite amazing how everyone finds something urgent to be dealt with just as soon as they realise a holiday is imminent. Most of the dramas I've dealt with today could have been handled a week ago.'

'What does your work entail?' asked Arnold, intrigued.

'What does it not!' Stuart gave a hollow laugh.

'My department is responsible for the welfare of ordinary families whose lives have been disrupted by the war,' Annie explained. 'We deal with temporary housing, welfare grants, provision of clothing and essential household items for those caught in the bombing, the placement and welfare of evacuees . . .'

'In fact,' Stuart added, 'anything that does not come under the headings of Fire, Police or Medical Services.'

'Fortunately,' said Annie, 'apart from making the necessary preparations in case of air raids, there has been no necessity to exercise many of my roles. I pray I shall never be called upon to do so.'

'It seems to be a very responsible job for one woman to take on,' suggested Derek Miles. 'How is anyone selected for such work?'

'I'll have you know you're looking at one of the first women law graduates in Scotland,' said Stephen, proudly.

'It was all a long time ago,' his mother dismissed the topic. 'Now then, what are you young people going to do to celebrate Hogmanay?'

'I rather thought you would want us to stay here,' said Stephen, tentatively.

'Nonsense! Your father and I are quite content to sit up together and welcome in the New Year on our own. Afterwards we shall go to bed – always providing Stuart's patients don't make a nuisance of themselves by falling down in a fit or having babies or whatever.'

'We could all go up to St George's Square,' said Audrey. 'Isn't that what people usually do here, on New Year's Eve?'

'Are you sure you're up to it?' demanded Derek anxiously. He appealed to Stuart. 'What do you think, Docter Beaton?'

'So long as she keeps well wrapped up and doesn't get too tired, why not? Go on and enjoy yourselves while you can.'

'I'll just go and get my coat,' said Audrey eagerly, before Derek could change his mind. 'Are you coming, Ellen?'

This holiday had turned into something of a nightmare for her. She didn't see how she could face further hours of trying to appear normal when she felt so unhappy. Maybe it would be better to be out in the streets with all the crowds. At least there she wouldn't have to make conversation with anyone, least of all Stephen. The wine at dinner had gone to her head and she was beginning to feel rather more cheerful even if she was slurring her words a little bit. Linking her arm through Arnold Piper's, she said, 'I think it's a splendid idea, don't you, Squeaky? Let's all go and have a good time!'

By the time they had walked to the Square, the young people were glowing from their exertions. The good food and wine within combatted the cold without, to excellent effect. They walked, Ellen supported by Arnold in the front, and Audrey and Derek bringing up the rear with Stephen. They had been singing the old favourites for most of the way to help them keep in step: *Pack Up Your Troubles, It's A Long Way To Tipperary, Cockles and Mussels.* Audrey began the first few bars of *There'll Always Be An England*, and was howled down by Squeaky. 'You'll get us all lynched,' he laughed, and immediately broke into *I Belong To Glasgow*.

Stephen appeared quite unmoved by Ellen's discomfiture. Apart from a polite enquiry after her burn, once his father had attended to it, he had made no further attempt to talk to her. He was enjoying the singing now, though. All five of them stepped out together in *The Lambeth Walk*, and it was to this tune that they entered the great open space where three of the city's major roads meet. Not a vehicle could be seen for the thousands of people milling about, crowding the footpaths and roadway alike.

It was a bright, moonlit night and despite the blackout there was enough light for people to find their way without too much bumping and barging. As the crowds became more dense the party formed up around the two girls to ensure that Audrey, in particular, came to no harm in the crush. Within minutes of their arrival a dozen clocks on the surrounding buildings could be heard whirring in preparation for their big moment. At the twelfth stroke the multitude erupted in a great burst of greetings, shouts and laughter. Stranger kissed stranger, lovers lingered over their embrace and children held up their arms to be lifted high among the crowds.

Ellen threw herself into Squeaky's arms and for a moment the whole world was blotted out as he swung her round in his strong grip. Then he set her on her feet and it was Stephen's turn to kiss her, which he did first with a rather diffident peck, and then hard on the mouth, holding the kiss for so long that she emerged breathless to find him staring down at her, a puzzled expression on his face.

'I've hurt you, Ellen,' he murmured, his words clear despite the tumult around them. 'I don't know what I've done, but please forgive me.'

He put his head on one side, reminding her of a pet dog asking to be taken for a walk. She couldn't help smiling.

'Friends?' he asked.

'Friends.' She nodded, and allowed him to place his arm round her waist.

Audrey was receiving a fair share of attention because of her condition. Seeing her in danger of being overwhelmed by the crush of people, a burly six-foot policeman, of the kind that only Glasgow is able to produce, steered them into a corner protected on three sides by masonry. From this vantage point they could see all, without being in any danger of going down in the crush. The first few bars of *Auld Lang Syne* were taken up by the crowd and soon arms were linked and voices joined in unison.

The war seemed worlds away. For one fleeting, bitter moment Stephen reflected that many of these people knew nothing of air raids, had never experienced the scream of falling bombs or that deathly hush in the moment before the high explosive was detonated. He glanced at his two friends and wondered what they were feeling at this moment.

With their arms around each other's shoulders, Stumpy Miles and Squeaky Piper were rendering at the tops of their voices a favourite ditty from the airman's repertoire, while those around them mouthed the words until they felt they knew them well enough to join in.

After a while the crowds began to thin and while the stalwarts linked arms and paraded around the square, determined to carry on with their revels until dawn, others drifted off to continue their celebrations somewhere out of the cold night air.

Stephen led his friends to a pub he had frequented as a student, in a back alley off Buchanan Street. They found the girls a seat and while Derek took his place beside them, Stephen and Arnold forced their way to the bar.

'Had enough?' Derek enquired of his wife. She had dark shadows under her eyes and looked a little pinched and weary.

Audrey, not wanting to be the one to break up the party, would have denied that she was tired had not Ellen insisted.

'If you two want to go on home, I'm sure the others will understand.' She appreciated how desperately Audrey wanted her husband to herself.

At the bar, Stephen extracted his wallet from his sporran, an action which amused Arnold Piper.

'I didn't realise you guys actually used those things,' he remarked.

'The sporran has a considerable advantage over trouser pockets, I can tell you,' replied Stephen, allowing the handsome fur-trimmed leather pouch to fall back against the folds of his kilt. 'You don't hear of too many pickpockets robbing a man with a sporran!'

Arnold could not help but admire the splendid outfit which Stephen wore with so much confidence. While part of his mind abhorred the notion of dressing so conspicuously, he had to confess to feeling a distinct pang that here was a garb he was not entitled to wear. Glancing around at the sea of customers, he realised that a large number of the men were similarly clad in Highland dress. Men who in normal circumstances would never stand out in a crowd, took on a powerful stance and an imposing presence when wearing their native costume. It was no wonder the Scottish soldier was held in so much respect by his enemies.

As he extracted a ten-shilling note from his wallet, Stephen noticed the stiff white card which Janet Fraser had given him.

'If we want to finish the evening in style, we could go along to this do at the Marlborough,' he suggested, showing Arnold the invitation.

'Janet Fraser?' Arnold lifted his eyebrows and rolled his eyes. 'I didn't realise you were so well in there.'

'Grateful patient,' Stephen explained, turning a little pink nonetheless.

'I wish she would show some gratitude towards me,' was the other's comment.

'Well, what do you think?' asked Stephen.

'Best ask the others what they want to do,' suggested the Squadron Leader as with great skill, born of much practice, he lifted three brimming glasses of beer, leaving Stephen to bring along the girls' port and lemon.

'Are you sure Derek and Audrey didn't mind our splitting up?' demanded Stephen, feeling that he had been found wanting in his duties as host.

'Absolutely certain. I think Derek only came along with us because Audrey wanted to see the crowds. I'm sure that they were longing to have time alone together.'

Ellen, squashed between the two men in the back of a cab, thought enviously of the welcoming fire in the Beatons' drawing room and wished it might be she and Stephen cuddled up before it now.

The cab shot along Pollokshaw's Road, around Queen's Park, and drew to a halt before the dimly illuminated front entrance to the Marlborough Halls on Langside Avenue.

Stephen paid off the cabbie and led them through the darkened doorway into the brightly lit, overcrowded entrance hall. He found an usher who directed them to one of the smaller ballrooms on the first floor.

The moment they stepped into the room, Ellen knew that they had made a mistake.

Stephen was all right. In his full Highland dress he was indistinguishable from many of the men present, those who were not wearing white tie and tails. Arnold too, in his No. 1 uniform with an impressive array of medal ribbons, could mingle unashamedly with all the other Service officers on the floor, but she herself had dressed for dinner that evening in a short rayon dress, bright red to enhance her fair colouring and cut severely in the current style to save cloth. Most of the women swirling around the floor in the arms of their partners were dressed in ball gowns of satin or velvet, a year or two out of date perhaps but carrying the labels of the finest fashion houses in Paris and London.

She shrank back, trying to pretend she wasn't here, as a willowy female wearing a stunning creation in close-fitting gold lamé hurried over to where Stephen stood, presenting his invitation card to the steward who guarded the door from intruders.

'Stephen!' she cried. 'I'd almost given you up. We've already started the buffet . . . you know what folk are at these dos. Absolute gannets! Do come along in and meet everybody.'

Janet Fraser paused for a moment to observe, 'Oh, are these your friends? I recognised Squadron Leader Piper immediately, of course,' she took Arnold's hand limply, 'but who is this?'

Arnold being the person she was addressing at that moment, he took it upon himself to introduce Ellen.

'This is Miss McDougal,' he explained.

'How d'you do?' said Ellen, realising that in her embarrassment her Australian accent was enhanced.

'One of our overseas cousins,' declared Janet, registering the other girl's dress disdainfully, her critical appraisal speaking louder than any words. 'What fun. Well, do come along and join in everything, won't you? You'll have to introduce yourselves to everybody . . .'

Grabbing Stephen by the arm, she swept him away into the heaving throng, leaving Arnold and Ellen to fend for themselves.

Arnold saw a waiter approaching carrying a tray of glasses.

'Can I get you a drink?' he asked.

Ellen, still smarting at the way in which Stephen had allowed himself to be commandeered by that ghastly female, replied, 'Yes, please, and keep them coming!'

She and Arnold took seats in an alcove where they could overlook the proceedings without feeling too conspicuous.

'I'm afraid I'm no good at this Scottish dancing,' confessed Arnold, watching Stephen weaving in and out in the intricate measures of a Strathspey.

'Nor I,' Ellen agreed, miserably. The earlier moment of reconciliation with Stephen had left her hoping that something might be retrieved from this disastrous evening. Now he had gone off again, without a word of apology either to herself or to his friend. What had the glamorous Janet got that she had not? She was very beautiful, Ellen supposed, in a jazzy kind of way. She had clothes and money, lots and lots of money. But surely Stephen was above chasing a woman for her bank balance?

Ellen accepted the fresh drink which Arnold had brought for her. She downed it swiftly, feeling more light-headed than ever. The music had changed to a selection from one of the shows. 'Oh, good,' she said, struggling to her feet and moving unsteadily into her partner's arms. 'This sounds like a waltz or something. Let's dance.'

'I can't tell you how pleased I was to see you come through that door,' Janet assured Stephen when he had apologised for being so late arriving. 'You're not the only guests who decided to see in the New Year at the Square before coming on here. Ours was rather a good do, nevertheless.

Pipers to welcome in Father Time, loads of balloons and streamers . . . it was great fun.'

As he trampled the remains underfoot, Stephen wondered where the fripperies had come from. After sixteen months of war, such little luxuries as balloons and streamers were very hard to come by. It occurred to him that they might have given amusement to a huge number of children whose lives had been made drab by wartime restrictions. The sheer selfishness of these 'beautiful people', as Ellen had described them, was beginning to get to him.

'Exactly who are all these folk?' he demanded of Janet as, in an interval in the dancing, she led him into a small ante-room. 'There are a few in uniform, I grant you, but a whole lot more who are not.'

'Including yourself?' she said, defiantly.

'Oh, but you know I . . .' He grinned, shame-faced. She was right, of course. No doubt many of the other men had shed their uniform for the occasion.

That did not wholly excuse the tremendous display of self-indulgence, however. Champagne and whisky flowed like water and it was clear that the buffet table, now a total wreck, had carried many exotic items of food which would probably never have graced the tables of ordinary people. Indeed the pheasant, shellfish and salmon under which the tables had groaned earlier on were the produce of wealthy Scottish estates, and those indulging themselves were for the most part people whose lifestyle ensured their cellars and larders were never empty.

'I want you to meet someone,' Janet said, indicating a small group of gentlemen in immaculate evening dress who had gathered beside a roaring log fire. The great stone fireplace looked as though it had been transported direct from some baronial hall.

'That's the head of Orbison's the ship owners.' She pointed out a corpulent, florid-faced man who looked as though he might have a heart attack at any moment. 'He made a fortune when he turned over his fleet of passenger vessels to the government to be used as troop ships. The weaselly little man next to him converted his women's clothing factory in Paisley for the production of uniforms and increased his company's profits by three hundred per cent in the first year. The two younger men are my brother and his partner.'

'The racing driver?' asked Stephen.

'The doctor,' she replied. 'Andy joined the RAF as soon as war broke out. If he couldn't race cars he was determined to fly the fastest aircraft going. Unfortunately, he drove a Spitfire into the ground a couple of months ago.'

Stephen was shaken by her bluntness. 'I'm sorry,' he stammered, 'I didn't know.'

'Why should you?' Janet demanded, bitterly. 'No one is interested in ex-rally drivers these days, and Andy didn't last long in his new profession. He wasn't a famous ace – why should you have heard?'

Wary now of making another unfounded assumption, Stephen asked, 'Is your other brother in the Service too?'

'Not him.' Janet laughed, hollowly. 'Daddy wouldn't hear of it. One son as cannon fodder was quite enough. There's the dynasty to consider, after all. Fergus escaped call-up by virtue of his medical practice. He's personal physician to a few people in high places.' She tapped her nose to indicate that the names were too important to mention.

If Stephen was meant to be impressed he certainly was not. In fact, he was beginning to wish he had never come. Simply associating with people who were busy lining their own pockets while others made sacrifices to protect their interests, made him feel dirty.

He studied his watch and looked around, seeking his two companions.

'Look,' he said, 'I should go and find Ellen and Arnold . . . the people I came with. It's really time we were going.'

'Not until I've introduced you to Fergus,' Janet insisted, and led him across the room.

The party in front of the fire broke up and, having introduced Stephen to her brother, Janet slipped her arm through that of Fergus's partner, a young man called Donald McKenzie, and took him out of hearing. While only half listening to her brother, Stephen kept his eye on the other pair and could not help noticing the professional manner in which McKenzie seemed to be giving Janet the once-over. Anyone might have thought she was his patient rather than a dancing partner.

Janet's brother was a suave individual, perhaps ten years Stephen's senior. He was as tall as Stephen himself but his sallow colouring, dark hair and eyes intimated a Latin ancestry. The name Fraser however suggested a solid Scottish background. Everything about Fergus oozed wealth and position. Remembering the home that he came from, Stephen wondered why he had needed to train for a profession in the first place.

'You're the fellow who sewed up Janet's hand, aren't you?' asked Fraser. Stephen found both his voice and his manner too smooth and patronising.

'All in a day's work,' he replied, brusquely.

'It was a neat job,' insisted Fergus, 'a cut like that might have left her with crippled fingers. Its good to see that the RAF employs medics who can do a decent bit of needlework. Specialist, were you, before the war?'

'No,' Stephen replied, 'I didn't wait to take my Membership finals. I was too eager to get into uniform.'

'That's a pity,' drawled the other.

'I'm hoping to rectify the matter in the spring,' Stephen added, 'always assuming we're not posted away from Prestwick beforehand.'

'I'll wish you luck then,' said the other. 'Any idea what you'll be specialising in?'

'I was thinking of plastic surgery, actually. I've done a little work with burns patients . . . thought it might be an idea to follow it up.'

'Splendid,' agreed the other. 'We could do with an anaplastics man.'

'We?'

'At the clinic. You'll have to look us up when this spot of bother is all over.'

Fergus fished in his breast pocket and drew out a small but expensively produced business card. Stephen gave it only a perfunctory glance before thrusting it into his sporran.

'Well, it's been good to meet you.' Fergus shook his hand and melted into the crowd.

Left alone at last, Stephen sought out his friends and found them dancing together in the main ballroom. He waited rather impatiently for the music to come to an end before walking on to the floor to fetch them.

'I don't know about you two,' he said casually, 'but I've had enough. What about calling a taxi?'

Ellen was furious with him. It had been at Stephen's suggestion they had come here in the first place. Immediately on arrival he had left them to their own devices and now, without a word of apology or explanation, he expected them to leave at a moment's notice.

Indignant, she deliberately turned her back on him and addressed Arnold. 'What d'you think, Squeaky?' she asked. 'Shall we have another dance?' The company had tired of the wilder set dances and were now content to glide dreamily around the floor to the slow foxtrot and the waltz.

Arnold danced well and Ellen followed his movements easily. Stephen, smarting somewhat from Ellen's rebuff, was forced to admit that the two of them looked good together. He sought out a waiter and ordered a whisky. Now that Janet had turned her attentions elsewhere, maybe he'd get a chance to dance with his cousin himself before the evening was quite over.

Chapter Sixteen

With the New Year came the worst of the winter weather. Snow lay thick on the ground in all parts of the country. Railway lines were blocked and whole trains disappeared in the huge drifts which gathered in railway cuttings.

Across the Highlands poles marking the edges of the mountain roads were buried completely as fall after fall of snow covered fences and walls, abandoned cars and lorries. Sheep froze to death on the hillsides, ponds and cattle troughs were solid ice, and all over the countryside wild creatures died for lack of food and water.

At the temporary RAF airstrip at Prestwick, the conditions were now appalling. With water frozen in the pipes, the ablutions were out of action for days on end and it was necessary to dig temporary latrines.

Stephen's surgery was filled daily with those suffering from the effects of sleeping in damp, poorly heated accommodation. So bad were conditions he treated two cases of mild frostbite in the first week of the New Year.

He was concerned that the men were unable to keep themselves properly clean and were reluctant to observe the usual rules concerning the ventilation of their quarters at night because of the cold. He made every effort to isolate those with infectious diseases such as influenza but became alarmed at the high incidence of skin disorders like impetigo and barber's rash, and the increasing number of cases of fungal infections of the feet. Orders were issued for the men to take special precautions to avoid cross infection, but in such difficult circumstances these were impossible to implement. He began to fear an outbreak of enteric fever.

Bertha Dorkins's contingent of female fitters and mechanics had, contrary to expectation, remained with 11 Group and transferred to

Prestwick with the rest. They had been allocated only marginally better accommodation off the field.

Together with the other WAAF personnel on the station, they had been housed in an ancient stone building situated about half a mile from the camp, which gloried in the name of Bellayre Mansion. It was a fortified house of the late-eighteenth century which had been brought up to date in the 1890s by some nouveau riche baron of industry with more money than taste.

Designed for the comfort of the occupying family and with little thought given to the staff below stairs, it was a warren of steep stairways and narrow passages. Most of the flooring was uncarpeted stone flags which were hard on the feet in normal times and freezing cold in winter.

The WAAFs' sleeping quarters were in the attic, sharing two to a room. This in itself might be considered luxury after spending most of their Service life in dormitories of at least ten beds. Had these rooms had any form of heating, the girls' stay at Bellayre might have been reasonably comfortable, but in below zero temperatures they were obliged to pile all the clothing they were not wearing on top of their beds in order to get any sleep at all.

So far as its young female occupants were concerned, the house had one saving grace. Because the attics were approached by a series of narrow stairways rising up from the rear of the building, there were so many routes which could be taken to and from the outside that it was perfectly possible for those wishing to be out and about after roll-call and lights-out to dodge the MPs making their nightly patrols.

Janet Fraser drew her sports car into the side of the lane and switched off the ignition. The air was crisp and cold. Stars shone brightly in the clear sky and the waning moon provided sufficient light for her to see clearly. There was no sign of the night patrol. They would be huddled beside the stove in the guardroom. If she completed the final two hundred yards on foot, she might be able to avoid detection. In her present state she did not feel able to face up to their questioning . . .

She had recovered quickly from her little operation and had taken the precaution of reporting in sick only to make sure that the eagle-eyed Medical Officer spotted nothing that would give her away. Her brother's partner had been perfectly sweet about the medical certificate. Influenza was a very satisfactory cover for what had really ailed her. She even had a bit of a sore throat and a temperature to make it more convincing.

Unfortunately, the drive from Glasgow had taken longer than she'd expected thanks to appalling conditions, and she had now overstayed her leave by several hours. To cap it all, what had seemed to be a mild cold in the head when she set out, had developed into a real fever and she ached from head to foot.

Slipping into the shadows cast by the wall of the great house, she bent double to avoid being spotted by anyone peering out from the guard-room: a tiny cell which had once been the butler's pantry. The MPs had a tendency to turn out the lights and draw back the blackout curtains in order to keep an eye on the stretch of lawn leading up from the main road.

She straightened up as she reached the rear door, feeling a powerful twinge in her back as she did so.

The pain in her lower abdomen was awful. She must have strained herself, hauling on the wheel through all that snow. That would be it. If she could just lie down in her bed she knew she would feel better.

She negotiated the last flight of stairs, staggered along the corridor to her room and silently turned the knob so as not to disturb her room-mate.

Doris was huddled under piles of coats and blankets and snoring gently.

Janet slipped fully clothed beneath the covers of her own narrow cot and lay in the dark, tense and uncomfortable. The pain had eased only slightly when she lay down and the cold served to increase her dis-comfort. After what seemed to her like many hours, she fell into a fitful sleep from which her room-mate was unable to awaken her when the rising gong sounded at six-thirty.

Stephen straightened up, removed his stethoscope and stripped back the covers.

He had been surprised to find his patient still fully clothed. In her haste to summon assistance, Doris Carter had not even thought to cover her friend's illegal return the night before by getting her into her pyjamas.

'Give me a hand to get her undressed, will you?' he requested of the other girl, who stood shivering and anxious just inside the door.

After Doris had reported to the WO1 that Janet was unwell, it had taken Bertha Dorkins only a matter of seconds to decide to send for the MO as a matter of urgency.

'Was she complaining of feeling unwell last night?' Stephen

demanded. His patient had a high fever and her chest was certainly infected, but he felt that there was something more. .

The other girl looked a trifle uneasy as she replied, 'We-ell, no. Actually, I didn't speak to her myself. I'd turned in before she came to bed.'

Stephen gave her an enquiring glance. Doris was obviously covering up for her friend. He turned back to his task.

Together they stripped the patient of her clothes and her room-mate dug out a clean pair of pyjamas from Janet's wardrobe. They found her underwear was heavily soiled. The odour of putrefaction which arose as the standard WAAF bloomers were removed reminded Stephen at once of the gynaecology unit at the Western Infirmary where he had spent three months during the course of his training. In that period he had had ample opportunity to observe, at first hand, the worst results of the work of Glasgow's back-street abortionists. Puerperal fever was a common result of operations performed by the ignorant and unqualified.

He turned to Janet's room-mate.

'Corporal – if we're going to work together you'd better tell me your name.'

'Carter, sir,' the girl stammered in reply.

'What's your first name?'

'Doris.'

'All right, Doris, we need to get Miss Fraser into a warmer place. Isn't there a bedroom where we can light a fire?'

'We've set aside one room on the floor below as an infirmary,' the girl replied. 'I'll go and see about having it made ready.'

She disappeared and Stephen returned to his examination. It took him minutes only to discover the cause of the trouble.

The abortion had been carried out in the crudest possible manner. Not all the contents of the uterus had been rejected, and it was the remaining fragments of foetal tissue which were causing the trouble. He'd have to operate himself, and for that he was going to need some assistance.

He contemplated sending for Devlin but discarded the idea immediately. The news that Janet Fraser had had an abortion would be all round the camp like wildfire. No, he would have to rely on the help of her friend . . . he just hoped that Doris was level-headed enough not to start fainting on him.

★

'Hello, feeling a bit better?' Stephen smiled at Janet, reassuringly as he removed the cuff of his sphygmomanometer and tucked her arm back beneath the covers.

She had remained semi-conscious throughout his efforts to remove the remnants of the abortion, and for a further twelve hours he had kept a close watch on her as the fever gradually subsided.

On hearing the door behind him open, he glanced round to see Bertha Dorkins standing in the doorway.

'Thought you might like a cup of tea,' she said, advancing into the room and placing the cup at his elbow. 'Milk and no sugar . . . that's right, isn't it?'

'Thank you, Sergeant,' Stephen replied formally. He had never quite managed to bring himself to address her by her Christian name.

'How's Fraser?' she demanded.

Doris Carter had been quite evasive when Bertha questioned her about what was happening behind the closed door of the infirmary.

'The fever has gone down,' said Stephen cautiously. 'But it was touch and go there for a time.'

'Influenza can be very serious, can't it?' said Bertha. 'I remember people dying like flies in the epidemic of 1919.'

'Yes,' he replied, making no attempt to disillusion the WOI. 'She ought to make a rapid recovery now that the crisis is past,' he continued. 'By rights Fraser should have taken another few days before returning to duty, but now she's here she might as well remain where she is, to convalesce. Either I myself or one of my orderlies will call in regularly to administer the drugs she needs, but perhaps you will allow Carter to continue to nurse her for the time being? I gather there's not a lot that anyone can do on the airfield just at present.'

In requesting Doris's services Stephen was trying to limit the damage to Janet's reputation. Carter was not a qualified nurse, but she understood enough to realise what Janet had been up to. In these past few hours he felt he had come to know the girl well enough to trust her to keep her mouth shut.

Stephen completed his examination and, realising that Janet was more aware of what he was doing than she had indicated while Bertha was present, regarded her critically.

'In my pocket I'm carrying the result of your pregnancy test,' he told her. 'There's not much point in discussing it now, is there?'

Sheepishly, she replied, 'No, I suppose not.'

'You do realise that what you have done is not only foolish

and dangerous but also illegal?' he continued severely.

'There's no danger now, is there?' she asked rather more anxiously.

'Oh, there's no permanent damage, if that's what you mean, but this must never happen again. I doubt you could survive the attentions of your expensive butcher a second time.'

'It wasn't done at Fergus's clinic, you know,' she said, defensively. 'I told you, I couldn't have my father calling his precious daughter a cheap whore.'

'So where did you have the abortion?' he demanded, trying to control his anger.

'It was an address that Fergus's partner gave me . . . I'm not telling you where.'

'If your abortionist is not reported to the police, he or she will be free to do the same again, to other women.'

'What alternative is there for a girl in my situation?' Janet demanded. 'If you doctors won't help, there will always be someone else who will . . . at a price!'

Stephen knew that what she said was true, but nevertheless he resolved to give her brother's partner a piece of his mind, should their paths ever cross again.

'Well, let's see what kind of a job your friend Doris and I have managed to do,' he countered brusquely. He carried out his internal examination with great care and finally declared her completely healed and fit for action.

'Doris has been an absolute brick throughout this affair,' he told her. 'You're lucky to have such a discreet friend. I hope you appreciate what she has done for you.'

He wrote out Janet's discharge certificate and handed it across the desk.

'You've been fortunate,' he warned her. 'To make no bones about it, you very nearly died.'

'I shall be eternally grateful to you,' Janet told him. She lowered heavily shadowed lids over her beautiful brown eyes, and smiled demurely. 'I promise I shall not trouble you again. Not with a similar problem, at any rate.'

Chapter Seventeen

Ellen, still smarting from her unsatisfactory reunion with Stephen, was ready to fall into Malcolm's arms when he reappeared, two days after her return to Aberdeen, as unexpectedly as he had departed.

They met outside the University building. Ellen had been waiting in the cold for fully ten minutes with the snow melting around her ankles and her sodden shoes turning her feet to ice. She saw him approaching from the town centre and ran to him with a cry of relief.

'I thought you weren't coming after all,' she said as she disengaged herself from his embrace. Holding him at arm's length, she gave him a careful appraisal. He looked thin and gaunt. There were signs of strain around his eyes and she thought that the area of grey at his temples had increased.

'Whatever you've been up to hasn't done you any good,' was her assessment.

'Nothing like a little gentle encouragement to keep a fellow on his toes,' was his response. 'Look, it's too cold to hang about out here. Let's go to that tea room.'

Inside, they found the table nearest the stove was unoccupied and made straight for it.

The waitress recognised them as regular customers now and without taking their order she appeared with a tray of tea and scones with cream *and* strawberry jam.

'It's only tinned cream,' she explained, 'but we like to keep a bit extra for our *specials*.' She gave Malcolm a knowing wink.

'You seem to have made a conquest,' Ellen remarked.

'Have I . . . have I really?' It was a pointed question and she knew exactly what it meant.

'Malcolm, I've got some news . . .'

'I wondered if we could make up for our lost Christmas,' he chipped in before she could tell him. 'How about going away just as we had planned? I have a few days' leave to come and there's absolutely no chance of my being called away again for a fortnight at least.'

He made no attempt to elaborate on the reason for this. There was no need for Ellen to know that his trawler had been so badly shot up on this latest mission that she was already under repair in dry dock at Rosyth.

'That would be rather difficult,' she explained. 'I've been trying to tell you . . . I'm to be transferred to Surrey on the eighth. That leaves me only four days to wind up my work here and catch a train South.'

'You don't *have* to go, surely?'

'Of course I do.' Ellen was quite indignant. 'I have to obey orders just as you do!'

'Can't you say it's inconvenient or something?' Malcolm demanded.

'I don't recall your telling the War Department, or whoever it is you work for, that it was *inconvenient* for you to stand me up at Christmas,' she retorted.

'That's different.' He was like a petulant little boy. 'I was engaged in work of national importance.'

'And I'm not, I suppose!'

'Not really, no. I can't see what difference a few more days will make to a bunch of cows. Anyway, once we're married you'll be having to give up all this veterinary stuff. I don't want to come home and find you've been trampled underfoot by one of your famous Clydesdales or had your throat torn out by a Pekinese!'

'Don't be ridiculous!'

Angrily, she slopped the tea into the cups and slammed the teapot down with such force that it rattled the lid. An elderly couple, the only other occupants of the tea room, stared, while the waitress reached for a cloth for mopping up the mess.

'For a start I'm not ready for marriage,' Ellen declared, heedless of their audience. 'Not that I recall your ever having asked, come to think of it. What's more, if you believe I'm going to give up seven years' damned hard work, getting to be a veterinary surgeon, in order to keep house for you and raise your snotty-nosed little brats, then you have another think coming. When I marry – *if* I marry – it will be on the understanding that I go on with my work. Just at the moment, that happens to be making a significant contribution to the war effort, one which affects the food supplies of millions of people. Set against your paltry little fishing smack and its clandestine adventures, I think my job has the edge, don't you?'

She slammed out of the shop, leaving a bemused Malcolm wondering what he had said to make her so angry.

'That'll be two and six,' said the waitress.

'Eh? . . . Oh, yes, of course.' He fumbled with a handful of change allowing the woman to extract the coins she needed.

'Little tiff, was it?' she asked, as she counted out the coins. 'I shouldn't worry, dear, they're all like that. Probably the time of the month or something.'

With his hands in his pockets, Malcolm strolled disconsolately down towards the harbour where he turned into a familiar hostelry. He was bound to find someone in here to help him drown his sorrows.

After two whiskies and a beer chaser he had convinced himself that it was all for the best. That last action had nearly been the death of them all. His number was bound to be coming up soon.

'Thought you might like some coffee.' Stuart Beaton pushed the door to with his foot and placed the tray he was carrying on the end of the desk.

Hastily, Stephen moved a scattering of papers out of his father's way and sorted them into a neat pile.

'That just about does it,' he said. 'I never thought I would get it finished in time.'

He rubbed his eyes which were sore from poring over his writing.

'Where's Mum?'

'It's her night for the ARP post. She didn't like to disturb you . . . wished you good luck for tomorrow in case she's not home before you leave.'

Stephen nodded his appreciation and stirred his coffee, thoughtfully.

'Don't you two get a bit fed up, sitting by a telephone all night, just in case something happens?'

'It's all in a day's work for me,' said Stuart, 'and your mother positively enjoys it. She comes home with all manner of stories about what goes on at the old Bus Depot! It's more like a club for the people of the night, down there.'

'But she works so hard at the Council Offices during the day . . . and you're both no longer young.'

'There's a few years' work in us yet,' scoffed Stuart, touched by his son's concern.

In the eighteen months since the outbreak of war, Glasgow's Emergency Services had remained on the alert night and day, the posts manned by volunteers for the most part. Only a scattering of enemy planes had crossed the Scottish coast in all that time and the ARP Wardens and Auxiliary Fire Fighters could be forgiven if they had lost some of their earlier enthusiasm for spending one or more nights each week in a cold gloomy operations room, instead of in their own beds.

Stephen began clearing the remainder of the books and papers from the desk.

'You'll be glad to have me out of here,' he said as he moved the pile into the attaché case which he had been carrying back and forth to the University during the past fortnight. 'I'll get these back to the Library in the morning.'

'When's your viva?'

'Tomorrow afternoon . . . I'm one of the first on the list so it should be all over by about three. I'll need to catch the eight o'clock train in order to be on duty on Saturday morning. The CO's been pretty decent about this leave, I don't want to be late back.'

'I wish I could have been of more help to you,' Stuart said, settling into one of the two comfortable leather armchairs placed to either side of a cast-iron grate in which the fire was almost out. He took up the poker and stirred the dying embers into life, placing a couple of logs and a few knobs of precious coal on the still red ashes, 'but you can see how busy we are now that the yards are in full production. Most of my time seems to be taken up by factory accidents. How do you think things have gone this week?'

'Oh, the written papers weren't at all bad. The one thing that can be said for the kind of work you get to do in the RAF is that it gives you a pretty broad perspective. You never know from one day to the next what you're going to encounter. I have been surprised this week just how many of the situations described have actually come up since I joined the Service.'

'Short of gynaecology, I suppose,' Stuart observed, puffing comfortably on his pipe.

'That too,' said Stephen with a grin. 'We have quite a few WAAFs on the base, you know.'

'Of course, I'd forgotten . . . but once they get pregnant they have to be discharged, don't they?'

'Yes, but it's not the pregnancies I have to deal with.'

Stuart looked up sharply. 'Good God, you don't . . .'

'Certainly not,' Stephen reassured him, 'but I can't stop the girls having a go at aborting themselves. There have been a few pretty messy cases just lately. It would make things simpler all round if terminations were to be made legal. At least that would put paid to the back-street abortionists.'

'It's going to be a long time before that happens,' said his father. 'Certainly not in my lifetime.'

'I'd better go up and get my uniform ready for the morning,' said Stephen. 'There.' He cast an eye around his father's desk. 'I think that's all of my stuff out of your way. Thanks for the loan of the study this week.'

'My pleasure, son.' Stuart was delighted that Stephen had decided to complete his Fellowship examinations. 'It won't be long now before you'll be able to call yourself *Mister*.'

'I'm not so bothered about the title.' Stephen grinned. 'But I wouldn't mind a Squadron Leader's rings and a few bob extra in my pocket every week.'

He picked up the case and went to the door.

'If you'll excuse me, Dad, I think I'll go to bed and read for a bit.'

'Not more textbooks, I trust?' Stuart called after him.

'Not likely . . . what I don't know now I never shall!' Stephen stopped at the parlour door and opened it a few inches. He could hear the voice of Alvar Liddell reading the nine o'clock news.

'Anything of importance, Audrey?' he asked.

'We've made another raid on the Ruhr,' she told him, 'and it seems there were some attacks on towns in the Midlands last night.'

'How are you feeling?'

'Tired and uncomfortable but otherwise OK, thanks,' she replied.

Audrey's baby was due in just a couple of weeks. Despite the threat of air raids, she had felt perfectly safe under Stuart Beaton's roof all along, and continually reassured Derek that there was absolutely no possibility she would be left to have her baby alone.

'I'll probably be away before you get up in the morning,' Stephen told her, 'so in case I don't see you before I leave for Prestwick, I'd better say goodbye now.' He stepped into the room, gave her a friendly peck on the cheek and retreated.

'Good luck for tomorrow,' she said, 'and when you see Derek . . . well . . . you know.'

'I'll give him your kindest regards.' Stephen gave her a wicked smile and dodged nimbly as she threw a ball of knitting wool across the room at him.

In his room, he folded his clothes and packed everything which he would not be wearing in the morning. He had decided to present himself for the viva next day in his best uniform which was hanging ready, on the back of the door. A clean shirt and tie were draped over his bedside chair.

He climbed into bed, selected a thin volume with a garish illustration of a murdered girl on the cover, and began to read. Soon his eyelids began to droop and as he relaxed in sleep, the book slid from his fingers and fell noiselessly to the floor.

The undulating moan of the air-raid siren roused him from his slumbers.

For a few seconds he believed himself back in his room in Doone House at Westgate. The bedside light was still on, giving a poor level of illumination except on his pillow but he dared not turn on the overhead light in case the blackout was not secure. He fumbled for his clothes, drawing on the shirt laid out ready for the morning and grabbing his uniform from its hanger behind the door. Taking the stairs two at a time he was still buttoning up his tunic when he reached the ground floor.

In the hall he found his father already clad in his uniform overcoat and helmet, with DOCTOR in white letters painted across the black steel. He lifted a heavy canvas haversack with a red cross painted on it, and slung it across his shoulders.

'I have to report to Boquhanrhan School,' he explained. 'Will you take care of Audrey? I imagine that your mother will be pretty busy down at the Depot.'

'Leave it to me,' Stephen answered as Audrey herself appeared and calmly settled in the cubby hole under the stairs which Annie had converted into a little sitting place with cushions and blankets, and a few emergency supplies. Stuart watched, amazed, as Audrey sat down and calmly got on with her knitting.

'She's taking it all very well,' Stuart observed as Stephen accompanied his father to the front door.

'You have to remember that this was happening day and night when we were at Manston. One gets used to it.'

'Well, I hope she's feeling as calm as she looks,' said Stuart. 'I don't want her going into labour in the middle of an air raid.'

'I'll be here,' Stephen assured him. 'And I have delivered one or two babies myself.'

Stuart thumped his son affectionately on the back as he glanced up at the sky which had suddenly become cross-hatched with searchlights.

Stephen, more accustomed than his father to this activity, waited for the beams to centre on one of the marauding aircraft.

'There's one,' he cried as a silvery glint was picked up first by one then two other beams. At once the anti-aircraft guns which ringed the city began to fire and the air was rent with explosions as the shells homed in on their targets.

Stuart ran down the steps, turned left into the Great Western Road and was quickly out of sight. Stephen closed the front door firmly behind him and went to see that Audrey was comfortable.

'I'll make a flask of tea,' he said, moving past the cubby hole and into the kitchen. 'It could be a long night.'

They had turned out all the lights except a forty-watt blue bulb in the entrance hall and the miner's safety lamp which Annie had acquired for their makeshift air raid shelter. By the light of the fire in the range Stephen found a kettle already nearly boiling on the hob. He made the tea and poured it into the thermos flask which Annie kept ready for just such an emergency.

Within minutes he was back, squeezing in beside Audrey as the bombs began to fall.

At first the explosions seemed far away . . . on the other side of the river, perhaps . . . but as they came closer, the gunfire too became more frantic and Audrey, who had been keeping up a cheerful conversation, pretending to be unmoved by the onslaught, threw her arms around Stephen's waist and buried her head in his chest.

Shells were exploding right overhead now indicating the proximity of the enemy planes. They heard a stick of bombs falling, much nearer this time. It sounded as if they had landed only streets away. The explosions shook the whole building to its foundations and in the aftermath they heard the sound of glass shattering somewhere in the house.

In the silence that followed all they heard was the familiar drone made by Junkers 88s, passing overhead.

With bated breath they waited for another stick of bombs to fall, but nothing happened. Then, out of the silence, there emerged the sounds of traffic moving at speed along the highway with the ac-companying clang of ambulance and fire engine warning bells. They heard the vehicles changing gear as they turned down the next road in the direction of the river.

Stephen lent Audrey a hand to pull her to her feet.

'It seems to be over for the moment,' he said, going to the front door and pulling it open. The movement required more force than he expected. He looked up and in the dim light saw that the door frame had been shifted by the blast and a deep crack had appeared, snaking up the wall and out of sight. Gingerly he pushed the door fully open and allowed it to swing back of its own accord. Satisfied that the damage was only slight and there was no danger of the wall collapsing, he stood outside on the top step. Audrey crept up beside him.

From where they stood, little could be seen of the damage which they knew must have been wrought upon those closely packed houses nearer the river.

A dull rosy glow was beginning to suffuse the night sky and the air was filled with the acrid smell of smoke.

'There must be people injured and needing help out there,' whispered Audrey, voicing Stephen's own thoughts. 'Hadn't you better go and see what you can do?'

'What about you?' he asked, anxiously. 'I promised Dad I'd keep an eye on you.'

'I'm OK,' she replied, though less confident than she cared to admit. 'I'll go in and try to sleep in the chair under the stairs . . . just in case they come back.'

He turned and led her back inside. He noticed that she was trembling and shivering too.

'Are you sure you're OK?' he asked again, wrapping a shawl gently around her shoulders. His keen eyes searched her face in the dim light of the hallway.

'Let's have a cup of that tea you made,' she said, reaching inside the cupboard and retrieving the flask.

She poured out the steaming liquid into two enamel mugs and ladled in heaped spoonsful of sugar.

'That's nearly a week's ration,' she grinned sheepishly, 'but it *is* an emergency.'

'Quite right,' he said, taking the cup from her and carefully ignoring the shaking of her hand which had caused a little tea to spill on to the tiled floor.

'Oh, dear,' Audrey sighed, thinking of Maggie Brown's polished tiles, 'I'd better get a cloth and wipe that up. Someone might slip.'

'Leave it,' said Stuart, looking up the staircase and noticing for the first time the lumps of plaster which had fallen from the ceiling above and now lay scattered all down the stair carpet. A fine white powder seemed to have settled on everything. 'It looks as though there'll be plenty of clearing up to do in the morning.'

'Stephen, I know you want to go out there and help . . . I'll be all right on my own, really I will.' As though to prove her point Audrey wedged herself back into the small armchair that Annie had provided, and resumed her knitting.

'There probably won't be another attack tonight,' Stephen said with apparent conviction. 'The ack-ack seemed to be pretty effective. I suspect that Gerry was just trying out the defences, in which case he might think twice about a return visit.'

As if to confirm his statement, the all clear sounded, its continuous unwavering signal bringing the assurance he'd hoped for.

'If you're absolutely sure you don't mind . . .'

'You go on, Stephen; you'll be more use out there than looking after pathetic little me.'

'You're not pathetic, and you're certainly not little,' he replied jokingly. 'If you're absolutely sure you are not going to produce Junior within the next couple of hours, I would like to get down to the Infirmary and see if they need any help.'

'I'm all right, really I am,' she assured him.

He went to the door, yanked it open and stepped out into the night. Despite her assurances he still felt guilty at leaving her there alone. He would just go the hospital, see if he could lend a hand for a while and nip straight back if the sirens sounded again.

Stephen strode quickly along to the church at the corner of Byres Road and turned down towards the University and the Infirmary. Now that he could see over towards the river, he realised just how much devastation must have been wrought at the shipyards and factories along the Clyde. Flames tore into the darkness above the Singer works where, close alongside, a wood yard was well ablaze. Other fires lit up the further bank of the river from Broomielaw down river to Greenock and beyond.

As he reached the bottom of the hill it became clear that the streets of closely packed houses had caught the full force of the bombing. Fire appliances were desperately trying to dampen down the flames from a shower of incendiary devices which had been dropped by the pathfinders before the main bomber force had dispersed its high explosives. Rescue workers waited impatiently for the signal to go into a demolished building to dig out those householders still trapped in the rubble.

'Here, laddie, lend a hond, will ye?'

A disembodied voice led him over to where a shop front, its glass blown out, had collapsed under the weight of the two storeys of tenements above.

'Where are you?' Stephen called out.

'Down here,' said the voice.

He crouched down and peered into the area which had led to the basement of the building. He found a white face peering out from beneath a pile of timber and stonework and realised that the man must have burrowed in beneath the rubble.

Pulling his steel helmet down firmly on his head, Stephen crawled in beside the man who was searching the small space he had made with a flashlight.

'I heard a wean greetin',' the man told him. 'Wull ye catch haud of this balk of timber? When I gie the word, thrust it up there.' He indicated a jumble of beams above their heads.

'Won't that dislodge the stuff on top?' asked Stephen doubtfully.

'Trust me,' replied his companion with such authority that Stephen could find no reason to oppose him. When the man said, 'Now!' together they thrust the timber upwards and pushed it into a vertical position.

They had formed a kind of wigwam some four feet high. It appeared to be quite stable. With more space in which to work it was only a matter of moments before the man gave a cry of satisfaction. Placing the torch on the ground, he began to haul on something he had spotted in the wreckage.

'Here,' said Stephen, 'let me look . . . I'm a doctor.'

At this the man turned and observed his assistant properly for the first time. What he saw was a young fellow in a rather dirty RAF uniform and regulation steel helmet. Only when he caught sight of the two thin rings on Stephen's sleeve did he appear satisfied that what he'd said was true. The man pulled back and allowed Stephen to take his place.

He reached into the mass of debris and felt the material of a dress or nightgown. He began to remove the larger lumps of masonry, handing them back one by one to the other man. After a few moments he had exposed enough of the woman's body to ascertain that she was dead.

As he turned away, unable to help her, they both heard a feeble whimper. Stephen returned to his task with renewed vigour. Soon he was able to shift the body of the dead woman, turning her on to her side. Folded in her arms, shielded from the debris which had fallen on them as the building collapsed, lay an infant of perhaps eight or nine months old.

Stephen examined the child by the light of the torch. He showed no sign of serious injury although his lungs were full of dust and he was clearly having difficulty breathing.

Taking a handkerchief from his pocket, Stephen wiped the chubby round face free from dirt. Then, holding one hand behind the baby's head, he breathed into the tiny mouth. The baby responded immediately, coughing and spluttering as the choked airway began to open. Twice more the doctor inflated the child's lungs by which time Stephen was satisfied that he could breathe on his own.

'I'm bringing him out now,' said Stephen, shifting his position to make room so that he could hand the baby back to his companion.

'Catch hold of him behind the head and under the bottom . . . just in case there are any internal injuries. We don't want to hurt him further.'

The man took the baby as Stephen had directed and moved back into the space they had created.

'I'd better get him down to the hospital right away,' said Stephen. 'There's nothing you can do for the woman, I'm afraid. She might as well wait until morning.'

'Hang on a minute,' said the other. He withdrew from his pocket a label on which he wrote a few words before tying it to the child's wrist.

'Best let them know where the wean was found,' he said. 'It may save time when they come t' identify him.'

Humbled by the man's display of common sense, Stephen, who would not have thought of any such thing, and would not have known the number of the building anyway, took the child in his arms and set off down the street.

Audrey sat in her chair starting nervously at every sound from the street outside. She had put on a brave face for Stephen but, in truth, she was worried. There had been a few twinges in her abdomen in the last half hour and a dull ache in the lower back, more akin to a period pain than the backache to which she had become accustomed in recent weeks. Surely she couldn't be going into labour already? Stuart Beaton had assured her that nothing would happen for at least another fortnight.

One thing was certain, she could not spend another minute cramped up in here.

Things had gone quiet outside. Maybe Stephen had been right . . . perhaps there wouldn't be a further attack tonight. She pushed open the parlour door, needing to lie down but unwilling to risk going upstairs to her bed.

The parlour table was a family heirloom of immense proportions. Annie had told her that it had belonged to Stuart's grandfather and father before being brought to Glasgow some years before. It was solid mahogany and stood firmly on four bulbous carved legs. It would surely hold the weight of the ceiling should the house be bombed.

Gathering pillows from the sofa and the shawl which Stephen had given her, she crawled in underneath and made a cosy bed for herself. Exhausted by her efforts she lay back and closed her eyes. In moments she was asleep.

Maggie Brown was returning form her mother's home in Bearsden when the sirens began to wail. Tommy had insisted on riding on top of the tram as usual, and they were right up front when the conductor came running up the stairs.

'Best get yersels doon the stair, missus,' he said briskly, ushering a half dozen other passengers to the lower deck.

'Aw, Ma,' pleaded her wee son, 'we'll no see the Germans ha'f sae good doon there. Can't we stay?'

Mrs Brown, who had never experienced an air raid in her life but had witnessed many scenes of total destruction on the newsreels at the local cinema, was in no mood to argue.

'You just get yoursel' doon them stairs this minute, Tammy Broon, or I'll skelp ye mesel!' she cried.

As the tram rumbled south towards the river it became clear to the driver that they were actually moving towards the danger. Pulling into the next siding, he stopped the vehicle and called out to his conductor.

'Tell them we're no goin' ony further the night,' he said. 'The subway station is just over the way. Mebbe they should take shelter there.'

The passengers, who were no more desirous of carrying on towards the shipyards than was the tram driver, alighted with little protest. For most of them this was an experience they had long awaited and had begun to think would pass them by. Filled more with curiosity than dread, they spread out along the road and watched in amazement as the first incendiaries straddled the warehouses down beside Fairfield's yard and lit up the whole scene in their magnesium-white glare.

The high-explosive bombs followed soon after and for a moment everyone just stood watching in awe as one familiar building after another, illuminated by the fires burning out of control across the whole city, crumbled into ruins before their eyes.

For a time Maggie and her son, having followed their fellow passengers into the subway station at Hillhead, crouched on the platform against the tiled walls and flinched as each new string of bombs shook the building. An empty train drew into the station and stopped.

The guard jumped out and came running along the platform towards them.

'This train'll no be movin' until the all clear, missus,' he said to Maggie, bending over her and helping the weary Tam to his feet. 'Why don't you and the wean sit in one of the carriages? I'll no drive her awa' wi'out letting youse know.'

Gratefully, Maggie led Tam to one of the more comfortable seats and was quickly joined by others of the tram passengers.

People began to chatter amongst themselves and soon perfect strangers were exchanging their life stories. Someone took out a harmonica and they began to sing . . . *Run Rabbit Run; Roll Out The Barrel; I Belong to Glasgow; Keep Right On to The End Of The Road* . . . all the old favourites that everybody knew. The louder the noise of bombs falling, the louder they sang. Were it not for thoughts of family and friends outside, in far more danger than themselves, some might have said it was the best night out many had had since New Year!

When at last the all clear sounded, many people seemed reluctant to move. Only when the guard indicated that the train would be leaving shortly, did they start to climb the stairs to the street.

Maggie Brown, ignoring the sounds and sights going on at the farther end of the road, grasped her son by the hand and darted across Byres Road and round the corner into Great Western Road. In her purse she had a key to the doctor's front door. Mrs Beaton wouldn't mind if she took shelter there for the remainder of the night. Something told her that there was no point in going to her own home down near the river. All she wanted now was to get her boy into the warmth and safety she knew would await her at number seventy-two.

The doctor and Mrs Beaton would be out helping, after the raid, but Mrs Audrey would be at home and glad of the company no doubt.

It had been a busy couple of weeks in the Beaton household. Much as she enjoyed having Stephen at home again, his presence did create a certain amount of extra work which had thrown the daily routine out of kilter. Annie glanced across at the neatly made up camp bed in the corner of the ARP hut and thought longingly of the odd hour's rest which she might get, as soon as Donald returned from his rounds and took over the telephone.

She busied herself at the filing cabinet while Donald McDermot prepared for the first of the half a dozen tours of their area which they would make before dawn. Wee Jimmy McLaughlin came bursting in, his Boys' Brigade uniform as always untidily slung together.

'Sorry, Mrs B,' he exclaimed, snatching up the *Evening Echo* and searching the back page for news of his favourite footballers. 'Practice went on longer than usual tonight . . . we've a special game on Saturday. If I hadn't waited until the end, I mightn't have been picked to play.'

'Now you are here, Jimmy,' said McDermot, 'you can run round to Boquhanrhan School with these Bulletins for the First Aiders.' He turned over a couple of leaflets showing the latest method of applying artificial respiration.

'I don't know about all this breathing into people's mouths,' he said. 'Turn the patient on his front then alternately press down on the thorax and raise the arms above the head . . . that was the old way. Very effective it was too. I have seen many fishermen saved from drowning by that method . . .'

Fearing that they were about to be treated to yet another of McDermot's reminiscences of his boyhood aboard an Aberdeen trawler, Jimmy swept up the pile of leaflets and made for the door.

'No hanging about out there, mind,' Annie warned. 'You never know when the alert might sound.'

'Fat chance,' the boy called as he slipped out through the curtained doorway.

She did not really mind how long he spent at the school, where several of his friends would be attending First Aid classes this evening, but she was anxious that such a young boy should be out after dark on his own.

'I'm not at all sure about using the Scouts and the Boys' Brigade as runners,' she had confided to Stuart on more than one occasion.

Stuart's laconic reply did nothing to cheer her. 'In six months' time these lads will be doing their basic training in one of the Services and a few weeks after that they'll be considered old enough to fight. Children grow up fast during a war,' he reminded her.

She knew that what he said was true, but it did not prevent her from worrying when she sent one of them out into the blacked-out streets.

At last Annie was alone.

She wriggled on the hard wooden chair, trying to ease her back into a more comfortable position. Resting her arms on the ancient wooden table, she caught her sleeve on a splinter and cursed loudly. They had done their best to furnish the little office, but the only new piece of equipment was the green filing cabinet beside the door. Apart from an old rug, supplied by Annie herself, all the chairs, and the appalling old desk had been left behind by the bus company from whom she had requisitioned the ARP Post.

Having read all the latest memos and bulletins and entered the date in the log, ready for her report at the end of the watch, Annie switched on the radio to listen to music broadcast from Bristol by the BBC Concert Orchestra. After a while, despite the uncomfortable chair, she found herself dozing off to the strains of Mendelssohn's Hebridean Overture. She felt her eyelids growing heavy and then, as her head began to droop also, suddenly started up.

'Those idiots have switched off the fan again,' she muttered, annoyed at the ignorance of some of her fellow wardens. She got to her feet and reached for a cord which hung beside the wall map. 'Someone is going to be found unconscious in here, one of these days,' she told herself as her fingers tightened around the cord. She switched on the fan and listened to the satisfying whirring of the blades for a few moments.

The red telephone began to ring.

'Clydebank, No.1 Depot.' She tried to disguise the tremor in her voice. Could this be it . . . could this be the attack which they had been expecting ever since the raids had begun on England, last autumn?

'Enemy aircraft reported in considerable numbers approaching from Fife Ness. Estimated time of arrival, your sector, twenty-one twenty hours.'

Annie acknowledged the warning and pressed the button which would start the siren. As the whining notes began to drown out all other sounds, her hand reached up automatically to switch off the radio.

McDermot, having completed his first tour of inspection, had been gratified to find that only two households had had to be warned of chinks of light straying through carelessly drawn blackout curtains. That was a record. He had just turned into the main gate of the depot when the siren began to wail.

'How long?' he demanded, thrusting aside the inner curtain and replacing it carefully behind him.

'ETA twenty-one twenty hours.' Annie prided herself on having at long last mastered the twenty-four-hour clock used by officialdom.

'Making for the Naval base at Rosyth, I shouldn't wonder,' said McDermot, importantly. 'They'll no' risk coming right across here . . . their escorts canna make it this far.'

Annie prayed that he was right.

The red telephone rang again.

She picked it up, listened intently for a few seconds and replaced the handset.

'They've passed the western outskirts of Edinburgh and are approaching Coatbridge.'

Suitably chastened, McDermot walked over to the huge wall map which lent the only patch of colour to that dreary room and traced the line of the approaching bombers.

'A quick raid on Ravenscraig steelworks and they'll be awa',' he told her confidently.

Anti-aircraft guns had been set up on the braes which formed the rim of the giant basin in which the city of Glasgow sheltered. Even as McDermot spoke, they opened fire, the exploding shells making the rickety ARP Post shake.

Donald switched out the lights and Annie pulled back the curtain from the doorway so that they could step outside.

The night sky had been lit up by a dozen searchlights and they could see the puffs of black smoke which marked the shells exploding around an aircraft caught in one of the beams.

Undeterred, the fleet of enemy aircraft continued on their course and even as Annie and Donald stood gazing upwards, the first baskets of incendiary bombs were released. The two wardens watched them tumble down to land in a spectacular display of fireworks along the banks of the Clyde. Instantly, the whole area was lit by the uncanny white glare of burning magnesium. Soon, as the fires took hold, the colours changed through yellow to orange until at last the whole sky was glowing deep crimson.

Once the trail had been laid, the following bombers released their loads on the shipyards and factories, paying no heed to the surrounding rows of ordinary little houses that would also be destroyed.

Annie had lived through the Great War of 1914, when the death and destruction had occurred somewhere else; when one might have been forgiven for taking the attitude that soldiers were recruited to fight and, if necessary, die in the conflict. This was a very different war, waged upon an entire nation. One in which women and children, the old and the sick, were equal targets. She shuddered and drew her coat close about her. Just then, both the telephones began ringing.

Stuart wandered around the school hall from one group to the next, repositioning a victim here, adjusting a bandage or a sling there. As he approached each group, he enquired quietly what steps they had taken to deal with the problem presented to them and ticked off on his sheet those who gave satisfactory answers.

'Mrs Beaton asked me to bring you these, sir.'

Startled at hearing his wife's name, Stuart turned to find Jimmy McLaughlin at his elbow, thrusting a bundle of leaflets under his nose.

'Thank you, Jimmy,' he said, taking them and stuffing them in the pocket of his white coat. He wore the overall partly to protect his decent suit from the dust rising from the parquet flooring, but also to make himself easily distinguishable from the crowd.

He regarded the boy with a steady gaze.

'Let me see,' he said, remembering a glorious September sunrise . . . could it really be seventeen, nearly eighteen years ago?

He had emerged from a terraced house somewhere in Crow Road, after a long night battling with this same young fellow who, despite his size, had resisted with considerable determination every effort on Stuart's part to ease him, yelling, into a hostile world.

'You'll be expecting your call-up papers soon, won't you, Jimmy?'

'Any day now,' the boy replied, drawing himself up proudly, at the same time straightening his tie and adjusting the white webbing over his black uniform jacket.

'What's it going to be . . . Senior Service, like your dad?' Jimmy's father had retired from the Navy as a Chief Petty Officer, after twenty-one years.

'Not likely, sir!' Jimmy was adamant. 'I'm going to be a pilot . . . Fleet Air Arm, of course,' he added, admitting to the compromise arrived at with his father.

'Well, good luck to you, son,' Stephen replied, shaking the boy's hand and smiling to disguise his dismay at this news. The survival rate of Fleet Air Arm personnel was far lower even than that of RAF fighter pilots. Had he brought young Jimmy into the world merely to be blown to pieces over the ocean . . . to finish up as scraps for seagulls?

'You'd better cut along back to the ARP Depot, Jimmy. Tell my wife I'll be staying on here for a bit, but that I've made arrangements to see that our lodger is not left on her own. She'll understand.'

'OK. Goodnight, Doctor.' Jimmy made his way across the hall, lingering here and there to exchange remarks with those of his mates who had volunteered as First Aiders. He pushed his steel helmet jauntily to the back of his head, knowing how his friends envied him this symbol of authority.

Stuart turned away to give his attention to the next little group, not even noticing when the boy finally left.

Once outside in the blackout, Jimmy turned back the way he had come and began kicking at a can that he had found lying in the gutter. Noisily he made his way towards the depot.

What was that? He paused in his pursuit of the empty can and stood still to listen. What he had heard was the distant moaning of an air raid warning, followed almost instantly by the much closer wailing of the siren on the depot's forecourt. He forgot the can and hurried on, anxious now to be at his post when the fun began.

As the guns began firing Jimmy stopped to watch as first one then another of the enemy bombers was caught in the searchlight beams. What on earth was the matter with those gunners? Why didn't they hit the jerries? They were plain enough targets. If he were up there in his fighter, he'd soon have them dancing about the sky, not knowing what had hit them . . .

He saw the first shower of incendiaries explode and light up the sky. The great clock tower looming over the Singer works shook as high-explosive bombs fell all around it. When the pall of smoke and dust had cleared, he was amazed to see the tower still standing dark against the fiery sky.

He was close to the depot gates now. No longer shrouded in darkness, the yard was filled with the sound of revving engines and the shouts of rescue workers and fire fighters. Even as he approached the office, Jimmy saw Annie Beaton appear, waving a piece of paper which she handed to the driver of one of the fire appliances. The remainder of the crew boarded the vehicle and within seconds it had left, its bell clanging to warn of its approach.

'Oh, Jimmy, thank goodness you're back.' She grabbed him by the arm and shoved him under cover. 'Where on earth have you been?'

The way she fussed, she sounded just like his mother. Petulantly, he muttered something about having to wait for a message from Dr Beaton and would have told her then what Stuart had said had she not interrupted him.

'It's not you I was worried about,' she said sharply, 'I need you to get down to the Mission Hall immediately. There's been a report of an unexploded land mine . . . it was spotted coming down somewhere in that area. There was a concert in the hall this evening and it's just possible that the audience is still sheltering in there.'

As Annie spoke, Jimmy's boyhood fell from him like a discarded cloak.

'It would be just as dangerous to turn a crowd of people out into the street . . . there's shrapnel and stuff falling all over the place,' he protested.

'They can take shelter in the crypt of the Episcopalian Church, next door,' she said. 'Get them out of the hall in as orderly a manner as possible, avoiding the north side where they think the mine landed. And, Jimmy . . .' he stopped just as he was about to pull the curtain back '. . . don't panic them. Just explain the situation quietly and get the conductor to order the move. They'll take more notice of him.'

She did not want to undermine his self-confidence, but she knew some of the people who would be at the concert this evening. They were unlikely to take orders from a seventeen-year-old boy.

Across the street a group of tenements had received a direct hit. A single fire appliance was being used to keep down the blaze from a shattered gas main while rescue workers helped the dazed and battered occupants from the formless rubble which moments before had been their homes.

Ignoring the warning shouts of fire fighters and dodging heaps of masonry and abandoned vehicles, Jimmy skipped over a tangle of hoses snaking across his path and ran on.

He covered the three blocks to the Mission Hall in minutes. Built of the red granite common to most of the public buildings in the area, the hall stood back from the road, fronted by a tree-lined grassy plot.

Jimmy paused before entering. Within this little haven, green amongst the bleak buildings all around, the tracery of branches was already burgeoning with new life and the scent of newmown grass still hung on the air despite the acrid smell of destruction all around.

High above his head he spotted the ghostly white blur of a parachute entangled in the uppermost branches of a tall lime tree. The massive façade of the Mission Hall cast deep shadows so that it was a few moments before his eyes became properly adjusted to the feeble light. He wasn't exactly sure what he was looking for. A land mine, Annie had said. No one had ever shown him a picture of a land mine.

At last he spotted it.

A huge metal sphere hung by the cords of its canopy of white silk from a single branch which, bowed under the massive weight, looked likely to snap at any moment.

Jimmy took the three steps to the heavy oak door in one stride.

Slipping inside, careful to avoid the escape of any light, he closed the door behind him, relieved to have put the solid wall of the building between himself and the monstrous weapon of destruction outside.

His entrance had coincided with the beginning of the slow movement of Elgar's Cello Concerto and when the squeak of the hinges was followed by the clunk of the heavy oak door closing, heads turned and angry looks accompanied his progress towards the rostrum.

He was obliged to tap the conductor on the shoulder in order to gain his attention. The music stopped . . . the musicians at least seemed anxious to hear what this white-faced young messenger had to say.

'I'm sorry to disturb you, Mr McMurdo,' Jimmy said. He used a stage whisper so that only the conductor and the front row of musicians could hear.

'There's a land mine caught up in a tree out front . . . you'll all have to leave.'

Some ears in the audience caught the gist of what he had said and those in front began to shuffle uncomfortably in their seats.

'What's that, laddie?' McMurdo asked.

'Mrs Beaton has sent me from the ARP Post. She says you're to use the rear exit and get everyone into the crypt next door. People are not to try to go to their homes until the police say it's safe.'

Seeing the conductor's hesitation, Jimmy added, more urgently, 'The mine might go off at any moment.'

He saw no point in elaborating upon what he had just seen. The thing was to clear the hall and answer questions later.

'I thought it best to continue with the concert when the raid started,' McMurdo told him, trying to justify his decision to carry on despite the bombing. 'It seemed sensible to keep folk here rather than have them milling about in the street. This building is made of solid granite . . . they can't be in much danger here.'

'My orders are to get everyone out, sir,' Jimmy persisted. 'Shall you give them the message or will I?'

'If it's that important,' muttered the first violin, 'I don't know why they didn't send a policeman to tell us.'

'They're all busy,' Jimmy replied, becoming more exasperated by the minute. 'You don't know what it's like out there . . .'

'All right, laddie, keep your hair on.' To his annoyance, McMurdo patted Jimmy on the head in patronising fashion and turned to the audience, tapping with his baton to gain their attention.

'Ladies and gentlemen, our young friend has come with a message from the ARP Post. We have to vacate the hall and take shelter in the crypt of the church until the raid is over. If you will kindly make your way, in an orderly fashion, out by the rear door, Jimmy McLaughlin will show you where to go.'

Trying to appear calm, people began to form up by the door and Jimmy, making his way to the head of the queue, recognised with some relief the familiar figure of Charlie Wernham, the warden of the Episcopalian Church.

'Will you lead the way, Mr Wernham?' he asked. 'I'll take care of the stragglers.'

There were gasps of dismay as, emerging into the narrow alley between the buildings, folk realised for the first time what had been happening whilst they were engrossed in their entertainment.

As they filed past him, Jimmy recognised many of his neighbours, people he had known all his life. He gave them a smile or a friendly word and helped the elderly, less agile people down the steps and into the gloomy interior of the crypt.

At the foot of the steps he turned, feeling a tug on his arm. He looked down upon a tiny old lady, seeking to attract his attention.

'Young man, I'm awfu' sorry,' she began, her hand trembling with the effort of supporting herself on a walking stick, 'but I've left my handbag in the hall. I canna do wi'out it, you see. It has ma glasses and ma ration book . . .'

'All right, Mrs Lavery,' said the obliging Jimmy, 'don't you worry about it. Just as soon as everyone is settled, I'll pop across and fetch it for you.'

He waited by the door of the crypt whilst people found themselves somewhere to perch. There were a few chairs stacked in one corner and the musicians began to hand these out. As he turned to leave, one of the violinists was tuning up in preparation for some lively Scottish music. To the strains of *The Riggs o' Barley*, he scurried up the steps and out into the night once again.

The deserted hall seemed larger and gloomier than ever now that all the people had gone. By the light of his torch he searched the rows of seats for Mrs Lavery's bag. At last he saw it . . . a large black leather handbag, hanging by its strap. He slipped between two rows of chairs to retrieve it and turned towards the exit.

At that moment the tortured lime tree gave up its fight. The bough snapped and the land mine tore through the remaining branches, bouncing on the concrete path before exploding. They said afterwards that you could have got a double decker bus into the crater that it made. Nor was there any shortage of rubble with which to fill the hole, for the entire front of the Mission Hall collapsed in the blast. Jimmy McLaughlin, clutching Mrs Lavery's handbag to his chest, was buried beneath tons of masonry.

It was two days before they dug his mangled remains from the wreckage and a whole week passed before the police were able to return the handbag to its owner.

Stephen kicked open the swing doors into the Casualty Department's waiting hall.

He was surprised to find groups of doctors and nurses standing around, apparently unoccupied. Whatever was happening out there on the banks of the Clyde, here at the Western Infirmary the emergency team of doctors and students awaited the expected casualties with growing impatience.

He carried the baby, now ominously silent, into one of the side cubicles and was followed by a somewhat indignant nursing sister.

'Just a moment,' she cried. 'You must report to the desk first.'

Stephen turned on her wildly. The atmosphere in here was unreal compared with the horrors he had just witnessed outside in the streets.

'The child is dying, Sister,' he said sharply. 'Fetch me some oxygen and get a pediatrics man down here right away.'

She would have protested further had not one of the doctors detached himself from the group and come over to join them.

'All right, Sister, Dr Beaton knows what he's doing. Fetch the oxygen.'

Stephen had freed the baby from its shawl and was stripping off the tiny garments. Recognising the voice, he looked up into the smiling eyes of his friend and mentor.

'I think there may be liver damage,' he suggested, omitting the usual greetings. 'See, here?'

He showed the Professor a dull area of bruising which seemed to swell even as they watched.

'He was crushed.' Stephen could not rid himself of the image of those bodies lying under the debris.

'The mother?' enquired the Professor.

'Dead. She was shielding the child with her own body. It was the baby's crying which led us to the spot,' Stephen explained as the Professor took over from him, running his fingers over the tiny form, searching for signs of further injury.

The Sister returned with an oxygen cylinder and they placed the adult-sized mask over the infant's face for a few seconds.

'His airways were choked,' Stephen explained. 'I did my best to free them.'

The oxygen was certainly improving the child's colour, but the swollen liver gave the Professor cause for concern.

'Did you manage to contact Mr Menzies, Sister?' he enquired.

'On his way.'

The Sister took the oxygen mask from Stephen.

'You go and have a sit down, Dr Beaton,' she said. 'I've asked a nurse to get you a cup of tea.'

'Yes,' agreed the Professor, 'you look as though you've had a severe shock, Stephen. Take Sister's advice, there's nothing more for you to do here.'

As he turned away from the couch the Sister called after him.

'I'm sorry I didn't recognise you, Doctor. You do look a bit of a mess.'

Surprised by her statement, Stephen glanced at himself in a mirror as he sipped his tea and was dismayed to see that his best uniform was torn and covered in mud and that his face was truly unrecognisable under its veneer of dust.

Then the door at the far end of the room flew open and a young woman in her early-twenties staggered in carrying a little girl. An ugly wound on the child's forehead had drenched both the casualty and the woman carrying her with blood.

Two of the students, who had been growing more and more restless as nothing at all seemed to be happening, rushed forward and relieved her of her burden.

The expression on their faces as they exchanged glances above the girl's head indicated all too clearly that the child was already dead.

The woman was led to a chair, weeping, while the students dealt with the body.

Stephen went over to the woman.

'Where have you come from?' he asked, thinking there might be further casualties at the scene.

'The Church Hall in Radnor Road. Call themselves a dressing station!' she cried angrily. 'There's no' a qualified doctor amongst them. Told me there was nothing they could do for wee Amy so I brought her here. I know'd that she'd be OK if I could just get her here!'

A nurse had brought a medicine glass of sal volatile which Stephen encouraged the woman to drink. She choked on the unpleasant-tasting fluid, but rallied soon after.

'Something should be done about it,' she continued bitterly. 'There are people bleeding to death down there for want of attention. There's nae doctors, only the Reverend looking after things. They've nothing to ease the pain. The screaming is dreadful . . .'

'I can't understand why the casualties aren't being brought in,' observed the Professor, who had been relieved of his tiny patient by the paediatric specialist.

'No doubt the roads are blocked,' said Stephen, a vision still strong in his mind of tall buildings crumbling into the streets. 'There's nothing else for it. If the patients can't be brought in, we shall have to go out to the dressing stations,' he declared, getting back to his feet. 'Who can I take with me?'

Immediately he was surrounded by a group of medical students all anxious to put their skills to the test.

'I must keep my specialist staff here,' said the Professor, 'but if you're willing to take along these young men . . .'

Stephen turned to the group.

'How many third-year men do we have?' Three raised their hands.

'Right, each of you pick a partner from these others.' On the fringe of the crowd he spotted a fellow whom he recognised as being the younger brother of one of his own contemporaries. 'Alan, you can be my assistant.'

He looked around him at the seven beaming faces. God knows what they think they're getting themselves into, he thought, memories of the carnage after the Manston raids still clear in his mind.

The Night Sister was hovering at his elbow.

'Is there anything I can do?' she asked.

'From what the woman said, there's a shortage of equipment. Can we have sheets, bandages . . . you'll know what's needed. They've almost certainly got blankets . . . and drugs . . . morphine . . . oh, and perhaps you would pack up a couple of sets of surgical instruments?'

'No student from this hospital will administer morphine without supervision.' The cold voice of authority was that of Sir Duncan Ware Roberts, Senior Consultant Physician, who had been summoned from his home on the outskirts of the city at the first alert.

'I will supervise the administration of the drug when necessary,' said Stephen, his natural deference to a medical superior giving way to exasperation.

'And who, sir, might you be?' demanded Sir Duncan.

'Flight Lieutenant Stephen Beaton, RAF Medical Services.' He rattled off his rank, knowing full well it would carry little weight with this pillar of medical conservatism.

'Lieutenant Beaton is one of my graduates,' explained the Professor. 'He has been working with Fighter Command for the past year and has had more experience than any of us in this kind of situation. I can't think of anyone more suited to command this operation, Sir Duncan, and I'll thank you not to interfere with my arrangements.'

Suitably chastened, the physician found urgent business elsewhere while one of the porters appeared with an ancient hand-cart of an ambulance which had lain for half a century in the basement.

'This should do to carry your supplies, *Mr* Beaton, sir.' The man grinned at Stephen, knowing full well that he was not yet qualified to use the title.

'Well,' he confided to his mates afterwards, 'he'll be Mr by the end of the week . . . you mark my words!'

The first all clear sounded as they threaded their way through streets unrecognisable even to those who had lived there all their lives.

Turning the corner into Radnor Road itself, they found a fire appliance had accidentally driven straight into a fifteen-foot crater and was standing almost vertically, balanced on its bonnet. The driver was dead. Several of the crew had been thrown out, one appeared to be seriously injured. The rest seemed merely dazed.

Stephen began unloading packages from the ambulance, thrusting them into the arms of the firemen and students. 'Take these on into the hall,' he commanded, while, with two of the students helping him, he lifted the injured man on to the trolley.

Inside the hall was utter chaos.

The Reverend Neil was doing his best to marshal the minor injuries into one corner where a group of Stuart Beaton's First Aiders were cleaning cuts and applying bandages as they had been taught.

Scattered about the room on mattresses and trestle tables were numbers of the more seriously injured. For the most part they lay quietly, but some groaned or wept in their agony. Each had been tagged in the prescribed manner with their identification and a summary of the suspected injuries. They waited now for transportation to hospital where the professionals could attend to them.

As Stephen's company entered, the Reverend Neil came forward, his arms outstretched.

'Thank God,' he cried. 'The ambulances have got through at last!'

'Unfortunately not,' Stephen was forced to admit. 'We can, however, do something to relieve your casualties on the spot. Can you show me to the most urgent cases?'

It took a matter of moments to allocate the students to their patients. 'I'm relying on you to oversee the work of your assistants,' Stephen told the senior men. 'Help one another . . . I'm here if you need me.'

Bearing in mind the Consultant Physician's warning about the use of morphine, Stephen tried to oversee the administration of the drug but it soon became clear that there was not enough time for him to watch as each injection was given. Soon he delegated his powers to the senior students. Some of the cases were so bad that if the morphine didn't kill them their injuries would. This way at least some of the agony would be relieved.

The work continued uninterrupted for some time. The second air raid warning and the subsequent bombing went almost unnoticed by those within the hall. The surgeons barely raised their heads even when, at last, a fleet of ambulances arrived to take the worst cases to hospital.

The first of the drivers came in, full of apologies for having been delayed while demolition workers had cleared a roadway for them.

'You'll carry on driving, despite the raid?' Stephen pleaded. 'Some of these people are in urgent need of major surgery.'

'We'll do our best, Doctor,' said one of the drivers. 'It's not the bombs we're concerned about, it's the condition of the roads. There's debris lying everywhere.'

They carried the injured out and loaded them into army-style ambulances, six stretchers to a vehicle.

Stephen turned to the clergyman.

'Mr Neil, can you get a couple of your workers to accompany the casualties, please? Ask them to ensure that the ambulances come back here as soon as they have dropped their load. If we have a great many more victims brought in now, we shall be swamped. It may be necessary to have people carried all the way to the hospital on stretchers, do we have any?'

The Reverend Neil indicated an assorted collection of stretchers which had been used for disaster exercises earlier in the month.

'It might be a good idea to start a convoy of stretchers off straight away,' suggested Stephen. 'They have all the beds and doctors anyone could want at the hospital.'

Neil, glad to have a specific job to do now that the doctors had taken over, went off willingly, gathering together the more robust of his parishioners to manhandle the stretchers.

At the ARP Post at the Old Bus Depot, Annie had been listening to a continuous saga of complaints throughout the night.

The biggest problem had been getting the rescue services to the sites where they were most needed. If appliances could not get close to a burning building, the only alternative was to link hoses from several pumps and transport the water from a greater distance. Along the river bank the problem was solved by lowering the hoses straight into the Clyde and pumping river water directly on to the fires. Ordinary hoses were not long enough for this purpose and it was necessary to link several together to obtain the required length. Unfortunately, different Fire Brigades employed different types of hose connectors. With a large number of appliances brought in from outlying boroughs, very few carried equipment compatible with that used on Clydebank.

Frustration mounted as, away from the river, the problem of water supply increased after each fresh wave of bombing. The number of fire hydrants damaged or destroyed was so great that water pressure was reduced to a trickle in some places. Annie found herself assuming her daytime role when she ordered out from the Council Depot the water-carrying tenders used for washing down the streets.

As a result of a brainwave of one of the wardens, she also persuaded her Roads Department colleague to send snowploughs out to clear debris from the centres of the streets, thereby making the passage of vehicles possible.

All of this took time. Meanwhile buildings burned and people lay dying in the rubble of their homes.

When Maggie Brown slipped the key in the lock and pushed open the front door of the doctor's house, she was surprised to find it stuck. She pushed harder and, when it did give way, crashed across the threshold, stumbling into the hall stand and sending ornaments flying in all directions.

She closed the door on herself and Tam, and switched on the hall light. It was very quiet in the house. Could it be that they were all out . . . even Mrs Miles?

She opened the door to the cupboard under the stairs. Clearly Mrs Miles had been sitting in there, for she had left her knitting.

She looked up the stairs and seeing the plaster and dust lying everywhere, knew that Audrey would not have gone up there.

There was only one place for her: the parlour. Even as she reached for the door handle Maggie heard a moan and scuffling noise from behind the parlour door followed by a plaintive cry. 'Mrs Beaton, is that you?'

Maggie pushed open the door, gently so as not to hit Audrey who in her anxiety to get help had hauled herself across the floor at the sound of movement in the hall.

'Oh, Mrs Brown . . . it's you.' Audrey sighed with relief. 'I thought no one would hear me.'

'What is it, my dear? Has it started?'

'My waters broke about half an hour ago,' Audrey gasped. 'I crawled in under the table when the bombing started again. I didn't know what to do to get help. I tried the telephone but the lines must be down.'

'I thought Mr Stephen was supposed to be staying in with you tonight?'

Mrs Brown pursed her lips, ready with her accusations.

'He would have done, but when the raid was so severe I knew he felt he could be more useful elsewhere. I persuaded him to go . . . he's at the hospital.'

The sirens began to wail again and soon they heard the bombs falling, further away this time.

Audrey shuddered as a particularly violent contraction racked her body.

'Here, you get in under the table again, lassie,' said Maggie. 'I'll go and get a few things we shall need. Tam . . .' to her small son '. . . just you come along wi' me. I'll find something for you to do . . .'

She spent a few moments rearranging the cupboard under the stairs so that the child could snuggle in with a book and pencils.

'Now you stay there,' she ordered. 'I don't want you under my feet all night.'

In the kitchen she gathered up towels and sheets just newly laundered, and put on the largest kettle to boil. From the kitchen drawer she withdrew a pair of sharp scissors and, taking a pan from the shelf, set them to boil until sterilised.

In the hall, she glanced up the stairs, tempted to go and get further supplies of linen, but seeing the extent of the fallen plaster, she decided not to risk it. All she could do was to encourage poor Mrs Miles and do her best to make her comfortable.

A glance into the cupboard showed her that Tam, wearied by the excitement of their adventurous journey, was curled up in the wee armchair, sound asleep.

Audrey, flat on her back beneath the table, pulled her legs up as pain tore through her again. Maggie knelt beside her on the floor and held her hand while she counted the length of time before the next contraction. Two, perhaps three minutes, no more. This child would not be long in coming.

From the kitchen she heard the kettle whistling.

'I'll make us a cup of tea,' she said, falling back upon that panacea for all ills.

When she returned she found Audrey with her legs bent at the knees and straining hard.

'It wants to come,' she gasped. 'There's nothing I can do to stop it!'

'Don't try,' said Maggie. Remembering her own experience of childbirth, she urged Audrey to bear down as the next contraction began and cried out with delight as she saw the head of the infant appear.

'Relax now and wait for the next one,' she advised, gently wiping the perspiration from Audrey's brow. The contractions came closer and closer together until Audrey began to think that there would never be anything else but this awful pain . . .

'Now . . . push . . . push . . . that's it! That's a good girl!'

The infant slipped out in a gush of bloody fluid which stained the sheets and the carpet around. There was nothing that Maggie could do to prevent it.

She caught the child up in her arms and placed it on Audrey's abdomen while she reached across for the strong thread and scissors with which she had armed herself.

It was a matter of moments before she had tied the cord twice and cut between the threads. She ran to the kitchen for a bowl and was only just in time to catch the afterbirth as it came away. The doctor would want to see that, she remembered, just to make sure it had come away clean.

Setting the bowl to one side, she wrapped the squalling infant tightly in a towel and laid it in its mother's arms.

'A beautiful little girl,' she said, smiling broadly.

Audrey, languorous in the aftermath of her ordeal, gazed at the tiny screwed up face and sighed contentedly.

'At least they won't want to send *you* up in an aeroplane to shoot down Germans,' she said.

Maggie collected the soiled sheets and towels from around her patient and made the best job she could of the bed beneath the table.

'Things have quietened down a lot,' observed Audrey, 'don't you think I should come out now?'

'Best stay where you are until the doctor comes,' Maggie suggested. 'You'll not be able to move in a hurry if the bombs start again.' She was doing her best to repair the damage to the drawing-room carpet. 'Have you decided what you're going to call her?'

'I don't know,' Audrey replied. 'Somehow I never thought about its being a girl. We've always discussed the baby as *he*.'

'You don't mind . . . about her being a girl, I mean?'

'Oh, no, I don't mind what kind she is, so long as she's healthy.'

Maggie bent over the infant who had ceased crying and was now gazing at her midwife with the astonished stare of the newly born.

Been here before has this one, she decided, and then as the child pursed it lips and extended its little tongue, 'Why, she's trying to smile already.'

Audrey watched the older woman's face, seeing in it all the loving and caring of mothers everywhere.

'I don't know what I would have done without you, Mrs Brown,' she said quietly. 'It's funny really . . . living in a house full of doctors and having to have my baby underneath the table.'

'With only a housekeeper for a midwife,' Maggie finished for her.

'I can't go on calling you Mrs Brown now,' said Audrey. 'Do you mind if I call you Margaret? It's such a lovely name.'

'My friends call me Maggie.'

'I hope we shall always be friends.' Audrey stretched out her arms to the woman to whom she had always given a wide berth until now. 'You must call me Audrey, Maggie.'

Whether it was the exhilaration of the birth or her extreme fatigue Maggie Brown did not know, but she found herself weeping, her normally stern façade quite melted away.

'I shall call the baby Margaret,' Audrey decided, 'Margaret Anne . . .'

This important decision made, she drifted into sleep, the child held firmly in the crook of her arm.

After a few minutes, Maggie crept outside to find that Tam was still fast asleep in his hide-out beneath the stairs. No point in disturbing him either. She went into the kitchen, refilled the kettle, and settled into the old rocking chair beside the range. Neither the all clear nor the whistling kettle disturbed her sleep. Had Annie not returned to the house ten minutes later, the kettle would have boiled dry.

Chapter Eighteen

Stephen and his team of students from the hospital worked steadily throughout the night and once the road link had been re-established, convoys of ambulances together with a steady stream of stretchers carried on foot removed the worst of the casualties for treatment elsewhere.

It was six in the morning before the last of the injured was sent on their way and the medics could begin to clear up the chaos into which the normally orderly church hall had fallen.

Ladies of the Church Hall Committee had appeared during the night and kept up a steady flow of cups of tea and sandwiches to sustain the workers. They now set to with brooms and brushes as Stephen packed the bags of surgical instruments, checking that nothing was missing.

The Reverend Neil, who had himself worked ceaselessly, thanked Stephen for coming to his aid.

'It was bad enough that our duty doctor never arrived,' he explained, 'but when we realised that the ambulances could not get through, all I could do was pray . . . and God sent you and your wonderful young men.'

Stephen, embarrassed, shook the priest's hand and murmured, 'In times like these we must all do what we can.'

He turned to his team and said, 'Thank you, everyone. You all did splendidly.' He was careful to direct his congratulations to the very young First Aiders and their elderly colleagues as well as the fledgling surgeons, who had performed miracles in the most difficult of circumstances.

A young girl, sixteen or seventeen perhaps, whose uniform overall was splattered with blood and whose face was nearly as white as her cotton blouse, sighed heavily and collapsed on to the nearest chair.

Stephen went to her, thinking she would faint.

She looked up as he approached.

'They trained us to staunch fake blood and immobilise limbs which were supposed to be broken,' she said, 'but no one ever told us what it would be like to have real, half-dead human beings under our hands.' She began to shudder and Stephen put his arm about her shoulders.

'It gets easier,' he said. 'Next time you will tackle things with greater confidence.'

She smiled at him, grateful for his encouragement, but Reverend Neil whispered, 'Pray God there will not be another time.'

The party of students set off for the hospital and Stephen, realising that he would have little time to prepare for his examination later in the day, made his way home. On passing the Boquhanrhan School he went inside to seek out Stuart.

He found his father busy tidying up after the night's ordeal.

'I thought you were going to have an early night.' Stuart grinned. 'I was very relieved when they told me you were at Radnor Park. Bad, was it?'

'Oh, you know . . . Neil was doing his best, but without a doctor on the scene the volunteers were a bit disorganised.'

'It was a Dr Lansbury who should have been on duty there tonight,' said Stuart. 'His house was destroyed in the first wave of bombing. He and his family were killed.' He paused, seeking some excuse for his own lack of foresight. 'When we made our plans, we never really considered such a possibility. We never envisaged such total chaos . . .'

Stephen recalled the words of the voluntary First Aider. 'No one can ever plan for every eventuality,' he said. 'There was no problem with getting fire appliances and ambulances through when we had the raids on Manston, but then, there were no tenement blocks in Kent to tumble four or five storeys of masonry into the streets.'

'It must have been the same in London,' observed Stuart, 'yet no one thought to get any advice from there. Annie tells me that the city bigwigs get together from time to time and discuss these matters, but it's at the level of the fire officers, the Air Raid Wardens and the medical services that the information needs to be shared . . .'

Stephen regarded his father with concern. He was on the point of collapse. An elderly man now, he ought to be thinking of giving up his practice and retiring to the coast as he had always planned to do, not spending his nights like this.

'Come on, Dad,' he said affectionately. 'It's time we were going home.'

They went by way of unfamiliar streets, from which many well-remembered landmarks were now gone forever. Here and there a damaged gas main still flared or a broken hydrant poured its life-saving water uselessly into the gutters. A heavy pall of smoke hung above the factories and shipyards of Clydebank and fine particles of soot and ash fell on them as they walked.

Streets of tall tenement houses into which the working classes of Glasgow had been crammed in their thousands for more than a century, had been turned overnight into formless mounds of stone and plaster.

Seeing some of the worst of these tenements in ruins, Stuart said, 'Annie and I have spent years trying to get these places demolished and rebuilt. Were it not for the loss of life, one might almost say that Hitler has done us a favour.'

'What will happen to the people left without homes?'

'If the scheme works properly, the women and children will all be out in the country by this evening . . . there is an emergency evacuation programme. The men will be housed in rest centres, hostels if you like, until the houses can be replaced. No doubt those who can afford to, will get away altogether. The city council has plans to requisition unoccupied property. It's your mother's job to see that people are rehoused as quickly as possible.'

'How's it all going to be paid for?' Stephen asked as they stepped over half a dozen hoses snaking across the roadway to where firemen were directing a steady stream of water on to a still smouldering building.

'There always seems to be money available when there's a war,' observed his father grimly. 'Think of the cost of just one fighter aircraft and consider how many decent houses could have been built with the money.'

'I suppose we should be glad that people are getting better medical attention than ever before,' Stephen mused. 'I presume that last night's casualties will be treated free of charge?'

His father nodded.

'Well then, if the government can find the money in wartime, why not all the time?'

'Too many vested interests.' Stuart sounded quite savage as he launched into his own particular hobby horse. 'It would mean continued pooling of resources and personnel after the war is over. Do you imagine most consultants would be prepared to give up their right to the ludicrously high fees they can charge now? Because that's what it would mean, if there was a permanent national medical service.'

They turned the corner into Dumbarton Road and saw with dismay that the public library had received a direct hit. The top two storeys had been demolished. The ground floor seemed relatively undamaged, however, and as Stuart and Stephen neared the scene, they saw that staff of the Council's emergency services headquarters were already gathering near a side alley which gave access to the basement.

When she saw her dishevelled menfolk approaching, Annie Beaton waved frantically.

'I thought you were supposed to be staying with Audrey during the raid,' she addressed Stephen accusingly. 'You might have known she would go into labour with all the excitement.'

'She insisted I go out and do what I could to help,' he protested, lamely.

'What's happened?' demanded Stuart. 'Has she had the baby?'

'Yes, and no thanks to either of you, both mother and baby are well. Maggie turned up quite by chance, seeking shelter from the raid. She seems to have done everything necessary.'

Annie was tired and cross. It was not like her to lash out in this way. She knew that the men had both been legitimately engaged with other problems. To her annoyance she felt her eyes fill with tears. With a defiant movement, she brushed them away.

Stuart grabbed her arm and pulled her towards him. Holding her close, he stroked her hair and pushed a few untidy locks back into place.

'Come on, old girl,' he said, gently. 'You can let go now . . . it's been a hard night for all of us.'

Her cheek felt wet against his own. He traced the line of her jaw with his fingers and kissed away the tears.

'From what you say, Audrey is all right. Steve and I will go home right away and check her over.'

Stephen, feeling like an intruder upon this moment of intimacy between his parents, bent down to retrieve a book from the rubble.

The cover had been destroyed by the fireman's jet, but the title page was still readable.

A History of National Socialism by Konrad Heiden. He threw it down in disgust and turned over another volume with his foot. *Germany – the Last Four Years*, by Germanicus. Was there no escaping them?

'Are you sure you should go to work in there today?' Stuart asked his wife, eyeing the damaged building with some suspicion.

'The surveyors reckon the ground floor is safe,' she insisted. 'The basement ceiling has been protected by an additional layer of concrete so it should be secure even against another attack. The demolition men say that it's quite waterproof down below. We'll be as comfortable there as anywhere.'

'But you've been up all night.' Stuart examined his wife minutely. There were dark rings under her eyes, her face was pale and her hair, lacking its usual lustre, hung limply and out of control. 'You look all washed out to me.'

'Thank you, kind sir.' Annie curtsied daintily, regaining her composure and smiling broadly. 'It's not every day a woman receives such a compliment.'

'Oh, come on, Mum, you know it's only that he's concerned about you,' Stephen protested in his father's defence.

'Well, there's no need to be. I shall be fine. There's a great deal of work to be done if we are to get all these homeless people out of the city before nightfall. Now do go along, both of you, Audrey needs you more than I.'

Stuart kissed her again and turned away reluctantly.

'Oh, and Stevie,' she called after them, 'good luck for this afternoon!'

Reminded of his appointment with the examination panel, Stephen glanced down at his battered clothing and smiled wryly.

'I hope there's enough water for a shave when we get home . . . I don't think that Sir Duncan Ware Roberts is going to be too impressed with my uniform, do you?'

'Don't tell me that old dinosaur will be on the MRCP panel?' His father was dismayed.

'He's the independent chairman.'

'Oh, well, no one is going to be bothered about appearances after the raid . . .' Stuart said, though his words lacked conviction.

'Sir Duncan will be. He and I crossed swords on another matter last night. I don't think I'm likely to find favour with him.'

Stephen noted the startled looks of two of the members of the panel as he entered the boardroom and took his seat. His friend the Professor, however, seemed unmoved by his appearance.

Despite a vigorous brushing by Mrs Brown, his uniform still showed all the signs of the previous night's activities. Nothing short of a visit to the dry-cleaner's would have put things right and there had been no time for that. Had it not been for the fact that one of his white shirts had gone late into the wash, he might still have been wearing the one he had stood up in all night, for his suitcase and its contents had been buried under the heaps of glass and plaster which covered the shattered upper rooms of number seventy-two and the Council's surveyors had not yet agreed that it was safe for them to go up to clear away the mess.

He had entered the boardroom in some trepidation, fearing that the events of the previous night would have driven all else from his mind. Once started on an account of his experiences with the traumas associated with crashed and damaged aircraft, however, he found that the words came easily.

'My only regret,' he concluded, 'is that in the earlier burn cases described, I had recourse to the use of tannic acid as the initial method of treatment. The patients had to undergo a series of painful operations to remove the hard surface formed, before the process of grafting could begin.'

Sir Duncan Ware Roberts looked up sharply. He might be a trifle out of date but he knew a thing or two about burns.

'Please explain yourself, Dr Beaton,' he interrupted. 'It has always been my belief that tannic acid is the correct treatment for severe burns. It is the only way to exclude both air and bacteria satisfactorily.'

'Unfortunately,' Stephen elaborated, 'burns, whether experienced by pilots or anybody else, are invariably contaminated with debris of all kinds and are never clean. Application of tannic acid simply serves to seal in dirt and bacteria, giving rise subsequently to suppuration. Experience has shown us that pilots shot down in the sea and consequently immersed in salt water, often for considerable periods of time, do better without the application of tannic acid. The new growth of skin around the margins remains soft and does not necessarily have to be removed before grafting can take place. In order to cover the open wounds to prevent secondary infection, sterile gauze and light bandaging are sufficient. The treatment was laid out in an article by Mr Archibald McIndoe in the November edition of the *Lancet*. I understand that a monograph has now been circulated throughout the Services, recommending this as standard procedure.'

Stephen had tried to make his response impersonal, but it was clear that Sir Duncan took his words as a direct criticism of himself.

He went red in the face and fumbled with the heavy gold watch attached to an impressive chain which was stretched tightly across his portly abdomen. 'Time is getting on, gentlemen,' he blustered. 'I would remind you that we have other candidates to see.'

Ignoring the chairman's implied dismissal, a thin-nosed, bald-headed individual whom Stephen recognised as the ear, nose and throat specialist with whom he had had more than one wrangle during his student days, leaned forward and hissed his question like a viper preparing to strike.

'Lieutenant Beaton,' he began, emphasising the lowliness of the rank, 'we are all aware of the circumstances of last night's air raid, but as you can see, most of us have been able to present ourselves suitably attired for this interview. Could you perhaps furnish us with some explanation as to why you appear to have spent the night in a midden?'

Before Stephen could even begin to explain, the Professor jumped to his defence.

'Dr Beaton took charge of a team of surgery students from this hospital which manned the casualty clearing station at Radnor Park Church Hall,' he told them. 'They all worked tirelessly throughout the night and are to be congratulated upon saving a number of lives. I for one am grateful to Dr Beaton for keeping his appointment this afternoon. There are those among us who consider that, under the circumstances, he might have been excused this further ordeal.'

He saved his summing up of Stephen's dissertation until the candidate had left the room. Apart from the chairman, not one member of the panel was inclined to disagree with his recommendation that Stephen should be elected to Membership forthwith.

As yet unaware of the outcome of the examination, Stephen returned to Prestwick immediately. Suspecting that he would be unable to find any trains leaving the badly damaged St Enoch railway station that day, he decided to cross the river at Erskine and managed to thumb a lift with a lorry as far as Largs.

He stepped down on to the road and drew in a deep breath of the fresh salt air before turning to give the obliging driver of the lorry a friendly wave. It was good to be away from the appalling stench of charred buildings and the choking dust.

It was quite dark now but in the east the sky still glowed with a reddish tinge above Glasgow, where many fires continued to burn out of control. The city would make a fine target should the Germans decide to repeat their attack tonight . . .

He found a public call box and asked to be picked up. It would take the driver twenty minutes or so to reach him so he went into a nearby café and ordered a cup of tea.

'You look as if you've had a rough time, son,' observed the proprietor, an elderly man anxious for news. 'Where have you come from?'

'I spent the night in Glasgow,' said Stephen, stirring his tea, suddenly weary. 'Didn't get a lot of sleep.'

'We watched it all . . . clear as day it was.' The man seemed suddenly ashamed of his recollection. At the time they had all stood around, chattering excitedly as each explosion added to the brilliance of the display. It had been just like the fireworks they always had to end the summer season. Suddenly serious, he asked, 'Bad was it?'

'Yes,' Stephen replied, 'pretty bad.'

'Much damage?'

'Clydebank will never look the same again.'

'Good job, if you ask me,' said the other. 'I grew up in a tenement just off Crow Road. A bomb was the best thing could have happened to that lot.'

'I doubt if the present occupiers would agree with you,' observed Stephen, coolly. He got to his feet and went outside, unable to put out of his mind the bewilderment and utter desolation on the faces of the homeless and bereaved people he had seen.

As the door closed behind him, he heard the man comment to another customer, defensively, 'After all, it was only the one night. They've had it night after night for weeks down in London. My wife's brother lives in Walthamstow. He's been bombed out of his house twice already.'

Stephen waited at the agreed pick-up point, anxious to be back in camp. He had had an overwhelming desire to give that man in the café a piece of his mind. What if the raid on Glasgow had been a one-off? To the people who had experienced it, it was devastating enough. A loved one has only to die once . . . a house can only be demolished once . . . whether it happens after a few hours or a few weeks of bombing, the result is the same.

Stumpy Miles was waiting anxiously for his arrival and opened the door of the station Humber as soon as it drew up before the HQ hut.

'Good God, Steve, you look as though you've had a night on the tiles,' he gasped when he saw the state of Stephen's uniform.

'You could say that,' he replied. 'Only thing was . . . most of the tiles were on the ground!'

'How's everything at home? I've been trying to get through all day but the lines to Glasgow seem to be down.'

'So you haven't heard?'

Stephen pictured his last sight of Audrey, comfortably tucked up on a camp bed which Annie had had brought to the ground floor for her.

The baby was at her breast and Stephen had wished he were a painter that he might capture forever this symbol of goodness, emerging from the midst of evil. Whoever else was to forget the night of 13 March, this little family would celebrate it, always.

'Everything's fine,' he said, smiling and grasping his old friend by the hand. 'Congratulations.'

'You mean . . . she's had it?' Derek was thunderstruck. 'But it wasn't to be for another couple of weeks.'

'You can thank Adolf for hastening the day,' Stephen told him. 'Your daughter was born at the height of the raid last night and Audrey and Mrs Brown managed the whole thing on their own.'

'But I thought . . .' Derek was going to protest that his wife should not have been left alone.

'She insisted that I left her and went to help out at the hospital,' Stephen interrupted him. 'When I did there was no sign that the baby was going to arrive early. Mrs Brown did a splendid job. When we got home after the raid, everything was in order. Dad gave both mother and child a clean bill of health . . . you have absolutely nothing to worry about.'

Derek's anxious frown remained despite Stephen's assurances.

'I wonder if the Old Man will let me off tonight,' he said. 'There might be a train . . .'

'Unlikely,' Stephen told him. 'I had to hitch a lift from Erskine, and I had my dad to drive me to the ferry. I suggest you wait until morning, the trains may be running again by then.'

Derek had to content himself with buying rounds of drinks in the Mess to wet the baby's head and every half hour he tried to ring through to the Beaton household. Eventually his patience was rewarded.

'Hello . . . oh, is that Derek?' Annie's voice sounded strained. It had been a long, eventful day. 'We've been trying to get through to you for hours . . . the line can only just have been connected. Did Stephen get back to camp all right?'

'Yes, he's here.' Derek was impatient to hear from his wife, 'How is Audrey? Is she able to speak on the phone?'

'Audrey? No, I'm afraid not.'

Derek's heart missed a beat. Why not? What had happened?

Annie was quick to explain. 'Everyone not engaged in war work of some kind has been evacuated from the city. Audrey was due to go out to Alexandria, but Stuart's brother drove down from his home near Oban to see if we were all right, and he's taken her and the baby back with him. There wasn't time to consult you first, I'm afraid. We tried to get through several times . . .'

Relieved, Derek hastened to reassure her.

'Just so long as they're all right,' he said. 'And, Mrs Beaton . . . thank you for looking after them.'

'Your daughter is quite beautiful,' said Annie, her voice softening at the thought of the tiny child she had handed to her mother, in the back of Hugh's Lanchester, no more than an hour before.

'Has Audrey given the baby a name?' Really, Derek thought, this was quite extraordinary, having to ask someone else what he was supposed to call his own daughter.

'Did Stephen tell you the circumstances of the birth?'

'That neither he nor his father was there at the time? Yes.'

'It was Mrs Brown who delivered the baby, so Audrey has called her Margaret,' Annie explained. 'She said I was to tell you that she hoped you didn't mind?'

'Mind? Of course not. It's a splendid idea. Will you give Mrs Brown my kindest regards? Tell her I'm looking forward to thanking her in person.'

'I will. Is Stephen there by any chance?' Annie asked, her voice conveying a certain excitement.

'Yes, he's here beside me. I'll hand you over.'

Stephen took the handset from his grasp.

'Hello, Mum.'

'Did you have a lot of trouble getting back, dear?'

'No, not too bad,' he answered. 'I managed to get a lift soon after crossing on the ferry.'

'Professor Dowson rang your father.' She had meant to lead up to this a little more dramatically . . . tease him a bit perhaps . . . but the effort of containing her excitement whilst she spoke with Derek had been almost too much to bear. 'He says that the interview went exceptionally well and that you will be hearing good news from him very shortly. Wasn't it kind of him to let you know?'

With two pieces of good news to celebrate that evening, it was hardly surprising that the two men got a little drunk.

'What'll you do now you're a fully fledged surgeon?' demanded Derek. 'Surely they'll have to promote you?'

'I should hope so,' Stephen replied with great satisfaction. 'With luck they'll find me something a little more demanding than rookies' bunions and bloody pregnancy tests!'

'It's good of your family to take my Audrey under their wing,' Derek slurred, eyes filling with maudlin tears. 'How far is this place Eisdalsa anyway? It looks no distance at all across the water, but I can't bloody well swim, can I?'

He traced the road from Campbeltown to Oban on the large wall map of the Firth of Clyde and the western seaboard. 'Isn't there some way of getting there without going back in to Glasgow?'

'There's a ferry from Wemysss Bay to Brodick, on Arran,' said Stephen, 'but I don't know if she runs now . . . with all the naval activity in the Firth. It's another short ferry trip then across Loch Fyne to the Mull of Kintyre. You shouldn't have too much trouble getting a lift north from there.'

He showed Derek the route he should take and the position of Eisdalsa, a little south of Oban. 'Tell you what,' he said, 'I'll get hold of my Uncle Hugh and tell him you're on your way. He might offer to pick you up . . . you never know your luck.'

A young Flight Lieutenant burst into the Mess. 'There's a red alert out . . . the beam is on for Glasgow again.'

This meant nothing to Stephen.

Derek enlightened him.

'The navigation beam used by the Luftwaffe; it can be picked up by our people at Coastal Watch. They're now able to give a very accurate assessment of the direction the enemy planes are taking.'

Suddenly remarkably sober, the two friends got to their feet and made for the door.

'I'm going to the control tower,' said Derek, 'we had a good view from there last night.'

With a sinking feeling in the pit of his stomach, Stephen followed, ascending the outside staircase to the glass-enclosed dome from which all flights in and out of the landing field were controlled.

Fires were burning over the city, the dull redness still in evidence despite the continued efforts of a dozen fire brigades from around the country.

'They'll not be needing too many incendiaries tonight,' observed Stephen. 'It must be as bright as day.'

He thought of the terrible scenes of the previous raid and shuddered involuntarily. He wished now that he had delayed his return. He could have done so much more to help, had he remained.

★

Stuart Beaton hurried on foot to his post at Boquhanrhan School. He didn't like leaving Annie on her own. If the raid got heavy she had promised she would get under the table. Thank goodness they didn't have to worry about Audrey tonight. She and the baby would be safe with Hugh.

The school hall was seething with activity. The volunteers had spent a busy day replenishing stocks of bandages and equipment. Now they knew what to expect, their systems for reception and treatment had been tightened up considerably and Stuart was pleased to find everything in readiness for what the night would bring.

The siren had sounded at a quarter to nine. It was now twenty past and still there was no sign of enemy bombers. The younger people were becoming impatient . . . were they coming or weren't they? Anticipating a repetition of the previous night, they seemed almost disappointed when the bombers failed to appear.

Suddenly the night was alive with gunfire. Searchlights again painted their patterns across the glowing sky and the first bombs began to fall.

Most of the activity was on the far side of the river, over towards Hillington.

'They'll be after the Rolls-Royce factory,' said one.

'Or King George's Dock,' said another.

As though to confirm this latter suggestion, a great sheet of flame leaped into the sky as the woodyard at Shieldhall was set alight.

As he watched the bombs exploding, Stuart could not help feeling relieved that it was the great industrial complexes which were tonight's targets. The yards across the river were huge and stood away from the major housing developments on that bank. It was bad, of course, but homes and people might fare better tonight.

A single throbbing aircraft engine, right above their heads, suggested that a straggler had missed his target and was seeking another. Even as they gazed skywards the incendiary bombs began to fall in a straight line along the length of the Dumbarton Road. Stuart threw the girl beside him down on to the pavement as one of the bombs landed on the school roof, its magnesium flare quickly setting a tarred felt covering alight.

He ran into the building, followed by the girl. He grabbed a stirrup pump and a bucket filled with water.

'Follow me with that sand, and get someone to bring up more water,' he shouted as he sped towards the stairs which gave access to the roof.

Out on the gently sloping tiles he could see where the bomb had lodged in a gutter and set light to an area of flat roof over an extension, a recent addition to the school's amenities. Bitumen had been spread to seal a leak, and was now flaring.

Stuart adjusted the jet and placed the cylinder in the bucket as they had practised a dozen times. With his foot clamped firmly on the rest, he began to work the pump with one hand while with the other he directed a fine spray on to the flames. He was only vaguely aware of the girl who had crept up beside him with a second bucket filled with water. He glanced over his shoulder and, seeing her there, swapped buckets.

'I'll get more,' she said, and disappeared.

The flames were dying now. He crept further forward, balancing on the tiles, and directed the spray on to the smouldering surface. The water ran out again. He turned, looking for another bucket, and as he did so, the flames suddenly shot upwards and, caught by the wind, seared the back of his jacket. He stumbled forward and the girl caught him in her arms, hauling him back towards the main wall of the building and the safety of the doorway.

The roof timbers were well alight now, there was nothing for it but to abandon their efforts and leave it to the Fire Brigade. Stuart sent the girl before him down the stairs, calling out as he did so.

'Clear the building, everybody out . . .'

In the intervening moments, while Stuart had been fighting his battle on the roof, the casualties had been arriving. A dozen or more people with a variety of injuries had gathered in the hall and were receiving First Aid.

'Get them all out . . . now!' Stuart shouted.

Every face was turned towards the staircase. Silently, they stared up at him in horror.

Stuart was frantic. Why did they not realise the danger they were in? What were they all gawping at?

One young man broke the spell by rushing forward and, using a blanket, smothering the smouldering jacket which hung in tatters about Stuart's shoulders. Only then did the doctor realise that he had been burned and with the realisation came the pain. The adrenalin which had given him the strength to shepherd his companion to safety had masked his own injury. He allowed the boy to remove the smouldering garment, gasping as his blistered skin was exposed to the air.

'Wring out a towel in water,' he said to the girl, then to the boy beside him, 'get everyone out of here . . . make for the Radnor Park Hall.'

He watched them go and turned gratefully to the girl who had returned with a dripping towel. She wrapped it around his shoulders.

'Can you walk?' she asked anxiously, swallowing the bile which had risen in her throat at the sight of Stuart's back. If he could not walk she would have to find a means of carrying him to hospital.

'Shall I see if I can find someone to help?'

'I'll be all right,' he assured her, 'let's get out of here.'

As they stumbled into the street the fire appliances were arriving. Stuart looked back at the building. Maybe it had been worth it . . . maybe he had arrested the flames sufficiently to save the main part of the building. He hoped so. He would need some compensating factor to account for the agony which was beginning to obliterate all else from his mind.

CENTRAL MEDICAL ESTABLISHMENT
ROYAL AIR FORCE

ATTENTION SQUADRON LEADER STEPHEN BEATON MRCS YOU ARE DIRECTED TO TAKE UP THE APPOINTMENT OF SURGEON AT *THE QUEEN VICTORIA HOSPITAL EAST GRIN-STEAD, SUSSEX.* REPORT TO THE SENIOR CONSULTANT SURGEON BY 1800 HRS ON 22 MARCH 1941.

Stephen stared at the sheet of paper in his hand.

'I don't understand how they could have got to know so quickly,' he told the CO. 'I only received confirmation of the Hospital Board's decision myself this morning.'

'Never be surprised at the wheels within wheels in this Service,' Calcutt said. 'For my part, I shall be sorry to see you go, Steve. The chances of our getting as good an MO to fill your shoes are very remote.'

'To tell you the truth, any rookie GP could handle the work I've been doing these past few weeks,' Stephen confessed. 'I must say that the prospect of working with McIndoe is a very pleasing one. I couldn't have asked for a better posting.'

'You'll be going without saying goodbye to Derek . . . his leave ends on the twenty-third.'

'Maybe we'll catch up with each other some other time. I suspect that Audrey will be happy to stay at Eisdalsa now that she's there. My mother is going to let her use our cottage for as long as she wants. It's about the best place she could be at this time.'

'I'll see you in the Mess in half an hour,' said Calcutt. 'The drinks will be on you this evening, Squadron Leader!'

Stephen dumped his suitcases in the hall and, sliding past the array of steel helmets and navy blue coats with their distinctive yellow insignia bulging from the overloaded hall stand, knocked on the parlour door before entering.

Annie looked up, startled. The senior warden for the area was in mid-sentence. The words died on his lips when he saw the son of the house, resplendent in his new uniform, filling the doorway.

Excusing herself, Annie made for the door and hustled him outside.

'Steve . . . whatever . . .' She looked distressed. It was not the welcome he had expected.

'What's going on?' he demanded.

'Oh, that.' She nodded in the direction of the parlour door. 'The library premises are undergoing repair. I offered our front room as a committee room, just for the time being.'

She seemed furtive. What was she trying to hide? he wondered.

'This is very unexpected,' Annie said, hurriedly. 'How long do you have?'

'No time at all, really,' he told her. 'The night train for London leaves at eight. I have to report to my new posting by six o'clock tomorrow.'

'New posting?' She still seemed agitated . . . whatever could the matter be?

'I'm joining Archie McIndoe at East Grinstead . . . plastic surgery. Isn't it marvellous?'

'Oh, Stevie!' She threw her arms around him and kissed him. 'I'm so pleased for you. It's what you want, isn't it?'

'I can't think of anything I'd rather be doing,' he said. 'Ever since I visited poor old Digger, and met McIndoe, I've had a sneaking ambition to work there. It's such a new and challenging field. Dad will be pleased, I'm sure.'

'It sounds like a wonderful opportunity,' his mother agreed.

'Where is he? Dad, I mean.'

'He made me promise not to say anything to you . . .' She seemed on the point of tears.

'What is it?' he demanded. 'What's happened?'

'It happened on the second night of the raids . . . after you left.'

'What happened? I thought the bombing was confined to the south bank of the river.'

'It was, but a stray stick of incendiaries fell on Dumbarton Road.

Stuart tried to save the roof of the Boquhanrhan School Hall and was badly burned.'

Stephen frowned.

'Why didn't you let me know? I could have come . . .'

'Your father made me promise not to tell you until it was all over. He's doing very well, so Sir Duncan tells me.'

'Duncan Ware Roberts?' Stephen demanded.

'Yes, I think that's the name.' Annie seemed surprised that Stephen should know the consultant so well.

He was on the point of making some disparaging remark about the man, but checked himself just in time. There was no point in alarming his mother unnecessarily. Ware Roberts was probably treating his father perfectly adequately . . . He thought of the discussion there had been around the boardroom table. Even if the man did use antiquated techniques he had a good reputation. Maybe there was no need to worry . . .

'Do you have time to visit the hospital?' asked Annie, relieved now that the secret was out.

'If you don't mind my pushing off right away?' said Stephen, searching her face which was drawn and anxious.

'I really should get back to my guests,' she told him apologetically. 'I'm sure Stuart would like to see you, despite his insistence you should not be worried about him.'

'I'll ring as soon as I'm settled in at East Grinstead.' He kissed her lightly on the brow. 'When Dad is recovered, you two should have a holiday, get off into the country somewhere . . . you both deserve it.'

'We'll see. It depends a bit on Adolf. Hopefully we have seen the last of him, but you never know . . .'

'Bombings or no, you and Dad have done more than your fair share. It's time you stepped down and let someone younger take over.'

'We must all do what we can,' Annie insisted.

Stephen was too familiar with that tone to consider any further dissuasion. Once it was made up, there was no way in which he could persuade Annie Beaton to change her mind.

Chapter Nineteen

Stephen was relieved to find that Stuart had been placed in a side ward of the general surgical unit at the Western Infirmary. The risk of infection, were he to be on an open ward, would have been much greater. His injuries were such that he could not lie on his back, but was forced to remain uncomfortably on his stomach, propped up by pillows to allow him to breathe. Stephen approached the bed with growing apprehension, fearing to upset his father by disobeying his strict instructions to Annie not to tell him about the accident.

He need not have worried for Stuart seemed pleased to see him. He's probably forgotten what he said, thought Stephen, drawing up a chair and sitting close by so that his father could speak to him more easily.

'What brings you back to Glasgow so quickly?' Stuart spoke with difficulty, his voice very weak. Stephen had to lean forward to hear what he said.

'I'm on my way to Sussex. I've been posted to East Grinstead.'

'McIndoe's unit?' In his excitement at this news, Stuart tried to raise his shoulders from the pillow, but the effort was too much and he fell back with a groan. 'That's absolutely marvellous. Aren't you pleased?'

'Yes. It came as quite a shock, though. McIndoe seemed to know the outcome of the exams before I did myself.'

'Dowson has been speaking to East Grinstead about my condition,' Stuart explained. 'I expect he mentioned you in passing.'

'No doubt.' Stephen nodded thoughtfully, unable to suppress a suspicion of collusion between the two surgeons. He had the distinct feeling that he was being manipulated, and although the outcome of their manoeuvrings had been exactly what he would have wanted for himself, he could not help wishing that he had been the one to make the moves himself.

'I couldn't have asked for a better posting,' he agreed, 'but it's come at a very inconvenient moment. I would have preferred to remain within call while you're in this state. Mother will have to carry the whole burden of your illness by herself.'

'They wouldn't allow you to do anything for me, even if you were to stay around,' said Stuart, 'and I know that Annie wouldn't want you to jeopardise your future by refusing this appointment. I shall be up and about again in no time. You'll see.'

'What's the extent of the damage?' Stephen wanted to know.

'They won't tell me,' said his father. 'But look for yourself.'

His back was covered with a single sheet. Stephen lifted it back, gently, to find the area covered with dressings dyed a distinctive yellow colour.

Tannic acid . . . Ware Roberts had used tannic acid despite all that had been said at Stephen's interview. He fought back a wave of anger.

'Both shoulders and the entire dorsal surface as far down as the coccyx,' was his estimate.

Stuart closed his eyes momentarily. It was worse than he had feared. Doped as he was with morphine, he had never been entirely sure what they were doing when they dressed his wounds.

Noting his father's distress, Stephen deliberately measured his next words.

'Looks as if they are doing a good job, Dad,' he said, with as much sincerity as he could muster.

After all, this would have been the treatment he would have used himself up to eighteen months ago. It had saved lives, even if it had cost the patients pain in the later stages of recovery. Stuart's burns covered an area of flat skin and the problems were not so great where digital movement was not involved. Severe scarring was inevitable, however. The saline treatment would have reduced that particular risk.

Stuart shifted uncomfortably.

'This is damned uncomfortable,' he complained.

'Doctors always make bad patients,' Stephen chivvied him. 'Looks like you'll just have to grin and bear it for a bit.'

'I wanted them to experiment with your famous saline treatment, but on advice from McIndoe they abandoned that idea. He seemed to think that without suitable equipment they could do more harm than good.'

Talking about his case seemed to rally Stuart. He became quite animated as he continued and his voice grew stronger.

'It seems that some young upstart of a surgeon put them all in their places about tannic acid a while ago.' Stephen squeezed his father's hand and smiled at this.

'Ware Roberts is in charge of the case,' Stuart told him. 'He was very much against any radical treatment, but nevertheless Dowson contacted McIndoe. It's nice to think that all these high fliers are looking after me.'

His tone was flippant but Stephen suspected that his father was rather pleased to be the centre of attention. 'It's a pity they weren't prepared to take a risk. I would have been happy for them to experiment . . .'

Determined not to allow Stuart to continue to fret about what *might* have been done, Stephen played down McIndoe's treatment.

'They place the patient right into a saline bath at East Grinstead,' he told his father, 'but they have had a lot of difficulties with getting the solution just right. It's rather early days yet for everyone to be using the method.'

He lifted his father's chart from the end of the bed.

'At least they don't have to worry about you taking a peek at this,' he said, studying the soaring temperatures with a worried frown.

'Running a bit high, is it?' Stuart asked. 'The sweating makes me darned uncomfortable . . .'

'A trace of infection, I should say,' Stephen replied, minimising the significance of what he saw. 'May be something to do with the pretty nurses.'

'You haven't seen the Sister!' Stuart rolled his eyes. 'She's guaranteed to freeze the blood, not boil it!'

'Do they let you up at all?' Stephen asked. 'You're able to walk?'

'I am quite able to stand,' he answered, 'it's only my shoulders that are badly damaged. I walked here on my own two feet from the school . . . didn't Annie tell you?'

He did not mention that when he had arrived, leaning heavily on the arm of his stoical female companion, he had been on the point of collapse.

'They won't allow me to move about too much at the moment, though, in case the dressings rub.'

In sterile conditions he would be better left without dressings, Stephen thought, but here, even in a side ward, his father was nursed by staff in contact with all manner of patients. Infection was undoubtedly their worst enemy.

'At least the burns haven't disfigured your handsome profile,' said Stephen, more light-heartedly than he felt. It was true that his father's face had escaped damage, but nevertheless it showed every sign of his ordeal. His flesh was grey, the skin transparent, the veins standing out alarmingly, the unhealthy pallor accentuated by purplish shadows beneath deeply sunken eyes.

Stephen could see that their talk had tired his father. He was in danger of overstaying his welcome.

'Look, I'll have to go now,' he said, reaching for his cap. As he moved to stand, Stuart caught sight of the rings on Stephen's arm for the first time.

'You've been promoted.' His eyes were shining. 'I'm so proud of you, son . . .' In his weakened state he had no control over his emotions and Stephen was distressed to see a tear trickle down his father's cheek.

He leaned over him and gently wiped the wetness away with the corner of the sheet.

'Behave yourself,' he instructed, the roles of father and son suddenly reversed. 'I don't want any reports about your being a difficult patient, you know. Just do everything they tell you.'

He stood over the greying locks, dull and lifeless because of Stuart's condition, but even now bearing a hint of their original flaming red.

Then he bent and kissed his father on the lips, something he had not done since he was a small boy.

'Goodbye, Dad.' He pulled on his gloves and settled his cap at the prescribed angle. 'I'll be back just as soon as they'll allow me.'

He couldn't bear to wait for a reply. Turning on his heel, Stephen walked out into the main ward, passing beds filled with the victims of the bombing. So engrossed was he in his own thoughts, that he nearly collided with Professor Dowson.

'Stephen, how good to see you! Well, I must say, you're looking a little more presentable than last time we met. Even the ENT man couldn't find fault with *that* uniform!'

As he spoke, he ushered Stephen into the Sister's office where they could not be overheard.

'You've seen your father?'

He nodded.

'The third-degree burns are not all that extensive. The problem is that there was so much dirt in the wounds . . . we did our best to clean him up but, as you can see, there is widespread infection.'

'Sulphanilamide?' It was a question, not a suggestion.

'We've tried it . . . not very effective, I'm afraid. There is, however, something new. We've had a small sample sent over from the States, for trials. Penicillin . . . ever heard of it?'

'I read something in the *Lancet* a while back,' Stephen recalled. 'Wasn't it discovered in England?'

'Yes, a chap called Fleming. It was the usual story. Queen Mary's, where he worked, couldn't find the necessary research and development money so it was taken up by some American concern.

'Stephen,' he continued, unable to find any way to sweeten the pill, ' I don't need to tell you that your father is very poorly. He's not a young man and the fever has worn him down. If we don't arrest the infection soon, his heart will not be able to hold out. This new drug is supposed to work quickly.'

Stephen nodded. 'I believe they're calling it a miracle drug?'

Dowson laughed. 'Well . . . you know the Americans.' Then, becoming serious once more, 'The chances are that Stuart will not survive without some extraordinary intervention. I'd like your permission to try this penicillin.'

'What does *he* say?'

Stephen understood the Professor's dilemma. Clinical trials always carried an element of risk. It was fine if the drug worked. If it didn't, then questions were asked and reputations frayed.

'I haven't asked him. Frankly he's in no state to make a rational judgement. I was waiting to speak to your mother, but I'm sure that she will go along with whatever you say.'

Stuart agreed. His mother had an alarming confidence in his own as well as his father's infallibility. She would go along with any decision he made.

It was what Stuart himself would want. Hadn't he only a short while before insisted that they should experiment if they wished?

'Go ahead,' said Stephen. He wrote rapidly on a scrap of paper and handed it to the Professor. 'That's my new phone number. You'll let me know how it goes?'

'Of course.' The Professor scanned the note he held in his hand. He smiled and called after Stephen's receding figure.

'So McIndoe caught up with you at last!'

'As if you didn't know,' Stephen murmured to himself. He turned to acknowledge the remark, saluted casually and hurried on his way. He would need to get a move on if he was to catch the London train.

There can be few sights on earth more beautiful than a Sussex woodland in the early spring. Leaving his luggage to be called for later, Stephen had decided to walk from the railway station to the hospital. He was in good time, and after travelling for more than twenty hours, needed to get some fresh air into his lungs.

Green hedges of holly and rhododendron shimmered in the noonday sun. Willows and birches carried a faint greenish bloom from their burgeoning foliage, while the oaks and beeches overhead remained starkly bare, their complex tracery of twigs and branches breaking up the sun's rays so that they fell in delicate patterns across the roadway.

Swathes of white wood anemones swept the forest floor, and here and there a primrose peeped from the litter of decaying vegetation, its delicate yellow petals set off by the dark green of bramble and the chocolate brown of last season's bracken.

Stephen swung along at a good pace, his weariness falling away as his limbs enjoyed the luxury of uninhibited movement.

The night express from Glasgow had been delayed at every major junction where trains carrying troops and armaments always took priority.

Most of Stephen's travelling companions had been in uniform. Many seemed battle-worn and all preferred to snatch a few hours' sleep rather than engage for any length of time in conversation.

For hours he had worried over his father's condition. Unable to contribute in any way to Stuart's recovery, he fretted over the treatment he was receiving and worried about the abilities of the doctors in charge of his case. When he did fall into a doze, it was to dream . . . irrational scenes from his childhood took him on a journey through a jumble of memories in which his mother was the principal character, his father a shadowy figure, always in the background. The psychiatrist in him suggested that the infant Stephen had resented the return, after an absence of two years, of a father whom all but Annie had assumed dead. Stuart had appeared, out of the blue, to come between the little boy and his mother. It had been many years before Stephen had been able to share the love he felt for Annie with his father also. How he regretted those childish feelings of resentment now, when it could be too late to make amends . . .

Turning a sharp corner in the winding lane, he came suddenly upon the hospital, lying behind a neat privet hedge, its entrance marked by tall brick pillars and its driveway already bordered by a cheerful array of daffodils.

On his last visit he had been coming to see Digger Sheen. Since Stephen's transfer to Prestwick, their correspondence had been spasmodic to say the least. He presumed that Digger was still here at the Queen Vic. Surely he would have let someone know if he had been discharged? At the prospect of seeing his friend again, after so long, Stephen quickened his pace.

In the past few months, the original hospital had spawned a small village of hutted wards to the rear, well away from the road. It was to this area that Stephen was directed.

He found himself in a spacious entrance hall with a cheerful-looking woman in a neatly tailored suit seated behind the reception counter.

'May I help you?' she asked.

'I have to report to Mr McIndoe,' he explained.

'You'll be Squadron Leader Beaton? Mr McIndoe said you were to join him in the bath house as soon as you arrived.'

He hesitated.

'Yes?'

'I walked from the station,' Stephen explained. 'Is it possible that someone might pick up my luggage?'

'There is a courtesy bus laid on for visiting hour,' she replied. 'I'll ask the driver to collect your cases.'

'Thank you . . . and where *is* the bath house?'

She called over a white-overalled orderly.

As Stephen and the spare young fellow confronted one another, each wore a bewildered frown. There was something about the scraggy form and the cheeky upturn of the mouth which stirred Stephen's memory. 'Baggy?' he demanded.

At the same moment, the other also recalled his early days in the RAF. 'Mr Beaton, sir. Fancy you remembering me.'

'What are you doing here?' Stephen asked, surveying this healthy specimen who stood before him and comparing him with the sickly fellow for whom he had once demanded treatment in a Service hospital, despite the fact that the man should never have been recruited in the first place.

'Medical Orderly, Second Class, Barnabus A. Gage, sir.' Baggy saluted smartly.

'No need to ask if you got over your spot of bother.' Stephen smiled. A healthier specimen than this wiry little man it would be hard to find.

'I thought it was the end of me when I found myself at Wroughton, sir. Up there on the Downs, in bed outside on an open balcony in rain or sunshine, with temperatures sometimes below freezing and at others eighty degrees or more. But it didn't matter. Did wonders for me, it did . . . all them eggs and the milk. Fat as a pig I was after six months of that treatment.'

'TB all gone?' It was an unnecessary question. Baggy would have had to have been quite clear of the tuberculin bacillus for six months before he would be allowed to work here.

'Not a whisper of a cough for ages,' Baggy confided. 'They still test me from time to time, and I gets an X-ray every few months, but I'm all clear, Doctor, thanks to you.'

'I'd say that the staff at Wroughton might have had something to do with it.' Stephen grinned.

'They'd never have got started had it not been for you insisting I was sent there.' Baggy was not to be contradicted. He knew where thanks were due.

'How long have you been an orderly?'

'Three months. I'm studying for my State Registration,' Baggy said proudly. 'It's heavy going. I was never much of a reader, but I remembers things once I've done them for myself . . . know what I mean?'

Stephen nodded.

'It looks as though we may be seeing quite a lot of each other,' he observed. 'I've been posted here for the foreseeable future. If there's anything I can do to help you with the studying, just let me know.'

'D'you mean it, guv'nor? Sir . . .' he corrected himself, quite overcome by the idea that Stephen might stoop so low.

'Of course. Now, point me in the direction of the bath house, will you?'

Stephen recognised the burly figure of his new boss immediately. With the stance of a prize fighter, his broad shoulders were hunched over as he appeared to be examining the plumbing of a large slipper bath. It was placed centrally in a treatment room and surrounded by all manner of equipment, most of which appeared to be for the lifting and handling of patients.

Stephen cleared his throat noisily to attract attention. McIndoe raised his head, peering over the edge of the bath through large horn-rimmed spectacles. Stephen, hard put to it not to laugh at this comical sight, was tempted to say in the words of a popular cartoon figure, 'Wot, no water?'

'Ah, Beaton.' The surgeon stretched himself to his full height which was to a little above Stephen's shoulder. 'Glad you could make it.' He wiped his grubby hands on the small towel that hung from his trouser pocket, and shook Stephen's hand warmly.

The younger man tried hard not to wince when the ham-like paw squeezed his own. It was difficult to believe that these were the hands which also had the delicate touch of the plastic surgeon.

'It's good to be here, sir.' he grinned.

'You don't feel that you've been hijacked?'

'I must admit that the suspicion has crossed my mind.'

'People with your degree of skill are hard to find,' McIndoe told him. 'Once spotted, they rarely escape me!'

Patting Stephen on the back, he led him outside and along a series of corridors to his own office.

'Grown a bit since you were here last?' It was a question. He really had no notion how long it was since he'd seen Stephen. Time meant nothing at all to this dedicated human being. He measured days by the number of treatments he could fit in and his months by the time each of his patients took to heal.

'Had the unit built to my own design,' he explained. 'At least we can isolate the burns victims from other patients so the risk of cross infection is minimised. More importantly, here in our own domain we can exercise a little leniency not allowed in the main wards. It may offend Matron's sensitivities, but there are very few rules out here in the Hutch.'

Stephen looked mystified.

'It's a name the boys have given the unit. They are McIndoe's Guinea Pigs and they live in a Hutch!'

Stephen laughed outright. Gaining in confidence in this easy atmosphere, he asked, 'What was all that . . . with the bath?' Never in his life had he met a surgeon who engaged in plumbing as a pastime.

'The saline treatment has proved successful in ninety-nine out of a hundred cases,' McIndoe told him. 'The patients do all right, but we are costing the Hospital Committee a fortune in copper piping. The trouble is, the treatment is most effective when the solution is kept circulating and the strength of the saline can be adjusted frequently. That requires a system of pipes and pumps. Some boffin has recently come up with a form of piping which is made using Ebonite. He's asked us to try it out.'

'Does it work?'

'At first we believed it was the solution to all our problems.' McIndoe ran the flat of his hand across his plastered down black hair. 'The Ebonite doesn't seem to be affected by salt, but after some use it hardens and becomes brittle . . . then it cracks. That's what I was doing – looking for leaks.'

Stephen had begun to understand that this was no ordinary posting. Nothing had prepared him for the fact that they might be expected to be plumbers and engineers as well. This would take a different type of dedication. He regarded his new job with growing interest.

'I want you to consider these first few weeks as a training period,' McIndoe said, suddenly switching to the purpose of their meeting. He regarded Stephen fiercely, perhaps seeking some sign of dissent.

Stephen smiled. It was no more than he had expected.

'I'm here to learn.'

McIndoe nodded briefly, relieved to find that neither Stephen's elevation to the status of registered surgeon nor his promotion to Squadron Leader had gone to his head.

'Well then, to begin with you will shadow my every move. Take notes if you must, and remember, I don't reckon to say anything twice. Later, I'll hand over a couple of cases for your own personal attention and we'll see how things go from there.'

He got up from his chair, wandered out into the corridor and collared the first person who happened to be passing.

'Orderly, show Squadron Leader Beaton to his quarters, will you?' And to Stephen, 'Dinner is at six-thirty in the canteen. Afterwards you can accompany me on my evening round. Take the time until dinner to settle yourself in.'

'Is Digger Sheen still a patient here?'

'On and off,' was the odd reply. 'He spends the time between grafts with his wife, down in Kent.'

'His wife?' Stephen's heart missed a beat.

'Didn't he tell you? They married soon after his fiancée came here as a nursing sister. Grace left soon after, to take care of her elderly aunt. The War Department couldn't insist on her staying once she was married. It's a waste of an excellent nurse, but at least Digger is well looked after when he's on home leave.'

'When is he due back?' Stephen swallowed his disappointment. He wondered if he should find time to go and visit his friends at Manston.

'Another three months or so, I think. You can check for yourself sometime.' McIndoe waved in the general direction of a stack of filing cabinets.

'Thank you, sir.' Stephen turned to the orderly. 'Sorry to keep you, Baggy. Lead on.'

★

It was a small, sparsely furnished room, not nearly so comfortable as the MO's suite at Doone House, but luxurious compared with the shoe box which Stephen had shared with Stumpy Miles at Prestwick.

The bed looked like standard WD issue for Service hospitals: narrow, with a sharp angle-iron structure and low to the ground. The mattress felt pretty hard but tonight, at any rate, he didn't think he'd have much trouble sleeping.

Beneath the window stood a plain deal desk with, alongside it, a small bookcase. The usual white wood and fibreboard wardrobe and chest of drawers occupied one wall.

Stephen regarded the wash-hand basin in the opposite corner as sheer luxury. He tried the hot tap. It ran cold for a few minutes, then warmed up rapidly. An adequate supply of hot water was one of the pluses associated with living in a hospital.

In the centre of the room someone had placed his two suitcases. The receptionist had been as good as her word, he must remember to thank her.

Stephen unpacked hurriedly, anxious to explore the remainder of the building before dinner. Forewarned is forearmed, he told himself, anxious not to show himself wanting in any respect when on his first crucial round of the wards with his new boss.

From his earlier visits to the hospital he had observed McIndoe to be easygoing with the patients, always ready for a laugh and a bit of banter, and prepared also to turn a blind eye to some of their pranks. This more recent encounter, however, had made him suspect that his chief, sparing himself nothing, would expect an equal degree of dedication to the job from his colleagues. Stephen had never been one to shirk his duties, but he was determined that the great man should think well of him.

He laid out his new No.1 uniform and a clean shirt. He would allow himself time for a shave and a wash and then he would take a quick look around the wards.

The hutted complex had been designed to ensure that those confined to bed for long periods should have the best possible outlook on the world. Most of the windows, larger than in the usual military style of temporary buildings, looked out upon the Sussex countryside and despite the criss-crossed tape, intended to prevent the glass from shattering during a bombing attack, the views were magnificent.

The wards radiated from a central block containing the treatment rooms and bathrooms, theatre, dental surgery and technicians' workshop. Nearby, a lounge and a dining room were provided for mobile patients and medical staff.

Having satisfied himself that he now had a general idea of the layout of the building, Stephen retraced his steps to the central core where the public rooms and offices were situated.

In the lounge he discovered a number of chaps wearing the bright blue uniform and red necktie of the wounded serviceman. They sat about in small groups or alone, playing cards, chess, dominoes, or reading. All totally engrossed in what they were doing, no one even looked up when Stephen entered.

At the piano, a lone figure tinkered with the keys. He would execute a popular tune with great precision for a few bars, improvise a little in a most professional manner, and then pass on to something else, never completing a piece.

Stephen moved towards him, intending to engage him in conversation when he next stopped playing. He had taken the fellow to be a victim of premature male balding until he was within a few feet. Closer inspection showed that the scalp had been torn or singed from two-thirds of his skull, leaving a heavily scarred cap of white and brown flesh. So startled was he by the discovery that Stephen's face must have betrayed his reaction to the sight of these terrible injuries. He felt guilt for the relief he experienced when he realised that the man was also blind.

'You're new, aren't you?' The pianist cocked his head on one side, like a thrush hunting for worms.

'Yes,' Stephen replied, startled by the acuteness of the man's undamaged senses. 'You play very well.'

The pianist gave a derisive laugh, somewhere between a chortle and a cry of pain, slammed down the lid of the piano, felt for his white cane and rose to his feet. He wandered away, tapping at the furniture and negotiating the hazards in his path with consummate ease.

'Take no notice of Fingers,' drawled a voice, 'he gets irritated when he can't remember the score.'

Stephen turned towards the high-backed wing chair from whence the remark had come. A pair of exceedingly long legs were stretched towards the grate in which a log fire burned cheerfully. A pad lay on the speaker's lap, but it was the hand holding the pencil which arrested Stephen's attention. It was like a bird's claw. The fingers were twisted grotesquely, their skin withered and darkened to an unhealthy-looking brownish colour. It was as though it had been tanned like a cow's hide.

In profile he was a good-looking fellow, possibly in his mid-twenties. His blond hair was neatly cropped and curled close to his head. His finely chiselled features, fair complexion and one piercingly blue eye, which was given an ethereal quality by the almost colourless lashes bordering it, completed the appearance of an angel from a fresco by Michelangelo.

The speaker laid down his pencil and turned to look Stephen full in the face.

The doctor was hard put to it to contain his astonishment. It was as though the man wore a hideous Hallowe'en mask which covered only one side of his head. The reverse was a mass of scarred and puckered skin in a variety of hues, ranging from purple through red to brown. From out of a bed of mutilated tissue peered the second blue eye, the only aspect of this profile which in any way reflected the reverse.

'Used to be a concert pianist,' the speaker continued, unabashed. 'I saw him performing at the Wigmore Hall before the war. Marvellous. You may have heard of him . . . Martin Dorrel?'

Still trying to come to terms with the apparition before him, Stephen was startled by the question.

'No, I can't say that I have. Never had much time for that sort of thing. I spent most of my time studying pre-war, in Glasgow.'

'I'd never have guessed,' replied the other with a degree of sarcasm which, coming from any other source, would have riled Stephen. He had become accustomed to being teased about his Scottish accent at Manston, but in recent months it had been he who was on familiar territory. The respite had blunted his wit, and right at this moment he could think of nothing with which to retaliate.

'Medic?' demanded the airman.

'How did you guess?' Stephen was beginning to sharpen up.

'Well, you appear to be in one piece, unlike the rest of us, and I do recognise the badge even though it's a while since I saw one of you guys in uniform.'

Stephen fingered the badge pinned to his collar: paired silver serpents winding around their winged staff.

'Are there no other RAF doctors here?'

'You're the only one I've seen, here in the Hutch at any rate. There were plenty at Halton, of course, but Old Mac came and got me out of there months ago. Name's Ed, by the way.'

He pushed out his right claw and Stephen took it gingerly.

'Beaton – Steve Beaton,' he said, turning the hand over in his own. 'Don't mind if I take a look, do you?' he enquired.

'Be my guest, Doc,' Ed replied. 'Not a bad job, is it . . . considering?'

Stephen looked closely, observing the manner in which skin grafts had been used to reconstruct the palm of the hand. By the addition of new skin the opposable thumb had been made to operate sufficiently well for Ed to be able to hold a pencil. Glancing at the pad on which his companion had been writing, he saw that the result was legible if spidery and laboured. He had seen worse handwriting amongst his fellow students.

'Poetry?' Stephen asked, noting the form that the script had taken.

'I do my best,' replied the other, turning the pad face down, unwilling to allow this stranger to see what he had been writing.

Stephen stood up.

'I'm just finding my way about,' he said. 'No doubt we shall meet again.'

As he turned to go, the other dropped his gaze to his work. At the door Stephen took a last look round. Apart from the empty piano stool nothing had changed from when he had entered the room. It said a lot for the morale of the place that all its patients were so intently occupied.

He was sorry that his encounter with the pianist had been brief and so unsatisfactory. It would be all the more difficult to make contact a second time.

'Well, what do you think?' McIndoe laid down his napkin and played with his butter knife.

Startled by the question, Stephen looked up from the remains of his treacle pudding, swallowed hastily and asked. 'About what, sir?'

'I understand that you couldn't wait for my evening round. They tell me you have already done your inspection.'

McIndoe kept a straight face and Stephen wondered if this was some kind of reprimand.

Colouring under the intense scrutiny, he explained, 'I just wanted to get my bearings. I hate having to ask directions when I can seek things out for myself.'

'A man of independent spirit,' observed McIndoe. 'Yes, I like that. So, do we meet with your approval?'

'From what I've seen so far, everything seems to work very efficiently.' Now that Stephen realised that McIndoe had only been pulling his leg, he allowed himself to concentrate on the subject in hand. 'I suppose it helped that you were able to design the layout yourself?'

'The Ministry of Works people were very difficult,' McIndoe recalled. 'I had to insist on doors wide enough to take a bed, and beds wide enough to take patients, cradles, and all the rest of the gubbins that accompanies the lads on their way to and from the bath house.'

'Those beds are a bit special, aren't they?' Stephen remarked. 'I've never seen anything quite so splendid. Did you get them made by Rolls-Royce?'

'From the price you might have thought so.' McIndoe grinned ruefully, recalling the arguments over the telephone with the *bowler hats* at the Ministry of Supply. 'I had to force one of the blighters down here to see for himself what we were faced with, before he would sign the order. I've never seen such a sudden change of attitude in any man as when that pompous little ass was confronted by our Eddie.'

'The poet?'

'Yes, that's him. At the time, he was receiving saline treatment three times a day and every movement was sheer agony. His third-degree burns cover forty per cent of his body surface, you know.' McIndoe paused, remembering the stoicism of his young patient under the primitive conditions of those early treatments. 'Anyway, this Ministry guy watched the entire operation of lifting Ed on to a trolley and off that into the bath, back to the trolley and back to bed. Without saying a word, he walked into my office, took out the order, signed it and gave it to my clerk to post! After that I had no problems getting anything I asked for.'

'I can see that the rubber wheels give a much smoother ride,' observed Stephen. 'I'm surprised you managed to get stainless steel tubing for the frames. I would have thought that would be unobtainable?'

'It is important that the beds retain as little dust as possible,' McIndoe reminded him. 'Cross infection is our worst enemy. That tubular steel was lurking in some warehouse in the Midlands and a very good contact of mine had it smuggled out to the factory which manufactures the beds. It pays to have friends in high places.' He grinned.

Stephen could imagine that Archie McIndoe had little trouble in that respect. He was well known as a fund raiser for important medical projects. Stephen could just imagine him charming the pants off some wealthy dowager with that extraordinarily attractive New Zealand accent of his.

'Well, if you've finished.' McIndoe rose from his seat, placing his neatly folded napkin in its silver ring. 'It's time we did the rounds.

Sister will be wanting to tuck the lads up for the night.'

They made their way to the first of the wards whose four occupants were seated around a central table playing poker. They looked up when the two surgeons entered.

With obvious relief one of the players laid down his cards, while another groaned, 'Oh, not now, Mac. This is the best hand I've had in weeks!'

'Sorry, fellers, I do need to have a word in private with each of you before lights out. Just go to your own cubicles, will you? Oh, this is Stephen – Squadron Leader Beaton to you lot. Until they think of something more appropriate,' he muttered, so that only Stephen heard. 'Mr Beaton has come to give me a hand with the surgery.'

'If you say so, boss,' said one of the young men, eyeing Stephen with suspicion. They were accustomed to receiving Archie McIndoe's undivided attention. This new bloke had better be good . . .

'Don't worry, Peter, he wouldn't want to make his first mistake on your miserable physog,' McIndoe chided, winking at Stephen over the head of the mutilated airman. 'I shall be doing your grafts at about 0600 hours. No midnight feasts for you tonight . . . and that goes for the rest of you.'

He checked out the four patients carefully. Stephen was impressed with the trouble he took with each of them to say exactly what was to happen the next day, what improvement he hoped for and the limitations of any work that was to be done.

'Only another twenty trips to the theatre for you, m'lad,' he said to the last one, 'and Peggy down at the Red Lion might actually fancy you!'

The fellow grinned, quite unabashed by this direct reference to his appearance. There was no pussyfooting around with these boys. Their wounds were there for everyone to see and the sooner they and everyone else came to terms with them, the better.

'Mum? Mum, is that you?'

The line was bad. There were mysterious background noises and his mother's voice seemed to come and go.

'Stevie, is that you? Oh, thank goodness you rang!'

Stephen's blood rang cold. His father . . . was he worse?

'Wonderful news . . . I saw Stuart tonight . . . Professor Dowson called me in specially. Your father's been so poorly the last two times I've been in . . . tonight he was sitting up in bed when I got there, reading a newspaper, would you believe? They have him supported in some kind of a sling thing . . . Oh, Stevie, he is so much better . . . I just couldn't believe there could be such a dramatic change.'

He could hear the tears in her voice now.

'Oh, Stevie . . . I've been so worried. I really thought . . .'

'But he's really OK now? What did Dowson say?'

'He said that it was early days yet, but that there seemed to be no reason why Stuart's burns should not heal perfectly well if they could prevent further infection. He'll be scarred, of course, but who's to know? Only me.'

Stephen's relief was so transparent that even at a distance of four hundred miles, Annie felt his tension ease.

'You knew, didn't you, Stevie?'

'That it was touch and go . . . yes.'

'When Professor Dowson said you had given them permission to try out something new, that was his last chance, wasn't it?'

'Dad had been complaining to me only minutes before that they hadn't used McIndoe's treatment for his burns, so I'm sure that, had he been in a fit state to decide, he would have wanted them to experiment with the penicillin.'

'Penicillin . . . that's the stuff. The Professor said it was from America. It's wonderful, Stevie . . .'

'How about you? Are you OK?'

'Oh, I'm fine. I've been too busy to fret. Ellen arrived last night . . . as soon as she heard about Stuart she took a couple of days' leave to see if there was anything she could do to help.'

Stephen experienced a stab of conscience. Ellen was fulfilling his duties. She was a better daughter to his parents than he was a son.

'Look, Mum, I'll try and get back . . . it's not up to Ellen. This has just come at such an awkward time . . .'

'Stuart wouldn't want you to neglect your work, dear. Even when he was at his lowest, he was talking about your new appointment. I think it would do him more harm than good if you were to do anything to interfere with that.'

'Have you been at the hospital all day?'

'No, not all the time. We've spent much of the day tidying up after the builders. The broken windows are boarded up and the men have put steel props in two of the bedrooms to prevent the ceiling collapsing. We can't use the top floor, and the first floor is so gloomy that I've made the dining room into a bedroom for the two of us.'

'That sounds like a sensible idea,' he told her. 'Is Ellen there?' he asked, wanting to thank her in person.

'She's just popped out to see one of her colleagues who's taking a short course at the University. I'll tell her you were asking after her. How is Sussex? Have you settled in all right?'

'I haven't really had time to find out,' he laughed, the burden of the past twenty-four hours lifted from his shoulders. 'Everything seems fine so far. I start work tomorrow.'

'Stuart is so proud of you. He's been boasting to all the nurses that you are rebuilding the faces of burned pilots.'

'A slight exaggeration. For the next six weeks I'm to be a student. Only after that will I be able to perform any surgery on my own.'

'Hugh telephoned. We were talking about opening up the cottage on Eisdalsa so that Audrey can live over there as soon as she's fit enough to look after herself. Apparently he and Derek have spent the day getting it ready for her to move in. Derek was sorry to have missed you, by the way. I had a brief word with him too. He says he will call in to see Stuart as he passes through on his way back to Prestwick. He had a terrible time attempting to cross the Clyde by ferry so he's coming back by train.'

'When you see him, will you tell him that Digger Sheen is married and is recuperating at the Vicarage in Manston? I hope to be seeing him and Grace very soon.'

'I'll make a note of that. Digger, did you say? Another Australian?'

'Yes, actually, Ellen's already met him. He was badly burned, way back . . . last year. Look, I'll have to go now. This is a public phone and there's a crowd waiting. Give Dad my love. I'll be back to see him as soon as I get the chance. God bless. And Ellen too, of course.'

When he put down the phone, Stephen's worried frown returned. It was good to know that his father was making such excellent progress. He just hoped that this miracle drug was as good as they claimed. Sometimes these things had disastrous side effects. That was the whole point about a trial, discovering the snags.

As he wandered along the corridor towards his own room, he heard a commotion coming from one of the wards. The door flew open and Baggy came rushing out. Seeing Stephen, he stopped for long enough to gasp, 'It's Ed, he's having one of his nightmares . . . can you fetch the boss, sir? I must go back and restrain him or he'll do himself an injury.'

'Can't I do something?' Stephen demanded.

'Best leave it to the boss,' Baggy insisted. 'He's the only one can calm him when he gets like this.'

McIndoe needed no second bidding. On hearing Stephen's message, he flew down the corridor, pulling on an ancient bathrobe over his pyjamas as he ran.

'Fetch me some Nembutal,' he called to Stephen as he thrust open the swing door.

Relieved that he had already learned the general geography of the building, Stephen found his way to the dispensary and sought out the required sedative. He hurried back to the ward to find the patient curled up on the floor, in one corner of the room, with Baggy cradling him in his arms as though he were a child. McIndoe was standing over them, talking very softly. It was a picture which Stephen was to hold in his memory until the end of his days.

Terror suffused that part of Ed's destroyed features which could still register any expression. His glance darted about the room like that of a wounded animal.

'OK, sir,' Baggy was saying, 'you've just had a bad nightmare. Old Baggy wouldn't let the monsters get you, now would he?'

Ed turned his wild eyes towards the diminutive orderly who held him pinned down with extraordinary strength.

'Baggy?' he demanded.

There was a look of relief on the face of both surgeon and orderly . . . he was coming out of it.

'Got it in one, sir,' Baggy replied, cheerfully, relaxing his hold now that the limbs had stopped thrashing about in an uncontrolled fashion.

Stephen waited just inside the door, undecided whether to go in.

The room was a shambles. Books and papers had been torn up and thrown about the room like confetti. The patient's chart had been torn from its clipboard and ripped into a dozen pieces, and the one rather attractive picture which hung on the wall opposite his bed had had its glass smashed as though some missile had been hurled at it.

Sensing Stephen's arrival, without taking his eyes off the patient, McIndoe reached behind him for the syringe.

'OK, old chap,' he said, calmly, 'we'll soon have you feeling better.'

Baggy released Ed's arm so that McIndoe could push back the sleeve of his pyjama jacket and swab a patch of skin in the crook of his elbow. He slid the needle in and slowly pushed the plunger. As the drug flowed into Ed's veins, he began to relax. In a few moments he was as limp as a rag doll.

The three of them lifted him and laid him on the bed. Baggy then took over, securing the patient's limbs with restraining webbing and lifting the sides of the bed to prevent him from falling out, should he come round before morning.

McIndoe bent over the prone figure, examining him for any self-inflicted damage.

'He'll do,' he said, satisfied at last. 'Well done, Gage, you handled that very well. Shouldn't you be off duty now?'

'Yes, sir. I was just saying goodnight all round when I found the Wing Commander in this state, sir.'

'You'd better cut along now and get some rest.'

'I'll just hang on for a few minutes, until the Night Sister comes on duty . . . if it's all the same to you, sir?'

'Please yourself,' McIndoe responded amiably. Then, turning back, his hand resting on the door, 'Thanks.'

Baggy might be a trifle small in stature but he had remarkable strength, as Stephen had witnessed, and now it seemed that he was also courageous enough to stand up to McIndoe. A very determined fellow, in fact.

Outside in the corridor the surgeon turned to Stephen.

'As you see, it's not only their bodies which have been destroyed. These lads are stoics when they are conscious but they dream – and God alone knows what their nightmares contain.'

'Do they have any psychiatric help?' Stephen asked.

'Only after they leave here, and only if it's patently obvious they need it. Here they have to depend upon amateurs like our friend Baggy in there.'

'Probably does just as much good . . . coming from someone they know and trust?' suggested Stephen.

'Maybe, but the real problem is that there aren't enough trick cyclists to go round in this Service. I've asked for support but they always manage to fob me off with some excuse or other.'

Stephen recalled family stories about his Uncle Hugh's difficulties, following the Great War.

'At least psychological disorders are recognised as a genuine illness now. They used to shoot men for desertion and court martial them for something they called "lack of moral fibre" in the last war.'

'As you say.' McIndoe dismissed both the subject and Stephen in one sentence. 'See you in the morning. I've asked the night staff to give you a call at 0600 hours.'

Stephen settled down to sleep with his mind in turmoil. His father was going to recover . . . that was wonderful news. It was good of Ellen to have gone to his mother's aid. Annie was very fond of her . . . treated her like a daughter . . . a woman needed a daughter . . . Look how Grace had given up her career to look after Mary Dobbie. Dear Grace . . . he hoped she was not regretting her marriage. It had been a shock to hear about it like that. Until today he'd held out some hope that she might change her mind, that there might still be a chance for him . . .

Stephen's eyes closed and he fell into a fitful sleep, punctuated by weird dreams. Grace, wearing a flowing gown, her hair blowing about in the wind, kissed the tips of her fingers and waved to him. Suddenly receding into the distance, she grew smaller and smaller until he couldn't make her out at all. He chased after her, feet sinking into a soft cloying substance which impeded his progress. As suddenly as she disappeared he caught up with her and turned her round. It wasn't Grace . . . it was Ellen. Ellen, her fair hair tossing in the breeze, her eyes shining . . . Content to bury his head in her comforting bosom, he relaxed at last into a dreamless sleep and was startled when, what seemed only a few minutes later, he was roused by the Night Sister, shaking his shoulder.

'It's 0600 hours, Mr Beaton. I was asked to make sure you weren't late in theatre.'

Chapter Twenty

'Miss McDougal, please.'

Stephen heard a muffled exchange and then a rather gruff male voice answered, 'Miss McDougal is busy at the moment. May I ask who's calling?'

'It's an old friend of hers . . . Stephen Beaton.'

Again the exchange of words. He heard the phone put down and shuffling of papers before a rather breathless Ellen came on the line.

'Stephen?'

'Ellen . . . how are you? I've been trying to get through for days. When did you get back?'

'Yesterday. It took simply ages on the train and I'm still feeling pretty whacked.'

'How was Dad?'

'Fine. His fever was quite gone when I saw him last and Professor Dowson told Aunt Annie that his burns should be sufficiently healed for him to be discharged very soon.'

'And Mum – is she OK?'

'Auntie is feeling the strain a bit. Thank goodness the Gerries have been leaving them alone . . . I don't think she could have coped if there had been any more raids. Apart from the obvious damage, the house is back to normal. I helped Mrs Brown to straighten things out on the ground floor so that their living space is reasonable. There's not much chance of anything being done to the upstairs. The builders have made it wind and watertight.'

'I don't know how to thank you for giving up all your leave like this.'

It had been Ellen's second trip North since his father's accident while he himself had been powerless to do anything more than make a few phone calls to the hospital and to his mother.

'Oh, it's nothing,' she protested, 'Auntie would have done the same for me.'

'Will you get any free time now you're back? I wondered if we might take a trip down to Manston . . . to call on Digger and Grace?'

Ellen's heart gave a lurch. It was the first intimation that Stephen had actually accepted his two friends were an item.

'I'd like that,' she said, cautiously. She did not want to appear too eager. Having become convinced of his lack of interest in her, she had no wish to have him accuse her of throwing herself at him just because her other romance had faltered.

Once she had settled into her new job, she had tried to put Stephen out of her mind. If it had not been for Annie's call to tell her about Stuart's accident she would probably have succeeded in carving out a new relationship with someone else. As it was, her time in Horsham had been interspersed with journeying around the countryside and her two periods in Scotland. She had hardly had time to get to know anyone.

On returning to Glasgow she had toyed with the idea of contacting Malcolm McGregor, but enquiries in that direction had led nowhere. Even the Rosyth number had yielded no information. Commodore Salter was away at sea and no one there had ever heard of Malcolm.

It was almost with a feeling of relief that she'd abandoned the idea. The disclosure that he considered that any woman he chose to marry should devote herself to his interests alone, had put her right off. Her own reaction to this had shown her in no uncertain terms that she did not love him. Any renewal of their friendship would have had to be on a platonic level and she didn't think that Malcolm would be willing to accept that a second time.

'I couldn't make it until the end of next week,' she explained now. 'I have to go down to Chichester for a few days and then there'll be more paperwork to complete up here.'

'How about next Thursday?' Stephen insisted. He really sounded very keen to see her.

'OK, will you pick me up here?' Ellen gave him directions.

'Right then, see you about ten o'clock if that's OK?'

'Sure.' And she put the phone down abruptly.

That's a pity, Stephen thought, wishing he had been able to add something more. Oh, well, he had waited this long to show her how much he enjoyed her company. Another week wouldn't matter.

★

'East Grinstead, RAF Burns Unit,' the receptionist answered. 'Hold the line one moment, Squadron Leader Beaton will take your call.'

It was four o'clock in the morning, she hesitated to disturb him so early . . . but it did sound urgent.

'Beaton.' Stephen's voice was still drowsy and muffled with sleep.

The caller spoke very rapidly for some minutes before pausing for a reply.

'Your most important priority is to alleviate shock,' Stephen instructed. 'Intravenous plasma will stabilise the body fluids. Apply nothing in the way of dressings other than sterile linen to cover the entire body . . . is that understood? No, don't attempt to dress the wounds at all.' There was a pause for the caller to explain his particular problem. 'You can help by clearing away as much of the debris as possible,' was Stephen's reply. 'If you can manage irrigation of the affected parts using saline solution, do that, but you must avoid cross infection at all costs. I'll ring you back when I've made some arrangements.'

He rang McIndoe's number.

'It's Lincoln. They have a bomber pilot, very badly shot up and suffering forty per cent burns.'

'In hospital?'

'Still on the airfield. It seems that the MO has heard a lot about this unit and decided we should be consulted before the local civilians took over.'

'What would be the quickest way of getting there?' demanded McIndoe.

'The fastest method would be a flight from Gatwick,' Stephen suggested. 'Including the road trip to the airfield, you should be able to make it in a couple of hours.'

'Tell him we'll send someone to collect his patient.'

Stephen redialled and relayed this information to the caller.

'I can't say exactly who'll be coming,' Stephen told him. 'Just keep your patient sedated until someone arrives.'

McIndoe joined him in reception, still pulling on his white overall. 'I thought Gatwick was a civilian airfield?'

'It was before the war. It's an RAF emergency landing strip now, used mainly for ferrying bigwigs about and so on. I was over there last week, hoping to get in some flying time. A couple of Lysanders are kept on the field, ideal aircraft for carrying stretcher cases.'

'They'll never let us borrow one of those,' McIndoe declared.

'I don't see why not,' Stephen insisted, 'pilots are a precious commodity these days. You've said yourself that the first few hours determine whether a man will be fit enough to fly again. If you get on the blower to Transport Command, I'll bet you can swing it.'

Another thought struck him. 'If they say they've no one to fly the aircraft, tell them I'll do it myself!'

'Can you?'

'Of course.' Stephen did not elaborate. He had never flown a Lysander but it was reputed to be one of the safest and simplest aircraft to fly. It probably wouldn't be necessary anyway. From what he had seen, the pilots on standby at Gatwick were twiddling their thumbs for most of the day.

'I'll see what I can do.' McIndoe started for his own office telephone. If he was going to grovel, he preferred to do it in private. At the door he called back, 'Meanwhile, get your kit together. Even if it means going by road, this is your case.'

Stephen's mouth fell open in surprise.

He was aware that from time to time, McIndoe had been called to attend to a casualty elsewhere immediately after an incident, but he had hardly expected to be called upon himself. Now, only four weeks into his training, Stephen was being asked to take the chief's place.

Excited at the prospect of working on his own again, he hurried off to the theatre and began to pack a bag with everything necessary to carry out the initial treatments. Since the call had come directly from the airfield, he could expect only the most primitive facilities on the site. It would probably be best if he took everything with him.

McIndoe reappeared while he was sorting out what was needed.

'I managed to talk them into it,' he said, omitting the details of the heated conversation he had just engaged in with a faceless bureaucrat at Transport Command. 'They'll fly you up to Lincoln but can't guarantee an immediate return flight with the patient. It seems that there's some kind of a flap on and they have several ferrying jobs for later this afternoon. They'll pick you up as soon as an aircraft becomes available.'

As McIndoe spoke, Stephen was continuing with his task. He opened the linen cupboard.

'By rights these should be packed in some way – cellophane, I suppose – to keep out dust.' He laid three of the folded sheets inside the fourth, making sure that those inside were fully protected. 'That's the best I can do for now.'

McIndoe nodded his approval and began checking over the rest of Stephen's supplies.

'It's time we had a "ready-to-go-pack" for these occasions.'

'It may prove fortunate that the aircraft can't wait for us at Lincoln,' Stephen told him. He fastened the carrying case and began sorting through his own instruments, checking them one by one before packing them into the old Gladstone bag. 'I didn't mention that the patient has fractures in both legs in addition to multiple burns. It may be necessary to operate before moving him.'

Baggy arrived to collect the equipment.

'I'm sending Gage with you,' said McIndoe, 'you might find him useful.'

'That's splendid, sir, thank you.' Taking up the Gladstone bag, Stephen gave Baggy a thumbs-up sign of approval and grinned broadly.

During these past weeks he had learned to value the skills of Baggy Gage and his colleagues. Their unstinting dedication to their duties, their cheerful approach to difficult and unco-operative patients, and their unwavering confidence in the surgeons' abilities to cope with the direst injuries, made for an air of optimism in which miracles could sometimes be performed.

McIndoe shook Stephen by the hand. 'Ring me when you're ready to leave Lincoln,' he said. 'I'll have an ambulance standing by at Gatwick.'

'Thank you, sir,' Stephen replied. 'I suppose we might need some more of your clout in getting us a ride home!'

'Don't worry,' said McIndoe, confidently. 'It'll all be fixed by the time you get there.'

Stephen turned to his orderly.

'Come on, Baggy, we'd best get going.'

They flew in low over the cathedral, just skirting the twin towers of the ancient building, and turned upwind to land at the RAF station on the outskirts of the city.

Stephen, seated beside the pilot, had concentrated on the controls throughout the flight. As they had followed the line of the Malvern Hills northwards, well away from any danger from enemy aircraft, he had taken over for a short while. The Lysander was heavier than the aircraft to which he had been accustomed, but she flew easily.

'Like driving a number twenty-five bus down Aldgate,' the pilot had observed as he took back the controls in order to make their landing approach. 'What's more, you can put her down on a postage stamp if you have to.'

The pilot gave his call sign, alerting the control tower.

'I have on board Medical Aid Unit, two passengers and equipment . . . over.'

'Land on No. 2 runway . . . No. 2 runway. Transport is laid on to collect your passengers.'

'Roger and out.'

The pilot concentrated now on his landing procedures and Stephen sat back, taking note of every move. There was no telling when he might be called upon to do this for himself.

As he had feared, Stephen found the medical facilities on the airfield to be primitive, despite the very young Medical Officer's obvious attempts to turn the wooden building into an efficient First Aid post.

'There was a brick-built medical centre here originally,' the Flight Lieutenant explained. 'But it was destroyed early in the war during a hit and run raid.'

He appeared quite overawed by the presence of a Senior Medical Officer and defensive about the poor facilities at his disposal. Stephen knew what it was like to be put in charge of a situation like this with absolutely no back-up from more experienced hands.

'I'll take a look at your patient right away,' he said, briskly. 'Perhaps you will show my Corporal the treatment room so that he can make preparations? Do you have anyone who might lend him a hand?'

An Orderly appeared at the Lieutenant's bidding, already clad in a white theatre gown.

'Take Mr Beaton's assistant to the treatment room, Wilson,' he ordered, 'and see he has everything he wants.'

'Sir!'

The Orderly led the way across the narrow corridor into a treatment room which showed every sign of recent, if hasty, tidying.

Baggy looked about him disparagingly.

'Got any disinfectant?' he demanded, eyeing the leather-covered couch with disdain.

'Already given it a going over, Corp,' said the other, cheerfully.

'So I see,' was Baggy's reply, as he tested the surface with his finger. It came away wet and stained where the drying had been inadequate.

'Now we'll do it all over again,' he declared. 'And, by the way, it's Corporal Gage to you, sonny.'

The casualty had been assigned to a small side ward. At first sight he did not appear to have such extensive burns as Stephen had been led to expect. His face seemed to be untouched and his bare shoulders and arms, which lay on top of the sheet, were blistered but the degree of scorching was minimal.

Stephen said nothing, but waited for his colleague to pull back the sheet which covered the lower part of the pilot's body. Both legs were charred black and the lower torso had several areas of severe burning.

Obeying Stephen's telephoned instructions to the letter, the MO had set up a plasma drip, over which a second Orderly hovered like a mother hen. The flying suit and undergarments had been removed and an attempt made to clean away fragments of cloth adhering to the charred flesh.

'You've given him morphine?' Stephen enquired.

'I had to stop him from thrashing about. He would have done himself even more damage.'

Stephen nodded his approval.

'You've done all you could in the circumstances,' he said, regarding his younger colleague with a careful scrutiny. This could not have been a pleasant experience for a chap who was, to all appearances, fresh out of medical school. Even Stephen had been shocked by the extent of the airman's injuries. It was a miracle he had survived this long.

'Now, what about the leg fractures?'

The MO hesitated to give his opinion. 'Without an X-ray one cannot be certain, but from the position of his legs before he was lifted out of the radio cabin, there are multiple fractures to both limbs.'

Even now the Lieutenant gagged when he remembered the charred bundle of humanity they had prised from the wreck of a Lancaster. It had been nursed home on three engines by the pilot, himself wounded, his co-pilot dead.

'How is it possible to get bones to heal without the support of healthy muscles?'

'It isn't,' said Stephen, decisively. 'It's not just the muscles, of course, it's the blood supply as well. There's no way we can save his legs. In fact, I shall have to amputate immediately if we are to save his life. He could well die from the shock of the operation, but I have no alternative.'

'Oh, God.' The young man bit his clenched knuckles.

'Yes,' said Stephen, in a feeble attempt to lighten the mood, 'prayers would be in order, I think.'

The amputation was one which Stephen had never been called upon to perform before. In a way it was a simpler matter than severing the limb at a lower level. His incision was right around the hip joint, leaving sufficient relatively undamaged skin from the inside of the thighs to cover the stump. Having tied off the major vessels as he cleared the connective tissues away from the joint, it was a relatively simple matter to dislocate the hip and separate the head of the femur from its socket. The second leg followed within a very short while.

As he worked, Stephen talked his way through the operation keeping all their minds on the technicalities of the task and not, for the moment at any rate, the patient's prognosis. His colleague proved to be an accomplished anaesthetist and Stephen quickly came to rely upon him to maintain the patient at a suitable level of unconsciousness.

'While we have him under,' he said, as Baggy removed the second leg from the scene, 'I think we'll have another go at cleaning up these other burned areas.' With a skill developed during the past weeks, he worked on the mutilated tissues of the lower trunk until he was satisfied that everything that could be done to clean the site, had been done.

Using the sterile dressing which they had brought with them, he covered the burned areas, and bandaged the neatly stitched stumps.

Before the general anaesthetic had worn off, Stephen had them lift the corpse-like figure on to a trolley draped in sterile sheeting. They wrapped the airman up like a parcel and pinned the loose edges of the top sheet so that all but the patient's head was enclosed.

When everything had been done that could be done, the two doctors made their way back to the MO's office.

The younger man was shaky and grey-looking despite the flush caused by working for so long beneath the hot overhead lighting. Stephen cast a glance around the room, seeking the medicinal brandy bottle.

'Filing cabinet, bottom drawer,' muttered his colleague from the depths of his armchair. It took seconds only for Stephen to pour a couple of stiff drinks.

The younger man stared into space for a long time, holding the glass at such an angle that Stephen feared the brandy would be wasted.

'Drink up,' he ordered, and zombie-like the other obeyed.

Suddenly he burst out, 'Why didn't he die? What sort of a life can a man live . . . like that?'

'He still may die,' said Stephen, gently. 'That is not our decision to make. It's up to us to do our best to keep him alive . . . and in that respect, you have done a good job. You have nothing at all for which to blame yourself. The man may thank you for what you have done today, or he may not . . . only time will tell.'

'What if he blames us for saving his life?'

'If he doesn't wish to live, he will find a way to die. It is not a decision we can make for him. Had he not been determined to go on living, don't you think he would have given up the ghost during the hours when you were awaiting my arrival?'

The Lieutenant stood up, refilled his glass and offered Stephen a top-up.

'I won't, thank you,' he replied. 'It's about time our transport arrived. Can you find out if they have any news of it?'

The MO rang through to the control tower.

'That was well timed,' he reported, slurring his words just a little. 'Ten minutes to touch down.' He picked up the receiver once again and spoke to the transportation officer.

'The ambulance is on its way,' he told Stephen, 'I'd better warn the Orderlies.'

'I'll just make a call to my people, if that's OK?'

'Be my guest,' replied the other, waving his hand towards the telephone.

Stephen glanced at his watch. It was gone seven in the evening. McIndoe would probably be at dinner.

He dialled the number. There was something at the back of his mind . . . he just couldn't put his finger on it for the moment.

McIndoe answered.

'How did it go?' he enquired.

'Well . . . he's still alive,' said Stephen, 'for now. By the way, I know this sounds daft but . . . what day is it?'

There was a chuckle from the other end of the line.

'I'm impressed with the strength of your concentration,' McIndoe observed. 'It's Thursday.'

'Oh, Christ!'

Stephen dropped the receiver into its cradle. He'd really done it this time!

★

It was as though they dared not give the patient in the single room attached to B Ward a name, lest by so doing they might somehow damage his chances of survival.

In everyone's mind he remained patient number thirty-two, until the day his parents arrived for their first visit.

'We have been told that our son is here.' The elderly gentleman was straight as a ramrod, tall, thin, with an elegant snow-white moustache, neatly trimmed. He looks just like some distinguished actor, the receptionist thought, wracking her brains to think who it was he reminded her of.

'What name, sir?' she asked politely.

'David Brownrigg . . . er . . . Pilot Officer Brownrigg.'

The girl seemed puzzled. She scanned the patient list. Oh, yes, of course . . . Pilot Officer Brownrigg. She paled, glad that she was not the one to have to tell them. 'Bed thirty-two . . . it's a little side room off B Ward.'

The tall man and his diminutive wife turned in the direction she had indicated.

'Just a moment.' The receptionist, having read a note attached to the name Brownrigg, called them back.

'Would you mind taking a seat? The surgeon, Mr Beaton, wishes to speak with you before you go in.'

The woman looked nervously at her husband. He gave her a reassuring smile, took her hand in his and led her to a wooden bench opposite the desk. The receptionist spoke in a low voice into the telephone.

Stephen arrived within moments.

'Good afternoon, sir . . . Mrs Brownrigg.' He shook hands with them both and led them along the corridor to his own small office.

'I don't know how much the authorities have told you about your son's injuries . . .' Stephen began, cautiously.

'Only that they are severe,' said the father. 'We assumed that he had been burned when we heard he had been brought here.'

'He has multiple burns on the lower part of his body,' Stephen told them. 'Fortunately these received attention very early, and will as a result heal satisfactorily.' He paused to give them time to assimilate the best news first.

The woman appeared to be relieved by this. Her husband said, 'I can't help feeling there is a but, Doctor.'

Stephen had thought long and hard about how he would tell the

339

relatives the dreadful details of their son's injuries. McIndoe, well practised in these matters, had offered to undertake the task for him but
Stephen had refused. Now he was beginning to regret that decision.

'You son's legs sustained the worst injuries. They received multiple
fractures from enemy bullets and were subsequently burned when the
aircraft caught fire. I'm afraid that it was impossible to save them.'

'Amputation?' The woman's voice was barely audible.

'I'm afraid so.'

'How much?' It was the man who spoke.

'At the hip . . . both legs.'

The woman let out a choking cry then stuffed her fist into her mouth
to stop herself from screaming. Her husband, chalk white, held her tightly
about the shoulders.

'But how . . . how can anyone live . . . like that?' she demanded
regaining some of her self-control.

'Many people do, Mrs Brownrigg,' Stephen assured her. 'I have met
men who have lived long and fulfilling lives with injuries as bad as your
son's. There are excellent wheelchairs these days. Artificial limbs are out
of the question in this case, I'm afraid, but that does not mean your son
cannot achieve some degree of mobility.'

Mr Brownrigg got to his feet.

'I think it is time that we saw David, Mr Beaton.' He spoke with
calm determination. 'Come along, my dear.'

He helped his wife to her feet and signalled Stephen to lead the way.

A white sheet covered both the boy's body and the large cradle where
his legs ought to be. He was conscious when they went in, but his eyes
wore the hazy look of one who had spent days in a drug-induced stupor.

As the parents moved forward into the tiny room, Stephen stood
back, allowing them this moment of privacy. They had been obliged
to don white gowns, caps and masks so that their son at first did not
recognise them.

'Davy . . . Davy, my darling . . . it's Mummy.' His mother sank down
on to the chair which her husband placed for her, and took hold of her
son's undamaged hand. She dared not look at the cradle bulging beneath
the covers. All she could think of was that this must be an extraordinarily
large sheet and that they must have difficulty getting hold of special sizes
in wartime.

'Mum? Dad?' The voice was weak, the brow furrowed with constant pain. He appeared ten years older than their son should look.

'We're here, David.' His father bent forward and shook his limp hand, gently.

'They told you?' He indicated the mound at the foot of the bed.

His mother recalled childhood games when he had made tunnels and camps using the furniture covered with old curtains.

A tear appeared in the corner of his eye.

'Oh, God, Dad.' His voice was suddenly stronger, more insistent. 'What are we going to do?'

'We'll manage, son.' The white head turned away from the light for an instant so that his son would not see the fear in his eyes. 'We coped with things in the past . . . we'll manage, you'll see.'

Silently, Stephen closed the door on the three of them. The old man was right. They would find ways of coping . . . somehow.

The early-morning sun penetrated the slats of the Venetian blind and a single ray fell across David Brownrigg's pillow. He squinted. The light was intolerable. Why didn't someone do something about it? He pressed the bell push resting beside his head.

A few short, quick steps in the corridor and the door flew open.

'My, but you're awake early,' said the nurse. She was a bundle of energy and still spick and span despite her night on duty. One glance about the room and she spotted the problem.

'It's a shame, isn't it?' she said, cheerfully. 'We wait all winter for a sight of the sun and then, when we get it, we rush to shut it out.' She manipulated the cords and the blind cut off the troublesome rays.

'There must be some way I could work those for myself,' said David. 'A kind of remote control.'

'No need when you have us here to do it for you,' she replied, brightly, circumnavigating the room, every action carried out with maximum efficiency, every movement full of purpose. He watched her with interest, glancing from time to time at the rather elaborate time-piece he wore on his right wrist. When she had finished, she straightened his sheet.

'Three minutes twenty-two seconds,' he told her.

'Pardon?' She stared at him.

'That's what it took you to do everything.' He grinned up at her from the nest of pillows by which he was supported. 'The other girls all take at least five minutes. You're new, aren't you?'

'I was apprenticed to a time and motion study engineer at Ford's before the war,' he told her, and thrust the watch beneath the covers. 'It's something to do,' he explained. 'I promise I won't pass on my findings to Matron.'

She grinned. 'See if I care.'

'I thought I knew all the night nurses,' he called after her. 'So tell me, where did you spring from?'

'I'm here on a training course. We're setting up our own burns unit soon at Halton, and some of us are here to learn the ropes.'

'Are you always going to be on night duty?'

'No. As a matter of fact, I finish tomorrow. Now, is there anything I can get you before I go off duty?'

'Well . . . there is something you could do for me, if you're likely to go anywhere near a public library during your time off . . .'

'A book you want returned?' she asked, stepping back into the room.

'No, something I want out, actually. I need information on electrical engineering . . . radio control . . . circuitry. Do you know what I mean?'

'I think so. My dad's a great radio enthusiast. He has masses of books and magazines. Is that the sort of thing you had in mind?'

'It would do for a start. All the WVS book waggon carries are historical romances and whodunnits.' David cast a disparaging glance at the yellow-covered novel on his bedside locker. 'The stories are identical, only the names of the characters change.'

'I know what you mean. I'll tell you what,' she had a sudden inspiration, 'I'm going home for a couple of days at the end of the week. If you could write down the things you want to know about, I'll get my dad to come to the library with me to select some books.'

'That would be marvellous. Thanks very much.' He watched her disappear into the main ward.

Left to himself he felt free to groan as the absent legs reminded him of where they ought to be. The healing stumps itched agonisingly and it took all his willpower to resist an overwhelming desire to scratch at the soft pink regrowth of skin.

When it came to her tours of inspection, Matron usually tried to avoid David's room. If she did not see the unruly mess of wires, switches, valves and metal boxes, nor experience the unmistakable stink of hot flux; if she could avoid noticing those little round burns in the sheets where hot solder had dripped off the end of the wire, she did not have to complain about it. It was a mercy someone had found him an electric soldering iron . . . she couldn't imagine what he would have done with a gas burner.

'Watch this, Doc,' David greeted Archie McIndoe who was accompanied on his rounds this morning by two Group Captains, one Air Commodore and an Air Vice Marshal.

David raise his hand in which he held a small rectangular device with a red knob situated on the upper surface. With one finger he depressed the knob and the curtains closed with a swish of the gliders. A second depression of the switch and the curtains opened again.

With the exception of one of the Group Captains, the Air Vice Marshal's Adjutant, who crossed over to the bed and took the proffered device, the medical brass hats appeared unable to see further than the untidy condition of the room.

'That's bloody clever,' the Adjutant declared, trying the gadget out for himself.

'Flying Officer Brownrigg has not been wasting his time in hospital, as you can see, gentlemen,' observed McIndoe, with a grin. He winked at Stephen who hovered in the background.

'What branch of the Service are you in, my man?' demanded the Air Commodore. 'Air crew, presumably.'

'Radio Officer, sir.' David drew himself up in the bed as best he could.

'His burns look just about healed,' commented the RAF's Senior Medical Officer. 'When will this man be returned to duty, Mr McIndoe?'

To be fair, thought Stephen, there was so much clutter on the bed that the Air Commodore might be forgiven for not noticing the absence of David's lower limbs.

McIndoe was not so forgiving, however.

'When someone produces a prosthesis which operates from the hip joint,' he replied, coldly. 'Flight Lieutenant Brownrigg has multiple third-degree burns to his lower trunk and both legs have been amputated. He will be ready for discharge in another month or so, provided his most recent set of grafts take satisfactorily. I think he's done his bit for the war effort, don't you?'

The Air Commodore looked most uncomfortable. He cleared his throat loudly and consulted his watch.

During this exchange, the Air Vice Marshal, who apart from his Adjutant was the only non-medical observer in the party, stood silently by. Now he leaned across the bed and took up David's gadget for himself.

For a moment or two he amused himself opening and closing the curtains. If the Commodore was impatient with his senior colleague, he struggled to conceal it.

'Did you have a book of instructions to make this?' the Air Vice Marshal asked.

'Not really, sir,' David replied. 'I sort of figured it out for myself.'

'Have you made anything else?'

'I've been working on a design for a self-propelling wheelchair, powered by batteries,' he replied. 'It's not gone past the drawing-board stage yet because I'm still waiting for the chair.'

The Air Vice Marshal wrote a note on his wrist. It was a habit of which his wife disapproved because she couldn't get the ink off his cuffs.

'I want to keep in touch with you, young man,' said the senior officer. 'I'll give Mr McIndoe my office number. When you are discharged, I may be able to find a spot for you.'

When the other officers withdrew, the Adjutant remained standing beside David's bed.

'You ought to patent that thing,' he advised. 'Otherwise you'll have some boffin pinching the idea.'

'Already in hand,' David replied. 'My girlfriend has taken care of it.'

'I suppose I had better get along,' said the other. 'It's been an honour to meet you, Brownrigg.'

He shook David by the hand, picked up the gadget and had another go at the curtains.

'Bloody marvellous,' he murmured as he replaced it on the bedside table and scurried away.

It was three months to the day after David Brownrigg's arrival at East Grinstead when McIndoe finally pronounced him ready to face the outside world.

He had at last been presented with the very latest model in wheelchairs, whose operation he had mastered in a matter of hours. The corridors of the complex had suddenly become far more hazardous for ordinary mortals. So silently and easily did it glide that there was no way of telling when Brownrigg's chair with its four-inch, generously tyred wheels would come upon you . . . or from which direction.

'We're taking a few Guinea Pigs out to the pub after supper tonight.' Baggy stopped him as he glided past, down the main corridor. 'The boss says you can come if you want to.'

'Oh, I don't know,' said David doubtfully. 'It's one thing to whizz around here in a wheelchair . . . but a country pub. Suppose there are steps and things?'

'No problem,' said Baggy cheerfully, 'we can always carry you if we have to.'

'That's just what I was afraid of,' declared the other.

'That pretty little Princess Mary's Sister is coming . . . she's promised to look after you.'

Baggy knew this temptation would be irresistible.

'Lucy . . . did Lucy say she was coming?' David demanded, unbelieving.

'Only because you are.' Baggy felt that a little subterfuge was in order if he was to fulfil his mission.

Lucy Spurling had not only brought David the books he needed, she had even persuaded her father to come and visit him. The two men had taken an instant liking to one another and spent hour upon hour involved in their discussions. Lucy understood nothing of alternators and oscillators, thermodynamics and semi-conductors. She quickly lost interest when the conversation turned to cathode rays and the future of television, but she had her own reasons for being pleased that the two men got on so well together.

She needed to have a friend at court when she finally presented her future plans to her mother . . .

Stephen had called Ellen directly he returned from Lincoln only to be told that she had been unexpectedly called out and would be unobtainable for several days. He wasn't sure what to think of this. Was it true, or had she merely persuaded a colleague to deliver the message in retribution for his thoughtlessness? Deciding it was the latter, he made no further attempt to contact her. He was too busy with his work now that he had been given his own list of patients. Also, there was a new love in his life!

Since returning to the South, Stephen Beaton had acquired a rather splendid old 1929 Bentley. She was an open-topped tourer in British racing green. Beneath the elegantly stretched bonnet, which was secured by a leather scrap, purred a magnificent four-and-a-half-litre engine.

This had been the vehicle of Stephen's adolescent fantasies. When he had discovered her, blocked up for the duration in a garage, the property of a Naval Lieutenant who would not now be home to reclaim her after the war, he could not resist the temptation to acquire her for himself.

But much as he loved her, for most of the time he was obliged to reserve the Bentley only for official journeys. She drank petrol and the allocation for any but RAF or hospital purposes was very small. As transport for his patients, however, the car proved to be an ideal vehicle and had earned the title of the most prestigious ambulance in Southern Command. David and his folding wheelchair were packed into the rear seat, together with two more members of the Guinea Pig Club, Eddie the poet and the pianist, Martin Dorrel. Baggy climbed into the front passenger seat.

As Stephen started the engine, David complained, 'I thought you said Sister Spurling was coming?'

'So she is,' said Baggy, 'we're picking her up from her digs down the road.' They drove out into the main road and a few hundred yards further on pulled up beside the waiting Lucy. Baggy hopped out to let her in beside the driver.

With Lucy Spurling firmly wedged between them, Stephen set off along the lanes, his back-seat passengers looking for all the world like surreal characters from a Salvador Dali painting.

For this, their first adventure into the real world, Stephen had chosen a quiet pub on the outskirts of a small village in the middle of the Ashdown forest.

The Sackville Arms, the first significant building they had come across for several miles, lay back from the road in a broad clearing. From the look of it, the battered red sign, bearing the armorial device of the Sackville family, dated back to medieval times, when the family was a focus of power in the land.

As it swung crazily from its elderly iron bracket, the sign complained noisily in the evening breeze. The party, glancing up at the sound, hurried inside least it should choose this of all moments to fall.

The bar was already half full when they arrived and there were cheerful exchanges between Baggy, a regular visitor, and the locals.

David, having been settled discreetly into his wheelchair in the pub's car park, was the least disturbing of the apparitions which then entered the saloon.

Over recent months the staff of the Burns Unit had set up such a friendly rapport with the landlord here that they had been able to persuade him to accept, without question, those of their patients who were approaching the time for discharge from hospital.

At first the locals had balked at the sight of these sadly mutilated beings, declaring that they put them off their beer, but after a time they became accustomed to seeing a man with half a face, claw-like hands, wired jaws or missing limbs, and on this particular evening welcomed the newcomers with open arms. The blind fellow who played the piano was with them, and that meant there would be a sing-song later on.

It had been Stephen's idea to acquire a set of gramophone records of dance tunes and ballads. At first the blind pianist had got up from his chair and left whenever anyone decided to play this mustic. Then, for a time, he had simply ignored it, not leaving the room when the gramophone started up but appearing to be asleep while the jazzy stuff was belted out. But one day, when he had the lounge to himself, Martin Dorrel had begun to tap out the tunes on the piano, quickly swinging into the rhythms he had heard and embellishing the mundane tunes with his own variations.

Up to this point, Martin had used music solely as a means of communicating his anger and frustration at his situation. It had not occurred to him that his talent could be his salvation from eternal misery and loneliness.

Suddenly he was a welcome guest at every gathering and never, ever had to buy his own beer!

Once the singing started, the men gathered around the piano, leaving Lucy and David alone beside the empty fireplace. It was the opportunity she had been waiting for.

'Have you heard from the chap at Central Command yet?' she asked, knowing that McIndoe had alerted the Air Vice Marshall to the date of David's discharge from the hospital.

'They've asked me to report to the Middlesex Hospital for a Medical Board, on the twenty eighth,' he replied.

She blanched. It was sooner than she had anticipated. Her own period of training would be completed on 30 June. It was unlikely that Matron would release her to accompany David to the examination, so close to her own departure.

'Has anyone said how you are to get there?'

'Oh, I expect they'll arrange an ambulance,' he said. 'The RAF isn't going to abandon me the moment I leave hospital, you know.'

He grinned at her, full of confidence, and her heart turned over.

'Have you thought how you will manage, once you leave the Queen Vic?'

'Archie suggested that, since they intend to give me some kind of a job, they might allow me a sort of batman-cum-nurse. As long as he's a good strong fellow, I'll be fine.'

'So the looking after side is being dealt with?' she persisted.

'Yes . . . I said so.' David looked at her curiously.

'I wanted to get that out of the way before I told you what I have been wanting to say for weeks.' Her voice was tender, eyes shining as he had never seen them before. Her touch, when she took his hand in her own, was cool and soft.

'I love you, David Brownrigg, and I want to marry you.'

Startled, he pulled his hand away as though he had been stung.

'You don't know what you're saying. How could a beautiful young girl like you contemplate a life with this?' His arms hung limply over the sides of the chair, emphasising the simple truth that he was only half a man.

'Tell me honestly,' Lucy said, ignoring his outburst, 'do you never think of me at all . . . in that way?'

He shook his head. He could have told her how he always listened for her step in the ward and strained to hear her voice amongst so many others as she went about her duties. He might have confessed to finding out in so many devious ways everything about her . . . her favourite foods, what she read, the places she visited and the people she knew. He knew all about her but had never allowed himself to think of loving her.

'I'm not a fool, you know,' she said, gently, taking his hand again and playing with his fingers as she continued to speak. 'Don't imagine I have not considered all the problems which we would have to face. I probably understand the physical side of things better even than you. Don't think either that I'm proposing this to you out of pity or with some charitable notion of sacrificing myself to a good cause . . . I'm not. My motives are personal and quite selfish. I love you.'

'That was quite a speech,' he said, eyes filled with amazement at what she was offering him.

'I've thought about it for a long time,' answered Lucy, happy to have opened her heart to him at last. 'Will you do something for me?' She crouched beside him, looking up eagerly into his face, her eyes brimming with tears. 'Just for a moment, I want you to forget what has happened to you. I'd like you to imagine that this is last spring. You are still a Radio Officer, just about to set out on a mission. We have met and fallen in love, and we are not going to see each other again for a while. What are you going to say to me?'

He gazed at her, trying to get his jumbled thoughts to clear.

'Well?' she urged him.

'I love you, Lucy,' he murmured. 'Will you marry me?'

'Yes, my wonderful David, I'll marry you. And we'll have a terrific time together . . . you'll see!'

They had started singing the real old timers now: *The Miner's Dream of Home, John Brown's Body, Home Sweet Home*. Alcohol-fuelled tears accompanied this last but as the landlord called time, Martin swung into *Good Night, Ladies* and Lucy wheeled the chair to the side of the piano so that they too could join in. With sparkling eyes and glowing cheeks, she and David held hands as they sang. Beside them on the piano stool, Martin Dorrel, sensing their closeness, touched their clasped hands and smiled.

'I think these two might have something to tell us,' he said.

Lucy looked startled, but David, unabashed by the incredulous looks on every side, announced, 'I want you all to share in our happiness tonight, chaps. Lucy has just agreed to become my wife.'

His words fell into a soundless vacuum.

Martin ran his fingers lightly over the keys and the notes of *For They Are Jolly Good Fellows* were taken up by the gathering, voices swelling as silence gave way to expressions of genuine good will.

Cheers and noisy congratulations followed, and with the pub doors firmly closed in accordance with the law, the landlord produced champagne he had been saving for some special event. He was unlikely to find a better moment for it than this!

Chapter Twenty-One

On the day of David Brownrigg's departure from East Grinstead, there was a general turn-out to see him off. The ambulance waited for him beside the door to the Accident and Emergency wing, while both staff and fellow patients made their farewells.

The Air Vice Marshall had been as good as his word. A place had been found for David at the Special Research Department of the War Office where his inventive skills could be put to good use and where his legless condition was no barrier to his making a significant contribution to the war effort.

'Good luck, pal.' Eddie shook him by the hand, his ghoulish grin portraying both joy and envy that one of their number had managed to escape to a real life in the world outside.

'Your turn next,' said David, smiling. 'When's your Board?'

'Couple of weeks . . . the twenty-fifth.'

'Our flat is just a mile down the road from the Middlesex,' David told him. 'Why don't you call in afterwards? The people in the office have the address. Lucy would love to see you.'

'I'll think about it . . . thanks.' Eddie was not going to commit himself. If the Board turned down his application to return to active duty he would probably be heading for the Thames, ready to throw himself in.

Lucy and David had married in a very quiet little ceremony held in the hospital chapel. Her mother had taken some persuading that her daughter was not sacrificing her life to some ill-conceived and totally impractical ideal. It had taken Lucy's father to persuade her that the lad had a future of any kind, but in the end it was David's own quiet determination that had won the day. Nevertheless, it was going to be a long time before Mrs Spurling was fully reconciled to her daughter's marriage and the fact that she was attached for life to a legless cripple.

'Thanks for everything, Doc.' David shook Stephen's hand firmly. There was no need for further words; they both knew that he might well have been written off by other medical opinion. Stephen remembered the young doctor who had questioned their right to prolong such an apparently pointless existence. If he could only see David now.

McIndoe stepped forward to say goodbye. He had seen many such departures, but it was still a wrench when his patients left him. There was always something more he felt he could have done, given sufficient time. No repair was ever perfect.

'Don't forget, if you have any problems at all with those last grafts, just get in touch and I'll arrange for further treatment. Give my love to Lucy.'

David had moved on down the line of nurses gathered to see their favourite on his way. They would miss his cheery personality about the place and even Matron, who should be rejoicing at the repossession of one of her precious side wards, admitted to a certain regret at David's leaving.

It was over at last.

Baggy and his colleagues lifted the chair into the back of the ambulance and secured it.

'You take good care of him,' Baggy told the discharged PT instructor whom they had found to act as David's nurse-cum-batman. He had spent the past two days shadowing Baggy, learning how to cope with his charge.

'If you don't,' the Orderly continued, 'you'll have me to answer to.'

'Don't you worry, Corp,' the man replied, 'I'll treat 'im just like a baby, I will.'

'Over my dead body,' David declared robustly, and on this characteristic nod of defiance the doors were closed on another chapter in the story of McIndoe's Guinea Pigs.

As Stephen and his boss watched the ambulance negotiate the entrance gates and wait to get out into the main road, they saw an old black Morris squeeze past it, turning into the drive. When Stephen read the number plate he could scarcely believe his eyes. It was his own old Morris Ten . . . the one which had been handed down from MO to MO at Manston, over the years.

'Digger!' Stephen strode up to the car and grasped the gloved hand that was thrust through the open window.

'How are yer, cobber? They said we might find you here!'

Stephen's glance shifted to the driver. As ethereal-looking as ever, despite the tired lines and the deep shadows around her eyes, Grace's hair was neatly dressed, as always, and her make-up perfect. Stephen felt that old tingling sensation at the base of his spine . . .

He leaned across and grasped her hand. 'How nice to see you both.'

'You're here for your next round of treatments?' Stephen held the door open for Digger to get out. 'The boss did say you were due to come in for another spell.'

He had intended to get down to Manston to see them, but somehow there never seemed to be an opportunity.

'I hope this is the last,' Colin Sheen wriggled his fingers and showed how the thumb on his right hand had almost total flexibility.

Stephen was not fooled by this.

'Now the other one,' he said, smiling broadly.

'Ah, well . . . that's another story,' drawled Colin, his Australian accent purposely drawn out.

'What's with the car?' Stephen patted the familiar paintwork affectionately.

'Canadians and Poles have moved in at Manston,' Digger explained. 'The WO couldn't persuade any of them to buy her, so I relieved him of his burden. An act of charity and no mistake.'

'Nonsense,' Grace declared, stepping out of the car. 'She's a wonderful old girl and goes for miles on the little bit of petrol they allow us.'

She went around to the boot to retrieve a suitcase.

Stephen, anticipating, got there before her and lifted it out.

'They tell me that congratulations are in order,' he said, trying to disguise any hint of chagrin. 'Your wedding must have been the best kept secret of last year.'

She had the grace to colour a little. She supposed that they should have told more of their old friends, but it had all happened in such a rush.

'Everything seemed to happen at once,' she explained. 'Auntie was suddenly taken ill just at the time when Colin was due to leave hospital. He was still pretty helpless and needed someone to look after him so the best solution seemed to be for us to marry straight away so that I could apply for a discharge and take care of them both.'

The words had come tumbling out as though she had rehearsed them many times. She made it sound more like a matter of convenience than a love match.

'So long as you're both happy,' Stephen said.

'Very happy,' Grace assured him, staring him straight in the eye, defying him to make any other assumption.

Inexplicably angry, he slammed the lid of the boot shut and they followed McIndoe and Colin in through the swing doors, where they were met by Sister. Horrified to see one of the surgeons acting as porter, she wrenched the case from Stephen's grasp and led her patient to his bed on B Ward.

'Perhaps you'd like to wait in my study until he's settled in?' Stephen suggested, pausing beside the door and allowing Grace to enter before him. The familiar scent of her perfume heightened his senses to an almost unbearable degree.

She glanced around, approvingly. Stripping off her gloves and scarf, she laid them on the desk and turned around to examine this very masculine, very private, abode. She had never before met Stephen on his own territory and realised now that she knew so little about him.

'You've made this cosy,' she said, approving his choice of colours and his taste in pictures.

'One needs somewhere to call home,' he replied.

She admired the print of a Lowry painting. Typical matchstick figures poured forth into deserted Sunday streets from an urban brick building. In simple strokes the artist had depicted a whole town and a huge population comprised of every imaginable type of character. On the opposite wall Stephen had hung a second print, this time a painting of young children playing in a Highland stream. A veritable garden of wild flowers tumbled down the grassy banks while in the distance purple mountain peaks seemed to tower threateningly over the charming scene in the foreground.

'That one is a bit chocolate box for some tastes,' he said apologetically, 'but it reminds me of my own childhood. See that older girl there . . . the one with the red hair? That could be my cousin Morag.'

'And I suppose the tiny urchin with mud on his knees is you?' Grace laughed that laugh which he remembered so well . . . the sound that had once held him spellbound.

'The painter is one of a group of artists called the Glasgow Boys. I don't know if you've ever heard of them?'

She shook her head.

'You seem to have a whole gallery of beautiful cousins,' she remarked, lifting down a recent photograph of Ellen from the top of the bookcase. In the picture her hand rested on the neck of a magnificent Clydesdale horse. Her golden hair blew loosely across her forehead and she was sweeping it away with one hand as she looked up, taken by surprise. Her smile was radiant, eyes sparkling with laughter as she gazed at the photographer.

Grace studied the enlarged snapshot for a moment, seeing more in it perhaps than Stephen himself had observed during all the months it had stood here on the shelf.

'What a strapping young woman she is . . . with shoulders like that, one can just imagine her being able to handle the biggest farmyard beast.' There was an edge to her voice. Did Stephen detect a note of envy in her words or was the remark meant as disparagingly as Grace seemed to intend?

'Did you take it?' she asked.

He nodded. 'It was a couple . . . no, nearly three years ago . . . before we were all scattered to the four winds. We haven't managed to get together again since last New Year's.'

'This *is* your cousin, isn't it? The girl who came to Derek and Audrey's wedding?'

'Ellen is an honorary cousin,' he told her. 'Her father's family were very closely connected with my mother's. Her people emigrated to Australia just before the Great War.'

The expression on Grace's face remained enigmatic. She gave the photograph one final scrutiny, and returned it to the shelf.

'How is Mrs Dobbie?' Stephen asked, grasping an opportunity to change the subject. He felt uncomfortable discussing Ellen with this woman who, whether she knew it or not, had once been the centre of his universe.

'Aunt Mary had a severe stroke . . . it was just after Christmas at a time when Uncle was as busy as he is all year,' Grace replied, haltingly, reliving the details of that difficult period. 'At first she was completely paralysed on her right side and lost all power of speech.'

Stephen thought affectionately of the gentle little lady who had treated them all as her own children.

'Uncle has been so patient with her these past months, and Colin has spent hours and hours working with her. Between them they have got her speaking again, enough for her to tell us what she wants, at any rate.'

'That's good,' said Stephen. 'It's more often the case that when someone has a stroke, they are put in a corner, as it were, and ignored. I'm sure that proper stimulation on a regular basis is the answer.'

'She has plenty of that, I can assure you. Uncle Andrew chats away to her all the time . . . so convincingly that you feel he is actually getting a response from her.' Grace's eyes filled with tears. It was the first chink he had seen in her armour. Stephen's heart bled for her, struggling to put a brave face on the way the fates had turned everything against her.

'And the Vicar, how is he?'

'Tired,' she answered. 'Poor Uncle Andy. He's a shadow of his old self. It's just as well that the population of the parish is now so small. He can just about manage his little flock. The Canadian padre asks him around from time to time, but he misses 11 Group. He was very fond of Group Captain Calcutt and all of you. At least he has Colin to keep him company. It stops him from being too depressed.'

'Do you do any work down at the hospital now? I wondered how David Lewis was getting on.'

Stephen had promised to keep in touch . . . another of the one hundred and one duties he seemed to have neglected.

'I have done a little, just recently. Colin has been much less dependent on me lately and Auntie is well catered for, so I thought I would offer my services for a few hours a week. Now I suppose there will be another long spell before Colin can safely be left to his own devices.'

Stephen nodded. Grace knew as well as anyone how long it would be before Digger's latest graft could be considered to have 'taken'.

They had covered their shared experiences now and an awkward silence fell.

Stephen leaped to his feet. 'Colin should be all settled in by now,' he said, hastily. 'Shall we go along and see?'

As Digger followed Sister along the corridor, they were both obliged to step aside to avoid Martin Dorrel. He swung his cane with alarming enthusiasm as he checked the familiar landmarks on his route to the lounge. In passing, he managed to whack Colin quite severely on the leg and the Australian let out a yowl.

'Digger . . . Digger Sheen . . . is that you?'

Colin stepped towards Martin, brushing his arm lightly to tell him where he stood. They clasped hands like long lost brothers.

'How're you, mate?' demanded Digger, his voice full of admiration

MARY WITHALL

for the blind flier's progress. 'Isn't it about time you were getting yourself out of here?'

'Any day now, so they tell me,' Martin replied. 'I'm for St Dunstan's next . . . they're going to teach me to read braille.'

'That's great, Martin. See you around,' Digger sang out as he was whisked off by Sister, anxious to get her patient into hospital blues before Matron caught up with her.

'With your permission, I'm going to ask Mr Beaton to perform this operation.' McIndoe grinned at Digger Sheen as he stepped back from the couch and allowed Stephen to examine the areas which he had marked out with indelible pencil.

The hand is the most delicate of all the instruments of the body and the grafting of skin to restore it effectively is a very tricky business. Stephen sensed that this was to be his final test.

'I suppose your apprentices have to practise on someone, Doc.' The Australian grinned. 'It's as well old Steve here should try out what he's been learning on me. I'm less likely to sue him!'

Truth be told he would rather have Stephen perform an operation on him than even McIndoe himself, but he was not going to let the old bastard know it. Stephen had already saved his life once. So far as Digger Sheen was concerned, his friend was the very best there was!

In the course of the year since Colin had been shot down, the superficial injuries to his face and neck had responded well to grafting. Apart from a certain puckering at the temple and jaw line, and a permanent yellowish coloration on the cheeks, there was little to spoil his ruggedly handsome features. His right hand and forearm, too, had responded well to treatment and his hand functioned sufficiently for him to be able to hold a pen or his cutlery, although it was unlikely he would ever again apply a wrench to his father's tractor.

The process had been a slow one. So delicate and painful were the procedures that only small areas could be tackled at any one time.

His left hand still resembled a claw. McIndoe, concentrating on getting at least one hand functioning normally, had not attempted any grafting here. Skin had regrown of its own accord but there was little elasticity in the horny replacement of the fingers curled across the palm, making the hand useless. To complicate the situation still further, between the fingers the regrown skin had formed a kind of web, peculiar to this type of injury.

Stephen, examining the hand now, was thankful that he had not applied tannic acid at the initial stage. Had he done so, there would have been no way in which the situation could be improved. As it was, by careful removal of the unacceptable skin growths, he should be able to rebuild the hand with at least a small degree of useful function.

It was hot under the lights.

Stephen lifted his head briefly so that the nurse could wipe beads of sweat out of his eyes. He returned to the hand and forearm, the only exposed part of Colin Sheen. The limb was strapped to an extension piece which jutted out from the operating table. He had removed the layers of horny skin over the palm of the hand with infinite care, and as he did so the fingers had relaxed so that each in turn could be straightened and clamped back to the table with sticking plaster. The intricate network of tendons, blood vessels and nerves was laid out before him and he was pleased to see that his initial work to repair the damaged members had been largely satisfactory. Stephen examined each of the tendons with great care and, finding one which had only partially regenerated, cut it cleanly across and made a new connection.

He looked up to see McIndoe following his every move with the greatest interest.

'Might as well get it right as we go along.'

The older man nodded in agreement.

'I think we're ready for the skin now.' Stephen indicated the layer of covering to be removed and a small section of Digger's abdomen was exposed by the Sister.

On it was marked the area of skin he was to remove for the graft. Before attaching the main portion of new skin, he took a number of small slices from the edge of the flap of abdominal skin and laid them along the inside edges of each finger, where the webbing of skin had been removed. He sutured these in place with minute stitches along the edges where the remaining skin was sound. Pieces of dry sponge were then inserted between adjoining grafts and the fingers bound tightly together.

Now it was time for the palm graft.

Stephen folded the graft back so that the open palm of the hand could be laid on the underside of the skin flap. The graft was stitched in place along three edges and then another piece of dry sponge was placed against the graft and both hand and skin graft bound tightly together.

The Theatre Sister was urged forward to spray the bandaged hand with sterile water until the whole dressing was completely soaked, the sponges swelled as the bandages tightened and in this way sufficient pressure could be exerted to ensure that the grafts would not move.

They bound him round with crêpe bandages to keep the dressing wet for as long as possible and to ensure that the hand could not move from its position, strapped it tight to the belly.

'That'll put paid to any of his shenanigans for the next couple of weeks,' observed McIndoe, quietly.

Stephen checked with the anaesthetist, startled to find that the operation had taken him nearly four hours.

Physically, the patient was in good shape. Now it would just be a matter of time, patience and great fortitude. The agony produced by the excessive pressure on the open wound would be excruciating. They all knew only too well how much pain the Australian was to suffer in the coming days.

Stephen did not ask McIndoe how he had performed. He would be judged on his results. In his heart Stephen knew that he could have done no better. For Digger's sake, he prayed that it had been enough.

For his part, McIndoe was satisfied with his pupil's performance. Whatever the outcome of the operation, it had been a masterly piece of work. There was really nothing more that he had to teach this young man.

He supposed that Stephen would now be looking forward to running a unit of his own, for that had been the purpose of training him, after all. Nevertheless Archie McIndoe would be sorry to see him go.

It was October again but a much quieter period than at the same time the previous year. News from the battle fronts abroad was not good but at least the air raids on Britain had become more spasmodic, and there was the satisfaction of knowing that Bomber Command was giving the enemy a pasting in return.

Archie McIndoe and Stephen Beaton stretched out on two of the wicker loungers which some benevolent friend of the hospital had provided for the patients. The Guinea Pigs were all tucked up for the night and it was that quiet time of day when the staff could sit back and dream a little of the future.

'The new unit at Halton will be taking on some of the more complex work that we have been doing here,' McIndoe announced suddenly. 'They're looking for a suitably trained specialist.'

'Won't they have trouble finding someone?'

'I've been asked to make a recommendation.'

He stuffed his pipe thoughtfully while keeping half an eye upon Stephen. He appeared to be anticipating some reaction.

The younger man seemed only mildly interested.

'What would you say to such an appointment?'

Archie concentrated on lighting his pipe, the flames from his hand-made brass lighter shooting up in alarming fashion. Made from the empty cartridge of a German machine-gun bullet, it had been given to him by one of his departing patients.

Stephen, startled by the unexpected suggestion, did not respond immediately.

'Well?' McIndoe urged.

'I hadn't thought . . . it never occurred to me that I would work anywhere but here,' he stammered.

'Don't you want to branch out on your own? You're not afraid of the responsibility, surely?'

'No, it's not that. It's just that I had thought we would go on working together. There's still so much for me to learn, so many ideas to be tried out. I have my mind full of details . . . ways in which we could be doing things better. I had hoped to bounce them off you, just as soon as you were satisfied with my own performance.'

'Well, I do have an alternative proposition,' Archie told him, relieved, 'but I was obliged to suggest the Halton job to you first, you understand?'

Stephen nodded, wondering what the alternative might be.

McIndoe continued, 'You are only the first in what I hope will be a succession of surgeons passing through here for specialised training.'

'You mean that this is to become an official training school?' Stephen asked, immediately interested in the prospect.

'It's not so extraordinary really. After all, we already have a succession of nurses passing through on short courses.' McIndoe leaned back, admiring the sunset and getting into his stride with his favourite topic.

'Eventually we are expected to staff every major RAF hospital with a team capable of treating burns patients and others requiring our particular skills. In the meantime we shall continue to go out on call to assist with the worst cases on the spot.'

'The RAF has, until now, relied entirely on civilian consultants for any plastic surgery required,' he continued. 'It appears they never included plastic surgery in their plans when setting up the RAF Medical Services before the war.'

'How incredibly short-sighted of them,' Stephen observed. 'Knowing how difficult it was going to be to replace good pilots, you'd have thought that the formation of a team of skilled people to deal with burns would have been one of their priorities.'

McIndoe poured out a glass of precious malt whisky from a bottle which Derek Ede down at the King's Head had kept back for him. Derek was another landlord who was a good friend to the Guinea Pigs, welcoming them into his bar and putting a little something special on one side, for the staff of the unit.

Archie was considering Stephen's comment.

'When plans were laid before the outbreak of war, I believe the RAF never conceived of the large numbers of aircrew who would survive air crashes, nor did they appreciate the degree of injury to which the men might be subjected. After all, in the Great War, and even in the Spanish Civil War, the only combat aircraft they employed carried a modicum of fuel and were only lightly armed. Even when they *were* shot up, they could usually still be landed, and as often as not the pilot's injuries were restricted to fractures and bruising.'

'But there are so many things which could be done to reduce the damage inflicted on the men,' Stephen declared vehemently. 'Digger's injuries were largely due to the siting of the fuel tank right in front of his face, while if David Brownrigg had been wearing fire-retardant clothing, we might have been able to save his legs.'

'So what it all boils down to,' McIndoe threw back the whisky and refilled his glass, offering the bottle across to Stephen, 'is that there is still plenty of work to be done here.'

'We can expect more call-outs now, with the increase in bombing raids over Germany. By rights one of us should always be on duty here, so I have a good case for retaining your services on that score alone.'

'Then there is the question of training,' he continued. 'If we are to have sufficient men to deal with the work in future, the courses must be condensed into a far shorter time than I've taken with you. That means both of us will have to become involved and the teaching will have to be more formal.'

Stephen welcomed the prospect of staying on at East Grinstead, working alongside McIndoe, experimenting with new techniques and trying out the million and one ideas that were racing around in his brain

. . that was what he really wanted to do. The appalling vision of himself pushing paperwork around a desk at Halton RAF Hospital, receding into the distance. This was where he belonged.

'Well,' demanded McIndoe. 'What do you think? Will you stay on?'

'Just try to get rid of me!' Stephen laughed.

Raising his glass so that the wheat-coloured, crystal clear liquid caught the rays of the setting sun, he gave a toast.

'*Slainte mhor,*' he said, tossing back his dram in a single swallow.

'Good health,' repeated the New Zealander, and followed suit.

Colin Sheen woke to another day of searing pain. The pressure on his hand was excruciating and now to make things worse the healing had begun, with its accompanying constant itch.

He longed for the moment when Sister would appear with her trolley load of dressings.

He heard the swish of solid rubber wheels upon linoleum. She would be here any minute now.

'Good morning, Digger,' the day staff greeted him cheerily. 'What sort of a night did you have?' The two girls folded back his sheets and the younger one prepared to give him his daily blanket bath.

The question was rhetorical. They drugged him so heavily to prevent any movement while sleeping that he remained comatose from ten o'clock at night until eight the following morning.

'Fine, thank you,' he croaked his first words of the day.

The sun, slanting through the window blinded him momentarily when he glanced in her direction. Another new face. He wondered what they did to the girls these days. None of them seemed to stay for more than a few weeks.

Each day they removed the outer crêpe bandages and damped down the tight dressings surrounding his grafted hand. The cool water gave instant relief, but almost immediately the swelling of the sponges applied even greater force and the painful pressure was upon him once more.

In the hours which followed he would try to focus on the outcome rather than on the present agony. It was the thought that he might soon have the use of both hands which kept him going. All he really wanted was to be back in the cockpit of an aircraft. If they wouldn't let him fight, he would go home and find a job piloting civilian aircraft of some kind.

Grace had driven over twice in the first few days, but petrol rationing prevented further visits before the end of the month. The journey across country by public transport took so long that they had agreed she would not attempt it.

He longed to see her.

She had suggested getting digs in the town and coming in every day, but he had insisted that she could not leave the old people alone for so long. Now he wished he had been more selfish.

She telephoned every day and the nurses took her messages of love and encouragement since he could not get to the phone himself.

During the afternoons, Martin played the piano in the lounge and they left the doors open so that Colin could listen.

The blind pianist played as well now as he had ever done while sighted. The stimulus of mastering the popular ballads his companions demanded had triggered memories of classical works, learned long ago. To help him, Archie had persuaded friends in the surrounding area to lend gramophone recordings by some of the most famous concert pianists and orchestras from around the world. It was only a matter of time before Martin was able to reproduce faithfully studies by Chopin and the piano concertos of Beethoven.

Eddie too played an important part in Colin's recovery. He would come to his bedside to read endlessly, throughout the day. He found the cheap fiction enjoyed by his fellow patients irksome and had introduced the Australian to authors such as Thomas Hardy and D. H. Lawrence, Oscar Wilde and J. B. Priestley. Colin liked the Hardy novels best because the lives of the people in those stories reminded him of the country folk of his own childhood in the outback. Their fortitude in times of strife, their simple pleasures and daily tribulations, recalled much of his own early life. While Wilde made him laugh and Lawrence caused him to think profoundly about human frailty in a modern world, it was Hardy who took him back and made him live again the carefree days of his youth. He thought more and more often these days of those endless horizons and cloudless skies and wondered whether Grace would ever settle out there under the Southern Cross. She had promised to go with him to Salmon Gums after the war, but they had agreed that the final decision about where they would live had to wait.

'Mr Beaton, there is a lady in reception wishing to see you . . . a Miss McDougal?'

The receptionist looked up at Ellen to check she had the name right.

Ellen nodded, beaming. She had thought about writing but had decided, after all, to surprise him.

'Ask her to wait there,' Stephen replied, 'I'll be along as soon as I can.'

He had been taking a final look at the result of a patient's most recent operation. McIndoe had made a fine job of rebuilding Eddie's nose. The features were much improved but the skin was still deeply pitted and discoloured, despite several attempts to improve it using Thiersch's grafts. Eddie's case was typical of those who had been treated initially using the tannic acid treatment to exclude all air.

He was no beauty, thought Stephen, but not nearly so ghoulish as when they had first met.

'Well, Eddie, it looks as if you're ready for your Board. I'll arrange for you to go up to the Middlesex during the next week or so and we'll see what they say.'

'Will they let me fly again, Doc?'

It was the question they all asked. Despite the months in recovery, despite all the pain and discomfort, he had never come across a single individual who was not desperate to have another crack at the enemy.

'I don't see why not,' Stephen replied, smiling. 'Your vision is fine, and as for the scars . . . well, everyone looks the same in a flying helmet and goggles.'

'I don't know how to thank you for all you chaps have done for me, Doc.' Eddie was uncharacteristically sentimental this morning. 'I'll never forget my time here.'

'We intend to see that you don't,' Stephen told him.

He extracted a type-written sheet from his drawer.

'It's an idea of Archie's,' he explained. 'We would like to keep tabs on all our patients . . . for research purposes, you understand. There will be a reunion every year. It'll be a chance for us to check on old wounds, and for you guys to renew friendships and sink a few pints at the local. What do you say?'

'Like a sort of club, d'you mean?' Eddie asked. He thought about it for a moment. 'The Guinea Pig Club.'

He stood up, the interview at an end. With his hand on the door knob he turned, presenting Stephen with a full profile of the injured side of his face.

'We could all wear little gold Guinea Pigs in our lapels,' he said, with only the slightest tinge of bitterness, 'just in case people fail to guess we've been burns cases.'

★

'Would you like to take a seat, Miss McDougal?' The receptionist indicated a row of hard-backed wooden chairs arranged along the far wall. 'Mr Beaton will probably be a while yet.'

Ellen seated herself and looked about her. Although these were only temporary buildings, an effort had been made to produce a bright, welcoming atmosphere. A tall vase of flowers stood on the reception desk and the walls were decorated with a number of tasteful watercolours.

She reached for a magazine, several months old naturally. As she turned the pages of the April edition of *Picture Post* she was intrigued to find that it contained a series of pictures of the Glasgow Blitz. One of these was a group of civilians in siren suits. Their steel helmets and respirator cases hung nonchalantly from the shoulder. The caption read, *The Civil Defence team from Clydebank after their visit to the Palace of Holyrood.* She stared at the photograph . . . yes, it was definitely Aunt Annie. She read on.

'You're Ellen, aren't you?'

She looked up, startled. The face was familiar but Ellen couldn't put a name to it.

'Grace, Grace Sheen now, though when we met I was Grace Dobbie . . . at Manston . . . Derek Miles's wedding, do you remember?'

'Grace . . . of course!'

So she had married her burned flier after all. Poor Stephen! If Grace was married and out of the running, who was keeping her cousin's thoughts occupied now? Ellen wondered. Clearly he had no interest in her, still treating her as a sister . . . he'd made that pretty clear one way and another. Ellen recalled the day he was supposed to pick her up from Horsham. He'd let her down then. Even if he had been detained through no fault of his own, he could have let her know . . . And there was that awful creature at the Hogmanay Ball. Stephen had paid her a lot of attention . . . was she his heartthrob now? In a sudden wave of apprehension she decided that her decision to come here had been a big mistake. Perhaps she should go now, before he appeared. She could always tell the receptionist that she had been called away on business.

'You seemed very preoccupied with that photograph,' said Grace. 'Is it of someone you know?' She sat down beside Ellen and craned for a view.

'It's a picture of Stephen's mother,' she explained. 'She was presented to the King after the Glasgow Blitz . . . she has quite an important role in Civil Defence up there.'

'What a handsome woman.' Grace studied the photograph with interest. 'She's not a bit like Stephen.'

'No, he takes after his father.' Ellen was ridiculously pleased to think she had the edge on her companion. 'All the Beaton men are tall and auburn-haired. Aunt Annie was very dark when she was younger. Her hair is silver-grey now, as you can see.'

'She looks like a very strong personality.'

'And very stubborn,' Ellen agreed. 'Despite having had her house bombed and her husband badly injured, she won't give up her job.'

'I suspect that Stephen takes after his mother in tenacity and strength of character,' Grace observed, struck by the way in which Ellen's voice had softened when he was mentioned.

'Yes,' she agreed, 'they're very alike . . . but he gets his medical skills from his father, of course. Uncle Stuart is a great surgeon.'

Grace regarded her coolly. This girl certainly wore her heart on her sleeve.

'Well, look at this . . . they said one young lady, not two! This must be my lucky day!'

Both women looked up as Stephen burst through the swing doors, the white tails of his coat flowing behind him.

Ellen was startled by the subtle alteration in his whole demeanour. He seemed older, more sure of himself. Whatever he had been getting up to in these past months, it seemed to have improved him.

She stood up to greet him, allowing him to brush her cheek with his lips. She could not help but compare this brotherly peck with the manner in which he lingered unnecessarily long over Grace's hand, and felt once again that frisson of annoyance that he could not see how much *she* craved similar attention.

'You're here for the great unveiling?' he asked Grace, casually. Clearly theirs was an easy friendship. There appeared to be an unspoken understanding between them.

'The bandages are coming off today?' she demanded.

'Yes. Don't get your hopes too high, though,' he cautioned. 'You know we'll be lucky if a third of the graft has taken.'

'I used to work here, remember!' Her sharpness betrayed her anxiety.

'Of course,' he murmured, apologetically, and gazed at her intently for a few minutes, recognising the strain in her eyes.

'You can go down to see Colin right away, if you want to. We'll not be removing the dressings until later this afternoon. He'll be pleased to have you to help pass the time until then. You'll find him rather pent up, I'm afraid.'

Grace nodded. She had been through all this before.

'Look, I shall have to be going,' Ellen's words cut through the heavy silence. She hoped she sounded convincingly casual. 'I can see that I've come at a bad time . . . I just called in because I was passing through East Grinstead and remembered you were here. I'm working out of Brighton at the moment,' she explained to Stephen, breathlessly. 'a project with sheep . . . on the South Downs.'

'Oh, no, you don't,' he forestalled her. 'I was thinking of hopping into town for a quick pint and a sandwich at the King's Head. Won't you come too?'

'Well . . . I could do with something to eat,' Ellen told him. 'I've been on the road since seven this morning.'

'Come along then, what are we waiting for?' He steered her towards the outer doors, looking back as he did so.

'I'll see you later, Grace.'

'OK.' She gave a tentative little wave. 'Goodbye, Ellen. See you again sometime.' Stephen lingered a moment longer to watch Grace turn and disappear into the depths of the building. She was a lonely, rather pathetic figure, he thought, and wondered whether, after all, she regretted the path she had chosen.

Grace approached Colin's ward with leaden steps. When she reached the door she braced herself, anticipating the anxiety and impatience with which he would greet her. If only this afternoon could see the end of it all. She said a silent prayer, pushed open the swing doors and, smiling broadly, advanced into the ward, greeting the inmates in the cheerful manner they had come to expect from her.

Outside, Stephen led Ellen towards his own car, displaying it proudly, like a child with a favourite toy.

The thought crossed her mind: He had disposed of one rival only to replace her with another. Well, at any rate, a vintage car should be easier to cope with than another woman.

'What a monster!' she cried. 'It must guzzle petrol.'

'Well, yes,' he agreed reluctantly, 'but I get a good allowance of petrol because we use her for ferrying the boys around. We try to get them out and about as much as possible, you know.'

Ellen suspected this was just an excuse for running the extravagant vehicle, but refrained from saying so. 'She's a magnificent machine,' she conceded, and watched as he twiddled the throttle lever on the steering wheel and then scurried round to the front to give a turn on the starter handle. As the engine burst into life and then settled to a soft purring, he adjusted the controls. She looked across at her own Austin Seven.

'Puts my poor little Ruby right in the shade.'

'Leave yours here,' he suggested. 'You can pick it up later. Hop in.'

Ellen scrambled in beside him, clutching ruefully at her silk stocking which had snagged on the running board.

'Oh, damn!' she exclaimed. 'That was my last decent pair.'

'Sorry,' cried Stephen nonchalantly. 'She's not exactly this year's model, you understand.'

'No,' Ellen replied rather more coolly, 'so it would seem.'

The bar of the King's Head was empty when they went in. It was a trifle early, Stephen realised, but a log fire was already glowing in the grate. The room smelled strongly of fresh polish which disguised in part the lingering odour of stale beer and tobacco smoke. Copper and brass ornaments glinted in the autumnal light which filtered through the ancient diamond panes of the tiny Tudor windows.

'This is lovely,' said Ellen, settling herself beside the fire. 'Do they do anything to eat?'

Stephen went to the bar and quietly negotiated beer and sandwiches. He was looking forward to hearing about his parents, and finding out what Ellen had been up to. No doubt some of the locals would be in later but for the moment they had the place to themselves.

'This is cosy.' Ellen stretched her legs to the blaze. 'It's what I always used to imagine an English pub would be like. We only knew about them from Christmas cards sent out from Mum's people in England.'

Stephen agreed with her. 'It's a pity we don't have bars like this in Scotland. Drinking is considered too serious a business up there for comfortable seating, carpets on the floor and curtains at the windows.'

'You're looking much better than when I saw you last,' she observed. 'Much more relaxed. The work must be doing you good.'

Remembering the trying period he had had when stationed at Prestwick, Stephen had to agree that things had improved since he had last seen her.

'I never really apologised for not turning up that time . . . you got my message?'

Ellen looked surprised.

'No, I never heard a thing. I just assumed you had been called away for some reason or other, though I did rather hope you would get in touch again.' She tried not to sound aggrieved. It was quite possible that someone at the Horsham office had forgotten to tell her.

'When I did get around to calling you myself, they said you'd gone to Chichester and I'm afraid I haven't had a chance to follow up on you since.'

'Well, we've met up again now and you certainly seem to be in blooming health. The job must agree with you.' She noted the laughter lines about his eyes and that particular sparkle in them which she had not seen since those early days before the war.

'When you start from such a low base as we do here in the burns unit,' he told her, 'almost any improvement made by a patient is viewed as a miracle. It does wonders for one's self-esteem.'

'Will you go on working in plastic surgery after the war?'

'Yes, I think so. There should be a lot of money to be made lifting the faces of rich Californian women!'

'You wouldn't really do work like that?' asked Ellen, horrified at the thought.

'From the rumours abounding in the medical profession at the moment, there's a real possibility that there will be a new State system here. I can't see anyone making much money as a surgeon under those circumstances.'

Stephen's grin suggested that he was pulling her leg but Ellen could not resist the challenge.

'I can't believe that you would even contemplate working with rich vain women while there is a single scalded child or burned fireman who needs your services,' she challenged him.

'Why should it bother you what I do?' he demanded. 'You'll be rushing back to Australia just as soon as the war is over. You won't give me another thought.'

'You couldn't be more wrong about that,' Ellen told him promptly. Foolishly she had let down her guard. Now she was obliged to qualify what she had said.

'I'll always be interested to know what you're doing . . . where you are . . . how far along the road you've got with those dreams you used to have.'

She lapsed into dreamy recollection. 'Do you remember when we used to sit up on the railway embankment at Kerrera, watching the sun go down . . . all those things we said we were going to do with our lives?'

'I remember.' Stephen's voice had softened, all the banter gone now. Suddenly she was aware of his eyes, gazing steadily at her.

'Did you mean that?' he demanded. 'What you said just now about wanting to know what I was doing, wherever I might be in the world?'

'Of course.'

'But why?'

'Because I care about you,' she replied. Stephen looked at her, oddly, as though seeing her for the first time.

Realising that she had gone farther than she'd intended, Ellen was relieved to see the arrival of the sandwiches.

'Only a bit of mousetrap, I'm afraid,' the landlord apologised. 'But I've put some of the wife's pickles with it. Hope that's all right?'

'That's fine, thank you,' she told him. 'It can't be easy catering for anyone these days.'

The cheese was real Cheddar and the bread home baked.

'You can't get a better meal than this,' Ellen pronounced, and sank her teeth into the crusty white bread with relish. 'Have you heard from your parents recently?' she asked, chasing the remainder of the cheese down with the last of her beer.

'Yes, there's a big argument going on about them retiring to Eisdalsa . . . have you seen them recently yourself?'

'I called in on my way South a week or two ago. I had to go back to Aberdeen to give a couple of lectures.' She tossed in the information casually. What was a part-time lecturing appointment in cattle rearing compared with Stephen's work? 'Your dad seems fine, apart from having lost a lot of weight. His hair has gone very grey . . . shock, I suppose?'

Stephen nodded, absently. What was that she had said about lecturing at the University? He was impressed.

'It seems to me we're both getting on with our careers despite the war,' he observed. 'Have they really asked you to lecture?'

Ellen glowed inwardly. She remembered Malcolm's disparaging attitude towards her work. At least Stephen appreciated her worth in that respect.

Thinking of Malcolm brought her up suddenly and as though he had been reading her thoughts, Stephen said, 'I'm rather surprised to find that you're not married or engaged or anything? You aren't, are you?'

Her heart missed a beat. Why did he want to know? Instantly she dismissed his question as just a cousin's interest.

'Or anything occasionally.' She grinned. 'Nothing more than that.'

Stephen seemed relieved.

'We must see more of each other,' he pronounced. 'Brighton isn't all that far away. I'll give you a call the minute I have some free time.'

Ellen decided not to hold her breath . . . she had been let down before!

'OK,' she said, 'any time you like. I shall be around for about a month. No longer. Then I'm up North again.' She looked at her empty glass and set it down on the table.

Stephen got up. 'Let me get you another?'

'No, really, I shouldn't . . . I have a long way to drive.'

He looked at his watch and gave a low whistle.

'How the time has flown,' he said, 'I didn't realise it was so late. I promised to be back in time for Digger's dressings to be removed. We'll have to get a move on.'

The green Bentley tore through the winding lanes, a damp mess of decaying leaves swishing under its giant wheels.

Ellen felt strangely exhilarated.

There had been a subtle change in Stephen's attitude towards her during the past two hours. Suddenly she had the impression that she was, after all, important to him.

It was nothing he had said. Rather, it was the solicitous manner in which he had helped her into her coat and handed her up into the car, gently tucking a rug around her against the chill wind. She had thrilled at his attentions, suppressing only with the greatest difficulty a desire to fling her arms around him and kiss him properly.

It was just after two-thirty when they drove in through the hospital gates. He helped her down and escorted her to the little Ruby.

'I'll give you a call,' he said, closing the door and waiting while she wound down the window. 'Perhaps we could have an evening in town sometime. What do you say?'

'I'd like that.' Her smile was absolutely radiant. 'See you soon, I hope.'

He looked on, thoughtfully, while Ellen manoeuvred the Austin out of the parking lot. The Ministry of Agriculture and Fisheries label in her rear window was still readable until she turned out into the road.

With an almost inaudible sigh, Stephen turned on his heel and made his way round to the first of the temporary buildings.

Chapter Twenty-Two

Ellen leaned against the stout flint stone wall of the sheepfold and watched admiringly as the little black and white collie darted in amongst the flock. The dog would brook no dissent, bringing any wanderer straight back into the tight pack of animals wending its way inexorably towards the fold.

Suddenly Ellen felt a wave of homesickness. She was reminded of Vicky, her father's Border Collie and her own devoted slave until the day she died. The smart little bitch, born and raised in Argyll, had bred a line of the finest sheepdogs in Australia.

It was mid-May, autumn back home. Ellen wondered what changes there had been in the four and a half years since she had left.

These rolling Sussex downlands were a far cry from the limitless pastures of Kerrera station. Here the grass was brilliantly green, in sharp contrast to the Spinifex on which her father's sheep survived. So sparsely covered were the paddocks of Western Australia, that even in spring-time, directly after the wet, the red tones of the sandy soil predominated over the green of the coarse grasses.

Ellen caught a whiff of salt-laden air, wafted in from the English Channel which she glimpsed through a gap beyond the slope of Devil's Dyke. The rolling, close-cropped turf was dotted with clumps of elder, ash and hawthorn, just coming into bud on this brilliant May morning. An occasional white line cut across the landscape, showing where the turf had been worn down to the chalk, describing the routes by which man and beast had roamed these hillsides for thousands of years.

'All right then, Miss McDougal . . . they're all yours!' The shepherd came up to her, breathing heavily from the steep climb.

Ellen moved in among the flock, examining each animal minutely and seeing that those who had not passed muster were filtered off into a holding pen. There were few of these, for Jethro Fulmer was an expert shepherd. Very little escaped his keen eye.

She finished her examination and Jethro released the bulk of the flock, signalling to the dog to guide them back on to the hillside.

From those in the pen she took samples of blood which she stowed carefully in her case.

'You must keep these animals penned, Mr Fulmer,' Ellen instructed, 'until I get the results of the tests.'

Had they told him three years ago that they were sending out a woman vet from the Ministry, Jethro would have been astounded to say the least. Now it seemed quite natural that this slip of a girl should undertake work formally considered exclusively a male preserve.

Since the outbreak of war, more and more women had appeared on the land, taking the place of farm hands who had left to join up. They were essential to the maximum effort farmers had been called upon to make to increase food production. In these days in which U-boats blockaded the approaches to every British port, it was up to the farmers to see that people did not starve.

'I'll take these samples away with me, Mr Fulmer,' Ellen said, snapping the locks on her instrument case. 'You should hear from me within the week.'

'Looking for anything in particular are you?' he enquired, watching with interest as one of the selected beasts rubbed itself vigorously against the sharp flint wall forming one side of the pen and then staggered as it crossed to a hummock of long grass and began to chew.

'Scrapie,' she replied, laconically. 'There's a mild epidemic in East Anglia. We're trying to discover how far the disease has reached.'

'I see that one's staggering a bit,' he observed, a worried frown on his face.

'Yes,' Ellen agreed, 'it's just possible that there are already a few cases here. I think it best to isolate them for the time being, until I get the results of the tests.'

Seeing his downcast expression, she smiled encouragingly. 'There are other reasons for an animal scratching like that,' she assured him. 'An infestation of nematodes would have the same effect. Anyway, if it is scrapie I shall want to use some new antibiotics we have been given for trials. I'm told the drugs are very powerful. The idea is to give injections immediately the disease manifests itself. Your animals would

pear to be in the very early stages, so we may be able to save even the
w that are already infected. Call me if you find any more suspects. I'll
e back in a week.'

She handed him her card and together they strode down to where
llen's little Austin Ruby stood gathering a thin film of chalk from the
usty track.

'I'll give you a start,' he said, grabbing the handle and going to the
ont of the car. Two strong turns and the engine sprang to life.

'Can I give you a lift to the house?' she asked.

The shepherd shook his head. Replacing his cap, he said, 'Best see if
ld Nell has got they buggers back up on Beacon Hill.'

Giving her a casual wave, he sauntered back the way they had come.
mile down the track Ellen was forced to stop and open a farm gate
hich straddled the road. As she did so, Mrs Fulmer came running out
f the shepherd's cottage, calling to her.

'Wait, miss . . . are you the vet from the Ministry?'

Startled, Ellen answered, 'Yes, is something wrong?'

'I was just talking on the telephone when I saw you coming . . .
ere's someone wants to speak to you.'

This was no surprise to Ellen. In the course of any day there were
equently requests to divert to some emergency. She had, as usual, left
list of her appointments with the girl in the office.

In the musty parlour, she found the receiver off the hook and lifted
e antiquated instrument.

'Hello, Ellen McDougal speaking.'

'Hi there . . . it's me!'

Ellen thrilled to hear his voice. 'Stephen, how on earth did you
anage to track me down?'

'I have a forceful way with telephone operators.'

'You nearly missed me . . . I was just leaving.'

'Finished for the day?' he demanded.

'Well, yes, as it happens,' she answered, mystified.

'Can you get yourself on to the five-thirty train from Brighton?'

She studied her watch. 'I suppose so . . . but I'm filthy from handling
eep all morning. I shall have to clean up.'

'Well, don't take too long. I've been given tickets to the Windmill
r this evening. It's a chance to take a few of the boys out to mix with
e general public. I thought you wouldn't mind being seen with them?'

Ellen recalled the terribly scarred faces which had greeted her recent
ur around the wards the last time she had visited the Queen Vic, and

shuddered inwardly. She could cope with the boys themselves, but ho
would she react to the expressions of the people they encountered
the theatre?

'I don't know . . .'

'Digger's up here ready for his Medical Board next week,' Steph
continued, oblivious to her indecision, 'so I thought we might join the
as a foursome.'

'Four?'

'Grace has been here, working . . . helping out during this rotten '
epidemic, actually. We have been very short-staffed.'

Setting aside her own reservations, Ellen said, 'I'll have to go no
if I'm to catch that train.'

'I'll be waiting for you under the clock at Victoria, OK?'

'All right. Until later then . . . goodbye.' She put down the phon
her heart pounding. She had seen Stephen no more than a dozen tim
during the year which had passed since their lunch at the pub in Ea
Grinstead. Usually they had been accompanied by others. The last tin
it had been Archie McIndoe and the patients when they had listened
a piano recital in Brighton given by Martin Dorrel. She wondered
tonight they would have any time alone together?

'I wondered if you had time for a cup of tea, miss?' Mrs Fulmer sto
watching her from the doorway.

Anxious to be on her way, Ellen would have refused, but when sh
saw the carefully arranged tray with its spotless white cloth and dain
bone china cups, she felt unable to disappoint the woman. She sat dow
on the overstuffed sofa and accepted the cup politely.

'I can only stay a moment,' she explained. 'I have another urge
appointment.'

'Everyone is so busy these days,' said her hostess, 'sometimes a who
week goes by when I don't speak to a soul other than Fulmer. I fi
myself talking to the hens for want of conversation.'

Ellen consulted her watch. It was barely two o'clock, she could allo
herself another fifteen minutes and still have time.

'Have you lived in these parts all your life?' she asked, settling ba
and accepting a second cup of tea.

The little band of Guinea Pigs arrived by coach. The vehicle, in the lig
blue livery of the Royal Air Force, proceeded to disgorge its unusu
passengers on to the pavement in good time for the start of the sho

here were two wheelchairs which had to be handled through the emergency exit and this held up the traffic in the narrow street. To the accompaniment of blaring horns and disgruntled shouts from other drivers and the stares of passers-by, who halted to watch their arrival, the men in their hospital blues descended to mingle with the crowd.

Some members of the public drew back appalled at their initial sight of these horribly scarred young men. Others, unable to contain their reaction, cried out. The voice of one very elderly woman spoke for them all.

'Oh, the poor dears!'

Clad in furs and hanging on the arm of a Brigadier in full dress uniform, a tall angular woman at the back of the crowd was overheard to criticise.

'How disgusting, allowing them out in public! I know they are heroes and all that, but really. Just to look at them makes you feel sick.'

Her escort released his grip, wishing to distance himself from her.

'What do you expect, Cynthia?' he demanded. 'Do you think they should be locked away out of sight, so as not to disturb your delicate sensibilities?'

She pulled an expression of disgust, ignoring the hostile faces all round her. The Brigadier moved forward and grasped the elbow of one of the wounded men who carried a white stick.

'Let me give you a hand, old chap,' he said quietly, intending to guide the blind airman through the crowd. 'It's a great show . . . I've seen it a number of times. I'm sure you'll enjoy it.'

The pilot, recognising the tone of authority and feeling the quality of the barathea uniform tunic of his helper, stepped back a pace and saluted, white stick tucked under his arm like a swagger stick. 'Thank you, sir. If you would just steer me towards the rest of the group . . . I believe we're in the dress circle.'

Startled, the Brigadier took a second look at his companion. Could he see a little after all? Satisfied that the man was totally blind, he asked, 'How did you know I was an officer?'

'Let me have a better look,' the airman said, his fingers wandering upwards to the Brigadier's shoulders. When they encountered the three pips and a crown, he dropped his hand in confusion. 'I beg your pardon, sir,' he said, reddening with embarrassment.

'Not at all,' said the senior man as they walked. 'It is I who should apologise for my countrymen . . . and women.' He glanced across to where Cynthia stood angrily consulting her watch, anxious they should not be late taking their seats. 'You're a brave bunch, confronting the public like this. Don't be put off by thoughtless remarks. People quickly become accustomed to disfigurement.'

'Where did you lose your leg, sir?' asked the other.

Startled that the blind man should have noticed, the Brigadier caught his breath. 'El Alamein,' he replied softly.

The airman nodded. 'You'd know a bit about it then. Disfigurement I mean.'

'Yes . . . a bit.'

They had rejoined the others. Baggy told hold of his charge's other elbow and winked at the Brigadier.

'I think we can manage now, sir. Thank you very much,' he said firmly.

'It was a pleasure,' said the old soldier and made his way to where his impatient wife awaited him. Poor Cynthia, so brave and solicitous in her attitude to his own disability, had displayed her anger at the injustice of it all by assuming an air of insensitivity to the injuries of others. A form of self-defence, perhaps? He took hold of her hand and led her toward the entrance to the stalls.

'Stephen Beaton, what a surprise!'

As they descended the crimson-carpeted staircase, it took him only seconds to spot Janet Fraser in the entrance, surrounded by a group of US Army Air Force officers. He supposed he should not be surprised. The Yanks seemed to have commandeered most of the more attractive Service women since they had begun to arrive in Britain in increasing numbers. President Roosevelt's declaration in December 1941 had changed the face of the war but it had also put most of Britain's male population very much on its guard!

'Good Lord, what a nuisance,' Stephen murmured. Ellen wondered if his annoyance was feigned.

They had met under the clock at Victoria Station, as arranged, but in the mad rush to park the Bentley and reach the theatre before the curtain went up, there had been little opportunity to exchange other than the most commonplace of remarks. Now, with the coach waiting outside to take the boys home, they had anticipated a late supper, just the four of them, before Ellen caught the last train for Brighton and Stephen gave the others a lift back to the hospital in the Bentley.

'Why, Stephen!' Janet Fraser repeated, forcing her way through the rush. 'And . . . Thingy,' she added, with a vague wave towards Ellen, what a surprise!'

'Janet, how are you?' Stephen enquired, stiffly. He had taken in at a glance her Flight Lieutenant's uniform and wondered by what miracle a WRAF WO2 could be so elevated simply by wielding a spanner, no matter how skilfully. Uncharitable thoughts crossed his mind, particularly when their reunion was suddenly interrupted by an irascible Colonel with a mid-western accent, who demanded to know what all the delay was about.

'Just saying hello to some old friends, Elmer darling,' she replied, threading her arm through his.

'This is Squadron Leader Beaton and . . .'

'Ellen McDougal.' She took his hand and gave him a weak smile.

Stephen, suddenly galvanised into action, remembered his manners. 'Flying Office Colin Sheen and Mrs Sheen,' he introduced his friends.

'Look,' said Janet, 'we're all off to the Regent Palace, why don't you tag along?'

Ellen tried to hide her crestfallen expression when Stephen turned to Colin and Grace and said, 'What do you think?'

'Just as you like,' said Colin. 'We were going to have to find some supper somewhere, might as well be the Palace as any other.'

'They have dancing there.' Grace bent closer to Ellen. 'So it won't be all that bad!'

Following Colin's marked improvement, there had been a number of occasions recently when the four of them had got together. If Stephen still harboured thoughts of Grace as anything other than Digger's wife, he was at pains to disguise them and as the months passed, the two girls had become friends.

'What did you think of the show at the Windmill?' The Colonel from Montana had taken it upon himself to entertain Ellen, while Stephen and Janet reminisced about their time with 11 Group.

'Very good,' Ellen replied, 'and the boys enjoyed it . . . that was the main thing.'

'Yes, poor guys. Don't suppose they get out and about much.'

'I understand that mixing in large social groups is all part of their rehabilitation.'

'Gee,' said the other, 'you're not a medic yourself, are you?'

'Not exactly.' She laughed at the alarm which the thought had evidently aroused. 'Actually I'm a veterinary surgeon,' she explained.

'That's a cute accent.' He leaned forward, his rank breath and

yellowed teeth betraying his life-long addiction to the Havana ciga.
which he had been chain smoking all evening. 'Where are you from?'

'Western Australia,' she replied, mind not really on their conversatio

'An Australian . . . gee, that's great. I've just come across from fightin
a war with your guys, in the Philippine Islands. They're a tough bunc
of cookies and no mistake.'

'Are you stationed near London?' she asked for want of somethin
to talk about.

'Not really supposed to say,' he replied with a conspiratorial wink
'but yes. A little place called Manston . . . near Margate.' His laboure
pronunciation did at least raise a smile.

'Oh, really?' she observed. 'Stephen was stationed there for a tim
during the Battle of Britain.'

The Colonel's expression changed immediately. He turned t
Stephen.

'Gee, Doc,' he said, puffing out clouds of cigar smoke, 'that was on
hell of a beating you guys took down there on the coast.'

Stephen caught the look of annoyance on Colin's face and answere
crisply.

'I think we gave a pretty good account of ourselves, considering ho
few of us there were and how many of them. It was during one of th
last raids that Digger here was shot down.'

'Yeah?' The American seemed unimpressed.

'Yes,' said Stephen, stiffly, 'for the second time. The ribbon he
wearing is the Distinguished Flying Cross, awarded after he ha
destroyed three enemy bombers and a Heinkel.'

The Colonel, whose breast was covered with an array of colourf
ribbons, took note of the single tiny strip of colour on Colin's tunic an
puffed out a perfect smoke ring.

Digger, rising to the occasion, summoned his best Australian accer
to drawl, 'That was one hell of a pasting you guys took at Pearl Harbo
mate.'

The American's colleagues exchanged uncomfortable glances.

Never at a loss for words, the Colonel leaned across Stephen to attrac
Janet's attention.

'You should take Miss McDougal here to meet your pa, Jan,' he sai
' She'd be interested in his new breed of cattle.'

Mortified at what the beautiful creature who was hanging upo
Stephen's every word would make of this suggestion, Ellen was covere
with confusion.

Seeing her suddenly rosy complexion, Janet remarked pointedly, 'Oh, is Ellen connected with farming? I might have guessed.' In an aside which was meant to be heard by the whole company, she commented rudely to Stephen, 'she might have modelled for one of those recruitment posters for the Land Army!'

The band began to play and Janet dragged Stephen to his feet.

'C'mon, Doc,' she demanded, 'how about a slow foxtrot for old times' sake?'

As they moved about the floor, performing the intricate steps with a proficiency born of countless station dances, Janet said, 'My brother Fergus often mentions you, you know. He was most intrigued when I told him you had gone to join the Burns Unit at East Grinstead. Apparently your Mr McIndoe is quite a celebrity.'

Stephen made no response to this but asked, 'Is he in the Services yet?'

'Fergus? No, not really.' Her manner was offhand. 'He acts as a consultant to the RAF in cases of facial injury, in the Scottish sector . . . much the same as your fellow, I assume. It allows him to maintain a hold on his clinic patients, while doing his little bit for the war effort.'

'Does he ever mention what he'll do if this new National Health Service comes into being?'

'Only to exclaim "over my dead body" whenever the subject is raised.' Janet laughed loudly. 'He declares he will go to America if medicine here is State-run. The Old Man's going crazy, because that would mean breaking up the family motor racing team.'

This total disregard for anything other than the most venal of motives sickened Stephen who soon found an excuse to lead her back to their table.

'I really think it's time we were going,' he said to the others. 'Ellen will miss her train.'

No one argued. Ellen jumped to her feet, relieved to be free from the uninvited attentions of the Colonel. Colin looked tired and Grace only too happy for them to be on their way home. In two days her husband had a Medical Board at the Middlesex Hospital. They would know then what the future held for them both.

The four friends walked abreast along the blacked-out pavements, to where Stephen had parked the Bentley in the Mall.

'You don't have to take the train back,' he said to Ellen. 'That was just an excuse to get away. I can drop the others off at the hospital and take you on to Brighton, if you like? It won't take all that long.'

Not relishing the thought of a journey alone, so late at night, she accepted readily and soon they were spinning down the A23 in grave danger of being run in for speeding by the highway patrol. Grace was quite relieved when at Purley they took the narrower A22, and Stephen was forced to slow down to a respectable speed.

At Ellen's direction, Stephen drew up by the white balustrade which marked the edge of the cliff.

Thirty feet below, Brighton's Marine Drive ran parallel to the shore. Even in the darkness of the night it was possible for them to distinguish waves breaking in a white line along the shingle and dispersing amongst the steel stakes and barbed wire defences which covered the beach.

Stephen turned off the engine, and in the silence which followed they could hear the shingle rattle as each successive wave receded.

'I'm sorry,' he said, lighting two cigarettes together and handing one to her.

'Whatever for?' asked Ellen.

'It didn't go at all as I'd expected.' He turned to face her, seeing her only dimly in the poor light of an early dawn.

Ellen drew heavily on the cigarette, inhaling deeply. 'The boys enjoyed the show,' she said. 'That was the main thing.'

'Did you?' he asked urgently, as though it mattered that she had got something out of the evening.

'Of course.'

'We should have refused to go with Janet to the Regent Palace,' he said. 'It was my fault. She's a woman who won't take no for an answer,' he added lamely.

'It didn't matter,' Ellen assured him.

'It did to me. Whenever we go anywhere together these days, other people seem to get in the way.'

'Not every time.'

'I've decided I don't always want other people around when I'm with you,' he said bluntly.

She was glad of the dim light which hid her expression. Her cigarette's flame was reflected in his eyes which seemed to be piercing the shadows between them. Gently he removed her cigarette from her fingers and stubbed it out in the ash tray. Then he drew her into his arms.

'I've been such a fool!'

'I wouldn't say that,' answered Ellen, smiling. 'You have had a lot on your mind for a long time.'

'Yes, that's a fact,' he agreed, 'but it's no excuse for taking you for granted. Somehow I've expected you to keep on turning up, with very little effort on my part.'

'People should be able to separate for long periods and then get back together without noticing the break,' Ellen told him. 'That's what true friendship is all about.'

'I'm not talking about friendship.' Stephen's voice was throbbing with emotion.

His lips found hers and lingered firmly for a few seconds until, breathless, she was forced to draw away.

He put one hand behind her head while the other sought to open her coat and slide inside. The softness of her breast through the thin material of her blouse was warm and inviting to his cold fingers.

Already Ellen was aroused, and in that moment would have done anything he asked.

'Good evening, sir. Havin' a little trouble with the vehicle, are we?' The constable touched his helmet politely, while peering in at them.

'Not really, officer,' Stephen stammered, taken unawares. 'Just seeing the young lady home.'

'Best say goodnight, then,' the constable suggested, 'and be on your way.'

Trying hard not to giggle, they both got out of the car.

'Of course, Constable,' said Stephen. 'I'll be off just as soon as I've taken the lady to her door.'

The policeman watched them cross the street and waited until Ellen had extracted her key and handed it to Stephen. Then the policeman continued on his beat towards Black Rock, walking away with measured pace.

'I love you, Ellen.' Stephen's words were spoken so quietly she strained to hear him. 'When this rotten war is over . . . do you think you could marry me?'

'Oh, Stephen,' she breathed, 'I thought you would never ask.' With scarcely a glance in the direction of the departing policeman, Stephen grabbed her again and kissed her passionately.

When at last they drew apart, they realised that they could see one another more clearly. Along the coast towards the Seven Sisters, the first light of day could be seen streaking across the horizon.

'Time for breakfast?' Stephen suggested, hopefully.

'I'm a dab hand at scrambled eggs,' Ellen said, remembering Mr Fulmer's gift from her hen house that afternoon.

'No bacon?' he teased.

'Only Spam.'

'You're on!' He slipped the key into the lock and allowed the door to swing open.

'This is it,' she said, selecting the right key from those he still held in his hand.

It was a large airy room, brightening by the minute with the advancing dawn. She had left before nightfall and the blackout curtains had not been drawn.

Ellen crouched down to light the gas fire. She had become quite chilled in the fresh early-morning air. For a time she stood with her back to him, warming herself as the fire bars began to glow. Glancing in the mirror above the overmantel, she saw that he was close behind her.

He drew off her coat and turned her around to face him.

Without speaking, she began to peel off her blouse and loosen her skirt. He drew the straps of her silk slip down to entrap her arms and undid her brassiere.

For a long time he gazed at her exposed breasts without moving, then lowered his head and kissed first one erect nipple and then the other.

As she slipped out of the rest of her clothes and stood before him naked, he knelt down, took hold of her by the buttocks and buried his face in the golden mass of hair between her thighs.

She slipped to the rug as he tore at his own clothes, but before he straddled her body he allowed his soft surgeon's fingers to trace its contours, arousing her to a point which made her cry out in her eagerness to have him take her.

Their coupling was urgent. Heedless of the hard floor, they melded as one being until, in a moment of exquisite agony, Ellen gave herself body and soul to the man she had dreamed of since girlhood.

After a while, he lifted her in his arms and carried her to the narrow bed in the corner. There they made love again, gently this time, slowly exploring each other's bodies, relishing each new intensity of feeling until, exhausted by the events of the day and the excesses of the past hour, they fell asleep in one another's arms.

The sun settled upon Ellen's eyelids and she opened them to find him staring down at her. Her lips parted as he kissed her firmly and then turned her over and whacked her soundly on the rump.

'Ouch,' she complained.

'What about those eggs?' he demanded.

'Give me a moment,' she said, pulling on a comfortable fluffy dressing gown. 'The bathroom's just down the passage.'

Stephen made some repairs to his appearance using the sink in the tiny kitchen alcove. He could do nothing about a shave, unless . . . He opened Ellen's surgical case and searched through the instruments, his hand coming to rest on an old cut throat razor and a leather strop. Working away steadily, and only nicking himself a couple of times, he soon completed his task. With yesterday's shirt tucked neatly inside his tunic and his tie properly adjusted, he looked quite presentable by the time she returned.

She looked from his smoothly glowing chin to the open razor on the draining board and grinned. 'The last time that was used was to clear an area of skin to give a cow an injection.'

'Lucky cow, it's a good razor,' he laughed.

He glanced at his watch and gave a low whistle. 'Look at the time! I'm afraid I'll have to skip the eggs after all. It's my day for ward rounds and Matron's a stickler for punctuality.' He caught Ellen in his arms. 'I'll ring you tonight, OK?'

'Lovely.'

She kissed him again, her head in a whirl and her heart dancing.

The waiting room was like a morgue. The white walls were unrelieved by any form of decoration, the only colour in the room supplied by a pile of dog-eared, out-of-date magazines which lay scattered on a low table in the centre.

Half a dozen RAF personnel sat or stood, in various degrees of agitation about the room, their individual apprehension combining to create an atmosphere of pervasive gloom and despondency.

Digger looked up sharply as the medical orderly returned. It must be his turn soon . . . they were running half an hour late as it was.

'Flying Officer Sheen, please.'

All heads turned in his direction.

Digger stood up, dusted down his tunic unnecessarily, and tucked his cap under his arm.

'Follow me, sir.' The orderly set off at a cracking pace coming to a halt at last before a door marked ADJUTANT.

The orderly rapped sharply on the door, opened it and ushered Digger inside.

The Administrative Officer was a white-faced individual, heavily scarred, with hollow cheeks and deep shadows beneath his eyes. One side of his face was badly puckered and a sickly brownish-yellow. It was easy to see why he was reduced to flying a desk.

From an ominously large pile of folders he extracted one.

'Sheen?'

'Sir.'

'Take a seat.' He indicated the plain wooden chair, set at an angle to the desk so that the light would fall full on Digger's face. Realising that this was some sort of a test, he concentrated on the officer, not allowing himself to be disturbed by the strong sunlight.

The Adjutant read rapidly, turning each page of Digger's well-stuffed file with a little grunt but whether of disapproval or satisfaction, it was hard to tell.

'. . . third-degree burns to hands, face and legs; gunshot wound in left leg . . . You shouldn't have much trouble getting your bowler . . .' Then, noting the RAAF insignia on Digger's tunic, he added jocularly, 'or should I say bush hat with corks?'

'I've come here for a flying category,' Colin Sheen protested, 'not a discharge.'

'Forget it,' came the reply. 'You haven't a chance.'

He made an entry in the file and placed the folder on a different pile.

'You'll have a full medical before your discharge. Just take a seat in the waiting room. We'll try not to keep you too long.'

Colin returned to the gloomy waiting room to find that things had moved on. Some men had disappeared and others had taken their place. He picked up another dog-eared magazine and tried to interest himself in 'ten ways in which to improve your approach to the fair sex'.

'Flying Officer Sheen?'

This time the orderly led him to a room which was clearly a doctor's surgery.

Here blood pressures were taken, columns of mercury blown up and held in place by lung pressure, reflexes tested and blindfold one-legged exercises carried out.

The general physician gave way to an ear, nose and throat specialist who blocked one ear and expected Digger to hear what was said from way across the room. Tuning forks hummed and tonsils and nasal passages were peered at with the aid of a pencil torch. The ophthalmic surgeon followed and in a darkened room Colin was tested on his reactions to flashing red lights and diagonal bars. He read the letter chart with one eye closed and interpreted the usual colour blindness charts more by familiarity than ability to see the hidden forms within. It was now past midday and the orderly suggested he might go and find himself a bite to eat.

'Be back in a couple of hours, sir,' he suggested. 'They should have some news for you by then.'

Digger found a pub in a tawdry little street behind the hospital.

'Beer and one of those sandwiches, please, miss,' he ordered.

He downed the beer and contemplating the empty glass, wondered if he should have another. Deciding against it, he glanced around him, his sandwich remaining untouched on the bar.

He was sick with worry.

What was he going to do if they grounded him for good? He'd never enjoyed being cooped up in an office and could not imagine himself on the ground staff of an active combat station like poor old Stumpy Miles. He felt fit enough to fly. Why not let him?

His thoughts must have given some expression to his features for the two barmaids, who had observed him with great sympathy when he entered the pub, now appeared concerned and approached him, diffidently.

'Give you a hard time at the Medical Centre, did they?'

'Eh? Sorry?'

'Lots of the boys come in here for a spot of Dutch courage or to drown their sorrows,' she explained, and placed a glass containing a generous tot of whisky on the bar for him.

'Here,' she said and, as he went for his wallet, 'it's on the house.'

'Thanks,' said Colin, and downed the spirit in one gulp.

He looked at his watch. Scarcely half an hour had passed but he knew that if he stayed, he would be drunk before it was time to return to the Centre.

'No reason for any weepin' and wailin',' he said, using the studied Australian drawl which seemed to please the girls. 'Just getting back me wings, that's all.'

He slipped off the stool, nodded his appreciation of their kindness and left, pulling his cap down tightly as he went. It covered much of the scarred area of his face.

The clear cockney accents of the barmaid followed him to the door.

'Poor bastard,' she observed to her friend. 'Fancy imagining they'll ever let 'im fly again.'

The Orderly led the way up a flight of carpeted stairs and came to a halt beside a door marked AIR COMMODORE CHARLES MASON. He tapped lightly, and on hearing the word of command opened the door and went inside.

'Flying Officer Colin Sheen, sir,' he announced, taking three smart paces towards the desk and handing the senior officer Colin's file.

'Right, show him in, Corporal.'

The Orderly saluted smartly and turned on his heel.

Colin smiled to himself. All this RAF bull was in sharp contrast to the homely way in which McIndoe's establishment was run. He understood now why Steve had turned down the offer of a job at Halton. He imagined the atmosphere there would be much the same as this.

The grey-haired man behind the desk hardly looked up when Colin entered the room. With a vague gesture he indicated the chair in front of him.

'Sit down, Sheen.'

He picked up Colin's file which now bulged more than it had earlier in the day. He read steadily for a few minutes, turning over first one sheet, then another. At last he put down the folder and gazed intently at Colin over the rim of his steel-framed spectacles.

'Apart from your scars you seem to be a hundred per cent fit, Sheen. Which would you prefer, an immediate discharge with a small disability pension or a posting to ground duties?'

'I'd like to return to my own squadron, sir. Flying, of course.'

The Commodore was expecting this . . . they mostly said the same thing.

Seeing the Medical Officer's doubtful expression, Colin added hastily, 'I can still fly all right, sir. I had a spin with a pal of mine last week . . . it went very well.'

They both knew he was lying. No one would have allowed Colin to take the controls unless he had been passed by a Medical Board. He had taken a trip over to Manston the week before and the Station Officer had given him a short spin in a trainer. His hands had never left the dual controls.

Ignoring his 'porky', the Commodore leaned across the desk and stretched out his arms.

'Grip my hands,' he ordered, 'hard as you can.'

Colin Sheen, raised on an Australian cattle station and fed from infancy on a diet of steaks, had been as strong as an ox before his injuries. Now he squeezed the MO's hands as though they were the rubber balls with which he had been exercising for months. Perhaps in his anxiety adrenaline was released to increase his power . . . perhaps the Air Commodore was feeling particularly kind-hearted . . . Colin would never know.

Mason quickly withdrew his hands.

'There's more strength there than I would have thought possible,' he observed, still rubbing his bruised fingers, out of sight beneath the desk.

He wrote a few words on the sheet in front of him and signed his name with a flourish.

'I'm passing you fit for non-operational, single-engined aircraft only,' he explained. 'If you are still this determined in six months time you can have another Board and I'll see if we can make you operational.'

Colin could hardly believe his ears. At least he could fly again. Six months would pass soon enough. He got to his feet and, replacing his cap, saluted smartly.

'Thank you, sir.'

'Don't you let me down, young feller. You prang some valuable machine and I'm the one will have to answer for it!'

'No chance of that, sir.' Colin was smiling broadly. 'See you six months from now.'

Chapter Twenty-Three

In the months which followed there was little enough time for Stephen and Ellen to meet, let alone make plans for a wedding. Stephen's work never let up sufficiently to allow him to take more than the odd day's leave, while Ellen found herself moved around the countryside to wherever her skills were most needed. She spent the autumn in Wales, the winter in Aberdeen, and it was not until the following spring that she found herself once again in Sussex.

Towards the end of May 1944, those living in the coastal areas of Southern England could no longer ignore the increasing numbers of armed forces gathering in their midst. In the shopping queues at the village store, waiting in line at the cinema on a Saturday night and in the bar at the local, the one word upon every lip was 'Invasion'.

Visiting Mr Fulmer's flock for a follow-up examination, Ellen found her road barred by military police and was forced to show her identification papers before they would let her through.

To either side of the narrow country road which ended at the farm gate and the shepherd's cottage there were tents . . . row upon row of camouflaged marquees and bivouacs standing in the shelter of the beech woods on the lower slopes of the Downs. Everywhere she looked, army vehicles of every description were lined up, and men, thousands of men, thronged the woods and exercised in the fields. Even above the roar of her own engine she could hear the shouted words of command.

'Invasion at last?' she asked Fulmer, catching hold of a white-faced ewe and grasping a handful of woolly skin into which she plunged the hypodermic needle with a skill born of thousands of hours of practice.

'This build up can't be for anything else,' he replied. 'They don't say nothin' but it's obvious, isn't it?'

'They won't cross the Channel in this weather, surely?' Ellen asked, glancing out at the bleak landscape. Rain, which had been falling steadily since before dawn, pounded down on the corrugated iron roof of the barn in which they were working.

'June's a funny month and no mistake,' Fulmer mused. 'I don't know where it got the reputation for being good . . . never known this first week be anything but wet.'

'It's laid flat the hay fields down around Henfield,' Ellen told him. 'I was out that way yesterday . . . farmer there wasn't at all pleased.'

'Gettin' the grain dry, that's the problem.' Jethro Fulmer nodded his grey head thoughtfully and pulled deeply on his pipe. 'Trouble is . . . if you stores it damp, starts sproutin', see.'

'That's the lot, Mr Fulmer,' she said at last, standing back to watch as the ewe she had been treating, suddenly released from restraint, sprang clumsily to her feet and scurried off to join the others. 'Let's hope that does the trick.'

'Well, they look a sight better than when you started the treatment,' he said, approvingly. 'Good things these antibiotics.'

'I hope so. Only time will tell.'

Ellen shook his hand warmly.

'I'll come out and get you started,' he suggested.

'No sense in both of us getting soaked,' she replied, 'thanks all the same.'

She slipped out into the muddy yard and stumbled towards the Austin. It took more turns on the handle than she'd expected . . . the plugs must be damp.

'Can I be of assistance, ma'am?' The drawl, familiar to her from countless Hollywood Westerns, was unmistakable.

She turned to find a burly American Sergeant of Marines standing beside the car. Without another word, he took the handle from her.

'Give her a bit more gas,' he suggested.

Ellen climbed in and adjusted the throttle. With the next swing the engine burst into life.

'Can I give you a lift, soldier?' she asked, lowering the window and leaning out.

'I'd be glad of a lift to camp, ma'am. If I'm not back by six o'clock they'll be sending out a search party. We're not allowed to wander far from home these days.'

'No, I suppose not.' Understanding the near paranoia about secrecy, she hesitated to question him although it was impossible to believe that the Germans could have been kept in ignorance of this massive build up of men and equipment.

'You must be here on official business,' he suggested, knowing the problem she would have had in getting past the guards.

'I'm a veterinary surgeon,' explained Ellen. 'I've just been treating a few sheep.'

'What's the problem – foot rot?'

So he knew something about farming.

She shook her head.

'Liver fluke . . . we're trying to control it by attacking the parasite at various stages in the life cycle. It's a bit of an experiment.'

'How many animals would there be in that flock?' he asked, gesturing towards Fulmer's sheep, huddled together on the hillside wherever a gully or a few bushes offered a little shelter.

'About four hundred?' she calculated.

'Is that so? Where I come from, you'd need an army of vets to treat all of our sheep.'

'Why,' she asked, rising to the bait, 'how many animals do you run on your ranch?'

'As many as three thousand head most years,' he told her, proudly.

'Is that all?' she asked disparagingly. 'Where I come from we don't call it a sheep farm with less than ten thousand head.'

He gazed at her, mouth hanging open.

'And where would that be, little lady?'

'A place called Kerrera in Western Australia.'

He fell silent and remained deep in thought until she set him down at the barrier.

'Well, thank you, ma'am,' he drawled as he alighted.

Ellen couldn't resist one final dig.

'Yes,' she said, grinning broadly, 'farmers down under run so many sheep, they're obliged to train kangaroos to work with the dogs!'

She slammed in the gear and pulled away, leaving the burly American, a puzzled expression on his face, standing in the middle of the road, staring after her.

'How many in that last batch?' McIndoe demanded, looking up from a pile of paperwork as Stephen entered his office and settled on the examination couch. He swung his legs up and placed his hands behind his head.

'Three serious cases . . . more than forty per cent third-degree burns.

The remainder can be sent straight on to Halton.' Stephen yawned and closed his eyes. He was exhausted

Ever since the Allied invasion of France on 6 June, the casualties had been mounting steadily and there seemed to be an endless stream of ambulances disgorging their laden stretchers at the emergency entrance.

'You know it's ridiculous sending all the cases here for assessment,' he declared. 'Half the chaps I've seen this afternoon could have been effectively dealt with at base hospitals, particularly now all units are supplied with the special burns packs. Things seem to have changed from the ridiculous to the even more ridiculous. The field hospitals used to think they could handle everything that came their way. Now they shunt every little scald and facial gun-shot wound straight to us no matter how trivial.

'What would you prefer – an over-zealous medic who sends us a chip out of a zygomatic arch or an ignoramus who retains a third-degree burns case to treat himself?' McIndoe could see that Stephen was tired. It was unusual for him to be so disgruntled.

His young colleague appeared about to go to sleep.

'Anyway, the Combined Forces have come up with the solution to your problem,' McIndoe went on. 'They've authorised an inspector to visit the field dressing stations to assess the degree of injury in burn and disfigurement cases, ensuring that patients are directed to the correct establishments for treatment. How would you like the job?'

Stephen hesitated. His eyes remained closed while he thought about what his boss had said. There was so much that needed to be done here. Mac was short-staffed as usual and he wasn't getting any younger. Stephen had been taking more and more work off the boss's shoulders as the weeks went by. To leave him now would be nothing short of desertion.

'They're giving you a converted transport aircraft,' McIndoe continued.

Stephen sat up, abruptly.

'You mean it's already decided . . . you've volunteered me?'

'Well, it seemed a nice way for you to end the war,' said his friend and mentor. 'A kind of bonus for giving up flying.'

'What kind of an aircraft am I getting?' Stephen demanded.

'A Dakota, redesigned for ambulance work. You're to have a pilot and radio officer and a couple of medical orderlies who can double up as crew. It will display the normal roundels of the Allied forces but will also carry some red crosses, prominently displayed. One hopes that at this stage of the war the enemy will be ready to respect the Geneva convention.'

'Think I might get a chance to fly her myself?' Stephen asked.

'I can't see how they could prevent you.' McIndoe grinned then added, 'Oh, yes, and you'll be operating out of Gatwick most of the time.'

'So the worst cases will still be coming here?'

'I should jolly well think so.'

Stephen wondered how much wrangling, how many hours of telephone conversations and face-to-face confrontations at Headquarters, it had taken for McIndoe to win this concession. Now they would at least have a chance with some of the most severe injuries . . . The war might be nearing its inevitable conclusion, but much of the new weaponry was more devastating in its effects than anything they'd had to contend with in 1940.

'I'm afraid that there'll be no time for you to take that leave you've been after,' McIndoe added, forestalling Stephen's next question. 'The Director General wants you to take over right away.'

'Ellen has been reassigned to the Western Highlands,' Stephen told him. 'She leaves at the beginning of the week. We've just about resigned ourselves to waiting now, until it's all over.'

This war had been particularly hard on the young people, McIndoe thought. His own way of life had left no space for such things as marriage and a family, but he could understand those who wanted the best of both worlds. Stephen had worked hard and had earned his happiness.

With Stephen's elevation to the status of consultant in plastic surgery, came promotion to the rank of Wing Commander. The change made little difference to him so far as his work was concerned, but it gave him a certain lever when it came to disputes with the MOs he encountered at the field hospitals.

'So many of these guys are prima donnas when it comes to decisions about patient care,' he remarked to Baggy when, following an argument which had lasted the best part of half an hour, he had finally persuaded a very reluctant Army Surgeon to release a seriously burned tank commander into his care.

'Anyone would think we were going around touting for business because not enough pilots are getting shot down!' he grumbled.

As with so many aspects of the profession these days, the activities of doctors in the three Armed Services seemed to have become merged. For the older men, those Medical Officers who had been in the Regulars in the 1930s, the distinctions were still sacred, but to those recruited for war service only, it mattered little whether they treated matelots, tank commanders or pilots, Free French, British or American.

Baggy finished preparing a hypodermic, staggering slightly and regaining his balance as the Dakota hit an air pocket and fell twenty feet in as many milliseconds.

Stephen injected the morphine and waited, holding his patient's unbandaged wrist while the drug took effect. He felt the pulse steady itself and then continue to beat in a more regular fashion.

'Try to get some rest,' he said to the mummy-like figure on the stretcher. 'We'll be back in the Sussex countryside in under an hour.'

The agonised expression in the man's eyes gave place to a dull sleepiness and his eyelids drooped.

Stephen replaced the blanket which was draped loosely over the patient and sat back in his uncomfortable canvas seat.

It was doctors such as that unco-operative MO he had just encountered, who would be the ones to oppose the new State Medical Service. Concerned for their own position and the fat fees they could command in peacetime, they would not wish to join the ranks of salaried staffs in the pay of the government.

Stephen remembered the way in which his father had been obliged to work before the war, relying upon his private patients' fees to pay the household bills so that he could give his services voluntarily to the Govern General Hospital. That system worked all right for those doctors the bulk of whose patients lived in the affluent suburbs, but it was a different matter entirely for the ones whose patients were drawn entirely from the working-class areas of the larger towns and cities.

Stephen Beaton could see nothing but good in the proposals being put forward for a salaried profession run by some central organisation. An equal distribution of medical staff and facilities across the country seemed to be the answer, if they were to cater for the medical needs of an entire population. It had worked during wartime, why not in the balmier days of peace?

Stephen watched Baggy seal a container of used instruments, destined for the steriliser back at base, and then carefully dispose of used dressings and the debris of their recent furious activity.

The once scrawny little chap discharged from a sanatorium five years ago, had filled out into a stocky figure whose short stature belied his exceptional strength. Good food and plenty of exercise, lifting and carrying helpless patients had, over the years, developed muscle and sinew concealed by his carefully tailored uniform and spotless overalls.

With a little encouragement from Stephen, Baggy had passed his trade tests with flying colours, and having had these converted for State Registration purposes, now held a position equivalent to that of a nursing sister, with the RAF rank of Flying Officer.

'What will you do when it's all over, Baggy?' Stephen asked.

'Seems to me there'll be plenty as will be needin' my 'elp for a long time to come,' he replied, nodding towards the silent figure on the stretcher.

'So you'll stick with nursing after the war?'

'Mr McIndoe said I ought to take training as an instructor, and sign on as a Regular,' Baggy told him. 'I was thinking of going ahead with that when this job come up.'

Stephen's head jerked.

'You mean, you actually turned down an opportunity like that to work with me?' He was flattered.

'Couldn't let you go off on your own without a proper nursing sister to 'elp yer, now could I?' Baggy grinned up at him. 'You an' me's a team, ain't we?'

'Yes, Baggy, we certainly are.'

Stephen was choked by this unexpected compliment. To cover his embarrassment he stood up.

'I'm going forward to take over the controls for a bit,' he said. They were approaching the Channel, the pilot could probably do with a break.

'Well, don't rock the bloody boat then,' observed his companion. 'You'll have matey 'ere fallin' off his stretcher and then that poncey MO back there really will 'ave something to complain about!'

Stephen eased himself into the co-pilot's seat and reached for a helmet.

'Everything all right back there?' asked Digger.

'Yes, patient's heavily sedated . . . he won't feel a thing till he's tucked up in the Queen Vic.'

They had allowed Digger to continue flying after his first six-monthly assessment and he had even progressed to piloting larger transport aircraft, though he was still not allowed to fly in combat. It had been relatively simple for McIndoe to have him assigned to the Burns Unit for special ferrying duties.

'Want to take her for a bit?'

Digger could see that the doc was tired. Usually a complete change of activity proved as good as a rest to Stephen. Half an hour at the controls and he was as relaxed as though he had had a couple of hours with his head down.

Stephen experienced the full weight of the aircraft under his hands as

Digger relinquished the controls. She was an easy bus to fly. The Yanks tended to make things reasonably comfortable for their air crews, unlike their British counterparts who designed war machines for their destructive powers alone, with little consideration for the men who operated them.

Digger loosened his helmet and allowed his mind to wander. They were approaching the North Sea coast. He looked down to see the Port of Zeebrugge, laid out like a model below the starboard wing. Merchant shipping plied the narrow waterways to and from the port under the protection of a fleet of small Naval vessels, while barges carried essential supplies inland towards the fighting line. It was a scene of activity no less furious than on that other occasion when boats and barges were preparing to sail westwards for an invasion which had never taken place.

Digger remembered the moment when he had realised he was off course and running out of fuel and instinctively his glance fell to the instrument panel. Everything in order there. With a sigh of satisfaction, he leaned back and scanned the great vault of the sky. Except for a single patch of white cumulus to the north-west, it was cloudless. The sea below sparkled in the evening sunlight, where intermittent flashes from the wave tops produced a strobe effect. He felt himself nodding off to the monotonous pulse of the mesmerising lights and sat up suddenly, to ward off an overpowering desire to sleep. His trained eye moved across that arc of the sky which was visible through the wide windscreen and he squinted as he looked directly into the setting sun. What was that?'

He leaned forward, craning for a better view. There was a dark speck coming towards them fast from out of that cloudbank. All his old instincts, heightened in that moment of recognition, took over.

'Aircraft approaching on the starboard side,' he told Stephen, and, not changing his relaxed tone one iota, 'I think I'd better take the con . . . just in case.'

The approaching aircraft did not show any sign of changing course. Digger spoke calmly into his microphone.

'Break out the guns,' he said. 'I don't like the look of this.'

The aircraft had been stripped of all armament save a pair of machine guns mounted one on either side, in the body of the aircraft. The two Orderlies, forsaking their medical duties to become air gunners, took up their posts.

'You'd best get back to your patient, Steve,' Digger ordered. 'Tell your men to prepare to ward off an attack.' Then, seeing the astonishment in Stephen's face, 'It's a matter of self-defence, old man. We don't want to be caught with our pants down.'

★

Horst Otto Steiner had reached his eighteenth birthday on the day they gave him his wings and sent him up on his first solo mission. He had been fed from childhood on the exploits of First World War flying aces and, more recently, on the amazing achievements of Luftwaffe pilots during the present conflict. His two elder brothers, whom he had worshipped, had already been sacrificed upon the altar of the Third Reich. Only he remained to uphold the honour of the family.

The Luftwaffe, short of both men and machines after six years of bitter fighting, could afford only the occasional lone aircraft to worry enemy shipping, reserving what air power it had for the protection of the home-land. Thus it was that on this mild evening in August 1944, Horst, patrolling the coastline for any easy mark, spotted a lone aircraft making for the Channel. As he dived out of the sun he recognised the distinctive outlines of a Dakota. A transport aircraft and therefore easy meat . . . no match at all for his Messerschmitt. He prepared to chalk up his first kill.

Those aboard the Dakota could now see the approaching aircraft more clearly. In silhouette she could have been been any one of a number of models. From this distance it was impossible to tell if she was friend or enemy. They were to have their answer when the aircraft suddenly levelled out and shot across the Dakota's tail, slamming a dozen bullets into the fuselage.

'Bit of a rookie,' Digger shouted into his intercom. 'He's firing wild.'

Stephen had seen the flash of a swastika as the attacker exposed the undersurface of his wing before swerving up and away. At the apex of his arc he turned, ready to make a second run in. The hospital livery of the Dakota was unmistakable. Digger realised with a sinking feeling that this man was determined to get them, regardless of any Geneva Convention.

Well, Baggy thought as his finger rested on the trigger of the machine gun, the Hun was due for a bit of a shock next time he flew by . . . provided, of course, he passed at the right angle.

They heard, rather than saw, the second attack coming.

'It's a Messerschmitt,' Digger shouted over the intercom. 'She can only fire forwards. Try to get her as she pulls away.'

He could hear the enemy plane screaming into a dive towards them. Baggy had handled a gun only once or twice in training. His colleague had had a good deal more experience. He had been tail gunner in a Lancaster before being shot down and relegated to non-combatant duties.

Once within range, the Messerschmitt let off another burst of gunfire, peppering the length of the Dakota with bullets.

Baggy tightened his finger on the trigger and as the enemy came into view, squeezed.

Taken completely off guard by the power and noise of his weapon, he allowed it to leap under his hands. There was no question of good marksmanship. By sheer good fortune, some of his bullets must have struck the Messerschmitt in its fuel tank for as the German aircraft flew out of range, they saw it burst into flames.

The pilot was making frantic efforts to escape, throwing back his canopy and falling backwards away from his aircraft. In that instant the Messerschmitt exploded in a ball of fire and as the parachute opened they could see that it too had been caught by the flames and was burning fiercely. Stephen was horrified to see the pilot's fall accelerating as the parachute was consumed by the flames.

He could hear their own Radio Operator calling for assistance.

'Mayday . . . Mayday . . .' followed by their call sign and location. They must have taken some damage up front.

'Keep an eye on our friend,' he said to Baggy, indicating the patient who had passed the entire episode in a drug-induced stupor.

He struggled forward, clearing the passageway of extraneous debris from the attack.

The Dakota was flying straight and level when he slipped into his seat. 'What's the damage?' he asked. Receiving no reply he glanced across at Digger. He was slumped over the controls, hands gripping the column with such ferocity that the plane maintained its course while flying blind. Blood was slowly forming in a pool on the map case strapped to his knee.

Stephen pulled him back, away from the control panel, and gasped in dismay. A bullet had entered the Australian's temple at an angle and emerged through the opposite cheek. His face, the one which McIndoe had laboured over for month after tedious, painful month, was a bloody pulp.

Stephen made a grab for the controls as the aircraft suddenly pitched and fell into a dive. Concentrating all his efforts now on regaining control, there was no time to think of his friend.

Everything felt sluggish. There must be some damage to the transmission. As he hauled back on the column, he began to feel some response and was relieved to see the nose come up level.

'Baggy . . . Baggy . . . Get up here fast, will you?' Stephen shouted over the intercom. Then to the Radio Operator, 'Tell them I've taken control and am going to land her at Manston.'

The familiar coastline was coming up fast.

There was the estuary of the Thames, the river crowded now with shipping since the war had moved away to the continent of Europe. In the distance, Southend pier, its central section destroyed to prevent its use by enemy invaders, stood out like a child's Meccano set against the reddening sky.

They were over the Isle of Thanet now. The flat fields were yellow with ripening wheat. The apple orchards, their trees paraded in regimental rows, awaited their turn for harvesting to begin, while here and there a tiny field of hops, survivors of the purge on all inessential crops, staggered under the weight of its blossoms.

Sick with worry that he would not be in time to save his friend, Stephen glanced anxiously at Digger, strapped tight into his seat, unconscious and clearly dying. Blood had seeped through the bandages, poppy red against the white cotton. He shuddered. They spoke of the poppies in Flanders Fields in the last lot. This time the poppies would grow among the apple orchards and the hop fields of Kent and everywhere where men like Digger were dying for the things they believed in.

They were talking him down now.

This was not the polished, standard Oxford English voice of a Stumpy Miles, but a sharp nasal intonation. From Brooklyn or Maryland? He could never distinguish one American accent from another.

'Come in, Dakota. You are free to land . . . Good luck, brother.'

Stephen tried lowering the undercarriage. The lever was stiff. Frantically he tried again, calling to the Radio Operator to lend a hand. Together they laid their full weight on the resisting metal bar until with a sudden jerk the apparatus freed itself and the lever moved.

Stephen breathed a sigh of relief and waved the Radio Operator away. He turned to where Baggy had been working on Digger. Miraculously the big Australian was still alive. His head was now swathed in bandages, only his eyes visible through a narrow slot. They were open.

Baggy had arrested the bleeding. Head wounds always bled a lot, Stephen told himself. In the heat of the moment perhaps his initial assessment had been wrong. Maybe Digger would survive after all . . .

'Get back to your seat and strap yourself in tight, Baggy,' he ordered. 'Hold on everyone . . . we're going in!'

With one quick glance at his friend, he began the descent. There had been no sign that Digger was even aware of their situation and yet

Stephen had the strangest sensation that that Australian's hands were hovering above his own on the control column.

He eased back on the stick as the wheels touched. It was almost as perfect a landing as Digger himself would have executed but as the wheels made contact with the ground the undercarriage gave way and one wheel strut crumpled under the weight. Still pounding along the runway, the Dakota lurched over on to her side, one wing tipping down to touch the ground. She slewed around, cutting into the grass on the side of the runway and throwing up a shower of mud and gravel. With a tearing sound and a loud screeching, she came to a halt, only yards from the end of the runway.

In the silence which followed, Stephen released his safety harness and went across to his friend. He could just feel a carotid pulse. Digger was still alive.

'Baggy . . . give me a hand here, will you!' he yelled into the microphone at his throat. To the Radio Operator he said, 'Help to get the stretcher case out, will you? Fast as you can.'

There was a strong smell of aviation spirit. They would not be safe until they were all clear of the aircraft.

Baggy came forward and together he and Stephen eased the pilot out of his seat and carried him through to the main cabin.

A fleet of recovery vehicles had screamed to a halt on all sides of the Dakota. In seconds they had the door open and the wounded tank commander was handed out on his stretcher.

'This man needs immediate attention,' Stephen told the medical team which had materialised in the open hatchway. He indicated Digger. 'He was shot up during the attack. The other patient is the burns case we were transporting to East Grinstead. Don't do anything for him at all . . . just keep him warm, OK? Thanks!'

With practised efficiency the Medics removed both casualties and an ambulance sped with them across the field to that same old infirmary in which Stephen had spent so many months, so long ago.

The Station Adjutant greeted Stephen as his feet touched terra firma.

'Wing Commander Beaton? We've been in contact with your people at East Grinstead as you asked . . . their ambulance is on its way. They only mentioned one casualty. Was someone injured in the shoot up?'

'The pilot,' Stephen told him, 'he took a bullet in the head.'

'That's tough!'

He looked over Stephen's shoulder, expecting to see another crew member. The Radio Operator had already made his report, so where was the co-pilot?

'We didn't have one,' Stephen explained. 'I took over the control myself when the pilot was wounded.'

The Adjutant looked bemused. An MO who could fly a Dakota . . these crazy Limeys never ceased to amaze him!

They had transferred Digger to the little hospital in Margate. With Stephen's assistance, David Lewis had done what he could to make him comfortable but since that early indication of a flicker of life, the big Australian had been slipping in and out of consciousness and now both doctors knew that his case was hopeless.

'We'd better let Grace know.' Lewis put words to Stephen's own thoughts. He had been dreading the inevitable, but now he knew what he must do.

'I'll go and fetch her,' he said. 'Can I get a car anywhere?'

'As luck would have it, the old Morris is standing outside in the car park. Grace left it at the garage for an overhaul. It should be ready to drive away by now.'

The familiar old car stood just where David had said he would find it. Stephen climbed in behind the wheel.

With heavy heart, he headed out along the familiar highway, driving between hedges heaving with the wild harvest of the Garden of England. Hazel saplings bent double with the weight of nuts ripening on their branches and hawthorn berries glowed like jewels in the narrow beam of his shielded headlamps. On the beech trees, leaves were turning to a crisp brown and the oaks and elms, caught by a sudden equinoctial gale, had already shed their foliage, forming a black tracery against the darkening sky.

The Vicarage lay dimly behind the yew hedge . . . not so trim these days, he noticed. Poor old Dobbie would find it hard to keep the garden under control now that Mary was unable to help him.

Perhaps it was a good thing it was so late in the evening. She would have gone to bed long ago. Dobbie could take his time in telling her.

Stephen knocked, half-heartedly at first and then, when there was no immediate response, more loudly. He heard a door open and a foot falling on the hard quarry tiles.

The door opened a fraction and Grace was standing there, already dressed for bed herself.

She hesitated a moment, peering at him in the gloom without

ecognition. Not expecting callers at this late hour, she was suspicious.

'Yes?'

'Grace.'

'Stephen . . . is that you?'

'Yes.'

She ushered him into the hall, full of apologies.

'We have to be so careful these days. A lot of funny people around t harvest time . . . they're not like the old hop pickers, a new breed ntirely . . .'

She stopped suddenly, aware of his discomfort, knowing in that noment that his mission was to bring bad news.

'Colin?'

He nodded, unable to form the words.

'He's had another crash?'

'No, not that . . . we landed at Manston a couple of hours ago. The ircraft was attacked. Digger was shot up . . . rather badly, I'm afraid.'

'Is he . . . ?'

'Not yet, but I don't think he can last the night.'

A dry sob caught in her throat.

'You'll take me to him?'

'Of course. You'll need a coat. It's getting quite chilly out there.'

She glanced down at her ragged old woollen dressing gown and a weak smile crossed her face. 'I'd better put something on.'

She went upstairs, leaving Stephen to explain to the Vicar what had happened.

'I'll come along too,' he said. 'Mary has taken her sleeping pill. She won't stir until morning. Grace might need me.'

How old and tired he looked. Stephen's heart went out to them. The ates had dealt them, all three, so many cruel blows.

Nothing was said as he retraced his route towards Manston. The interior of the car became quite warm with the three of them aboard and the windows shut fast against the damp night air. There was a mustiness from he elderly leather of the seats but it was mixed with some other scent. Stephen sniffed, remembering suddenly, and despite the sadness of the moment, a smile played about his lips. Shep still lingered here. After all hese years, the smell of wet dog was almost overpowering.

At the hospital, Lewis came forward to lead Grace to her husband's edside. They had replaced Baggy's bandaging but still the whole head was swathed and only Colin's eyes were visible. Closed now as though in repose.

Grace touched his hand which lay limp upon the counterpane. He was warm. She stroked her fingers across his palm.

Dazed, as though emerging from a distant place, he opened his eyes and in them was a hint of recognition.

'Gracie?' His voice came out as a hiss between the wires they had used to replace his shattered jaw.

She bent closer to hear what he said.

'Salmon Gums . . . will you go . . . tell them . . . about . . . us?' He was drifting again.

She bent her head over his hand, tears dripping on to Matron's pristine sheet. Then she lifted the hand to her lips, just brushing the tips of his fingers.

'I love you, Colin . . . don't leave me now . . . not after everything . . . I'll take care of you . . .'

His eyes were open again. The look in them was filled with compassion. The bandages moved as he tried to speak, but no sound came out. She read the mouthed words.

'Promise me?'

'I promise,' she said.

'I love you,' he mouthed again.

Grace had no idea how long she had sat there. She was aware of her uncle speaking quietly, holding his prayer book but reciting the words by heart. After a while, Matron came along and touched her on the shoulder.

'Come along, dear, there's nothing more that anyone can do for him now.'

She rose to her feet, took one last lingering look at the figure lying on the bed and collapsed into Stephen's arms.

'I took a hand in the rearing of young Stephen here, from when he was just a few days old.' Hugh Beaton took a sip from a well-charged whisky glass and glanced over the top of his gold-rimmed spectacles at his nephew.

'Born at the height of one World War and qualified at the beginning of another, who is better equipped than this young feller and those like him . . .' he glanced around the company, taking in Stephen's cousins, friends and colleagues '. . . to decide how the world should be run?'

Iain and David Beaton exchanged glances.

Iain raised his eyebrows as if to say 'He's off again', while Millicent, their mother, hovered between her pride in the family gathered about her and dread of what her husband would say next!

Hugh now addressed the bride.

'I couldn't say that I knew your father well, Ellen. He was part of another generation, older than us. To Stuart and I, he and Annie's brother Dougal were figures to be revered and worshipped from afar. I can't tell you how proud it has made me to be asked by Jack to stand in for him at his daughter's wedding. So, ladies and gentlemen, on behalf of the father of the bride, I would like to propose a toast of: the bride and groom.'

The toasts were drunk, there was a buzz of conversation, a clink of cutlery and the occasional burst of laughter.

Annie drank in the atmosphere of this marvellous old house as thirstily as one finding an oasis after days spent lost in a desert.

It really was very good of Millicent to have her home turned upside down like this . . . but then, Annie thought, she and Hugh had always regarded Stephen as an additional member of their own family. Had Stuart never returned from that disastrous voyage, she had no doubt that Hugh would have taken on the role of father on his behalf.

She glanced along the table to where Stuart sat beside Millicent. Retirement had made a new man of him. Already the deep shadows under his eyes had faded and he had lost that gaunt expression which had so haunted her during the final stages of the war.

Annie felt sure that they had done the right thing, selling up the house in Glasgow and returning to the island. What a blessing it was that her brother had purchased the old quarrier's cottage on Eisdalsa when he had had the chance. It was hers and Stuart's now.

The house needed quite a lot of modernising, of course, but they had nothing better to do with their time. She had plans for a garden and had noticed Stuart riffling through his father's old Gaelic books. No doubt he would find some new literary project to keep him occupied in the days ahead.

Stephen looked so distinguished and handsome, she thought as she regarded the happy couple at the head of the long dining table. She had had quite a job to persuade him to wear his uniform. He would have chosen to wear the kilt, but in the end all the boys had agreed to wear their uniforms, and very smart they looked too. The dull khaki and light blue, mixed with a smattering of navy here and there, seemed to highlight the more colourful tartans.

After six years of war and with all manner of restrictions still remaining, the women had been presented with the greatest problem. Beneath those unfashionable made-over dresses, lurked knickers and slips made of parachute silk. A few, those fortunate enough to know an American soldier, wore the coveted new nylon stockings, but for the rest shapeless lisle hosiery was all that was available.

Annie and Millicent had contributed a few of their precious clothing coupons so that the bride could have a proper trousseau.

Ellen, an austerity bride in a sensible tailored suit, softened only by her frilly blouse of pale blue chiffon, was no less beautiful than if she had worn a bridal gown. Perched on her gleaming gold hair she wore a neat little pill box of a hat made of feathers dyed to pick up the colour of the Parma violets she had pinned to her lapel.

Stumpy Miles, performing his role of best man to perfection, read out a number of dubious greetings telegrams which had the men roaring with laughter and the ladies blushing only slightly beneath their flower- and fur-trimmed hats.

'There's one rather special cablegram here,' he said, suddenly bringing the noisy exchanges to an abrupt end. 'It's from the steamship *Ocean Star*, somewhere in the South Atlantic.'

SORRY NOT WITH YOU ON YOUR SPECIAL DAY STOP GRACE SHEEN IS ABOARD EN ROUTE FOR AUSTRALIA STOP BOTH SEND CONGRATULATIONS STOP SEE YOU IN MARCH STOP MCINDOE

Archie, on his way home to visit his family in New Zealand, had not forgotten them. Ellen reached for her husband's hand beneath the table and gave it a squeeze. She knew how much Stephen would have wanted all his friends to be here today and had a sudden vision of Digger Sheen as she had last see him, proudly boasting that he would be getting a transfer to Bomber Command at his next Medical Board. She thought of Grace, standing between Stephen and herself, pale and listless, as they watched his flag-covered coffin lowered into the ground, to rest forever amongst his comrades from Manston Field. Brushing away a tear, she tried to concentrate on what Stephen was saying. Digger would not wish to see her weeping on her wedding day.

They had called on the Dobbies before coming North, hoping to see Grace before she left. The old people were taking her departure very well, but they were going to miss her for the next three or four months.

Ellen and Stephen had promised to go and see them as often as possible. Now that they had rented a little house on the outskirts of East Grinstead it would be quite easy for them to pop down to Thanet from time to time. The house would be their home for the remainder of Stephen's appointment at the Queen Victoria Hospital.

Ellen had arranged to join a small veterinary practice in the town. She was rather looking forward to exchanging herds of cattle and flocks of sheep for poodles and pussy cats. It would make a pleasant change, for a while at any rate.

Audrey Miles had to admit that she had found Eisdalsa a remote and alien place when she had come here, after Margaret was born. At first the dark nights had bothered her. She had found it difficult to sleep for the absolute silence. When she had first taken up residence in Annie's cottage, she had felt very isolated but the old people who still lived on the island had quickly become her friends and there had been a surprising number of visitors coming and going during those war years. Soon she had come to appreciate the tranquillity of life and the comradeship which living in such an isolated situation could bring.

After VE Day, she and Derek had settled in the South London suburb where she had been born. Although she was happy to be once again in familiar surroundings, she knew that she would always hold a special place for Eisdalsa in her heart . . . they would be back in years to come, she decided now, as she soaked in the familiar view. They would come for holidays whenever they could get away. It would be nice to think that some time they might even buy one of the ruined cottages and fix it up as a holiday home . . .

Stephen was on his feet now.

'Ladies and gentlemen, my wife and I . . .' He was hooted down by the noisy comments of his friends. 'My wife and I,' he repeated, 'would like to thank you all for joining us on this most important day in our lives.

'Ellen and I met when we were kids, out in the Australian bush. She was a wild little monkey who could ride a horse and rope a steer as well as any man. She certainly outclassed me . . . and I hated it!'

There was laughter from all around the room.

'I never saw her wearing a skirt until Christmas 1938. Even on the day I met her at Central Station, when she first came over from Australia, she was wearing slacks . . . and very becoming they were too. Although I didn't know it at the time, that was when I really fell for her. I was a goner from that moment.'

They exchanged smiles and she touched his sleeve, her fingers playing across the embroidered rings on his uniform jacket.

'Her skills at training horses were applied equally successfully to me. First of all she ignored me, then she allowed me to chase after her until she caught me!'

They laughed. If only that were true, Ellen thought to herself. The fact was, it had been he who had ignored her . . .

'I want to thank my aunt and uncle for turning their house over to us for this event. It's the only place in the whole village with a room large enough to hold more than twenty guests.'

He raised his glass and took a sip of wine. 'Millicent and Hugh, thank you.' He toasted them. 'I would like to say how sorry I am that Ellen's parents could not be with us on our wedding day. We have had plenty of messages from them and shall be going out to see them as soon as travel becomes easier. Who knows? We might even stay there.'

Annie jerked her head up at this. He had never made any such suggestion before. She supposed there had always been the possibility they might emigrate, filled with foreboding now.

As though reading Annie's thoughts, Stephen turned to her. 'Don't worry, Mum, the world is getting smaller all the time. Soon it will be possible to fly to Australia in two or three days. It will be no more of an adventure than taking a train to London.'

She nodded, smiling bravely through the tears which were gathering. He was right, of course. After all, they hadn't seen much of him for the past six years.

She should be used to his absences by now. The one thing she could be sure of was that he would never neglect them. Stephen would always come back some time, no matter how far or for how long he went.

'We none of us know,' he was saying, 'what the future holds in store. There are exciting things happening here and enormous challenges for those willing to take a chance.'

For a moment he paused, considering the gathering of medical men assembled in the room.

'I'm willing to bet that whatever comes of this new Health Service, it won't stop us from doing our job in the best way we know how. So let's leave it to the politicians to work out the details. After all, it's not the Ministry of Health we should be fighting. Poverty, ignorance and disease are the old enemies. They are always going to be with us, no matter where we go in the world.'

The atmosphere had become a little heavy . . . they were all looking far too thoughtful for a wedding feast.

Stephen brought his speech to a sudden halt.

'I'd like to propose a toast to the future. Good luck to us all – I think we're going to need it! The future!'

They threw back the dregs remaining in their glasses and stood up. In the general bustle as tables were cleared and furniture pushed back against the walls, Ellen and Stephen mounted the stairs to the room where she had spent the previous night.

As they stood gazing out at the wild November afternoon, great waves were bursting in showers of spray all along the shore. Towering purple cumulus moved up from the south-west, threatening a stormy evening, but where the sun shone from behind the hills of Mull the sky was ice blue and pink in the dying light.

Ellen sighed deeply.

'My dad used to describe all this,' she said. 'We'd be sitting there in the stifling heat, with the fans whirring overhead and the flies buzzing, and he would talk about how green it was and about the colours of autumn and the pictures formed by clouds gathering over the sea . . .'

Stephen pulled her into his arms.

'Happy, Mrs Beaton?' he asked.

'What do you think?' was her reply.

'Oh . . . I love you, my Ellen.'

He kissed her hard on the mouth.

'Did you mean it?' she asked, pulling back from him and studying his face.

'What?'

'About staying in Australia?'

'Who knows?' he replied, holding her tighter. 'Anything's possible.'

They heard a fiddle tuning up down below. It sounded as if the *ceilidh* was about to begin.

He kissed her once more and took her hand.

'Come on,' he said, 'we don't want to miss any of the fun. I only intend to get married once in my life!'